FIRST TIME

A LESBIAN ANTHOLOGY

VICTORIA RUSH

COPYRIGHT

For the uninhibited...

VOLUME ONE

THE GIRL NEXT DOOR

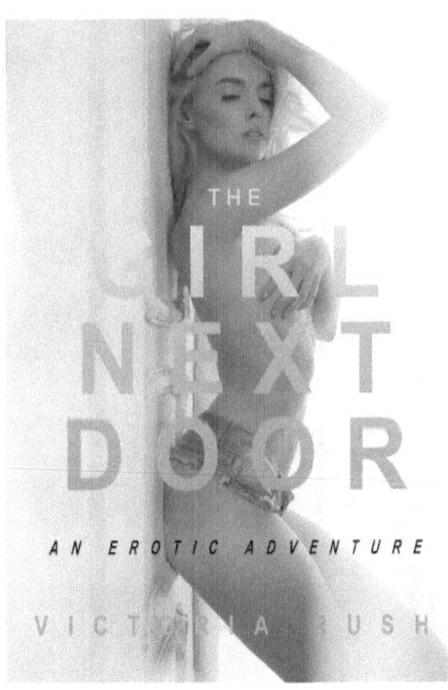

1
———

KEEPING UP WITH THE JONESES

I'd always considered myself a good neighbor. I'd kept my property in good repair, exchanged pleasantries whenever our paths crossed, and tried to respect everyone's personal space. But there's only so much privacy one can maintain when your homes are separated by a modest wooden fence. Especially when you live in a two-story house.

From my master bedroom balcony, I had a commanding view of my fellow residents' backyards. It didn't take long to figure out who lived in each abode, and everybody's predilections. Whether they liked to skinny-dip in their pool, sunbathe in the nude, or cavort in their hot tubs, it was pretty hard to hide from prying eyes.

Not that I made a point of spying on my neighbors. But the ones on my immediate west side were unusually reclusive. I knew they had a single teenage daughter because I'd seen her playing in the back-yard when she was younger. But unlike all the other neighbor kids, she hardly ever left the house. She never got on the school bus rounding the neighborhood, and she rarely swam in their large in-ground swimming pool.

On the few occasions that she did venture into the water, it was always in a full-piece swimsuit. I watched her blossom over the years from a skinny pony-tailed girl to a full-figured, voluptuous young woman. With her shapely figure, long blonde hair and full sensuous lips, she looked like a young Marilyn Monroe. The perfect girl next door.

But I couldn't help feel sorry for how she'd been sheltered by her parents. There were no gentleman callers, no prom dates, no giddy sleepovers with her schoolmates. With her home-schooling, who knows what other worldly pleasures she'd been denied? The more often I caught fleeting glimpses of her, the more intrigued I became with her. I'd shamelessly spy through my shutters to catch a glimpse of her patting her wet body dry after a dip in the pool.

Counting the years since she'd fully developed, I figured she was approaching college age. One night, I knew a change was in the wind when I overheard her parents whispering on their back patio.

"We've got to let her go *one* day, Frank," a woman's voice said.

"I know, but college is such a huge step," a middle-aged man replied. "She hasn't been on her own her whole life."

"Abby's a smart girl," the woman said. "We've taught her well. She'll be fine. Besides, she's a grown woman now. If you ever want grandchildren, she'll eventually need to find a mate. Emory's a good Christian college. It won't be that big a leap for her."

"But it's halfway across the country—"

"There comes a time when every young person needs to spread her wings. This is Abby's moment to begin making her own way in the world."

"Miriam—"

"I've been thinking," the woman interrupted. "Summer's almost over. Why don't we take that trip to Europe we've been putting off for so long? We can have some time to ourselves and give Abby a little space to start looking after herself. That way it won't be such a shock when she leaves home."

"How long did you have in mind?"

"Two weeks. Enough time for us to do a little sightseeing and for Abby to get used to being alone."

"What if there's an emergency?"

"Aunt Jenny's only a half-hour away. Plus, Abby's got her driver's license and already knows how to cook and clean up after herself. How much trouble can an eighteen-year-old get into in two weeks on her own? We can call her every day if you're that worried."

The man sighed.

"All right, hon. I suppose we're going to have to let her be on her own one way or the other."

"Good. Because I've already booked the plane tickets for next week."

2

———

STOLEN GLANCES

In the days leading up to her parents' flight to Europe, all I could think about was Abby. She'd finally be alone, free to express herself and do anything she wanted. At the very least, I hoped she'd spend a little more time in her backyard. A late-summer heat wave had struck the city, and there'd be plenty of opportunities for her to take a refreshing dip in the pool. Maybe she'd been secretly harboring a two-piece swimsuit or — God forbid — planning a skinny-dip after dark. Either way, I'd be glued to my balcony in hopes of stealing another glance at her sweet, nubile body.

But after her parents left, I was disappointed to see her resume her sequestered ways. One day she left the house to pick up groceries and a couple of days later a middle-aged woman I presumed to be her aunt visited for a couple of hours. But during that first week, she ventured into her backyard only a few times to sunbathe in her one-piece suit. By the middle of the vacation fortnight, I began to despair of seeing any part of her beyond her bare legs.

One night as I was getting ready for bed, I noticed her bedroom light was on later than usual. Our windows faced each other on the same side of our house, but she'd always kept her curtains drawn for privacy. Tonight though, I noticed a sliver of light emanating from a

crack in the canopy. I crept up to the side of my window and separated my blinds with two fingers, then peered across the narrow
laneway.

Abby was sitting at her desk, peering at a computer screen. She
was wearing a light nightgown, and I could see the outline of her full
breasts from the backlight of the computer through the gauzy material. The screen was flickering with some kind of moving image, but it
was hard to make out what she was watching from my distance about
twenty feet away. I reached into my nightstand and pulled out a pair
of binoculars that I kept on hand for occasional neighbor spying.

Raising the field glasses to my eyes, I gasped when I adjusted the
focus and zoomed in on her. The image on the screen was a porno,
showing a man and a woman having missionary sex on a bed! I tilted
my binoculars down a few inches and saw Abby had her legs spread
apart with her hand moving in a strange thrusting motion between
her thighs.

She's masturbating while watching the video!

I've never pulled my clothes off my body so quickly in my entire
life. I stripped off my jeans and dropped my panties to the floor and
immediately began circling my clit. My pussy was already soaked in
excitement, as my juices ran down the inside of my legs. I struggled to
steady the binoculars with my left hand as I furiously tribbed myself
with my other hand.

As Abby watched the video, her mouth parted and I could see a
pink flush on her cheeks. Her tits bounced up and down under her
skimpy negligee as she rocked gently in her chair, while she thrust
her fingers between her legs in rhythm with the lovers on the bed. I
was just about to come when the man in the video lifted himself off
his lover and stood by the side of the bed while she began to perform
fellatio. Suddenly, Abby removed her hands from between her legs
and lifted a strange green object in front of her face. It was a large
cucumber!

Poor girl, I thought. *She doesn't even have a proper vibrator, having to
resort to common household vegetables to get off.*

But what she did next soon made me forget about her deficiency of sex toys. She placed the end of cucumber in her mouth and began sucking on the tip, imitating what the woman was doing in the video. Then she moved her left hand back between her legs and began moving it rapidly up and down. I could see her body shaking in obvious pleasure as she sucked on the green phallus.

This girl is going to make at least one Christian college boy very happy.

The man in the video placed his hands at the side of the woman's head and began deep-throating her. I could see his butt cheeks contracting as he thrust his hips forward, while Abby mimicked his movements with her own rocking action on her chair. Suddenly the man stopped thrusting as he held the woman's head tightly against his stomach.

Abby pulled the cucumber out of her mouth and thrust it between her legs, then arched her back and moaned. I didn't realize that her window also was ajar a few inches, and the sound carried clearly over the small space between our houses. I'd hardly paid any attention to my own pleasure up to that moment, but when I saw her coming, I thrust my fingers into my snatch and gushed all over my hand, biting my lip to stifle my own screams of euphoria.

Abby rested for a minute with the cucumber still embedded in her pussy, then she grabbed the computer mouse and the screen flashed a few times before she settled on a new video. I turned my binoculars back to the monitor and noticed this time the video was of two naked women scissoring on the floor. Abby paused for a moment as I saw her eyes widen and her mouth part in surprise. Then she grabbed the cucumber with two hands and started pumping it into her cunny.

Fuck, that's hot! She likes women! Thank God.

My mind was already racing with thoughts of how I could entice her into my bed. But right now, I needed something in my *own* honeypot. I reached back down into my night table and pulled out my favorite vibrator, then I turned it on maximum and plunged it deep into my snatch. Abby and I were both fucking ourselves watching other women getting off, but suddenly Abby looked up and turned her head in my direction.

Had she noticed the movement in my window? I froze with the vibrator buzzing away in my pussy, suddenly aware that I was standing stark naked in front of my window with the shades half open. As she stared in my direction and squinted her eyebrows trying to detect any sign of intrusion, I suddenly came at the thought of her seeing me. My orgasm consumed me, and I struggled to remain motionless as my upper body quaked and quivered in powerful convulsions. I stared back at her, praying she hadn't noticed me.

When she returned her attention to her screen, I suddenly became aware of the dim glow that was being cast in my own room from my open bathroom door. I quickly walked over to the bathroom and turned off the light, then returned to the edge of the window and peered through the blinds. When I looked back up at Abby's window, she'd pulled her curtains and I could only see the faint shadow of her voluptuous body standing behind the sheers.

Fuck! I cursed.

Whether she'd been distracted by the flickering light in my room or she'd noticed me watching her, was unclear. Either way, I didn't care. I'd finally seen her magnificent body in all its glory, and we'd shared a powerful moment of pleasure together. And now that I knew she was sexually active and attracted to girls, I had other plans. I was already thinking of how I could escalate our secret rendezvous.

3

____

LAYING THE BAIT

I had difficulty sleeping that night thinking about what had happened between me and the girl next door. Beyond my obsessive thoughts of seeing Abby playing with herself, I couldn't help wondering why she'd left her window ajar. Had she just been trying to get some fresh air from the stifling heat of the day? Had she simply forgotten to close her curtains all the way? Or had she left them open *intentionally* hoping I'd see her?

Had she been watching *me* also all these years?

My mind raced with fantasies of fucking this shy vixen. Even though she was all grown up, she'd probably never felt the delicate touch of another man or woman. Her mother was right—Abby needed to find her own way in the world, and soon. College would be crawling with thousands of predatory men trying to take advantage of such a beautiful innocent girl. She needed to be educated in the ways of tender lovemaking before getting a rude awakening.

After watching Abby fuck herself with the huge cucumber, I rushed downstairs to retrieve one from my own fridge. I was startled at first by the feel the cold vegetable in my pussy, but it didn't take long to warm up inside my steaming love tunnel. There was something about the texture and feel of the cucumber that made it feel almost like a real cock. Unlike my vibrator, it had a certain sponginess to it. It had the firmness of a man's hardon, but it was flexible like the real thing. The lack of artificial vibration, far from being a detriment, actually was a welcome change from my oscillating dildo. It felt like a real man inside me—just a better hung one. Maybe Abby wasn't so deprived after all. As I lay on my bed with splayed legs replaying the image of Abby pumping her pussy with the giant legume, I got an idea.

I watched for any sign of movement from Abby the next day, but her curtains remained closed and she didn't venture outside. I still harbored hope that the little glimpse she'd provided me the previous night wasn't just a coincidence. At dusk, I repositioned my bed against the opposite wall so that it was directly facing my window. Then I opened my blinds half way and slid the window open a few inches. I turned on my night table lamp so that it cast a soft glow over the covers. Then I took off all my clothes and lay face up on top of my sheets and closed my eyes.

If Abby happened to glance out her window, she'd see me stark naked, looking like I'd fallen asleep trying to catch a break from the heat. But I had a lot more than just *sleeping* on my mind tonight. I squinted through half-closed eyelids at Abby's window for over an hour but didn't see any sign of movement. It was approaching 10:30 p.m., and I assumed she'd soon be getting ready for bed. Eventually, I saw some flickering light coming from behind her curtains.

No, Abby! Look out your window, not at your computer! I'll give you a much better show than any of those pornos, and it'll be the real thing.

I squeezed my thighs together in frustration, then remembered what had brought her to her window yesterday. I leaned over and turned my night table lamp on and off twice in rapid succession, then I leaned back down. Through the corner of my eye, I could see her shadow moving behind the thin curtains. Then I noticed the corner of the drape open on one side and a dark figure blocking the light from her room. She was looking out her window! I knew she could see me clearly across the laneway in the soft illumination of my bedroom in the pitch dark of night. Now it was just a question of whether I could maintain her interest.

I shifted my position as if I was having a restless dream while keeping one eyelid open just enough to see her outline through the window. She didn't move. But I had to be careful. I didn't want to make it look like I was luring her into some kind of a trap or make her feel uncomfortable. I still wasn't sure that she'd seen me yesterday or that she knew I'd seen her. I needed to maintain the illusion that I was sleeping, or at least that I hadn't noticed her watching me from across the laneway.

I lifted my right hand off the bed and let it flop on my stomach like I was unconscious. Then I began to shift my hips in rhythmic movements as if I was having an erotic dream. It was electrifying to know that Abby was watching my naked body just as I had watched her the previous night. After a few minutes of suggestive hip action, I felt daring enough to begin fondling my tits. I cupped my left breast and began pinching my nipple while continuing to sway my hips. Abby was locked in position by the edge of her window. I knew I had her. Now it was just a matter of pulling her in.

After a few more minutes of squeezing my breasts and writhing suggestively on the sheets, I began to move my left hand down my stomach towards my pussy. I paused for a moment with my fingers on the edge of my pelvic bone while I lifted and swayed my hips. My bare pussy throbbed in anticipation of my touch. The thought of Abby watching me perform my tantalizing tease was intoxicating, and I felt the wetness accumulating on my lips.

I glanced out the corner of my eye and detected some movement of the curtain near the bottom of Abby's window. Her hips were swaying in synchronicity with mine behind the curtain. She was getting just as turned on as I was! I spread my legs further apart and moved my left hand slowly down over my pubis. Trying to play with yourself while pretending to be asleep was more difficult than I thought, and I wasn't sure how much longer Abby would buy the ruse.

But it no longer mattered. As long as I had a captive audience, I intended to make the most of it. I'd give her a show she'd never forget while enjoying something I'd never experienced before. I'd taken this whole spying-on-the-neighbors thing to a whole new level. When I finally touched my clit, I flinched in pleasure. My button was already poking out from under its hood and it was flaming hot. I mixed in the juices from my sopping pussy and circled my nub as I lifted and swayed my hips for my private audience.

I could have come right away, but I wanted to savor the moment and make it last. Plus I had a lot more in mind for the education of my innocent voyeur. I could feel the juices running down my vulva onto my ass, and I moved my other hand between my legs and began to fuck myself with my fingers. My pussy began to make sexy slurping sounds and I moaned loudly as I felt the pleasure rising in my belly.

Suddenly, I heard the sound of Abby's window sliding open as she shifted her weight a few inches away from the edge of her window. She'd obviously heard my muted moans through the glass and wanted a clearer connection. The drapes parted a little further, and I could see the full outline of her hourglass hips against the backlight of her bedroom. Before the curtains closed again to a narrow sliver, I caught a glimpse of a dark patch between her legs.

Of course she'd be unshaven, I thought. *She probably doesn't even know what all the girls are doing these days in terms of intimate grooming.*

Her natural appearance made me even more turned on, and I fucked myself harder as I imagined kissing her furry mound. My orgasm was getting closer, and I began thrashing my hips on my bed while I circled my clit with one hand and fucked myself hard with the other. Abby's curtains parted a little further, and I saw her hand moving between her legs under her thin negligee. That was enough to put me over the edge, and I screamed like a wild animal as I came. I no longer cared if Abby thought I was asleep or not, I just wanted to let the pleasure pour out of me. I heard a little peep emanate from Abby's window and I saw her knees buckle as her chest jerked in rhythmic spasms behind the curtain.

My contractions lasted for almost a full minute as I clamped my hand inside my pussy, giving Abby a full view of my naked body in the throes of ecstasy. After I finally calmed down and stopped moving, I noticed Abby was still standing at the side of her window with the curtains slightly parted.

That's my girl, I thought. *Stay there, baby. Momma's got a lot more where that came from.*

I flipped over, stretching my arms and legs lazily, and lifted my bare ass in her direction.

If you like the front of my body, wait till you see my backside.

I was proud of how I'd maintained my body tone for my age. Regular workouts at the gym and the yoga studio had kept my ass firm and round and tight. I spread my legs slightly to give Abby a glimpse of the dark tunnel between my legs, then I began to raise and lower my ass, beckoning her in. It felt sexy showing her my backside, but from my prone position, I could no longer see what she was doing in her window.

I reached over to my nightstand and tilted my phone up against the front of my clock radio, then twisted it until I could see Abby's reflection on the screen. The dark glass provided a perfect view of the illuminated window across the dark passageway. I wasn't sure if she could see my reflection as well, but it must have been obvious what I was doing, and she didn't flinch away.

Now that I'd reestablished our two-way line of communication, I returned my attention to my aching pussy. I slid my hands under my hips and spread my legs further apart, then placed my fingers under my mound and began fingering myself with both hands. I was still at the height of arousal from my last orgasm and knew it wouldn't be long before I came again. As I began to hump my bed, contracting my buttocks in rhythm with my hands, I heard some moans emanating from Abby's window.

At this point, I had no more interest in carrying on the illusion that I was half asleep. I lifted myself up on all fours and spread my ass cheeks to show Abby my soaking snatch. She had a commanding view of my open pussy and ass, and I leaned my shoulders down on the bed so she could also see my tits hanging between my legs. I reached around with my left hand and plunged my fingers into my cunt while I jilled my clit furiously with my other hand.

I was grunting like a wild animal at the thought of Abby watching me fuck myself from behind. But there was still one thing missing. I reached under my pillow for the cucumber that was still coated with my slippery juices and slammed it into my ass.

I bet this is something you haven't yet seen in one of your pornos!

I looked in the reflection of my phone and noticed that Abby was no longer standing at the edge of her window, hiding behind the curtains. She had pulled them aside and was standing in full view of the open window, with the backlight from her room shining through her flimsy negligee. I could see her full breasts bouncing on her chest as she rubbed her pussy frantically.

She was moaning without abandon now, and I joined her in our shared pleasure. My orgasm hit me without warning, and I couldn't help screaming her name as I gushed onto my hands and clamped down on the cucumber embedded in my ass. Abby screamed out loud too, and the whole neighborhood must have heard our cries of ecstasy as we climaxed in glorious union.

I knew now, that this was going to be the start of a glorious friendship.

4

───────

HEAT WAVE

When I woke up the next morning, Abby's curtains had been pulled back and I could clearly see into her room. A small four-poster bed was neatly made up with pink throw cushions and linens. A tall bureau sat next to it with a collection of stuffed animals resting on top. In the far corner, a large pink dollhouse sat unused on the floor. Overhead, a fan with Alice-in-Wonderland leaf-shaped blades whirled quietly on the ceiling. Other than her computer desk and bookcase filled with high school home-study books, it looked like a typical young girl's bedroom frozen in time.

But for most of the morning, there was no sign of Abby. I wasn't sure what to make of the conflicting signals. She'd finally opened a portal to her world, which couldn't have been a coincidence. But why was she being so coy staying hidden? Was she feeling embarrassed about the intimate moment we'd shared the previous night? Had she noticed me watching her in the reflection of my phone on the night-stand? Why would she open her drapes if she didn't want me to see her?

Just before noon, I heard the front door of her house open and close, and I rushed to my living room to peek out the window. She climbed into a Toyota Echo sitting in the driveway, then backed up and turned in the direction of downtown. Was she going to visit her Aunt? Was she heading out to replenish her groceries?

Or was she going to the police station to complain about her peeping Tom neighbor?

For the next couple of hours, I paced my house second-guessing whether I'd pushed the envelope too far. I still wasn't entirely sure she was even of legal age. What if she'd taken a *video* of me? Could that be used to prove that I was some kind of criminal, trying to lure an under-age child into illicit sex? My mind raced with all manner of scary scenarios, with patrol cars screeching into my driveway and burly policemen hauling me off to jail.

After a couple of hours, my heart rate finally returned to normal when I realized the cops would have already arrived at my door if she'd intended to report me. But I knew I had to be far more discreet in my outreach efforts going forward. There could be no more private nude shows, at least until I verified she was eighteen. I used the free time waiting for her to come back to formulate a plan.

I figured it couldn't be easy for her cooking her own meals for the first time in her life. It must be overwhelming having to cook and clean and look after that big house all by herself. I resolved to bring her a ready-made dinner that night. If she was amenable, I'd invite her over to my place, where I could take care of all the details and free her from having to worry about cleaning up. But what kind of food did she like? What does a sheltered home-schooled teenager like for dinner?

After some deliberation, I decided to bake her a chicken casserole. Chicken was pretty safe, and if she didn't accept my invitation, it would be easy for her to simply heat it up in her oven. I could toss a fresh salad as a side, and offer her a glass of wine to help her relax. But not until I verified her age. I probably wasn't the only nosy neighbor checking out the comings and goings in the neighborhood. The last thing I needed was to get either one of us in trouble for underage drinking. Or underage sex.

Jeesh. How could I broach that subject delicately?

I decided to run out to stock up on fresh groceries, and when I returned I noticed Abby's car in her driveway. I hurried inside and rushed upstairs to my bedroom. When I peered out my window, I saw that Abby had closed her drapes again.

Now what? I thought. Is she having second thoughts about what she'd seen last night? Had she only opened the window to let in a little fresh air from the oppressive heat?

I walked onto my balcony and peered into Abby's backyard. It was quiet as a mouse. If she planned to retire back into her shell, I had one last chance. There was no harm in being neighborly by offering to share a meal I'd baked. At least this way, I could confront her directly and see if she was as interested as I was in her. For the next hour, I focused on preparing the casserole, while keeping my eyes and ears open for any sign of activity from next door.

Just as I was placing the baking dish in the oven, I heard the distinctive sound of someone diving into a pool. It sounded like it came from Abby's side, and I raced upstairs to peer out my balcony into her yard. When I glanced at the pool, I saw Abby's unmistakable form swimming across her pool.

But this time, she was wearing a skimpy yellow two-piece swimsuit. I watched her tight round bottom wiggling through the water as the yellow shorts clung to the crack in her ass. As she turned her body from side to side, the side of her firm breasts rose tantalizingly above the edge of the water before plunging again below the surface. I was absolutely mesmerized watching her magnificent figure slide through the churning water.

After four or five laps, she stopped at the end of the pool closest to me and lifted her head out of the water, then shook the drops from her hair. She glanced up in my direction and I quickly slunk back behind my bedroom door. I was sure she'd seen me staring at her again, and I cursed myself for being such a pussy. This cat and mouse game, as sexy as it was, was getting tiring.

I went into my bedroom and pulled a racy romance novel out of my nightstand then turned the chair on my balcony towards Abby's house and sat down. If she caught me peering in her direction, I didn't care. I was simply catching some sunshine on a warm day while enjoying a good book. If she chose to run around in a skimpy bikini, that was her business.

When I returned to the balcony, Abby was standing by the side of the pool toweling herself dry. She seemed to linger longer than usual patting her breasts and the area between her legs, and I could have sworn I saw her glance up in my direction again. I tried to hold my gaze on my book, but I wasn't reading a single word. I peered over the top of the paperback, trying to cover as much of my face as I could get away with.

Abby walked over to the side of her pool near her back fence where two chaise lounge chairs rested, and she reclined one of them to a flat position. Then she placed her towel on the cushions and lay down with her backside pointed directly in my direction.

You little tease, I thought.

The ball was now in Abby's court. She was being just as sneaky and calculating as I'd been. Now it was *her* turn to put on a show for me. At first, she simply lay quietly on the lounge, pretending to soak up the sun. But after a few minutes, she began to shimmy her hips in the same manner I had the previous night. I smiled as I parted my legs, my pussy flooding with juices. I suddenly wished that I'd placed some kind of barrier between me and the narrow railing spindles of my balcony to provide more privacy. But I dared not move for fear of missing a single twitch of Abby's exquisite body.

After a few minutes of rolling her hips seductively, she shifted her arms from over her head and rested them at her sides beside her ass. Then she lifted her hips and moved her right hand under her pelvis.

Holy Fuck! I gasped out loud. *She was going to finger herself in plain view, just as I had yesterday!*

There was no longer any doubt that she'd seen me watching her the previous nights. She was going to torment me in exactly the same way I'd done with her. I glanced around at my fellow neighbors' properties to check that we were alone. It was a hot weekday afternoon, and most people had either retreated inside their air-conditioned homes or were lying around their fenced-in pools.

Abby had chosen her lounging position carefully, close to the back fence where no one else could see her besides me. Had she also purchased that skimpy yellow bikini today to drive me even more crazy?

I raised my right leg and bent my knee to provide a modicum of cover, then I unzipped the front of my shorts and thrust my fingers under my panties. As I watched Abby's fingers moving in the tight cleft between her legs, I circled my clit and groaned in delirious pleasure. My shorts already had a giant wet spot creeping down the front of my pant legs, as I dripped like a broken faucet watching her play with herself.

I could see Abby's buttock muscles flexing as she humped the chaise lounge cushion. She was faced away from me, so it was hard to see the expression on her face, but I remembered the sweet look of ecstasy I'd seen two nights ago. I looked in front of her to see if there was any reflective object where she might watch me like I had with her last night, but there was none. Apparently, she was content to give me a one-way show.

But then she turned her head to the side and flitted her eyes in my direction. I could tell that she was trying to disguise the fact that she was peeking at me out the corner of her eyes, and I laughed when I realized how obvious it had been when I tried a similar feint last night. I lowered my book and spread my legs as far as I dared as I rubbed my soaking snatch furiously. We both stared at each other for a moment, then her lips parted and I could hear soft moans wafting up to my balcony. This time I couldn't wait for her. I jerked in my chair and pulled my legs together as I came all over my wet hand in my shorts. I groaned out loud from the pleasure sweeping over me, as I shook and convulsed in my chair.

She must have seen me in the throes of orgasm, because within seconds, she suddenly straightened her legs and pointed her toes, and she clenched her cheeks together as her upper body began to shake. We didn't take our eyes off each other the whole time we both came. The feeling of our first direct visual connection was electrifying, and I spasmed in my chair for almost a full minute as I watched

the pretty girl in yellow release her inhibitions for the whole world
to see.

Two hours later, I knocked on the front door of Abby's house carrying my ready-made casserole. It took quite a while for her to come to the door, and I began to worry that I'd scared her away. If I were in her shoes, I'd be a little nervous too about making direct contact with someone I'd shared such an intimate, but heretofore remote, relationship.

Maybe her parents told her not to open the door for strangers, I thought. *Come on, Abby. You can do this. I won't bite.*

About sixty seconds later, I heard some footsteps approaching the door from the other side, then I saw the view hole flicker as she looked through the spyglass. She hesitated for a moment, then swung the door open.

"Hi," I said. "I'm Jade, your next-door neighbor."

Abby's pupils dilated as big as saucers. Whether it was from excitement or nervousness, I couldn't be sure.

"Yes," she said. "I recognize you. I've seen you...*around.*"

"I hope you don't mind this little intrusion. But I saw your parents leave for a trip a few days ago and noticed that you were all alone. I thought I'd be a good neighbor and bring you a little gift."

I held the covered baking dish in my outstretched arms.

"That's very thoughtful," Abby said. "What is it?"

"It's a little casserole I threw together. It's already cooked. You just need to put it in the oven for thirty minutes to warm it up."

Abby reached out and accepted the dish, then we paused awkwardly for a moment on the doorstep.

"If you'd like, we could share it together," I said. "If you want to come over to my place, I could throw together a nice side salad and we could get to know each other a little better. We've been neighbors for quite a while, and I heard rumors that you'll be heading off to college soon. I'd love to hear about your plans."

Abby hesitated as her eyes fluttered considering the offer. She must have known I had other designs, beyond sharing a meal together.

"Um, okay," she finally said. "When's a good time?"

"How about seven?" I said, trying not to betray the rush of excitement coursing through my body.

"Okay, I'll see you then."

Abby smiled at me, then she closed the door. I practically skipped back to my place with thoughts of what lay ahead that evening.

5

THE SWEETEST WINE

For the next two hours, I busied myself preparing for Abby's visit. Fortunately, I'd replenished my fridge earlier in the day and had most of the cooking already done. Now it was just a matter of cleaning up the house and getting myself ready. I washed the sheets and placed some extra cushions on the bed, then cleaned the washroom and hung some fresh towels. I wasn't sure if Abby would make it this far, but I wanted to make everything as welcoming as possible if she did.

Then I had a long shower, dried my hair, and put on some skinny jeans and a silk blouse. I knew I was overdressed for a casual dinner, especially on such a hot day, but I wanted to highlight my best assets in hope of attracting Abby's attention. I considered going braless, but at the last minute erred on the side of prudence over provocation. I didn't want to be too obvious or make Abby feel like I was coming on too strong.

When my doorbell rang at seven that evening, I rushed to the door and took a deep breath before swinging it open. Abby looked more beautiful than ever in matching pastel shorts and blouse, with tasteful leather sandals. Her shimmering blond hair was freshly washed, and she'd applied some light lipstick and mascara that highlighted her natural beauty. My eyes lit up as she stood on the doorstep holding a beautiful bouquet of long-stemmed tulips.

"Abby," I said. "Come in. You look...*lovely*...this evening."

Abby stepped over the threshold and presented the flowers to me.

"Thank you, they're gorgeous. How did you know tulips were my favorite?"

"I didn't, but they're my favorite too. I thought I should bring something..."

I took the flowers from Abby's hands and motioned toward the other end of the house.

"Come to the kitchen while I place them in a vase. Are you hungry?"

"Yes, definitely," Abby said, smiling at me softly. "It's been a while since I've had a good home-cooked meal."

I led Abby into my kitchen and filled a tall vase with water.

"Where did your folks go for vacation?" I asked.

"France, mostly. They were going to spend a week in Paris, then a few days on the Mediterranean coast before taking the train to England and flying back from London."

"How lovely. I hear the French Riviera is beautiful at this time of year. May I ask why you didn't join them? It would have been a perfect going-away gift."

Abby shook her head and shrugged her shoulders.

"They didn't ask. Maybe they just wanted a little alone time. I've been a bit of a handful all these years, with the home schooling and everything. This is the first time any of us have had a real break from one another. Maybe they wanted to make sure I could look after myself before sending me off to college."

I nodded my head as I sprinkled some flower food into the vase.

"College is a big step, especially for someone who hasn't had any prior public education. Are you excited?"

"I have to admit I'm a little scared *and* excited."

Abby watched me for a moment as I clipped the flower stems and arranged them in the vase.

"Do you mind my asking how you knew my parents were going away?" she asked.

I stopped for a moment and looked up.

"Yes, I guess that was a little forward of me. I actually overheard them talking one night on your patio by the pool. Voices carry pretty easily up to my balcony on a quiet night."

"Is that how you knew my name too?"

I placed the vase in the middle of my dining room table then looked up at Abby.

"Yes, sorry if I've been such a nosy neighbor. But it was nice to put some names behind the familiar faces. We've lived next door to one another for so long and never been formally introduced."

Abby frowned as she shifted position uncomfortably.

"My parents are a little overprotective of me. I think it was their religious upbringing. Not wanting me to have any unholy influences, and all that."

"Well there's a lot of *sinful* activity out there," I said, smiling at Abby. I placed a head of lettuce on the cutting board in the middle of my kitchen island and began chopping it into little pieces. "Is that why you so rarely ventured out of the house also?"

"You mean into our backyard, using the pool?" Abby said.

"Among other things."

"After I started developing, they didn't want me exposing my body. When they bought the house, it came with the pool. But they thought I'd be desecrating myself if I exposed too much of my body to strangers."

I shook my head as I sprinkled the lettuce leaves into a salad bowl.

"It's a shame, because you have such a lovely figure. I don't see any harm in displaying your God-given features, if you do it in a tasteful way. I was glad to see you sharing a bit more of yourself by the pool yesterday."

Abby looked away from me and blushed.

"Did you like the new swimsuit?"

"Oh, yes," I said, pulling a large cucumber out of the fridge and plopping it on the cutting board. "I enjoyed it very much. You looked absolutely ravishing in it."

Abby blushed a deeper shade of crimson and turned her body to look through my kitchen window into my backyard.

"You have a lovely home. I see you have a pool also. Do you use it very often?"

Watching Abby stand by the window made me think she'd stolen just as many glances of me swimming half-naked in my pool as I had of her.

"As often as I can. Especially in this summer weather. It's a great way to cool off from the heat." I grabbed a large paring knife and began slicing the cucumber into thin slices. "I especially enjoy swimming in the nude after dark. The water feels magnificent on my naked skin."

Abby shifted uncomfortably as she glanced toward her own backyard.

"That sounds like fun, but my parents would kill me if they ever caught me doing that."

My pussy began to moisten at the thought of watching Abby's naked body snaking through the water.

"You've still got a few days before they return. You should try it. It's very invigorating."

"What about the neighbors? There's not much...*privacy*...with us all huddled so close together."

I smiled at Abby's double entendre. I was beginning to enjoy our little game of verbal brinkmanship.

"If you do it quietly with the lights off, no one will notice. Except maybe the ones who've been watching you ever since you've grown up."

Abby turned around when she heard me pull the casserole out of the oven.

"The dinner smells delicious. Thanks for having me over."

"It's been a pleasure getting to know you, Abby," I said. "Please, have a seat." I uncorked a bottle of wine and paused as I held the open bottle over her goblet. "Are you old enough to drink?"

"I just turned eighteen last month."

"Well we'd better start getting you acclimated," I said, breathing a huge sigh of relief. "God knows, there's going to be plenty of spirits flowing once you get to college."

For the next hour or so, Abby and I made small talk over dinner, talking about her course of study and plans after college. Neither of us broached the subject of what we'd seen and done over the last couple of days, but by her second glass of wine Abby had loosened up and begun to talk about dating. When I started clearing the table and placing the dishes in the sink, she offered to help clean up.

"How about if I do the washing and you help me dry?" I said, handing her a dish towel.

As I filled the sink and leaned over to pour some soap in the water, I caught Abby stealing a glance at my ass.

"So you like boys, then?" I asked.

"I suppose so, but my parents haven't let me go on any dates yet. I'm not sure I'm ready though."

"Really?" I said, passing her the wet casserole dish. "You're eighteen, in the prime of your life, and just about to head off to a place that will be teeming with eligible bachelors. What's your hesitation?"

"I don't know," she said, rubbing the inside of the baking dish gently with her towel. "Lately, I've been finding myself more attracted to...*women*. I'm beginning to wonder if I'm—"

I turned around to face Abby and gently took the casserole dish from her hands and placed it on the counter.

"Abby, you're a smart, beautiful, sexy young woman. Anyone will be lucky to share your love. You'll know when the moment comes what the right decision is..."

I leaned toward Abby's face and hesitated as we peered into each other's eyes. Abby closed the distance and placed her lips softly against mine. Our hips moved together, and I placed my arms around her back and pulled her closer. My mind began spinning as we both moaned in each other's mouths.

I wanted to fuck her right then and there, and it was tempting not to lift her up onto my kitchen counter and pull off her shorts. But I glanced through my kitchen window and realized that we were far too exposed to prying eyes.

"Let's go somewhere where we have more privacy," I said.

I took her by the hand and led her upstairs to my bedroom, then gently lay her down on top of my comforter. I kneeled down beside her and propped myself over her body as I drew my right thigh up between her legs and pressed it against her warm pussy. Abby took in a sudden breath of air, and we gazed into each other's eyes as I lowered my face onto hers. As we kissed passionately, I pressed my mound into the soft flesh between her legs. Abby moaned into my mouth, and her breathing became ragged.

After a few minutes, I lifted myself up and began unbuttoning her shorts, but Abby placed her hand over mine to stop me. I feared that she might be having second thoughts, but then she leaned forward and glanced out my bedroom window.

"Do you mind if I close your blinds?" she said. "I know my parents are away, but it'll make me feel more secure. You never know who else might be watching from a distance."

I smiled and nodded knowingly.

"Of course," I said. "This time, there'll be no one but the two of us."

Abby got up off the bed and walked to the window, then turned the shutter handle to close the blinds tightly. When she walked back toward me, I stood up and blocked her before she reached the bed. Then I looked into her eyes and began unbuttoning her blouse. She looked straight back at me as I separated her blouse and peered at her breasts. She was wearing an old-school brassiere that pulled her breasts tightly together, and I stared at the cleft produced by her large bosom. I reached around her back with two hands and unclasped the latch of the bra, then I raised it and gasped.

Abby had the most beautiful breasts I'd ever seen on the female form. Full and plump, they were perfectly round and firm, sitting high on her chest. If I didn't know better, I might have thought they were surgically enhanced, but of course she was far too young and sheltered to have gotten anywhere near a plastic surgeon. Her areolas were small and dark, with thick nipples protruding almost a full inch off her chest. I cupped her tits with both hands then buried my face shamelessly between her magnificent mountains.

When I lifted my head, I sucked gently on each of her erect nipples. Abby placed her hands behind my head and moaned softly as I licked and stimulated her sensitive teats. I wanted to feast on her like a suckling baby, but the throbbing clit in my wet pants reminded me there was much more to enjoy. After a few minutes of kneading, suckling, and playing with her melons, I finally pulled myself away and kissed her on her lips.

"You're exquisite," I said, looking into her eyes.

"Jade," Abby panted. "Take me. I've been waiting for this for so long."

I pulled Abby's blouse off behind her back, then lifted her bra over her shoulders and threw it softly on the edge of the bed. Then I unbuttoned the front of her shorts and pulled them over her round hips and let them fall to the floor. I was surprised to see her wearing plain white granny-panties that extended almost up to her belly-button.

Jesus, I thought. *I'm going to have to take this girl to the mall to get her properly outfitted for college. This is no way to present herself among trendy university students.*

I placed my fingers under her waistband and slowly pulled her panties down over her stomach. When the band got half way down her abdomen, a tuft of light brown hair puffed out, forming a perfect triangle in the cleft between her legs.

She really hasn't been touched down here at all, I thought.

My mouth watered at the thought of feeling her downy pubic hair against my face.

Abby's legs quivered as I pulled her panties over his hips and lowered them to the floor. I kneeled down in front of her and untied her sandals, as I rolled my head softly against her bush. I could hear Abby panting above me, and I smiled in the knowledge that she was enjoying being touched by another woman for the first time.

When I finished untying her sandals, I placed my arms around her thighs and kissed her on her mound. I breathed in the fresh sweet scent of her pubic hair and closed my eyes. There was something about her natural beauty that was driving me absolutely crazy. As I kissed and nuzzled her soft muff, I raised my hands and cupped her ass.

"God," I muttered audibly, when I felt her firm round cheeks.

Her ass was even more perfect than her tits, if that were even possible. I desperately needed to see her full body in all its naked glory. I stood up and took a step back to look at Abby. She stood with her hands beside her hips, her tummy shaking in anticipation and excitement.

"You're stunning, Abby," I said, taking a long pause to soak up every curve and valley of her magnificent figure. "You're even more beautiful than I imagined."

Abby stepped forward and began clumsily unclasping the buttons on my silk blouse, then I took a step back and motioned for her to stop. I slowly unfastened the buttons myself, taking my time to sexily remove every stitch of my clothes while her eyes grew wider and wider and her stomach fluttered in obvious excitement. When we were both finally naked, we took a moment to appraise other's bodies, then we pressed our bodies together and began kissing passionately.

Abby was a clumsy kisser, unsure what to do with her tongue, and I slowed her down to teach her the proper technique. I placed my hands gently on the sides of her cheeks and began by softly kissing the sides of her lips. I nibbled her lower lip for a few seconds, coating it with my saliva, before inserting my tongue gently into her mouth and swirling it softly inside her. Then I placed my hands beside her head and pulled her into me, turning my face and head to probe her sweet, pliant mouth. As we rubbed our tits and pussies together, Abby's breathing grew heavier and heavier.

I desperately wanted to thrust my fingers into her box and feel her wetness in my hand and give her her first real live orgasm. But I kept reminding myself this was her first time with another lover and that she deserved a tender and measured first experience. After five minutes of passionate kissing, I separated myself again and grabbed Abby's hand and led her to the bed.

I lowered her softly onto the covers, then lay beside her on the bed. We turned and pressed our breasts together and kissed gently for the longest time. I just wanted to feel her delicate skin against mine and breathe in her sweet aroma. My mind spun in a drunken stupor, I was so elated to be finally holding her in my arms.

But there was so much more I wanted to do with her, and before long we separated again and I slowly began kissing my way down the front of her belly. I could feel Abby's stomach shaking the closer I got to her honeypot, but when I reached her mound, I stopped and kissed her soft muff for several seconds. It had been so long since I'd seen or touched a full and natural pubic patch, I reveled in the softness of her downy fur.

Abby twisted and raised her hips, begging me to go lower, and I gently spread her legs apart. I could smell the sweet aroma from her cunny and knew that she wanted me to touch her there. But I began by kissing the insides of her thigh, tantalizingly edging my way up toward her steaming kitty. I wanted to take me time and give Abby the most amazing sexual experience of her life.

When I finally reached her apex, her thighs were already coated in her juices. I placed two fingers over her opening and ran them along the sides of her slippery labia. Abby had a beautiful pussy, with full and plump outer lips framing tight, symmetrical inner lips. Everything about her was like she'd been molded by God himself to create the perfect female form.

Abby whimpered as I played with the outer edges of her flower, then I slowly inserted two fingers into her hole. She grasped my fingers tightly as I pressed them into her, then I began to slowly finger-fuck her as I watched her head roll from side to side in delirious pleasure. I couldn't believe that I actually had my hand inside this gorgeous angel, giving her a pleasure she'd never yet experienced. How lucky was I to be the first one to touch her virgin garden?

Abby began rolling and thrusting her hips more vigorously, and I began to fear she might come before I had a chance to taste her nectar. I lowered my head between her legs and placed my mouth over her throbbing clit, then I sucked her nub between my lips. Abby gasped and raised her hips off the bed, pushing her pussy harder into my face. It felt glorious to finally feel her in my mouth, and I danced my tongue over her clit as I listened to her squealing in unbridled pleasure.

"Yes!" she moaned. "Suck me, Jade. Please suck me. I want to come in your mouth."

I almost came myself when I heard her mention my name, and I clamped my thighs together, trying to give my aching clit some direct stimulation. I could feel Abby's clit hardening in my mouth as her hips thrashed and pressed against my face. I knew she was close when her whimpers turned to squeals, and I curled my fingers toward me, stimulating her G-spot. Suddenly, she lifted her hips off the bed and grasped the side of my head with two hands and squeezed my ears tightly.

"Jade!" she screamed. "I'm coming! God, I'm coming!"

With one final guttural groan, she paused and held my head between her legs as she jerked and spasmed against my drenched face. I could feel the inside of her pussy clamping down on my fingers in rhythmic contractions, as I cradled her softly, savoring every pulse and squirt of her quivering body.

6

TWO BECOME ONE

Abby and I lay quietly on my covers after she came, kissing and caressing each other, as her breathing slowly returned to normal. I ran my hand over her torso, marveling at the size and firmness of her breasts. Even lying down, they pointed high and proud on her chest, like the twin pyramids of Giza. I cupped and squeezed and pinched them, like a child with playdough.

"Are you sure you these things aren't surgically enhanced?" I said, pinching my eyebrows in amazement.

"Are you kidding? My parents would never let me debase what God gave me."

"Well thank you, God, for bestowing this beauty with such perfect and natural gifts. You're really a work of art."

I traced my hand further down her belly and ran my fingers through her soft pubic patch.

"I love your muff, too. It's so soft and...*pure.*"

Abby looked between my legs then placed her hand gently on my mound.

"Really? I noticed most of the girls in the videos are shaved like you. You're so smooth—there's no stubble like when I shave my underarms."

I smiled at Abby's delightful innocence.

"I used to have it waxed off, but a few months ago I chose to have all my pubic hair removed with laser treatment. Let's hope the trend with intimate landscaping doesn't change anytime soon, because there's no going back for me."

Abby caressed my mound softly with her hand, then pushed her fingers lower between my legs.

"I like it," she said. "I can feel *all* of you."

I watched Abby's eyes widen as she ran her hands over my bare vulva.

"You know I spied on you a couple of nights ago watching those videos. It was super-hot. Did you leave your drapes and window open on purpose?"

Abby lowered her gaze shyly as she caressed my inner thighs softly.

"Yes. I was kind of hoping you'd notice me. I've been spying on you for years. Watching you get dressed in the morning, sleeping at night..."

I placed my hand under Abby's chin and lifted her face so I could peer in her eyes.

"Is that what you were doing *last* night too?"

"Yes," she sighed. "You were so beautiful and sexy, I couldn't take my eyes off you."

"Did you like the little show I put on for you?"

"Yes. You were very naughty."

"Apparently, we both have a certain affinity for long green vegetables."

Abby blushed, then pressed her tits against me. Her hand circled over the back of my ass as her fingers probed between my legs.

"What can I do for *you* now?" she said. "I want to give you the same kind of pleasure you just gave me."

"Well actually," I said, lifting myself up off the bed. "I had a little something in mind that I think we might *both* enjoy."

I slithered down toward the other end of the bed and positioned myself between Abby's legs.

"No fair!" Abby said, trying to raise herself up. "It's *your* turn. Shouldn't I be the one on top this time?"

I pressed Abby back down onto the bed and smiled.

"There's a lot of ways to have sex besides the missionary position, young lady. Remember that video you were watching the other night? How would you like to try that?"

Abby began to roll and lift her hips seductively.

"Mmm—yes, please. I want to feel you. I want to feel you...*fucking* me."

I raised my eyebrows, then a wide grin stretched across my face.

"You're so naughty. I *like* a naughty girl."

"Show me how you do it, Mommy," Abby said, continuing the role play. "Show this innocent church girl the ways of the world."

"Fuck, yes," I growled.

I pulled her hips toward me and scissored my legs under and around her midsection. When our pussies touched, we were both sopping wet, and I could feel the heat radiating from Abby's oven. She moaned loudly when our clits connected.

"Oh, Abby, I've dreamed of doing this to you for so long. Let Momma cum all over your sweet cunny."

I got up on my knees and pushed my steaming pussy against Abby's hairy snatch and began grinding our hips together.

"Fuck," Abby panted. "That feels so good. Fuck my cunt with your beautiful bald pussy!"

I couldn't believe Abby was talking dirty to me, which turned me on even more. I lifted her right leg off the bed and placed it between my tits as I humped my pussy between her legs. I could feel her wetness coating both of our thighs and our pussies made sexy squishing sounds as our labia rubbed together. Abby's tits shook like two huge Jello molds as she looked between her legs watching me fuck her.

"God, yes!" she panted. "Fuck me, Jade. I want to watch you come like you did for me. I love you."

When Abby said those words, I felt a surge of energy through my body and my pussy tingled in excitement. I pushed my mound hard against hers and wrapped my arms around her extended leg on my chest.

"Abby!" I said, looking straight into her eyes. "I'm going to come baby. I'm going to come all over your sweet virgin cunny."

My climax poured over me like a tidal wave. I pulled Abby's leg hard against my chest and squirted my love juices into her gaping hole.

"Fuck," I screamed. "I'm cumming, Abby! I feel you between my legs. Come with me!"

Abby suddenly opened her mouth like she was gagging, as a deep red flush swept over her chest above her tits.

"Yes," she screamed. "Feel me, Jade! I'm cumming with you. Ohhh, yesssss!"

Abby grabbed my hips and pulled me toward her as we thrashed and ground our pussies together, screaming and panting in ecstatic union. I could feel Abby's fingers digging into the sides of my buttocks as her hips jerked and spasmed in concert with mine. All the while, we never took our eyes off one another. When we finally stopped coming, I held Abby's leg tightly against my chest for another minute as I savored the feeling of our wetness comingling between our joined pussies. Then I collapsed onto the bed beside her and exhaled deeply.

"That was incredible!" Abby panted. "I feel blessed that you're my first."

I turned my body toward Abby and kissed her gently on her lips.

"I'm the lucky one. You're an angel sent down from above. I've never felt—"

I stopped myself before I said something I'd regret. Abby was just starting out in her voyage of exploration, and she was just about to head off for college. It was unfair of me to harbor any expectations beyond our little fling.

"You mean..." Abby said. "You feel it too? Do you—"

I placed my finger over Abby's lips, then I pushed myself back so I could look at her directly.

"You've got your whole life ahead of you, Abby. I'm almost old enough to be your mother. You deserve to experience all the wonders of youth and explore your sensuality with other young people. Some day, long after you've graduated and found your footing in the world, you'll find your soulmate. We'll always have a special connection, and I'll always be your friend, forever."

Two streams poured down Abby's cheeks as her face contorted in pain.

"Does this mean we can't be...*lovers* any longer?"

I pulled Abby toward me and hugged her close to my body.

"We'll always have this special bond, Abby. But I want you to be free to fall in love with other people, to find that special someone you'll be perfectly yoked with. Right now, I think it's mostly the hormones talking."

"What do you mean?"

"Well, when two people make love and have an orgasm together, there's some special hormones that are released that causes them to have certain feelings for one another. It's called the love hormone— oxytocin. Nature, or God, provided us with this so that we'd be more likely to stay together and raise the children that often come after coupling, to ensure a more successful family unit."

"But...we're women. We can't have children this way."

"It's the same hormone, no matter who you're with. And it's a very powerful hormone, like a drug. You'll find it has a similar effect with other people you're attracted to. Don't rush into love—let it find you."

Abby snuggled closer to me and kissed my neck.

"Well whatever those hormones do, I like it. If we can't be lovers, can we at least be *friends with benefits* a little longer?"

I pushed Abby away from me and opened my eyes in mock surprise.

"So that's it? You're going to dump me just like that? Wham, bam, thank you ma'am?"

Abby looked at me coyly and traced a circle around my nipples with her fingers.

"Not exactly. I was hoping we could do a little more whamming and bamming, at least before I go off to college. I'm guessing there's a few more things you can still teach me..."

I flipped Abby over onto her back and pulled myself on top of her.

"You're damn right there is. In fact, I did have something else in mind if you're not too tired and already spent."

"Are you kidding? I'm eighteen! I can come all night with you if you'll let me."

"All right then," I said, getting up off the bed. "You just wait here and keep that pretty little pussy of yours warmed up for me. I've got a little surprise for you."

I hurried downstairs and ran into the kitchen and flung open the fridge. Then I opened the crisper and looked at the special collection of cucumbers I'd purchased at the grocery store earlier today. I picked out the longest and thickest one and bent it gently between my two hands.

This one will do just fine, I thought.

I ran back upstairs holding it behind my back and skipped into my bedroom like a kid on Christmas, stopping a few feet from the bed with a huge Cheshire grin on my face.

"What?" Abby said, a big smile spreading on her face. "What are you hiding behind your back?"

I slowly pulled my arm around in front of me and held the giant cucumber up triumphantly in front of me.

Abby looked at me teasingly and shook her head.

"But we've both already tried that. I thought you were going to teach me something new!"

"Oh, but there's so many ways we can use a big dildo like this," I said, crawling onto the bed between Abby's legs. Let Mommy show you how else one can savor fresh cucumber."

I placed the sprout against the inside of Abby's thigh, and she flinched from the cold texture on her warm skin. Then I slowly slid it up the inside of her thigh until it pressed against her pussy. She gasped when it touched her, and I began to slide it up and down over her wet slit.

"That feels good," Abby purred.

"It feels even better when it's *inside*," I said. "But you already knew that. This is what I mean about experimenting with other people. You really won't know for sure if you just like women until you've felt a man's throbbing cock inside you."

Abby looked up at me, surprised.

"So you don't just like girls?" she said.

"I consider myself *pansexual*," I said. "I like to have sex with the right person in the moment. But I have to admit, I do have a special fondness for women..."

I thrust the tip of the cucumber into Abby's hole and she took a sudden intake of breath.

"Yeah?" I teased. "You like that? There's more where that came from."

As I pushed the cucumber further inside her, I watched it stretch and push her labia apart the further it went.

"Uhnnn," Abby groaned. "Yes, Jade. Fuck me. Fuck me with your big cock."

I began to pump the cucumber in and out of her as I watched her head roll from side to side in pleasure. She thrust her hips in a matching humping action as she fucked and squeezed it in her tight box.

Damn, I thought. *This girl is going to make one hung dude very happy some day. But right now—she's all mine.*

"Deeper," Abby panted. "Fuck me deeper with your big cock, Jade."

I already had about seven or eight inches buried inside her and could feel the end of it pushing up against some resistance.

"It won't go any deeper," I said. "I don't want to hurt you."

Abby tilted her head up and peered at me holding the other end of the vegetable.

"You've only got it half way inside me," she said, teasingly. "It seems a shame to waste so much of it."

I smiled at Abby knowing we had the same idea.

"You're reading my mind, girl. I had no intention of wasting the other half."

I lay down on the bed and spread my legs facing Abby, then I slithered my pussy towards hers and inserted the other end of the cucumber into my slit. As I pushed myself toward her, I could feel the cucumber pushing deeper inside me. Abby groaned as she felt the pressure of it pushing inside her from my movement.

"God, yes!" she panted. "Fuck me, Jade. Fuck me with your big green cock."

I continued twisting and pushing the cucumber inside me until it filled me up. When our pussies finally touched, Abby and I both moaned, then we began rocking our hips together as we fucked the big dildo from opposite ends.

"Ohhh, Uhnnn," Abby groaned, as I clamped down on the dildo and thrust it inside her pussy.

We alternated squeezing and releasing the cucumber within each of our pussies, exchanging the feeling of being fucked and fucking our partner. This was something I'd never experienced before, and I closed my eyes focusing on the incredible sound and feel of the giant cock sliding in and out of our pussies as we ground our clits against one another. Within a few minutes, I felt that familiar sensation rising within me and knew I couldn't hold out much longer.

"Baby," I called out to Jade. "I'm going to come again. Let me feel you gush all over my cunt as we come together. Are you ready?"

"Yes," Abby panted. "I'm going to come all over you. Fuck me hard!"

I sat up and placed my hands beside Abby's hips, pulling her toward me in rhythmic movements as I thrust the cucumber deeper inside her. It was an incredible sight watching the thick green phallus going in and out of her splayed pussy as I fucked her like a man. As I felt my orgasm take hold of me, I squeezed Abby's buttocks and pulled her crotch hard against mine.

"Come for me, baby," I cried. "I'm going to come inside you now. Feel me, Abby," I yelled. "I'm *cumming!*

Abby and I both screamed each other's names as we gushed all over the slick cucumber embedded deep within our pussies. I could feel the walls of my pussy contracting as it gripped the fleshy dildo, and my clit twitched against the hard, cool skin of the vegetable. It was the most incredible feeling coming together with Abby, joined as we were with the juicy object between us.

We shook and panted and whimpered for several seconds, as we climaxed together. When we both came down from our highs, I pulled the wand out of our pussies and lay down beside Abby at the head of the bed. I placed the slippery cucumber between our tits and slid it sexily between our breasts, then I sucked on the end that had been in Abby's pussy.

"Mmmm," I said, looking teasingly into her eyes. I much prefer my cucumbers this way than in a salad."

***

For the rest of the week, Abby and I played and made love with each other, trying our best to stay out of the public eye. I was mindful that her parents would be returning from vacation soon, and I didn't want any nosy neighbors spilling our little secret. We pulled the blinds shut then slept together, ate together, giggled together, and bathed together. And we fucked each other deliriously, right up until the last moment.

After her parents returned, we continued our remote affair through our adjoining windows at night, with nobody the wiser. On the day Abby left for college, she snuck over to my place and gave me one last, long lingering kiss. Then I didn't hear from her again until she returned home for the Christmas holidays. Although I missed our secret trysts, I smiled whenever I thought of her, knowing that she'd finally found her independence.

***

Also by Victoria Rush:

CLICK FOR MORE INFORMATION

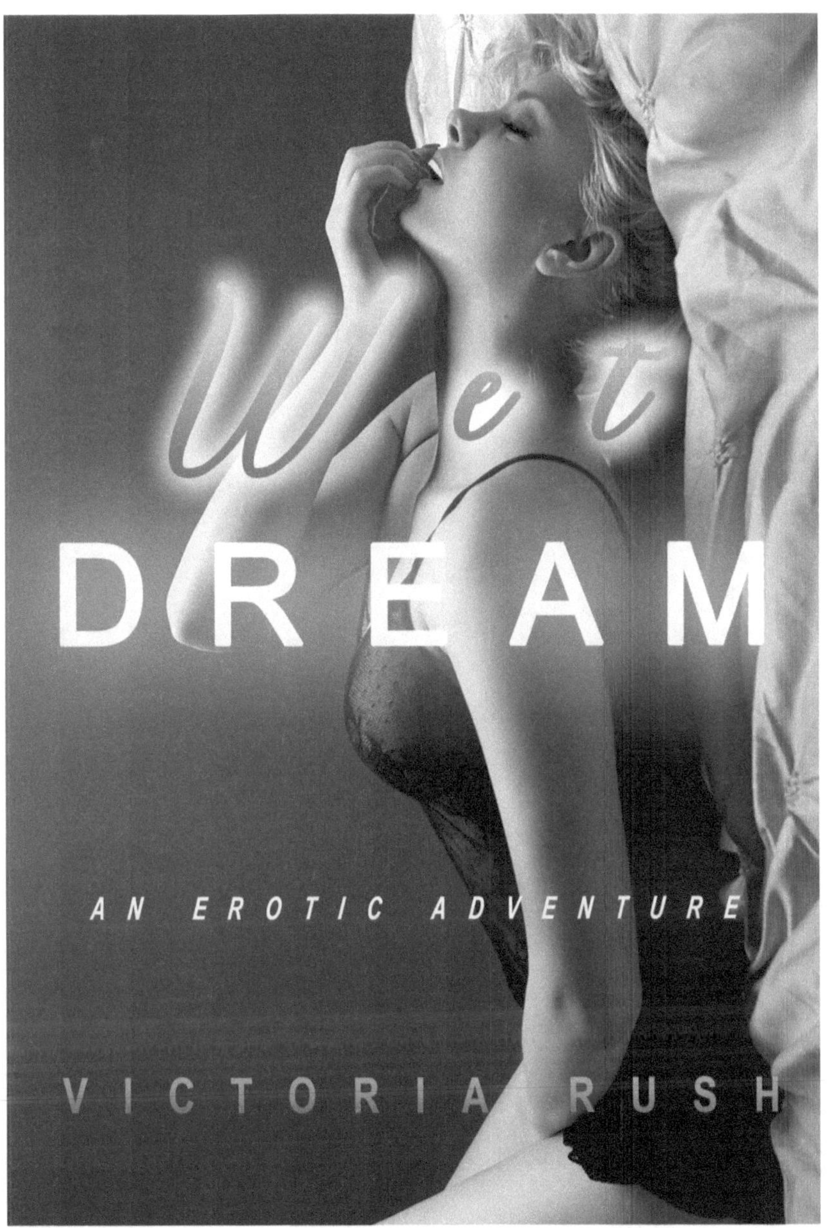

There's only one place you can live out your wildest fantasies...

Artificial intelligence never felt so real...

Everybody's an exhibitionist in disguise...

Books 6 - 10 in the bestselling series - now 60% off.

VOLUME TWO

THE HABIT

STACKED

I never particularly enjoyed going to the library. Beyond the hassle of dealing with crosstown traffic to get there, it always seemed such a chore to find what I was looking for. Whether I was searching through the card catalogue, the microfilm reels, or even asking the librarian, everything moved at a snail's pace. Having to search through the stacks, access the hard copy, then flip through all the pages to pinpoint my reference material—it all seemed so archaic.

Searching online was so much more efficient. From the comfort of my home office, I could tap in a few search words and within a couple of clicks, get exactly what I wanted. Unfortunately, today, I had no choice but to do it the old-school way. I needed to reference some old newspaper ads to get some ideas for a design project I was working on, and only the library went as far back as I needed.

At least I could count on a relatively quiet environment to do my research. Normally, there were few distractions to get in the way of completing the task at hand. People seemed to respect the rules of public decorum in a library more than other public places like the movie theater or a restaurant. Freed from trilling cell phones and loud side chatter, everybody went about their personal business quietly and politely.

But, today, as I walked toward the microfiche department, something unusual caught my attention. A nun in full regalia stood at the reference desk talking with the librarian. There was something about her manner of dress that seemed out of place among the casual jeans and shorts that other library patrons wore. Her black and white hooded frock stood in sharp contrast to the colorful and largely bare-skinned wardrobe of the other customers.

Like many other bystanders, I caught myself slowing down to stare at her. I saw a few people whispering and snickering amongst themselves as they pointed at her, and I began to feel sorry for the woman. Why should we judge her any differently, I thought, for quietly practicing her faith? There was something admirable about anyone in today's age who could so thoroughly dispense with the material and ego trappings of the modern world.

I was about to continue on my way minding my own business, when the nun turned around. She was much younger than I expected, perhaps in her early twenties, and absolutely stunning. The only part of her that I could see was the front of her face from her chin to her eyebrows. The rest of her head was covered in a white balaclava and hood that draped past her shoulders. She wasn't wearing any makeup, which only seemed to magnify her beauty.

Her pretty face was highlighted with plump rosebud lips, high cheekbones, and soft brown eyebrows. But the feature that stood out most prominently was her eyes. Her irises had an arresting—almost haunting—azure blue color, glimmering like glacial pools surrounded by the snow white hood encircling her head. She could have been a supermodel, and for all I knew, maybe she was. How someone that stunning could turn her back on all the temptations and opportunity that would have fallen into her lap, was a mystery to me.

Now I was even more intrigued by this stranger, and as much as I wanted to respect her privacy, I simply couldn't take my eyes off her. The librarian handed her a piece of paper and as the nun headed in the direction of the stacks, I followed a safe distance behind. Her billowing robe covered her body almost to the floor, but I could tell from the tight cinch of her belt around her waist that she had a slender figure under her heavy clothes.

As she walked toward the stacks, I tried to discern the shape and contour of her body, but her heavy vestments wouldn't betray what secrets lay beneath. But this only added to her allure. It was what I *couldn't* see that made her even sexier. I began to undress her with my eyes, imagining a model-perfect figure to match her face, and bit my lip trying to stifle my rising passion. As my panties began to moisten, I felt ashamed responding to this innocent creature in this way, but I couldn't stop.

Get a hold of yourself, girl, I admonished myself, under my breath.

When she retreated into the narrow space between two tall stacks, I stopped by a chair and placed my hand on the backrest for support. I could hear my breath escalating in excitement and had become weak in the knees. I'd never encountered another person—man or woman—who'd had such a powerful and visceral effect on me. I pulled out the chair and sat down, pretending to look through my purse so as not to be obvious that I'd been following her.

There were some loose textbooks in the middle of the table, and I grabbed one and opened it, pretending to read. I had no idea what the subject matter was because my focus was blurred trying to watch the nun's movement out of the corner of my eye. My pussy was burning in excitement, and I crossed my legs and rubbed my thighs together, trying to give my aching clit some direct stimulation. If there hadn't been so many people around, I would have torn off my clothes and cum within seconds fingering myself.

The nun stood in front of the stack tracing her finger over the spine of some books, trying to cross-reference the call numbers with the paper the librarian had given her. Her eyebrows pinched together in confusion, and for a moment I considered going over to offer some help. But I wasn't sure I could even talk, let alone make any sense, I was so smitten by her beauty. When she leaned forward to take a closer look at one of the books, I squinted to see if I could catch the protrusion of her bosom. But there was nothing to be revealed. It was almost as if she had multiple layers under her clothes to camouflage any hint of her female form.

Those Catholics sure know how to design a uniform to conceal a woman's shape. But I suppose that's the whole point. To minimize the possibility of any temptation—from within or without.

She was wearing a virtually impenetrable barrier to the outside world. My mind began to wander, wondering what kind of undergarments she might be wearing. Was she wearing a traditional corset or a push-up bra? Granny panties or boy-shorts? Nylons or bare legs? Or maybe nothing at all?

You could get away with just about anything under all that get-up, I thought.

I could feel the wetness beginning to spread in the crotch of my tight jeans, and I squeezed my legs together to pull the inseam harder against my throbbing clit. When the nun kneeled down close to the floor to pull a book from the bottom shelf, I couldn't stop myself.

I wish she were kneeling over my face. Oh, how I could give her a taste of earthly delights.

I began to wonder if she'd ever felt the loving touch of another man or woman. Or if she'd even touched *herself*, for that matter. I didn't know much about a nun's vows, but I knew they had something to do with remaining chaste and renouncing most worldly pleasures. It was hard to imagine having no sexual feelings, but if they kept their bodies covered in this manner, it would certainly minimize temptation. The nun never seemed to look beyond her direct field of interest or make eye contact with anyone other than the person with whom she was transacting. Perhaps she'd been trained this way, because there were plenty of scantily clad attractive young men and women scattered about the room to distract one's attention.

Suddenly, she stood up and placed a book under her arm. Then she walked to the rear section of the stacks and turned to walk down the rear aisle beyond my line of sight. After a few moments, I stood up from my desk and went into an adjacent column of stacks to see if I could trace her movement. I pretended to search for a book but instead looked through the space between the shelves to peer through the stacks. I saw her black robe moving to the far rear corner of the library, where she sat down on a large upholstered reading chair.

I grabbed the largest book I could find then headed in the direction of the nun. Not wanting to appear too obvious, I stopped at another upholstered chair about thirty feet away, turned slightly in her direction. I sat down and crossed my legs, then opened the large book on top of my knee. I laughed at my lame attempt at subterfuge, but at least it afforded a modicum of privacy while enabling me to continue spying on my new obsession.

As I peered over the spine of my book at the nun, I struggled to see what she was reading. I couldn't make out the title beyond the large cross appearing on the front cover.

Jesus—is she reading a version of the Bible? Now I'm definitely going to hell for having lascivious thoughts about a devoted woman while she's praying!

But there was no turning back. I was fascinated by this angelic beauty and couldn't take my eyes off her. As she read her book, I studied her face closely from the side. She had flawless alabaster skin, soft rosy cheeks, and a slender, perfectly-straight nose. Whenever she blinked, I could see her long, full eyelashes fluttering over her iridescent eyes. Her expression rarely changed, but every now and then I'd see the edges of her lips curl upwards in a gentle smile as if taken by a passage of her book.

How I'd love to feel those lips smiling around my love button, I thought, feeling my clit tingling in my tight jeans.

The more I looked at her, the more aroused I became, until it was impossible not to touch myself. Having the advantage of elevated padded armrests flanking me on both sides and a large reference book propped up on my legs, I was concealed in my own little cocoon. As long as I was quiet and careful, I could do just about anything I wanted on my chair and no one would be the wiser.

I looked around the room to ensure no one was watching, then I slowly uncrossed my legs and unzipped the front of my jeans and slid my fingers under my panties. But even with the front unzipped all the way, it was hard to reach far enough down into my tight jeans to reach my clit. My fingers pressed against the tight canvas, making it impossible to provide enough room to move around comfortably.

I braced my left arm on the armrest and lifted my hips up slightly, then shimmied my hips just enough to pull my jeans about one inch away from my opening. Now I finally had a little room to operate. My panties were thoroughly soaked, and as I began to circle my clit with the middle finger of my right hand, I had to clench my jaw to stifle my moans. When I redirected my attention back toward the nun, I caught her looking up at me before quickly peering back down at her book.

Shit! I thought. *Had she caught on to what I was doing? She probably runs into all manner of perverts exposing themselves to her whenever she leaves the safety of her convent.*

I froze with my hand down my pants, wondering what to do. The nun seemed to have refocused her attention on her book. My shifting position had probably distracted her temporarily. She couldn't possibly know what I was doing, walled off the way I was. I looked around the rest of the room to make sure I was clear, then slowly resumed fingering my sopping wet pussy.

As I touched myself, I watched the subtle changes in the nun's expression while she read. Her serious countenance made her appear even more model-like, as if she was posing for a camera.

Did she know I was watching her? Did she sense I was turned on by her? If she had, wouldn't she have excused herself?

Was she enjoying being watched?

As I watched her quietly reading, my mind raced thinking of all the dirty things I wanted to do to her if I could get her out of that habit.

What a funny term for a piece of clothing, I thought. I suppose it signifies her taking on a new form of habitual life. Whatever the garment's etymology, I was rapidly gaining a habit of my own for this sexy girl.

Forgive me, Lord. Forgive me the sins of my flesh.

As I began to feel the pleasure rising within me, my legs began to tremble, and I steadied my book on my thighs to disguise what was happening behind my armrests. As I neared my climax, my mouth unconsciously opened and just as I felt my orgasm take hold of me, the pretty nun looked up at me again. She must have known what I was doing from the tortured look of ecstasy on my face, and I looked away in embarrassment.

But I'd passed the point of no return and could no longer hold back the floodgates. As I jilled my clit furiously under my book, I felt the first wave of pleasure sweep over me. I fought to stifle my moans, gagging on the open air with my mouth wide open. I tried to remain as still as possible as the orgasm washed over me, but with each contraction, my chest heaved spastically in my chair.

The fact that I had to disguise the incredible pleasure radiating throughout my body only magnified its intensity. As I sat shaking uncontrollably in my chair, I thought the contractions would never end. I couldn't look at the nun for fear of betraying what was happening, so I peered straight ahead into the blurred text of my book.

When my contractions finally stopped, I slumped down in my chair and exhaled heavily. In my effort to disguise my orgasm, I hadn't realized that I'd been holding my breath the entire time. I panned the room to make sure no one else had witnessed my silent pleasure, then slowly zipped up the front of my jeans.

As I readied myself to silently slip out of the library, I noticed the nun shifting position in her chair for the first time. She crossed her legs and I saw a sliver of skin appearing under her frock above her shoes.

Was she giving me some kind of signal that she knew what I'd done and that she approved? Surely, she'd be discouraged from revealing any more skin in public beyond the small amount of her face?

After a few moments, I noticed a gentle bobbing of her upper foot over her leg.

Was she just indicating that she was happily engaged in her book? Or was this her way of revealing that she was really happy under her habit?

As I peered over the top of my book and watched her more

closely, I noticed that her hips were also squirming in her big armchair.

She's rubbing her thighs together as I was earlier, trying to stimulate her clit!

It was hard to be certain, because she continued staring expressionless straight ahead toward her book, but I noticed her eyelashes were fluttering more rapidly than normal. When her lips suddenly parted a few millimeters, there was no longer any doubt.

She was masturbating herself under her gown in plain view of the entire library! I looked around the room to see if anyone else was paying attention, then looked back at her face. Although she never directly returned my eye contact, the subtle changes of her facial expression and body movements told me everything I needed to know. As she rubbed her thighs together more firmly, her legs began moving more rapidly under her heavy tunic. The bobbing of her foot on her knee steadily picked up pace, and her face began twitching almost imperceptibly.

Suddenly, a deep flush fell over her cheeks and her back pulled away from her chair as the cloth of her habit rippled in shockwaves. She was cumming under her habit, and I was the only one to witness it! I jammed my hand into my panties and came hard again as I plunged my fingers into my soaking snatch. I'd never witnessed anything so sexy in my entire life. As I watched her sitting erect in her chair, spasming from her orgasm, my own pussy clamped down over my fingers in sympathy with her.

Although the pretty nun and I never spoke or made further eye contact that day, something told me this wouldn't be the last I was to see of her.

2

———

OBSESSION

For the rest of that day, I couldn't shake the pretty nun from my thoughts. It wasn't just her celestial beauty—there was something about her veiled appearance that got me worked up. Now that I knew she had sexual feelings, my mind raced with a million questions.

Was this the first time she'd acted on her impulses? Did she masturbate frequently in the privacy of her own room? Or had she simply gotten turned on watching me play with myself? Did she come to the library often for this express purpose? Was this her only safe outlet for expressing her sexuality? If so, why did she choose to live such a sheltered life, if she harbored such strong earthly desires?

But mostly, I just obsessed about what she *looked* like under all her formal vestments. As soon as I got home, I tore off my clothes and imagined our bodies bending together in every possible position. I imagined sucking her and licking her and fucking her, making her come in every possible way I could conjure. I fantasized about making her moan and scream in ecstasy, as I worshipped every square inch of her gorgeous body.

After I came for about the tenth time that day, I lay in my bed exhausted and naked, thinking about how I might see her again.

Searching for her at the local abbey was out of the question. They probably wouldn't even allow me to *talk* with her, and if so, it would only be through the front gate for a limited time. And my chances of running into her elsewhere in the Chicago area were practically nil. For all I knew, the library may have been the only sanctioned area outside the convent that she was allowed to visit.

My only chance for seeing her again was at the library. I knew that today's encounter might just have been a lucky happenstance, but I hoped that our silent tryst had awoken a primal urge within her that she'd want to revisit. My only hope was that she'd return to the library again soon and that this time we'd have a chance to connect on a more personal level. If so, I had no intention of letting her slip through my fingers again. At the very least, I hoped we could have a coffee together to give me a chance to get to know her a little better. I fell asleep that night imagining her lying beside me, our bodies intertwined, her skin still dewy from making love to me all day long.

The following morning, I headed out early to be at the library for opening time. I didn't want to take any chance that I might miss my blue-eyed nun if she had the same idea as me. If I had to stay there all day every day for a month, I was ready to do whatever it took. I packed my laptop to work on client projects in case she didn't show up, but if she did, I planned to be ready. I wore a mid-thigh skirt and my favorite cream-colored silk blouse, with absolutely nothing on underneath. As I walked up the front steps of the library, feeling the cool morning breeze wafting up against my bare pussy, my nipples hardened, producing two protrusions in my blouse.

If she wants more of this, I thought, *I'll really give her a show today.*

When the library opened, I searched every floor and every corner of the facility, but the nun was nowhere to be found. I hadn't expected to see her right away, so I found an open table near the chair where she'd sat yesterday and flipped open my computer. But as much as I tried to concentrate on my work, I kept glancing over at the vacant chair, thinking about what had happened yesterday.

I glanced around the room to make sure no one could see my computer screen, then I typed in the search phrase *videos of nuns having sex*. I paused before hitting the Enter key, then added the word *lesbian*. I didn't want any men polluting my fantasy. A video titled *Confessions of a Sinful Nun* popped up. I clicked the pause button, then inserted my headphones into the audio jack so I'd be able to listen to the video privately. The video was different from most other pornos, with top-quality cinematography, multiple attractive characters, and a real forty-minute story arc.

This should distract me for a while, I thought.

The video began with the mother superior at a convent informing a young nun that two other nuns had missed communion, asking her to search the surrounding grounds for them. The pretty nun headed out along a trail in the woods, and after a few minutes heard the sound of two women giggling in a sheltered glade. She peered through the branches and saw the two nuns fondling each other under their habits. It didn't take long for them to remove most of their clothing, until they were wearing nothing but white stockings.

As one of the nuns lay on the ground, the other one straddled her face, grinding her bush into the nun's mouth. While she humped the girls face, she turned her body and began fingering the other nun's pussy. Before long, the nun on top began to shake, as her breasts quivered on her chest. "Oh yes!" she said, pulling the other girl's head tighter against her pussy. "Right there!" Just as she came on the other girl's face, the mother superior suddenly walked up behind the pretty nun and asked her if she'd seen anything. The other girls overheard the conversation and quickly scampered away, while the third nun covered for them.

If convent life is anything like this, I thought, *no wonder my blue-eyed nun felt the need to travel so far afield to escape the overprotective clutches of her abbey.*

The video was part of an extended series, and as I watched each clip, I fingered myself quietly under my desk. For over an hour, I took myself to the edge of climax, slowly backing down each time. I wanted to save myself for my *own* special nun if she came back. But when one of the scenes introduced a sister resembling the one I saw yesterday, I couldn't hold back any longer. I was just about to cum when a familiar black and white figure emerged from the stacks about twenty feet away.

It was the same blue-eyed nun from yesterday!

She walked directly past my desk looking straight ahead, carrying another book under her arm. She sat in the same chair as yesterday and opened the book on her lap, then peered up over the binding in my direction. Her eyes widened when she recognized me, then she quickly crossed her legs and directed her attention back to her book. I glanced at the chair I sat in yesterday and was disappointed to see that it was now occupied. But from my vantage point just a little further away, I actually had a more direct view of the nun. And from her seated position directly in front of me, she had a clear view of knees and skirt at crotch level.

This could actually work out better than I expected, I thought.

But as the nun kept her head buried in her book, feigning disinterest, I began to wonder if we'd crossed signals.

Had I frightened her away yesterday with my bold overture? If so, why hadn't she just gotten up and moved to a location where I wouldn't be such a distraction?

When her foot started bobbing again on her knee, her intention became clearer.

What a sly fox. She's signaling her interest in me through her body language.

I closed my computer lid to give her an unobstructed view of my upper body, then unbuttoned two buttons on my blouse to reveal my cleavage. As my breasts pressed firmly against the silk fabric, I could feel my nipples hardening once again. The nun looked up from her book and did a doubletake, before directing her attention back down toward her book.

"Yes," I whispered under my breath. "Did you like that? Give me a little more of your attention, and I'll *really* give you a show."

The nun had her head down, but I could see her long eyelashes fluttering in excitement against her brow. I knew she must have been torn between her vow of celibacy and her desire to engage me more directly.

She just needs a little more incentive, I thought.

I shifted position in my chair and spread my legs two feet apart. A few seconds later, she peered up, and I wobbled my knees under the table to redirect her focus. When her eyes dipped under my desk, they widened in shock when she saw my bare pussy exposed under my skirt. This time, she didn't look away.

As I spread my knees further apart, she stared straight into the junction of my thighs. I reached under the table with my right hand and hiked my skirt up a few more inches. She now had a clear, unobstructed view of my bare, glistening pussy. She froze for a moment, staring between my legs, then peered down again into her book, as a flush fell over her cheeks.

I smiled, knowing how conflicted she must have been between her pact with God and the tug of raging hormones racing through her system. There was something about the frustration she was experiencing that made this even more of a turn on. I looked around the room to make sure no one else was looking, then I placed my fingers over my clit and began to circle it slowly.

If she looks up again, I'll make it impossible for her to turn away this time.

I squeaked my chair, and within a few seconds, the nun's eyelashes lifted above her book again. When she saw my hand between my legs, her leg straightened over her knee and her book wobbled on her lap. As I placed my hand over my vulva and began to rub it over my slit, I could feel my juices spilling out of my pussy, coating my thighs and ass. The feeling emanating from between my legs was sublime, magnified all the more knowing my pretty nun was getting just as wet as me under her heavy habit.

As I began to feel my passion rising, my mouth opened unconsciously, and seeing the look of unadorned pleasure on my face, the nun's lips parted also. Recognizing that we'd made sustained eye contact for the first time, I felt an electric charge go through me, and I pressed my fingers tighter against my snatch. I could have come at any moment, but I wanted to savor this for as long as I could.

When her eyes dipped back under my table, I slipped my middle fingers into my opening and began to fuck myself as my two outer fingers slid up and down the inside of my thighs. I wanted to bring my other hand under the table to massage my clit directly, but it was too dangerous. It would have been far too suspicious for any onlookers to see a woman squirming in her library chair with two hands pumping under the table.

Instead, I pressed the palm of my hand against my mound and shimmied my hand up and down over my button while I pressed my two fingers as deep as I could into my hole. The nun was now bouncing her eyes up and down between my face, my bouncing tits, and my cavitating legs under the table. Her foot began bobbing more rapidly on her knee and I could see the front of her frock rising and falling as she breathed heavily.

For the first time, I could make out the bulge of her breasts under her gown, and although they were heavily concealed by all the layers of fabric, I could tell she had a plump set of tits. As I fantasized about sucking on them, I increased the pace of my finger-fucking and spread my legs wider, until they were almost a full one hundred and eighty degrees apart.

As my orgasm began rising within me, my mouth gaped open and I nodded, indicating that I was about to cum, and the nun did the same. Whether she was feeling the same sensations under her robe, or was simply mirroring my expression in sympathy with me, I wasn't sure. When my climax finally poured over me, I thrust my hand hard against my mound and clamped down over my fingers.

As the pretty nun watched the look of ecstasy wash over my face, I pressed back against my chair and sat shaking in a spastic seizure for a full thirty seconds. When my contractions finally abated, I sat up in my chair with my fingers still embedded in my pussy, savoring the heightened sensitivity inside my warm cavern.

When I finally regained my senses, I realized that I'd been so lost in my own pleasure that I'd temporarily lost focus on what the nun was doing. I wasn't sure if she'd managed to rub one out herself, or if she had just been concentrating on enjoying my show. But when she uncrossed her legs and spread her knees apart, her plan soon became apparent. A few moments later, her right hand disappeared from the edge of her book and I noticed some movement under her gown in the area between her legs as the textbook in her lap begin to shake.

Clever girl! It looked like she'd cut a hole in the side of her frock so she could have direct access to her private areas.

The movement under her gown began to take on a familiar and steady pattern as she began to squirm in her seat. Our eyes met once again, and her lips parted as her chest began to rise and fall more rapidly.

Fuck! I thought. *She's actually going to let me watch her come this time!*

I pushed my fingers harder into my pussy and began shimmying my palm against my clit again. But this time, I paced myself so I could cum with her. As her movements under her robe increased in intensity, I sped up my movements in kind. We were staring directly into each other's eyes now, and I could tell she was getting close.

When she nodded her head to me signaling that she was about to cum, I couldn't stop myself from moaning as my second climax took hold of me. The nun's thighs pulled together as she hunched forward in obvious climax, and I gushed all over my hand as the contractions inside my pussy sprayed my love juices all over my thighs and ass. I clenched my face trying to stifle my moans, but a few pitiful whimpers escaped. At this point, I didn't even care if anybody noticed what I was doing. I was on my own special wavelength with the pretty nun across the aisle, and for now at least, we were the only two people in the room.

After a few seconds, the nun's body relaxed and she lay back against her chair. The book resting on her lap popped up as she pulled her hand from between her legs, then she smiled at me softly and closed her eyes, laying her head on the backrest. I looked around the room to make sure no one else had witnessed our silent affair, then I pulled my sopping fingers out of my cunny and cleaned them with some wet wipes in my purse.

There was no way I was going to leave the library alone today without at least talking to the pretty nun. When she stood up from her chair ten minutes later and walked toward the stacks to return her library book, I quickly collected my belongings and followed her. A dribble of lubrication run down the inside of my thigh as my pussy pulsed in excitement, knowing I was about to have my first real contact with the blue-eyed beauty.

SISTERS

When I entered the row where I saw the nun go to return her book, she was bending forward squinting at the call numbers on the spines of the shelved books. I stepped forward and tilted my head down slightly, smiling at her.

"You know you don't actually have to reshelve library books when you're finished with them," I said.

She stood up, flushing in her cheeks when she recognized me.

"Oh—yes," she said, in a soft voice. "I just figured the librarians can use all the help they can get. There's so few of them looking after such a big place."

My heart raced as I listened to her talk. She was even more beautiful up close than I imagined. She had flawless unblemished skin, and her azure-blue eyes penetrated me like a laser, deep into my soul. Completing the angelic imagery, her melodious voice reminded me of the virtual assistant on my phone, lulling me with its lilt.

I glanced at some of the book titles on the shelf in front of her and the category banner at the side of the stack.

"You're a fan of historical fiction?" I said, trying to break the tension.

The nun glanced at the marker, then smiled as she turned her book cover around for me to see.

"Not usually. Normally I stick to scripture and other Christian themes. But the title of this one intrigued me."

"*Jesus and the Riddle of the Dead Sea Scrolls*," I said, reading the title of her book. "That certainly sounds like it qualifies."

"I think its miscategorized. It's really more of a critique of the Bible, suggesting that the Dead Sea Scrolls offer a somewhat different explanation for the events surrounding the time of Jesus."

"Sounds interesting," I nodded. "What was your impression of the book?"

"I...kind of lost interest after the first few pages," the nun hesitated, looking away. "I guess it didn't exactly fit in with my world view."

She looked at the laptop bag slung around my shoulder and peered back at me with her piercing eyes.

"How about you? What were you reading today?"

"Oh," I said, momentarily caught off guard. "I wasn't actually reading anything specific today. I just like to come here every now and then to find a quiet place to work on some...personal projects."

The nun turned to face me directly, holding her book over her breast like a schoolgirl.

"What kind of work do you do?"

"Freelance graphic design mostly. Book covers, ad copy, corporate logos, that sort of thing." I looked at the pretty nun's smock and frowned. "Pretty superficial stuff compared to your life's work, I would imagine."

"You mean *this*?" she chuckled, pinching her gown and pulling it away from her body a few inches. "I think most people imagine the life of a nun to be one of the most boring vocations possible for a young woman."

"I wouldn't exactly choose that word. I imagine you have plenty of spiritual and emotional stimulation in your chosen field."

The nun nodded gently and sighed.

"Yes, there's plenty of that. Perhaps not as much intellectual stimulation as in your field, though. That's part of the reason I like to come to the library. There are lots of other—*perspectives*—to be found here."

Now I was the one who could feel a blush spreading over my cheeks. I paused, wondering how I could steal a few more private moments with her.

"I'd love to learn more about your life. It's all so mysterious. Do you have time for a coffee? You could enlighten me on spiritual matters, and I could regale you with all the fascinating logos I've worked on."

The nun chuckled, then paused to contemplate my offer.

"I'm not sure you'll find the life of a cloistered nun terribly interesting. I'm sure you have a far more fascinating life. Coffee might be breaking the rules though. I'll be happy to share some fruit juice with you."

I smiled, beginning to realize how pure and unspoiled she was.

"Fruit juice it is. I know a quiet spot not too far from here."

I extended my right hand slowly.

"I'm Jade."

The nun extended her hand and clasped mine softly in hers. My heart thumped in my chest, sending a surge of hormones racing to my pussy.

"Sister Caroline," the nun said.

"Should I address you as Sister, Caroline, or Sister Caroline?" I asked, unsure of the proper protocol.

"Sister is fine."

"Pleasure to meet you, Sister. May I offer you a ride to the coffee shop?"

"Sure. It's got to be more comfortable than the two buses I took to get here."

The pretty nun and I continued making small talk on the way to the coffee shop, with neither one of us broaching the subject of what had happened between the two of us earlier at the library. When we got to the coffeehouse, I ordered two fruit juices and we found a quiet corner of the shop near the fireplace with two upholstered chairs.

"This is a cozy little spot," the nun said. She closed her eyes and took a deep breath through her nostrils. "And the smell is divine."

"I thought you didn't like coffee?"

"This aroma is bringing back the memories. After taking my vows, I gave up a *lot* of little pleasures I'd almost forgotten."

We paused for a long moment smiling at one another, then the nun took a sip of her juice.

"Do you mind my asking what kind of vows you've taken?" I asked. "I'm ashamed to admit that all I know about nuns is what I saw in the movie The Sound of Music."

"We could do worse than that in terms of public perception," the nun chuckled. "That was another one of my favorite things from my previous life, to steal a phrase. I always admired Julie Andrews. I think her depiction of a nun's life is partially what drew me to it."

My eyes crinkled, recognizing a common bond. I was rapidly developing more than just sexual feelings for Sister Caroline.

"You know you look a little bit like her," I said. "The same piercing blue eyes, soft pretty features..."

"You're far too kind, Jade. But to answer your question, we take three separate vows for poverty, chastity, and obedience."

"Obedience in terms of adhering to scripture?"

"Actually, the obedience part pertains to our promising to follow the rules of the abbey and the guidance of our abbess."

"Abbess?"

Sister Caroline chuckled.

"That's mother superior, to our Sounds of Music fans."

"And the poverty part? Is that why you can't drink coffee?"

"That wouldn't be breaking the rules, per se. But we're expected to follow a life of austerity once we enter the abbey. The menu at the abbey is kind of bland, but you get used to it pretty quickly."

I paused, unsure how to broach the delicate third subject.

"And the chastity part? Was that something that you had trouble adjusting to also?"

"At first, no. We actually go through a ceremony where we're literally betrothed to Jesus. Once the temptations are removed in the sheltered confines of the abbey, you soon learn to not think about the temptations of the flesh any longer."

"And when you *leave* the abbey?" I said, finally addressing the elephant in the room. "How do you manage the temptations then?"

"I was doing fine," she said. "Until I saw you."

I paused, looking into the nun's eyes with a pained look on my face.

"Sister..."

"I think perhaps you should call me Caroline. It feels a little strange under the circumstances you calling me sister."

"I agree," I said. "Caroline. I like that name. It's soft and pretty—like you."

"I was thinking the same about you, Jade. It's been hard for me to take my eyes off you. It wasn't just because..."

I leaned forward and placed my palm over Caroline's hand resting on her armchair.

"I'm sorry about being so forward," I said. "I couldn't resist. From the moment I first saw you, my body seems to have a mind of its own whenever I'm around you. And then when I saw you reacting to me the way you did—"

"Was it that obvious?" Caroline said.

"Not to anyone else in the library."

"I hope not. Otherwise, my abbey's switchboard will be flooded with calls from outraged Christians."

"You were very...*proper*," I chuckled. "I'm quite sure I was the only one who noticed that you were enjoying more than just your book in your chair."

"Not nearly as much as *you*," Caroline said, her cheeks flushing a deep shade of crimson. "It was a lot more—*obvious*—how much pleasure you were experiencing on the other side of the room."

Hearing Caroline acknowledge our sexual connection for the first time suddenly sent a flood of juices pouring out of my pussy. I crossed my legs, feeling the moisture coating the inside of my thighs.

"You have that—*effect* on me," I said. " I think I could have just as easily—*enjoyed myself*—just watching you. I barely even needed to touch myself."

Caroline smiled at me warmly, as I noticed her bosom begin to rise and fall in silent excitement.

"I'm glad you did though. You're beautiful—everywhere. When I first caught you squirming in your chair yesterday, it was like a different power overtook my body."

I squeezed my thighs together, pinching my clit between my legs.

"While you revisited another one of those earthly pleasures you'd almost forgotten?"

"Yes," Caroline said. "And not just once. I've revisited those pleasures several times since yesterday. You're a difficult image to shake from one's memory, Jade."

As I crossed my legs trying to contain my rising passion, I felt the juices pouring out of my opening, dribbling down the crack of my ass.

"So what do we do now?" I asked. "Keep meeting for clandestine rendezvous at our local public library? Sooner or later, someone's going to catch on to us."

"I think you're right," Caroline nodded. "We're both taking unnecessary risks."

I looked around the coffee shop and noticed many people suddenly turning away. It was apparent that the pretty nun in her black habit had become the center of everyone's attention.

"Why don't we go somewhere where there aren't so many prying eyes? I can make us some more fresh juice at my place. That is—if you don't need to get back to the abbey right away..."

"What time is it?" Caroline asked. "I don't have a watch."

I pulled my phone out of my purse and tapped the screen to wake it up.

"Ten fifteen."

"It's still early," she said. "I might not be missed until the afternoon communion..."

For the entire duration of the twenty-minute drive back to my place, Caroline and I didn't say a word to each other, the sexual tension was so thick between us in the car. As she looked out her passenger window watching the passing scenery, I squeezed my thighs together, trying to keep my throbbing pussy from completely soaking the underside of my skirt.

When we got to my house, I opened the front door and invited her in. She looked around my living room and nodded approvingly.

"You have a lovely home," she said. "Tasteful and understated, just I expected."

"I wouldn't have thought you'd expect anything *understated* about me after today," I laughed. "Come to the kitchen and let me see if I can fix you up something more to your liking."

I led Caroline to my open kitchen and offered her a bar stool at the large central island.

"What do you feel like?" I asked. "Water, juice—or maybe something a little stronger? I don't suppose you're allowed to partake in certain other types of spirits?"

"We do occasionally partake in communal wine," Caroline chuckled, "so long as it's been properly consecrated first. Hopefully I won't be struck down for drinking something other than the blood of Christ, this one time."

"White wine it is then," I said, pulling a bottle of chardonnay from my fridge. "We don't need any more judging eyes upon us today."

I placed two wine glasses on the counter and filled the goblets halfway, then sat down beside Caroline.

"To rekindling forgotten memories," I said, holding my glass in the air.

Caroline tapped her goblet gently against mine, then took a small sip from the glass.

"There's been one other thing I've been meaning to ask you," I said, peering up at her white headdress. "Why is your hood white? Don't most nuns wear a black veil?"

"You're not the only one who's asked me that," she said. "Nuns normally go through a period of testing when they first enter the religious order, called a postulancy. For the first couple of years, we wear a white veil, signifying that we're still novitiates, or novices. Once we pass this initial test, if the nun and the abbess agree that the monastic life is what they desire, we take our final vows and receive the traditional all-black habit."

"So you're still—*testing* the waters, then?"

"I suppose so. I'm getting pretty close to the end of my postulancy period. My mother superior will be expecting me to take my final vows soon..."

"Do you feel ready?"

Caroline paused for a long moment with a pained look on her face.

"I thought I was. Until I met you. Then suddenly, my thoughts were no longer so pure..."

I set my glass down on the counter and stared into Caroline's eyes, imagining how conflicted she must have felt at this moment. We paused for many long seconds peering at one another, then she leaned her face toward me unconsciously. I quickly closed the distance and placed my lips against hers gently. As she closed her eyes, she pressed her mouth harder against mine.

I swiveled my stool until I was facing her directly, then I brought my right knee forward, parting her legs. As Caroline's mouth opened, I felt her cool breath on my face. I pushed my tongue gently into her, tasting the sweet vestige of wine on her lips. Within seconds, we were holding each other in a passionate embrace, pressing our bodies tightly together over the bar stools.

"Jade," Caroline panted, pulling away momentarily.

I looked into her eyes, trying to divine her intentions.

"Caroline," I said. "Do you feel ready?" I repeated.

She peered through glistening eyes at me and paused for only a moment.

"Yes."

Then she leaned forward and closed her lips around mine.

4

UNCLOAKED

C aroline and I kissed awkwardly on the bar stools for a few moments, then I pulled away and suggested we go upstairs where we could be more comfortable. As I led her by the hand through the hall, I felt an electric charge running through my body knowing I'd soon see her disrobed. But when we got to my bedroom, I paused looking at her habit, unsure where to start.

"I feel a bit uncomfortable touching your gown," I said. "Some-how, it just feels—*blasphemous*. I don't know how..."

Caroline smiled softly at me, then reached her hands up behind her veil.

"I can see how it might seem a bit daunting," she said. "Let me show you how I take off my armor."

She turned around and reached under the pleated fold behind her hood, then removed a hidden safety pin holding the two sides together, closing the pin and placing it in her pocket. Then she flipped up the back of her veil and unclasped another safety pin holding the inner flaps together. Then she turned around and lifted her hood off her head. Underneath, she wore a white cotton head-dress covering her ears, neck, and the rest of her head.

I stared at her as she disassembled her wardrobe, mesmerized by the multiple layers of strange regalia. She looked so pure and innocent bound up in her tight white hoodie.

"Is there somewhere I can keep my veil?" she said, holding the white hood in front of her.

"Yes," I said, hanging it delicately over the back of my chair so as not to wrinkle it.

When I returned, she had her hands behind her head, slowly untying some more connections.

"Can I help?" I said, frustrated by the slow pace of her undressing. "Two people might make this go a little faster."

Caroline chuckled then turned around. At the back of her head, I saw two cotton ties holding her headdress together.

"You weren't kidding about the body armor," I chuckled. "They've really got you all tied up in this thing, don't they?"

"It's not as bad as it looks," Caroline said. "It's actually quite comfortable. You get used to it pretty quickly."

I untied the cotton bows at the back of her headdress, then gasped. Her hair was shorn down to short stubs, revealing an almost bald head.

"Are you *sure* you want me to take this off?" Caroline said with her back still turned to me.

"Yes," I said. "More than ever." I looked at the back of her hoodie and saw some more clasps. "What now?"

"Remove the safety pin holding the flap at the back of my neck."

I reached up and found the pin and gently slid it out under the band.

"Good God," I said. "How do you manage to get all these pins in and out every day without stabbing yourself? Or do you just sleep in this thing?"

"Heavens, no," Caroline said. "We're expected to keep our habits in pristine condition. That would produce far too many wrinkles. I actually sleep in the nude most of the time."

My pussy pulsed at the thought of soon seeing her naked body.

"I'm dying to see you that way. How do we get the rest of this stuff off?"

"There's just one more pin to remove," she said. "At the bottom of my collar, you'll find another one holding the two flaps together."

I found the pin and removed it softly.

"Done."

Caroline turned around and smiled at me.

"Are you sure you're ready for this?" she asked.

"Yes," I said. "I want to see *all* of you."

Caroline reached behind her neck and removed her large oval collar and handed it to me. Then she reached behind her head and pulled her headdress forward off her head. When she showed her bare head for the first time, my eyes widened as big as saucers. Her baldness accentuated her soft features and beauty, reminding me of a young Sinead O'Connor.

"Caroline," I said. "You're stunning."

I leaned forward and kissed her on her lips and she pulled gently away.

"Don't forget about the wrinkling thing. I want to see you naked just as much as you do, but I've got to be presentable when I return to the abbey. Let's get the rest of these clothes off so we don't have to worry about it any longer."

She handed me the headdress and collar and I placed them flat on my work desk along with the pins. Now she stood before me wearing only her long black robe. The slow reveal was driving me crazy, and I could feel my pussy pulsing between my legs, anticipating what lay beneath.

Caroline threaded her fingers between the two sides of a long sash on the front of her gown, then pulled the strange garb over her head and handed it to me. Divest of the extra garment, I saw a long string of black prayer beads hanging down the side of her gown from her belt.

"This is called the scapular," she said.

"No wonder I couldn't make out your shape under your gown," I said. "How many layers do you have on this thing anyhow?"

"Just one more."

She reached around her back and unbuckled her belt, then handed it to me with the beads attached.

"Now the rosary..."

"Are you sure I won't get struck down by lightning touching this?" I joked.

"Let's hope not. But just to be safe, you might want to handle it by the belt only."

I held the belt out in front of me, being careful not to let the beads touch the ground, then laid it gently on my desk beside the other garments. When I returned, Caroline paused, looking at me unsteadily. I could tell she was a little nervous about revealing any more of her body.

"May I do this part?" I said, seeing the zipper running down the front of her tunic.

"Yes," she said, softly.

I slowly pulled the zipper down from under her chin and noticed that she wasn't wearing a bra.

"No undergarments?" I said, somewhat surprised.

"Not today," she said. "I wanted to feel...sexier. Normally, I wear an undershirt, bra, panties, and nylons. Something told me I might need to remove my habit a little faster today..."

I paused, realizing she was completely naked under this final layer. I stared into her eyes as I slowly pulled the zipper down. Listening to my heart pounding in my chest, I wasn't sure which one of us was more nervous. When the zipper reached the bottom of its travel, I pulled the upper halves of her tunic apart and peered down at her chest. When I saw her breasts, I gasped.

"Oh, God," I murmured.

Caroline's breasts were full and firm, standing in two perfect circles high on her chest. I reached in and cupped them with my hands and squeezed them gently, stepping forward and kissing her hard on her mouth. I could feel her chest rising and falling as she breathed heavily, blowing a soft breeze through her nostrils onto the sides of my cheeks. When I moved my thumb and forefinger over her nipples, I felt them harden, and she gasped in my mouth. As I rolled them gently between my fingers, she pressed her body firmly against mine.

We kissed for a few more seconds, then I moved my hands around the sides of her back, down toward her buttocks. As I ran my hands over her cheeks, they quivered in my hands and I pulled her toward me more tightly. When our mounds touched, we both let out a moan, and I felt Caroline's muscles contract in my hands as she pressed her mound against me.

"Jade," she panted. "This is all I've been able to think about. I want to make love to you."

She stepped back a couple of feet, then pulled her arms out of her sleeves and dropped her gown to the floor. When I saw her fully naked body for the first time, it took my breath away. She had a slender but shapely hourglass figure, with barely an ounce of fat anywhere on her body. Her whole body was white as fresh snow, except for a light brown triangle of pubic hair between her legs. I reached down and picked up her habit and folded it over the back of my chair, then returned to behold my pretty angel.

I stepped forward and ran my hands down the sides of her body, feeling the curvature of her hips, then I cupped her face in my hands and kissed her softly. Her body was shaking next to me, and as I touched her back, I felt goosebumps on her skin.

"Are you chilly?" I said.

"Maybe a little," she said. "I'm not used to being out of my habit for this long. Maybe I'm a little nervous too..."

"It's okay," I said. "We can take this slow. Let's get you under the covers where you'll be more comfortable."

I pulled the covers down from the edge of my headboard and gently sat Caroline on the side of my bed. Then I kneeled down on the floor between her legs and untied her black shoes and placed them beside my nightstand. With my face so close to her kitty, I could smell her sex wafting up from between her legs, and I wanted to pull myself into her so badly.

But I lay her down on the bed and pulled the sheets and comforter over her, then stood up. As she lay on my bed looking up at me innocently, I began to unbutton my blouse. Her eyes widened when she saw my full breasts pull away from my shirt, and I quickly pulled my arms out of my sleeves and threw my blouse on the floor.

"I'm not quite as worried about wrinkling as you are."

"Neither am I right now," she said. "Just get out of those clothes and get in here."

I quickly undid my skirt and dropped it to the floor. Even though Caroline had seen my naked vulva from across the library floor earlier, she was surprised to see my bare mound. Her eyes widened as she took in my body, squirming seductively under the covers.

"Now *you're* the one who looks pure and clean," she said, staring at the bare space between my legs.

I pulled off my shoes, then climbed in under the covers next to her.

"I'm sure I'm nowhere near as pure as you," I said, snuggling close to her. "But speaking of clean, I am feeling a little crusty from all the bodily discharges I produced watching you earlier today. Do you mind if I have a quick shower?"

Caroline wrapped her arms and legs around me and squiggled closer to me under the covers.

"Now?" she said. "You'd leave me to my own devices after teasing me so thoroughly?"

"Well if you don't think you can wait the five minutes it'll take me to clean up, you could always join me in the shower."

I turned around and opened my nightstand drawer.

"Or you could keep yourself amused with these other devices while I'm gone."

Caroline's eyes widened as she took in my collection of sex toys.

"Are those what I think they are?" she said.

"You've never used one?"

"Nothing quite so...elaborate. I've experimented using bottles and sundry pieces of fruit before, but these look a lot more —*sophisticated.*"

I looked into Caroline's eyes and smiled a wide grin.

"You're in for a real treat then," I said. "But first, I want to have my *own* way with you before you get too attached to mechanical devices. Come, let's have a quick shower together to get cleaned up. It'll warm you up, too."

I threw the covers back then we scampered into my ensuite washroom, giggling like two little girls. I adjusted the water temperature in my shower until it was nice and warm, then I pulled Caroline under the spray. As the droplets bounced off her bald head and streamed down her face, I pulled her toward me and kissed her hard on her mouth. We rubbed our breasts together under the slippery water, clasping each other's buttocks, grinding our mounds against one another.

Caroline moaned gently, and I began to lower myself slowly down her body. As the water poured over me, I kissed her under her neck, tasting her sweet flesh. When I reached her chest, I paused to give each of her breasts plenty of attention, sucking and flicking her hardened nipples with my tongue, cupping and squeezing her tits between my two hands. The further I moved down her body, the more she moaned and whimpered, her stomach quivering in excitement from my touch.

It was obvious to me that she'd never been touched in this way by another person, and I savored every square inch of her magnificent, unspoiled body. When I got to her bush, I sucked the water droplets off her thatch like dew on the morning grass. Then I knelt down on the tiled floor, gently spread her legs, and kissed her pearl. Caroline gasped, grabbing the back of my head, and pulled me closer toward her.

"I thought you said we were going to get *clean* in here," she panted.

"That's exactly what I'm doing," I said. "I didn't say *how* we were going to get clean. Do you want me to stop?"

"God, no!" she said, pulling my head harder against her crotch.

When I slipped my tongue around her button and began to lather her with my serpent, Caroline threw her head back and moaned loudly.

"Yes, Jade," she whimpered. "Lick me. Lick me clean with your tongue."

Caroline's sexy comments surprised me, emboldening me to go further. I cupped her ass with my left hand and began trilling my fingers against her opening. Caroline bent her knees and tilted her hips, encouraging me to go further.

"Yes—take me," she said. "I want to feel you inside me."

I slipped my middle and forefinger into her cavern, and she pushed her hips down until my hand was buried inside her up to my knuckles. As she began humping her hips against my hand, I sucked her lengthening nub into my mouth.

"Oh God, yes," Caroline panted. "Suck me, Jade. It feels so good."

As her humping action increased in intensity, she pulled my head harder against her pussy. I could tell she was getting close, so I curled my fingers against her G-spot and flicked my tongue more rapidly over her rubbery clit. When I slipped my pinky finger further down her perineum and placed it over her anus, she gasped.

"Yes!" Caroline panted. "Jade, I'm going to—"

Suddenly, she emitted a guttural scream and pushed her muff hard into my face, as I felt her vagina and rosebud pulsing against my fingers. As she came into my mouth, I held her firmly in my hands, savoring her sweet nectar as the water streamed over my face.

"Jade—Jade—Jade!" Caroline panted with each pulse of her pussy. "I'm cumming! Oh—I'm cumming into your sweet mouth!"

It was odd to hear someone screaming in the throes of ecstasy without using any curse words, which just added to my excitement. As I felt the water streaming down over my ass and mound, my pussy quivered along with Caroline's. When she finally stopped shaking atop of me, I stood up and kissed her passionately, as the water streamed down over our faces.

Caroline wanted to return the favor, but I just wanted to get her back into bed as quickly as possible. I let her run the bar of soap over my body and between my legs, but I made sure to not get too worked up. There was so much more I wanted to do with her when we had the full and free roam of each other's bodies. When we were both thoroughly clean, we stepped out of the shower and toweled each other dry, then we scampered back into my bedroom and dove under the covers.

We kissed and intertwined our legs awkwardly for a few minutes, then I pulled myself away.

"Are you thoroughly warmed up now?" I said, looking into her eyes.

"Yes. You've practically brought me to a boil."

"Good," I said, throwing back the covers. "Because this is going to need a little more space."

Caroline pinched her eyebrows together and began to raise herself up.

"What did you have in mind? It's my turn to—"

I placed my hand on Caroline's chest and gently pushed her back onto the bed.

"It's okay," I said. "This is for *both* of us."

I lifted her knees off the bed then gently pressed her legs forward and apart until her thighs were resting on top of her chest. Then I moved my body forward and pressed my mound against hers.

"Uhnn!" Caroline grunted in surprise when our clits touched.

"Yes, Jade!" she said. "Make love to me."

She lifted her head and peered between her legs. Both of our buttons were hard and erect, protruding like little pencil erasers toward one another. I lowered myself slowly and swayed my hips over hers, watching out nubs bending and flexing in a playful little sword fight.

"Oh God," Caroline panted. "That feels so good! Stroke me, Jade. Rub me...*fuck* me!"

I widened my eyes and gasped at Caroline in mock astonishment.

"You dirty little girl," I said. "I sure hope no one else is listening right now. Otherwise you could be in a lot of trouble."

"So do I," Caroline said. "But right now it hardly matters. Take me. There's only one place I want to go right now."

I lay my body on top of Caroline's and began to grind my pussy into hers as we kissed passionately. For the first time, I felt her tongue press into my mouth, and we sucked and nibbled on each other as our hips gyrated together. I wanted to make this feeling last, but I was already so worked up from making Caroline cum earlier, I could feel my orgasm rising quickly within me.

I grunted into Caroline's mouth as my juices poured out of my cunt, coating her bush and thighs with my lubrication. I could feel myself getting close, and I pulled my face up so I could look at Caroline's face. As my mouth and eyes widened signaling my impending orgasm, Caroline suddenly began panting louder.

"Yes, Jade," she said. "*Cum* for me. I want to watch you cum all over me."

I lifted my body up in one last strain and thrust my pussy hard against hers.

"Caroline!" I screamed. "I'm cumming! I'm cumming in your sweet pussy!"

Caroline's pupils suddenly dilated and she called out my name.

"Fuck, yes!" she screamed with me. "I feel you! I'm cumming with you, Jade! Oh God—it feels so good!"

Suddenly, I felt a hard spray jetting up against my vulva as Caroline squirted her love juices into my opening. Feeling her cum against my pussy was too much. I swung my body around her and clamped our boxes together in a scissor position. I wanted to feel our pussies connected as we were cumming together.

"Uhnn—Caroline," I grunted. "Come in my pussy, baby! Fill me up with your sweet nectar!"

I pulled her leg up toward my chest, grinding our cunts together, feeling my contractions gripping my entire body. We jerked and heaved our bodies together for a full minute, watching the look of tortured ecstasy wash over our faces. When we were completely spent, I collapsed on the bed beside Caroline, panting and sweating. We lay beside one another for a long time, holding and caressing each other, then Caroline finally turned toward me.

"What time is it?" she asked.

My eyes widened and I shook my head.

"Oh no," I said. "You can't..."

"I have to," she said. "The abbess will begin to worry if I'm not back soon."

I looked at Caroline through glistening eyes.

"But I don't want to let you go. I wanted to feel you fall asleep in my arms."

I turned my head toward my nightstand, thinking of how I could entice her to stay a little longer.

"And besides, you haven't even tried any of my toys. I had a few special ones in mind for you. When can you come back?"

"I don't know if I can," Caroline said. "These library excursions were meant to be temporary. I'm supposed to stay within the abbey. That's the whole point of my vows—to abstain from worldly temptations."

"But I thought you hadn't decided yet? Hasn't this changed your thinking at all about continuing on your life of abstinence?"

"It has, but I'm not ready to give it all up just yet. I need a little more time to think—"

"Can I visit you at the abbey at least? I just need to see you. I can't just let you walk out of my life forever."

Caroline looked at me with a pained expression and shook her head.

"It's too dangerous. People will notice there's something different between us—"

I reflected back to the videos of the naked nuns I watched earlier in the day.

"Is there somewhere I could meet you then, where no one would notice? Can you ever leave the grounds temporarily?"

"Not really."

Caroline paused for a long moment.

"But—"

"Tell me," I said. "I'll do anything, as long as I can see you again."

"There might be one way," she said. "But it's very dangerous..."

"What? Tell me!"

"I might be able to sneak you into the abbey for a short time. There's a secret passageway that we're not supposed to know about. A few other novices and I occasionally use it to slip outside to go for a walk. But we'd have to do it at night, and we'd need to have a signal."

I paused for a moment, thinking how I could notify her when I was near.

"How about if I hoot like an owl? There's plenty of those around here. Will you be able to hear it from inside the abbey?"

"I'll keep my window open," Caroline nodded. "But not tonight. The abbess will be watching too closely. Let's do it tomorrow night, just after dusk. Hoot three times in succession, so I know it's you. But be sure to do it convincingly, so it sounds like a real owl. I'll meet you at the south gate at the edge of the forest."

"I'll watch YouTube videos and practice all day," I said. "Will I be able to stay the night? I want to feel you in my arms when I fall asleep."

"Possibly. But you'll have to stay holed up in my room until the following night. Then you'll have to leave. It will be too dangerous for you to stay more than one day."

"I promise," I said, feeling my heart beating again in excitement. " Even one more day with you will feel like a lifetime. I just hope you'll reconsider your vows so we can see each other again. I don't want to lose you."

Caroline turned her body to face me and kissed me softly.

"You're so sweet, Jade. If anything could pull me away from the ascetic life, it's you."

Then she paused as she smiled into my eyes.

"And bring some of your toys. That might help."

5

———

MOTHER SUPERIOR

The next twenty-four hours seemed like an eternity, as I waited to see Caroline again. All I could think about was her radiant face and her pale, supple skin pressed against my body. I'd gone online and practiced my owl imitation as promised, standing in front of my mirror contorting my face and vocal chords, until I thought I'd gotten the pitch just right. As long as nobody saw me huddled in the surrounding woodland, I was confident I'd be able to pull it off.

An hour before dusk, I collected my belongings and drove north toward the remote address Caroline had given me. When I got to the monastery, there was a long drive leading up a hill, protected by a wrought-iron gate. I parked my car on a side street and tried to find a pedestrian access point, but the entire estate was surrounded by a tall iron fence topped with pointed finials, with locked gates all around.

Caroline had warned me about the barricade, so I removed a heavily padded blanket from my tote bag and flung it atop the spikes. I threw my purse over the fence then awkwardly pulled myself up the front of the fence and swung my legs over the top. I could feel the finials poking through the blanket into my stomach and chest, and swung my legs over the other side and fell onto the manicured lawn on the other side.

"These guys don't fool around," I murmured, feeling like a cat burglar invading a hallowed ground.

I made my way up the hill, trying to stay under the cover of the many mature trees scattered over the estate. When I got to the top of the hill, I saw a tall, steepled church flanked by two four-story block buildings. Caroline told me she was in the west residence, so I moved to that side of the compound and waited about thirty feet behind the rear entrance under a large elm tree. There was no sign of any activity on the grounds, which just added to the spookiness of the scene.

What the hell have I gotten myself into? I thought, looking around the quiet estate. *If anybody sees me, I'll stick out like a sore thumb.*

I'd worn special clothing to not be too conspicuous, and with my long dark pants, black sneakers, and black turtleneck, it just added to the cat burglar mystique. As the light dimmed over the estate, bats began darting over the dark sky and I heard rustling in the branches overhead.

This place is creepy, I thought, wondering if this was an omen of bad things to come.

But as dusk fell, I began to hear the familiar hooting of owls in the surrounding woodland, and as I listened to their calls I prepared to alert Caroline. At precisely nine-fifteen, I let out my signal.

"Hoo—hoo—hoo," I called out in my best falsetto.

Within seconds, a nearby owl returned my call.

"Hoo—hoo—hoo," I repeated.

Almost immediately, the owl hooted back.

If I can trick a real owl, I thought, *hopefully I can blend in with the rest of the local fauna.*

I waited five minutes, watching the back door to Caroline's building, but there was no sign of movement.

Had her abbess suspected something different about Caroline when she returned to the abbey and was keeping a closer eye on her? What if she can't get away?

I repeated my owl signal two more times, then I saw the back door swing open a few inches and Caroline stuck her head out, motioning for me to come in. I looked around to make sure the way was clear, then I scampered toward the door and jumped inside. Caroline and I kissed for a moment, then she pulled away with wide eyes.

"Jeesh—" she said, "do you think you could have made more of a racket out there? You've probably woken up the entire western wing!"

"It wasn't just me," I protested. "Apparently, there was another amorous owl out there competing for my affections. We had quite a little conversation going on for a while there."

Caroline giggled, then pulled a folded habit from under her cape and handed it to me.

"What do you want me to do with this?" I asked.

"We're going to need to disguise you, in case we run into anyone. It's only three floors and a short walk to my dorm, but I don't want to take any chances."

"Oh my God!" I said. "As if we haven't already broken enough rules. Now you want me to pretend I'm a *nun*?! God will surely strike me down before I get to your room."

"I'm sure he'll understand, under the circumstances," Caroline said. She removed the long tunic component from the pile. "Put this on first. Do you remember how it goes?"

"I've replayed your undressing ceremony in my head only about a hundred times since you left," I chuckled.

I stepped into the toga, then pulled the sleeves over my arms and zipped up the front.

"Good," Caroline said. "Now for the scapular."

She handed me the long flap draped over the front and back of the habit, and I pulled it over my head.

"Now the guimpe..." she said, handing me the large white collar.

She placed it around my neck and fastened it with the safety pin behind my back.

"Almost done," she said, handing me the white headdress. "Do you remember how to put on the wimple?"

"Of course," I said, placing my face through the hole in the front, then pulling it up under my chin and over my head.

"We won't worry about tying it at the back," Caroline said. "We haven't got far to go. It should hold until you get to my room. Now for the veil."

She lifted a black hood from my hands and placed it over my headdress, fastening it with two velcro tabs on top of my head.

"Why do I get a black one?" I asked.

"You're going to be a fully professed nun for tonight," she said. "You'll attract less attention this way."

"No prayer beads?" I joked.

"Let's not push it," she said. "You're already living on borrowed time as it is."

Caroline paused, as she looked at me approvingly.

"You know, you look quite suitable in a habit. Are you sure you don't want to consider joining our monastery full time? At least we'd have a chance to be together more—"

"I don't think I could manage the chastity part of your vows very well," I kidded.

"What now?" I said, looking up the stairs.

"Follow close behind me," Caroline said. "If we encounter any other sisters along the way, just keep your head down. Hopefully, nobody will recognize that you're an outsider."

"And if I am?"

"Well improvise."

"Is that where the lightning comes in?"

"Quite possibly."

I shook my head as I followed Caroline up the three flights of stairs, then she opened the door leading to her floor's hall and peered through the crack.

"All clear," she said. "Remember—stay close behind me."

I paused, reaching out to grab her arm.

"Shouldn't the more senior nun lead the way? Won't it look unusual for me to be following you?"

"Don't let that uniform go to your head, my lady. Just follow my instructions and we should be fine."

Caroline swung the door open and stepped out into the hall, then began walking down the corridor with her hands embedded under the sides of her gown. I mimicked her movement, holding my purse tightly against my abdomen, walking three feet directly behind. When we were about halfway down the hall, another nun suddenly turned the corner about a hundred feet ahead of us and began walking in our direction.

My heart raced in fear thinking I'd be detected, and I scurried up closer behind Caroline.

"What do we do now?" I whispered. "Surely she'll recognize that I'm not part of the congregation!"

"Just be calm and keep your head down," Caroline said.

I lowered my head, feeling my loose headdress falling down over my eyebrows, and I lifted my hand to push it back. After we'd closed the distance to about fifty feet, the nun stopped and turned to one of the residence doors and nodded gently toward us. Caroline returned the gesture, then the nun entered the room and closed the door behind her. Twenty feet ahead, Caroline stopped outside another door on the opposite side of the hall and quickly pulled it open motioning me inside. I scampered into her room, and after Caroline checked both ends of the hall to be sure no one else was watching, she slipped in and closed the door behind her.

We giggled quietly, then I pressed her body against the door and kissed her passionately on her lips.

"That was a close one," I said. "Do you think the other nun suspected anything?"

"I don't think so, but just to be extra careful we're going to have to be super-quiet as long as you're in my room. The horarium has ended for the day, so we've got the rest of the night to ourselves."

I leaned in toward Caroline and slipped my knee between her legs, pressing my thigh against her crotch as I kissed her. After a few seconds, she stepped away, pinching her eyebrows.

"Wrinkles!" she said.

"You've *got* to be kidding me," I said. "Don't you have an iron? They must provide *some* appliances to make your life easier—"

"We do. But it will just be easier if we get out of these clothes. Besides, I've been dying to see you naked again ever since yesterday."

"You don't have to ask me twice," I said, eager to get out of my religious garb as soon as possible.

We helped each other remove our garments, then Caroline hung and placed everything carefully in her wardrobe closet. When we were both naked, we pressed our bodies together, mashing our breasts and mounds against one another, kissing passionately. I moaned unconsciously from the delirious feeling of holding her close to me again, and Caroline pulled her face away, lifting her finger to her lips.

"Sh!" she said. "Not a peep. This place is like crickets at night. You can hear everything."

"That's easy for *you* to say," I whispered. "I don't know how I'm going to possibly contain myself around you."

"Well then, I guess you'll just have to do *me* first," Caroline smiled. "I've had more practice keeping quiet around here."

She looked at my large purse resting on the floor and widened her eyes.

"Did you bring some of your toys for me to play with?"

"I did," I said, smiling at Caroline mischievously.

I picked up my purse and placed it on her narrow bed, then pulled out a large purple dildo with a V-shaped extension near the base.

"This is one of my favorites. It's called a rabbit vibrator."

I pointed it up and turned the dial at the base of the dildo. The purple shaft began to vibrate and the tip of the dildo began to wobble in circles, as a ring of beads midway along the shaft began to rotate.

"Those don't look like prayer beads," Caroline said.

"No, but I think you might find them divine in an entirely different sense of the word."

Caroline looked at the animated device, widening her eyes.

"Do I put it *inside* me?"

"It works best that way. The oscillating head twists and turns, providing a heavenly form of stimulation against your G-spot."

"G-spot?"

"That the place inside you where I tickled you with my fingers yesterday."

"Oh yes—I remember that very well. That was the first time you took me over the edge."

Caroline placed her fingers over the strange rubbery protrusions on the side of the dildo. "What do *these* do?"

"Those are the rabbit ears. They provide direct stimulation to your clitoris while the shaft is pumping and churning inside you. The combined effect is really quite something."

"I can see how you were worried I'm might become too attached to these devices." She reached into my bag and pulled out a leather harness with a long red phallus attached to the front. "What about this one?"

"That's what's called a strap-on dildo. It's something I can use to—um—*make love* to you like a man."

"Do women *do* that to each other?" Caroline said, pinching her eyebrows together.

"Some do. It can actually be quite fun, when you're in the right mood."

Caroline glanced in my purse seeing a variety of other sex toys and shook her head.

"Where do we begin? You've brought so many—"

I pushed Caroline gently down on the bed and lay on top of her.

"First, I want to touch and feel you with my *own* body parts," I said. "I've been dreaming about tasting your sweet body for the past twenty-four hours."

I rubbed my tits against Caroline's and ground my pussy into hers, thrusting my tongue into her pliant mouth. As her breathing escalated, I began kissing my way down the front of her body toward her pussy. I played with her breasts for a few minutes, pinching and sucking her nipples, then I drew my tongue over her quivering tummy until I reached her pubic patch. I flapped my face over her soft bush, breathing her fresh scent deep into my nostrils.

The lower I went on her mound, the wetter her patch became until my face rested between her slickly coated thighs. When I placed my tongue over her clit and licked it like a lollypop, Caroline gasped. I looked up between her legs and she tilted her head down toward me.

"*Now* who's being the noisy one?" I said.

As we peered into one another's eyes, I took her jewel into my mouth and began dancing my tongue over her hard shaft. Caroline bit her lip and scrunched her eyes, trying to keep quiet. It was such a turn-on seeing her face contort in private pleasure as I nibbled on her fiery love button. Her mouth opened wider with her rising passion, and I placed my fingers at her opening, preparing to thrust them inside her. But she reached out and placed her hands over mine, stopping me.

"Wait," she panted. "I want to feel you...*fuck* me...if you're going to be inside me. Can we try your strap-on sex toy?"

I lifted my head and smiled at Caroline like a Cheshire Cat.

"I thought you'd never ask," I said.

I quickly got up off the bed and wrapped the leather harness around my hips then rocked my hips in the air, flapping the big phallus sticking out from my mound.

"Is that what a *real* man's penis looks like?" Caroline asked, wide-eyed.

"More or less," I said. "This might be a little larger than most, and it has a few extra features distinguishing it from a regular cock."

I tapped a button on the side of my belt and the penis suddenly began bouncing and oscillating from side to side. Caroline's eyes grew even larger, and she tilted her hips up toward me.

"Yes, Jade," she purred. "Fuck me with your big man cock. I want to feel you inside me."

My pussy pulsed and I felt a dribble of lubrication run down the inside of thighs. I ran my hand over the slick patch then rubbed it over the top of my phallus, simulating a masturbation effect.

"Mmm," Caroline said. "I think it will feel even better *inside* me. Stop playing with your cock and put it inside me."

Caroline's dirty talk was getting me even more turned on, and I kneeled on the bed between her legs and placed the tip of my artificial cock over her opening. I rubbed it up and down her slit for a few seconds then I pressed the head against her clit. She rocked her hips forward to provide more friction against her love button and moaned softly. I looked into her soft blue eyes then grabbed her hips on both sides and slowly inserted the cock into her cunny.

"Oh, God yes!" Caroline panted. "Fuck me with your big cock, Jade!"

I thrust my pole deep inside Caroline's pussy and began pulling her hips toward me as I fucked her harder. Her tits bounced up and down on her chest with each thrust of my hips, and she began swinging her head from side to side in pleasure.

"It feels so good, Jade!" she said, seemingly no longer concerned about how much noise she was making. "Fuck me harder. Make me cum all over your big cock!"

I could feel the base of the phallus rubbing against my own clit as I thrust in and out of Caroline, and before long I began to feel the familiar pangs of an orgasm rising within me. I reached to the side of my belt and pressed the vibrator button, suddenly feeling the device throbbing between my legs. I pushed my hips hard against Caroline's vulva, grinding the oscillating phallus against her clit.

"Oh God, Jade!" she panted. "You're going to make me cum! Here it comes—I'm cumming Jade!"

I looked down between her legs and saw her spraying all over my artificial dick as I pumped in and out of her. Feeling her love juices dripping down under my belt into my own pussy soon put me over the edge too.

"Caroline!" I panted, trying my best to keep my voice to a whisper. "Cum on me, sweetie. I feel you. Momma's coming with you!

I thrust my big dildo into Caroline's spasming pussy for a full thirty seconds, then I fell on top of her, kissing her passionately while I continued to pump my cock into her, savoring the slippery wetness between both of our legs. After a few minutes, I pulled out and lay beside her, kissing her face and neck softly.

"That was incredible," Caroline panted, looking into my eyes. "Those toys really *are* addictive, aren't they?"

"They can be. That's why I like to use them in moderation. There's still nothing quite like the natural feeling of skin on skin."

"Mmmm, I agree," Caroline purred. "Speaking of which, I think it's *your* turn for some good old-fashioned skin-on-skin lovemaking. What can I do for you now?"

"Well, now that you mention it, there *was* something I had in mind.."

I removed my harness and placed the strap-on dildo on the corner of the bed, then swung my legs over Caroline's midsection and shimmied my hips up toward her head. When I got to her shoulders, I lifted my legs and placed my knees on opposite sides of her head. I paused for a moment, watching Caroline stare at my dripping wet pussy, then I slowly began to lower myself toward her face.

Just before I touched her lips, we heard a loud rapping noise on Caroline's door.

"Sister Caroline," an older woman's voice said from the other side of the door. "Is everything all right in there? I heard some unusual noises. May I come in?"

"Um—one minute, Mother Margaret," Caroline called back, her eyes wide as saucers.

She raised herself up off the bed and whispered for me to hide in the closet. Then she went to the wardrobe and opened the doors, putting on a terrycloth robe. I quickly picked up my purse and slipped inside, retreating to the far corner behind the hanging frocks. Caroline closed the door quietly behind me, and I peered between the narrow slats with frightened eyes. Caroline lifted her bedcovers and threw the rabbit vibrator and strap-on dildo under the sheets, then straightened her robe before heading to the door. I couldn't see her and the other nun from my vantage point, but I overheard the conversation clearly.

"Good evening, Mother," Caroline said. "Everything is fine. I was just preparing my bed to go down for the night."

There was a long pause, and I looked around Caroline's room to make sure all of my belongings were out of sight. Fortunately, she'd had the presence of mind to hang my clothes in the closet, so for all intents and purposes, it looked like she was alone.

"May I come in for a moment?" Mother Margaret said. "I'd like to inspect your room to ensure everything is in order."

"Of course. But I don't think you'll find anything out of place. You know how neat and fastidious I am."

"I do," Margaret said. "This won't take long."

I heard some footsteps moving toward the closet, then a nun wearing an all-black habit passed by my door. I crouched lower under the hanging robes and held my breath so as not to be heard. The mother superior looked around Caroline's room and noticed a bump in her covers and bent over to smooth them with her hand. Her eyes widened when she felt a hard object under the covers, and she swung the covers down, revealing the rabbit vibrator.

"What's this?" she asked.

"It's a—" Caroline paused, trying to think of how she could explain the strange object, "...*massager*. It helps loosen up my tight muscles when I get cramps."

"*Really*?" Margaret said, in a condescending tone. "You know most electric devices are banned from use in this abbey. But I might make an exception in this case, depending on your need. Show me how you use it."

Caroline looked at the mother superior in shock as her mouth tipped open.

"It's okay, my child. I merely want to see how it relieves your —*pain*."

Caroline picked up the vibrator by its purple shaft and twisted the control knob on the bottom. The vibrator began whirring and twisting in her hand, and she placed it against the back of her neck, turning her head from side to side, simulating the relaxation of her shoulder muscles.

"That's quite an interesting device," Margaret said. "May I see it for a moment?'

Caroline hesitated, then turned the vibrator off and handed it to her superior.

Margaret held it up in her hands for a moment and twisted it around in her hands.

"Why is it shaped like a *penis*, I wonder?" she said. She ran her hands over the tip of the phallus. "It appears to be anatomically correct—except for these strange flaps on the side. Where *else* have you been placing this massager to relieve your pain?"

It was obvious to me that Mother Margaret knew full well how the sex toy was designed to be used and that she was enjoying watching Caroline squirm as she tried to explain why she had it in her possession.

"Just my shoulders and back, mostly," Caroline said.

"*Mostly*?" Margaret said. "Show me. Take off your robe and lie down on your bed and show me how you use this thing to stimulate your muscles elsewhere on your body."

Caroline froze as she looked at the mother superior with a terrified look in her eyes.

"Go on, child. I'm *ordering* you. By your vows, you must follow all of my instructions. Let me help you off with your robe."

Mother Margaret stepped behind Caroline's back and pulled her robe off her body, then threw it on the base of the bed.

"Please continue, Caroline," she said. "Lie down on your bed and place that massager where it is designed to go."

Caroline lay down tentatively on the bed and began to rub the dildo over the sides of her body.

"*Lower*, my child. I think it's meant to go lower."

Caroline traced the vibrator down the side of her body until it rested on the side of her hips, then she pushed it into the sides of her buttocks, pretending to massage her hip muscles.

"Now, bring it—*inside*," Margaret instructed. "Between your legs. Place the purple penis between your legs."

Caroline paused for a moment, and the mother superior nodded for her to continue. She pulled the vibrator over her thigh and placed it awkwardly between her legs, rubbing it up and down softly over her slit.

"Yes, my child. Doesn't that feel better than using it to massage your neck or shoulders? Now, I want you to turn it on."

Caroline lifted the dildo above her hips and turned the dial part way. The vibrator began humming softly.

"*All* the way," Mother Margaret said.

Caroline twisted the dial clockwise until it wouldn't go any further. Suddenly, the penis became fully animated, twisting and oscillating noisily in her hand.

"Now place it between your legs, and let's see how pleasurable this massager can really be."

Caroline placed the tip of the humming vibrator at her opening and gasped.

"Does that feel better, Caroline?" Margaret said. "Is this massager relieving your stress in your nether regions?"

"Yes," Caroline panted.

"I think it's designed to massage your *insides* too," Margaret said. "I want to see you insert it into your private area. You've had far too much stress built up these past few months. Let's see if this special massager might relieve you of some of your burden."

Caroline paused for a moment, then inserted the tip of the vibrator into her slit. I could see the oscillating head turning and dancing over her opening, tickling her clit. As her long eyelashes fluttered in obvious pleasure, I couldn't help reaching down between my own legs to play with my own clit. There was something incredibly sexy about watching her masturbate herself while being watched by such an austere authority figure.

"*Deeper*, my child," Margaret said. "Press it deeper inside you. Feel the phallus filling you up, massaging your deepest regions. Relax and enjoy the stimulation of your special massager."

As Caroline inserted the dildo deeper into her pussy, I could see the rabbit ears flapping along the side. When she pressed the ears directly against her clit with the oscillating dildo embedded all the way inside her, she grunted loudly.

"Yes, Caroline," Margaret said. "Doesn't that feel better? Is that relaxing all of your muscles now?"

"Yes, Mother," Caroline panted, beginning to hump her hips, thrusting the vibrator in and out of her. "It feels...very good."

"Continue, my child," Margaret beseeched her. "Continue massaging your inner regions to see if you can relieve *all* of your stress."

"Yes Mother," Caroline panted, beginning to lift her hips off the bed as she hammered the dildo in and out of her.

It was the sexiest thing I may have ever witnessed, and I bit my lip trying to stifle my moans as my juices poured over my hand trilling between my legs.

"Oh Mother," Caroline said. "I can feel it—beginning to—ease my pain. It feels very good."

"Yes, my child. Push it harder up inside you. Make sure it reaches all of your sore muscles."

Caroline lifted her hips high over the bed and pulled the vibrator as far into her as she could, holding the vibrating ears tight against her mound. I could see the wings flapping wildly against her clit as she opened her mouth at the height of ecstasy. Suddenly, she grunted loudly and began shaking her hips uncontrollably.

"Uhnnn!" she grunted. "Oh God, I feel it, Mother!"

"Yes, my child," Margaret said. "Feel his blessing sweeping over you. You are truly filled with the spirit of Jesus."

Watching Caroline cumming so hard in front of the mother superior unfurled my taps, and I gushed all over my hand as my pussy clamped down over my fingers. It took a superhuman effort to not utter a sound, as I jerked silently in the darkness of the closet.

Caroline held her hips up in the air as she spasmed in a long and sustained orgasm for many seconds. When the wave finally passed, she flopped back on the bed, panting heavily.

"There now," Margaret said. "Doesn't that feel much better?

Perhaps we can find a good use for this automated stress-reliever after all."

Margaret kneeled on the bed and took the dildo out of Caroline's pussy and inserted it into her mouth, sucking her juices seductively from the shaft.

"I've been feeling some built-up stress of my *own* lately..."

As she knelt on the base of Caroline's bed and began to lift the front of her habit, she suddenly paused and ran her fingers over the covers. Feeling something else under the covers, she pulled them back all the way, revealing the strap-on dildo.

"What have we here?" she said, looking at Caroline mischievously. "Have you been using these special massagers with some of our other sisters? I think perhaps it's time I reminded you who's *really* in charge around here."

As she began to remove her habit, Caroline glanced toward the closet doors. I wasn't sure if she could see me peering back at her, but I sure as hell could see her and the mother superior vividly. And I was about to get the show of a lifetime from my dark little peephole...

VOLUME THREE

WEBCAM CHAT

1

CYBERSURFING

After my playdate with the dominatrix, I felt I needed a breather to regain control over my sex life. My little excursion into the world of BDSM had been fun, but being whipped and hog-tied by a domme had its limits. Now it was *my* turn to set the terms of engagement. I wanted to be back in the driver's seat and branch out beyond one dominant partner.

One lonely night at home, I sat down in front of my computer and began searching for some online fun. I wanted something different from the run-of-the-mill porn—something more engaging. I needed something involving a live, two-way interaction. With a real person, someone with whom I could share a genuine, passionate, if only temporary, relationship. A virtual *fuck buddy*, for want of a better word.

I typed in the search words *webcam sex chat* and a bunch of listings popped up for live online chat. I clicked on one labeled *LiveGirls*, and a gallery of videos showing scantily-clad women touching themselves filled the screen. I tapped one of the thumbnails, where a live stream showed a pretty girl lying facedown on a bed, wearing only a thong. As she swayed her hips from side to side, she looked over her shoulder suggestively toward the camera. Beside the video window, a flurry of comments filled the chat box.

Spread your legs, someone named bigjohn said.

Nice ass, hornyjoe commented.

Can I see your tits? guest34 pleaded.

All the while, the pretty brunette ran her hands across her concealed breasts and rolled her hips in the same robotic manner. For a moment, I was hypnotized like everyone else by her lithe and sexy body. But as attractive as she was, I had no interest in joining what amounted to a public strip show. I was just about to exit the screen when I noticed a button for Private Chat.

Let's see if she's any more engaging one-on-one, I thought.

I clicked the button and a Join Now window covered the stream.

Jeesuz, I cursed. They never make this easy.

I filled in the required fields for Username, Password, and E-mail, then clicked the button. The next screen presented me with a choice between selecting ten free credits or buying a package of credits starting at fifty dollars.

So that's how it works, I thought. *It's not much different from a real strip club. As long as you're stuffing their stockings with cash, the girls are happy to put on a show for you.*

I'd never paid for sex of any kind, and I wasn't about to get started now. I didn't want to chat with someone who was only in it for the money. I backtracked to the main search screen and adjusted my search phrase to *free amateur sex chat* and clicked Enter.

A fresh set of listings popped up, including an intriguing one named *SexRoulette — free webcam live chat*. When I clicked on the link, a window came up with two side-by-side blank video screens. I enabled my laptop cam and mic, then I clicked the Start button. Suddenly, a live feed of me sitting half-naked in my bathrobe appeared in the left window, while some naked guy stroking his dick appeared in the right window.

Horrified to see that my face was showing, I quickly tilted my screen down and cursed out loud.

What's the matter? the naked guy typed in the chat box. *You're very pretty. Can I see your face again?*

I paused for a moment, realizing that he could hear me, then I clicked the microphone button to mute my mic. I wasn't prepared to carry on a live audio conversation with some naked guy. For that matter, I wasn't interested in carrying on a sex chat with *any* man.

I clicked the Next button and a different naked guy appeared with his legs spread wide apart, revealing another erect, throbbing cock. Every time I clicked Next, a different naked man appeared, pulling on his pud. As amusing as I found the experience of scrolling through a bunch of men's penises, the thought of chatting with one of these nameless guys turned my stomach.

Where were all the girls? I thought. *Are only guys interested in naughty online chats?*

I scanned the site and noticed some links across the top for different chat rooms. The default setting was for Mixed, but I could also choose between Guys, Girls, and Couples. Intrigued, I clicked on the Couples link, and a new window popped up showing a woman bobbing her head between a man's knees while his hand typed on a computer keyboard beside him on the bed.

Hi, the man typed in the chat window. *Wanna play?*

I paused for a moment, wondering if it might be fun to watch a hetero couple going at it.

Maybe some other time, I typed, before clicking on the Girls tab.

A new window popped up requiring me to verify that I was over eighteen years of age (*only to view girls??*) then I was redirected to a different website showing the familiar gallery of naked girls from the LiveGirls site. When I clicked on one of the images, a similar video and chat screen appeared. Another pretty young girl perched half-naked on a bed, while a bunch of anonymous viewers made lewd comments, 'tipping' her occasionally with tokens. Whenever anybody tipped her enough tokens, she bent over and waved her ass in front of the camera.

What the fuck? I thought. *Is it only professional girls who want to chat online?*

I clicked out of the website and was about to pull my vibrator out of my nightstand for some quiet alone time, when I decided to give it one last try.

There's got to be other lonely girls who are looking for a quick hookup with like-minded women.

I went back to the main search page and typed in *lesbian online chat*. Near the top of the listings, I noticed a site titled *SapphicChat — girls only free online chat*.

That's what I'm talking about, I said out loud, clicking the link.

Another side-by-side video setup appeared on the screen with a chat box underneath. I enabled my cam and carefully positioned my laptop lid so that only my torso was visible, then I pulled my robe tightly around my neck to cover myself up. There'd be no more skin showing until I was able to qualify a suitable candidate.

I clicked the Start button, and within a few seconds the adjacent window flickered with a live stream showing a fat woman lying on her bed with her droopy boobs hanging down by her waist.

Yikes, I said, quickly clicking the Next button. I felt bad judging the visitors so harshly, but it wasn't much different from other dating apps. If you didn't feel the chemistry right away, everybody just moved on.

After a few seconds, a new image filled the sender window. This time an older woman sat in front of her computer with her elbows propped up on her desk. Deep folds of flesh hung from her neck and upper chest as she peered sadly into the screen.

Wow, I thought. *These online forums really bring out the lonely girls.*

I toggled through the list of online visitors until an image appeared showing a younger girl sitting cross-legged on her bed, wearing a tight V-neck sweater. Her breasts were full and plump, and although her face was partially hidden off-screen, I could tell from the downiness of her bare legs in a mid-thigh skirt that she was considerably younger than me. I parted my legs unconsciously as my pussy throbbed in excitement.

Finally. A sexy girl who wants an authentic online chat.

ASL? I typed, wanting to be sure she was of legal age. The last thing I needed was to have the police breaking down my door for engaging a minor in online sex.

19, curious, Houston, she typed. *You?*

Nineteen? She barely looked of age. I'd have to vet her more carefully if things went much further.

I paused for a moment, wondering how I wanted to present myself. I didn't want to scare her away by revealing my true age if she was looking to hook up with someone younger. But she had to lean at least a little bit toward girls if she'd engaged me this far.

28, bi, Milwaukee, I stretched the facts on all three aspects.

She paused for a moment holding her hand over her computer keyboard, then the video screen suddenly went blank and a new visitor came online.

Touché, I thought. *I guess this works both ways. My fellow online surfers can be just as rash and judgmental as me when it comes to who they find attractive.*

Obviously. I hadn't measured up in her eyes. But had I been too old, not the right sexual orientation, or was it my *body* she didn't like?

I peered at my image in my webcam feed and looked at my tightly-bound boobs wrapped up in my bathrobe. I'd been slouching a bit, and the heavy terrycloth robe wasn't doing much justice to the shape of my bosom. I spread the lapels of my robe a few inches apart and lifted my chest. My ample cleavage shone through the opening, revealing the roundness of my breasts.

That looks better, I smiled, nodding at the sexy reflection. *If this doesn't hook them, I'm really losing my mojo.*

The next visitor appeared to be another young girl seated on a chair in front of her computer. She only showed the lower half of her face, but from her tight skin and smooth neck muscles, she looked to be in her late teens or early twenties. Her tight T-shirt had a wish-bone-shaped "C" emblem on the front. In the background, two small double beds sat on either side of her small room.

Hi, I typed, deciding to take a more measured approach with this new visitor. *What brings you to this crazy place so late at night?*

Just bored I guess, she responded.

Me too, I said. *This is my first time doing something like this. I'm used to meeting people the old-fashioned way.*

Boys or girls? she typed.

It was obvious that she was fishing. I had no idea what the right answer was, so I decided to play it safe.

Both, I guess. *But I prefer girls. How about you?*

I like boys... she typed. *But lately I've been finding myself unusually attracted to my dorm mate.*

Oh, I said, happy to hear she tilted both ways. *Where do you go to school?*

University of Chicago.

My heart skipped a beat when I realized how close she was to me in the real world.

What are you studying? I said, trying to steady my nervous hand as I typed.

I'm enrolled in the BA program, so right now it's mostly liberal arts. I'm just in my first year, so I haven't really decided on my major yet. I'm thinking maybe Communications...

She's barely eighteen! I thought. *My pussy throbbed at the thought of uncovering more of this pretty co-ed.*

What kind of career were you thinking of?

I dunno. Public relations, marketing, maybe television.

On the production side?

I suppose so. Somewhere behind the camera. I don't think I have prime time face.

You should let other people be the judge of that. From what I can see so far, I think you're very pretty. The combination of good looks and good communication skills will give you quite a leg up in that field.

Thanks, she said, tilting the camera up a little higher on her face. She smiled a broad smile, revealing perfectly-straight, pearly-white teeth. *What about you, what do you do?*

I'm a freelance graphic designer.

So you design websites and stuff like that?

A little bit of that. But I do more corporate work like logos, editorial layouts, that sort of thing.

That sounds interesting, the girl said. *I guess we both have an interest in communications of sorts...*

I paused for a moment, wondering how much longer I wanted to focus on the professional sides of our lives.

It looks like we share an interest in another form of communicating too. ;-)

LOL. This isn't the kind of communications my profs talk about.

I'm a little surprised to hear that, I said. *The world is rapidly adopting new forms of social media every day. Perhaps you can consider this as a type of vocational training.*

Except most people who come to this website are interested in only one thing.

You mean meeting people? I teased.

In a manner of speaking...

Are you testing the waters here because of your roommate?

Maybe. I didn't realize I had such a strong attraction to girls until I met her.

Have you shared your feelings with her?

Gawd no. She has a boyfriend. It could get very uncomfortable around here if I came on to her too strongly. We have to share this small room for the rest of the year and perhaps for the rest of our college residency.

Two charged up bodies in a small space can make for a combustible mixture. Do you think she's attracted to you also?

Not by the way I've seen her and her boyfriend go at it. I can't tell you how many times I've come back to my room to find a sock on the door.

Poor thing, I thought. *It doesn't sound like she's got much of an outlet to express her real feelings. I better tread lightly.*

Maybe you just need to be a little more suggestive when you have some alone time with her. You know, wear skimpier clothes to bed, come back from the shower naked. That sort of thing. If she's interested, she'll soon let you know.

It sounds like you have a little more experience with girls, she said. *Are you lesbian?*

Now we're getting to the crux of it, I thought. It was kind of fun playing the role of the girl's online mentor.

They say everyone's somewhere on the continuum, I said. *I'd say I'm about a nine, but I seem to be moving more to the right with each passing year. Men don't really do it for me any longer.*

The chat window paused for a moment as the girl seemed to process what I said.

What's it like? she said. *You know, being with a woman?*

Crikey, I thought. *How do I answer that without sounding like some kind of stalker?*

That's an interesting question. It's different in so many ways. Woman like different things than men. We're more focused on building the relation-ship. Men are mostly just interested in sex.

Aren't women interested in that too?

Yes, of course, I laughed. *We just let it happen more—organically.*

Organically?

We let it happen naturally, as our feelings for one another grow stronger. Instead of just jumping on the biscuit, in a manner of speaking.

You mean kind of like what we're doing right now?

I was beginning to feel a strange attraction to this girl. Beyond the pretty outside package, she had a sweet innocence to her.

I suppose, I said. *We lesbians generally like to get to know our partner a little better before jumping into bed with them.*

Do you mind my asking how that works when you do get together? I mean, it's not like regular boy-girl coupling...

All this tip-toeing around the edges of sexy talk was beginning to stir some new feelings inside me. I was enjoying the process of educating this young girl on the nuances of lesbian relationships.

It's not so different, when it comes right down to it. We have the same sensitive parts. We just use them a little differently.

Do you miss the penetration aspect of the relationship?

Maybe it's time to stop being so nuanced, I thought.

Who says we have to forego the penetration aspect?

Oh, sorry—the girl said, as I saw a flush roll over her face. *It's just that without a penis involved in the equation...*

There are lots of ways us girls can enjoy penetration without a man.

Strap-on dildos, two-sided phalluses, using sex toys. I'm guessing you've tried one or two of these before?

Well, yes. I have a vibrator I play with when my roommate is away. But I had no idea women used them together like you said.

Oh, yes. There are lots of interesting ways we make our own fun.

You're getting me pretty worked up talking about it. Can you tell me how you use a two-sided phallus?

Suddenly I became acutely aware of the wetness that had been accumulating between my legs. This innocent but sexy banter had been getting *both* of us worked up.

Well, usually it starts with us lying on our backs with our butts facing one another...

Mmm, the girl typed.

Fuck! I thought. *It's happening. I'm actually seducing a young college girl online!*

Then we insert the two ends in each of our pussies and push our bodies together...

The girl's left hand wandered below my line of vision as she began to squirm in her seat while pecking her keyboard with her other hand.

All the way? she asked. *Do you touch your bodies together?*

Usually, if the dildo isn't too long. That's where it really gets fun. There's nothing so electrifying as feeling your lover's peachka pressed up against your own.

God, that's so hot!

And wet. ;-)

You're making me very wet right now.

I spread my legs and began strumming my clit with my fingers at the thought of the pretty co-ed getting turned on by my explanation.

Are you touching yourself? I said.

Yes. Are you?

I am now.

I wish I could touch you the way you're describing right now.

If I could reach out through my screen, believe me, I would. I'd love to show you what it feels like to make love to a woman.

Can I see your breasts? They look very full and sexy.

I thought you'd never ask.

I pulled my robe apart and let the shawl fall around my shoulders.

OMG! the girl typed. *They're gorgeous. Do you mind if I ask how old you are? Because those are the most beautiful tits I think I've ever seen.*

I paused for a moment trying to decide how young I wanted to pretend to be. The last thing I wanted to do in the heat of the action was scare away another online partner because she thought I was too old.

Everybody tells me I look ten years younger than my real age, I thought. *She'll never know.*

That's very kind of you, I said. *I'm twenty-five. But before we go any further, I should probably ask you the same. If you're in your first year of college, you must be barely legal.*

I turned eighteen two months ago.

Like I said. Barely legal.

We're two consenting adults.

Since we're getting to know each other so intimately, can I ask your name? I don't want to have sex with a faceless, nameless person.

I'm Holly.

Pleased to meet you Holly. My name's Jade.

That's a lovely name.

Yours too, I said. *Holly and Jade. I like the way they go together.*

I'm imagining us going together in more ways than one.

Damn, girl, you're making me soaking wet. Can I see a bit more of you too? I want to let my mind run all over your sweet body.

The girl reached up over her shoulders and pulled her T-shirt over her head. Then she reached behind her back and unclasped her bra. When she pulled it off her shoulders and threw it on the floor, I gasped. Her breasts were smaller than mine, but stood firm and erect on her chest. But far more fascinating, was their *shape*. They were far pointier than most, pressing straight out toward me like two fleshy obelisks.

Mmm, I typed. *Those are mighty succulent boobies you have, Holly.*

Not as full and appetizing as yours! she returned.

I love their shape. I could suck on your pointy nipples all day!

I'd like that, Holly said. *You're going to make me cum pretty soon if you keep talking to me like that.*

That's not the only part of you that I want to suck, I said, starting to rub my clit more quickly. *I want to take your sweet nub into my mouth and watch your twist all over my face.*

Yes, Jade. I want you to suck my clit. Make me cum all over your face.

Oh Baby, I said. *Let me see and feel you cum. I'm pressing my fingers inside you now...*

Fuck, Jade. I can feel you inside me. I'm going to cum...

As I watched Holly writhing in her chair, my mouth opened unconsciously, imagining her riding my face.

Yes, baby, I said. *Cum in my mouth. Let it go.*

Suddenly, a deep flush spread over Holly's chest and she began jerking wildly in her chair.

Ohhhhhhh, she typed. *I'm cumming Jade!*

I hadn't been concentrating very much on my own feelings up to this point, but when I saw Holly coming, I thrust my fingers deep into my pussy and gushed all over my hand. While I watched her jerking in her chair, my tits jiggled spastically on my chest as the tremors spread throughout my body.

After a long pause, Holly began to type again.

That was incredible! she said. *I haven't had an orgasm that powerful in a long time.*

You should try this girl thing more often, I typed. *It's even better in real life. Maybe you and your roommate can find a way—*

Suddenly, Holly's face turned to the side and a panicked expression fell over her face.

I think she's here! she typed. *Someone's at the door!*

Oh no—not now, I thought. *Just when we were establishing such a strong connection.* I banged away at my keyboard, fearful of losing her forever.

Can we do this again some—

Holly's video stream suddenly went dark as she signed out of the program. I was sad to see her go, but at the same time I was thrilled to have made such an exhilarating connection my first time online.

I'm going to have to try this again very soon, I thought, closing my laptop with sticky fingers.

2

FULL DISCLOSURE

After my chat with Holly ended so abruptly, I stayed online for more than an hour hoping she'd reconnect and continue our conversation. But I knew that if her roommate had returned to their dorm, she'd be hard-pressed to find any privacy for the rest of the night. Their single room was so tiny that it would be impossible to find any place for a private conversation, let alone an online sex chat.

For the rest of the night, I fantasized about her roommate barging in to find her masturbating in front of her computer, then tearing off her clothes to join the innocent college girl in her lesbian discovery. If anything could persuade a straight girl to stray to the other side, surely it would be the sight of the winsome co-ed getting off watching other naked women. I came many times that night imagining all the fun the two of them might have discovering the joys of lesbian love-making for the first time.

The following night, I was eager to get back online to see if I could reconnect with Holly. Even though I knew my chances were slim, if she found herself alone again and was in a similar frame of mind, I hoped she might have the same idea. Around the same time that evening, I logged back into the SapphicChat site and began toggling through the gallery of online visitors.

I found a few interesting candidates, and for a short time I engaged in some playful banter with a closeted housewife from Texas, then a curious divorcée from California, then a sexy dyke from Delaware. On any other day, I might have been enticed to remove my clothing and begin another erotic online encounter, but after a few minutes of superficial conversation, I found myself clicking the Next button in search of my innocent college girl.

I was just about to reengage with the Texas housewife when a familiar silhouette filled the visitor chat window. She was sitting cross-legged in the middle of her bed wearing a tight T-shirt and shorts with her face out of the frame, but I recognized the contour of her breasts instantly. Her pointy tits pressed against the soft fabric of her shirt, barely concealing the two tubers of mouthwatering flesh. My pussy throbbed at the sight of the familiar swellings.

Holly? I typed on my keyboard.

Who's this? she responded in the chat box. I was wearing a different outfit this evening, and with my face off-camera, it was obvious she didn't recognize me.

It's Jade. I've been thinking about you so much since our chat last night.

She stretched her legs out on opposite sides of her laptop and leaned her body forward to type on her keyboard. This only accentuated the elongated shape of her breasts, highlighting the meaty areolas at their tips.

Me too. I wasn't sure if I'd find you again. Sorry for cutting you off so suddenly last night.

I completely understand. Did your roommate catch you in the act?

I was able to get myself pulled together pretty quickly. But she must have sensed something was up from the look on my face. Plus, I'm sure the room was saturated with the scent of my sex by the time we finished.

The thought of Holly's scent filling the room made my pussy weep, and I spread my legs unconsciously, feeling the moisture between my legs.

Did you tell her what you'd been doing?

No, I made up some lame-ass excuse about researching a term paper.

Too bad. If anything might swing her the other way, it would be the sight of her pretty roommate getting off watching other girls.

I dunno. I'm still afraid what she might think. I could smell her boyfriend's cologne all over her when she came back. I don't think she's interested in me that way.

Give it time. It's still early in the semester. She probably just needs to get a bit more comfortable around you. Your irresistible personality will eventually win her over.

So you're saying my body's not enough? ;-)

Don't be silly. Your figure is exquisite. I paused for a moment, contemplating whether to take our online conversation to the next level. *Though I still haven't seen your entire face. Don't you think we've come far enough to show the rest of our bodies to one another?*

Holly hesitated with her hands over her keyboard. For a moment, I thought she might hit the Exit button in fear of revealing her real identity.

I guess so, she said. *But I'm kind of wary about my showing my face in a public forum like this. You never know who might be recording us. I'd be horrified if somebody posted this online and my parents saw a clip of me masturbating online one day.*

I know how you feel, I typed. *I've been having the same concerns. Why don't we open a separate private chat. Do you have Skype?*

Yes, Holly said. *I use it to chat with my folks every couple of weeks.*

What's your username? Mine's gigi84.

Is that the year you were born? I thought you said you were twenty-five!

Ok, full disclosure, I sheepishly typed. *I might have stretched my age a little bit. But everyone tells me I look much younger than I really am.*

It's cool, Holly said. *Everybody has a secret identity online. I never would have guessed your age. You certainly have the body of a 25 yr old!*

Sexy enough to entice a college girl into an online affair with a middle-aged woman?

That's not middle-aged! You're barely through the first trimester. But to answer your question, yes. My Skype ID is ucgrad22.

LOL. I'm trying to slow down the clock and you're already looking ahead. Shall we log out of here and start a new Skype chat?

C u in a few minutes, sexy momma! Holly said, signing off with a playful kissing emoji.

As her image disappeared from the video window, my pussy pitter-pattered at her playful description of me. I couldn't wait to have her all to myself on a private webcam link, and I quickly exited the webpage and signed into Skype. I searched for *ucgrad22* and a profile pulled up with a thumbnail image of a pretty teenager wearing sunglasses against a seaside background. I clicked on the image and a new chat window opened, giving me three options. I could leave a text message in the chat box at the bottom of the screen, or I could send her an audio or video call request.

What the hell, I thought. *I think we're well past the preliminaries.*

I tapped on the video button and as my video stream went live, the sound of an electronic call warbled through my speakers. While I waited for Holly to pick up on the other end, I adjusted the angle of my camera so that it focused with a close-up of my face. I'd chosen to wear some skimpy lingerie this evening, and I didn't want to be too presumptuous right out of the gate. Besides, I was eager to see Holly's full face, and I figured if I set the tone, that she might follow.

After a few seconds, the bottom half of the screen filled with the familiar image of Holly's chest in her tight T-shirt. I smiled when I saw her, and she quickly tilted her screen up so that I could see her face also. My heart immediately began accelerating, not only because she appeared so close, but also because she was absolutely stunning. She had large doe-eyes, a cute upturned nose, and long auburn hair falling over her shoulders. With her bright green eyes and sprinkling of little freckles, she looked like a dead-ringer for the actress Emma Stone.

"Can you hear me?" I spoke toward my laptop's onboard microphone.

"Yes," Holly replied. "Oh my God, Jade—you're gorgeous!"

"Not bad for a thirty-five-year-old?" I smiled.

"Not bad for a twenty-five-year-old!" Holly beamed back at me.

"You're not too shabby yourself, young lady," I said. "Those eyes are to die for. Has anyone ever told you that you look a bit like—"

"Yes, I know. Emma Stone. I get it all the time. I think it's just the red hair and freckles. We gingers are always getting compared to one another. Amy Adams, Bryce Howard, Lindsay Lohan—I've heard them all."

"Sorry," I said. "I didn't mean to compare you to anybody. You're gorgeous and unique in your own right."

"No worries. It's just that I used to get teased quite a lot when I was younger."

"Not so much anymore, I bet."

"Thankfully, I seem to be outgrowing it."

"I bet you turn a lot of heads from both boys and girls on campus."

"I haven't been paying much attention. I've been focusing primarily on my studies. I don't get out much..."

"Oh my God, girl. You don't know what you're missing. With a face and body like that, you could have your pick of the litter. You could make your roommate super-jealous by bringing home a hot new boyfriend every night of the week."

"Except I'm not really into guys right now. Though I will confess, I *was* fantasizing about phalluses most of the night."

"Oh? Do tell. Real or pretend ones?"

"All your talk about strap-on dildos and double-sided cocks got me worked up all night. As soon as Jen left in the morning, I took out my vibrator and have been playing with it most of the day."

My pussy throbbed at the thought of Holly jilling herself with a dildo, as I felt a dribble of lubrication run down the crack of my ass.

"Same here. Do you have a favorite?"

Holly leaned over her bed and reached into the night table beside her bed. She pulled out a plain flesh-colored plastic dildo and held it in front of the screen for me to see.

"I just have this one. I actually pulled it out of the trash can at my house a few years ago. I think it belonged to my mother. I've been too nervous to go to an adult store to look for one of my own."

"Jeesuz, girl," I said, staring at the prehistoric sex toy. "That looks like something straight out of the eighties. Vibrators have become a lot more sophisticated over the last few years."

I reached into my side table and pulled out my favorite rabbit vibrator and held it up for Holly to see.

"This is one of my favorites. It's called The Rabbit. It twists and rolls on the end to provide an exquisite form of internal stimulation. But best of all are these little rabbit ears."

I tweaked the two silicone flaps with my fingers.

"When you turn it on, they vibrate and flap directly against your clitoris, providing the most intense type of stimulation you can imagine. The whole thing is made of super-soft silicone, so it almost feels like the real thing when it's inside you."

Holly stared at the multi-colored vibrator with wide eyes, then glanced back at her plain plastic dildo.

"I'm feeling pretty inadequate right now. Can you show me how it works? I mean—just turn it on so I can see how it moves?"

"Of course," I said, happy to indulge Holly's curiosity.

I held the vibrator vertical and turned it sideways so she could see the rabbit ears in profile view, then turned the device on. As it began making a low humming sound, a circle of beads swirled just under the transparent surface.

"See these circulating beads? They provide a sensation unlike any man can deliver."

Emma stared at the strange contraption and nodded.

"I can imagine. How else does it move?"

I pressed another button, and the tip of the dildo started rolling in small circles.

"Holy shit!" Holly exclaimed, with wide eyes. "That thing really is unlike any other cock, isn't it?"

"So you *have* experienced a real penis, then?" I said, probing for more details about her sex life.

"Well yes, just a few times in high school with a boyfriend in my senior year. But he wasn't endowed nearly as well as that thing!"

"It's a little bigger than most men's cocks, I suppose. But here's the best part." I tapped another button on the base of the vibrator and the rabbit ears started fluttering against the side of the shaft. "Can you see that," I said, pointing toward the flickering ears. "That's something else no man's cock can hope to emulate. The combined effect of these three actions will send you over the moon."

"Oh my God," Holly said. "I'm already soaking wet at the thought of having that thing inside me. I don't suppose you'd be willing to demonstrate it working for real? I mean—*inside* you?"

By this time, the insides of my thighs were coated with slippery lubrication emanating from my pussy and my clit was burning in need of some direct stimulation.

"It would be my pleasure—literally."

I unplugged my laptop and carried it with my vibrator to my bed. Then I sat up with my back resting against the headboard and placed the laptop between my legs about two feet away so Holly could see my entire body from my hips to my head.

"Mmm, I like what you're wearing tonight," Holly said, admiring my lacy camisole and matching boy-shorts panties.

"I wore it just for you," I purred, cupping my breasts and pinching my nipples through the thin fabric.

"I wish I were there to touch you like that. I want to caress every square inch of your body."

"Likewise," I said, spreading my legs further apart. "Can you take your T-shirt off so I can see your beautiful breasts while I play with myself? I've been fantasizing about seeing you naked again for the last twenty-four hours."

"Absolutely," Holly said. "In fact, let me get completely naked so I can enjoy myself properly while I'm watching you."

Holly pulled her shirt over her head as her pointy tits jiggled on her chest. Then she raised her ass and pulled her shorts over her ankles, revealing a completely bare pussy.

"Oh my God, Holly," I gasped, staring at her sexy slit and puffy labia. "Just when I thought you couldn't get any more perfect. That might be the prettiest pussy I've ever seen."

"I bet you say that to all the girls," she teased.

"I have to admit that I love every woman's vulva. But yours looks unusually—*pristine*. Almost like it's never been touched. Are you sure you've been with boys before?"

"Only a few times," Holly laughed. "Not as many times as I've used my vibrator."

"Well that skinny little thing isn't much thicker than a toothbrush. No wonder you look like you've barely been touched down there."

"My boyfriend in high school was pretty small too. I didn't know they came any bigger. Show me how that big dildo fills you up, Jade."

I had planned on giving Holly a slow striptease to get her in the mood, but when started talking dirty, I practically tore my panties and camisole off.

Holly paused for a moment as her eyes darted over her screen, appraising my body.

"Holy fuck, Jade! *You're* the one with the perfect body. I'd die to have your curves. You look like something straight out of some men's magazine centerfold."

"Or *women's*," I chuckled. "Hopefully this body works for both sides of the aisle."

Holly traced her right hand down the front of her stomach and began circling her fingers over her clit.

"It's definitely working *this* side of the aisle, I can assure you."

"Mmm, Holly, you're making me very wet."

"Wet enough for that big dildo to slide up inside you?"

"Let's see," I said, placing the end of the vibrator against my opening. I tapped the oscillating function button and the tip of the dildo began rolling over my slippery labia. As I began to insert the dildo inside my hole, Holly leaned in closer to the screen.

"Damn," she panted. "My boyfriend's cock never did anything like that. It was mostly straight in-and-out action. Usually pretty fast."

"You have no idea how good real lovemaking can be," I purred. "The trick is to take your time and let the passion slowly build. Only after you've been properly teased and stimulated, is it time for a pounding. The pleasure is so much more intense when you let it build to a boil."

"You're sure bringing me to a boil right now," Holly said, rolling her fingers over her slit. "Show me how you enjoy the rest of that special dildo. I want to watch you squirm and moan."

I raised my knees higher off the bed and tapped the second button on the vibrator. As the rotating silver beads glistened in the nightlight from my side table, the shaft slowly disappeared inside my cavern as I pushed it further inside me.

"Fuck that's hot!" Holly panted, her big doe eyes widening even further. "What does that feel like inside you?"

"It's like nothing else," I moaned. "The feeling of the beads caressing the inside of my walls while the rotating tip presses against my G-spot is simply indescribable. You've got to get one of these for yourself to truly appreciate it."

"I'll be going to my corner sex shop as soon as it opens tomorrow," Holly grunted, slipping her fingers inside her pussy. "You've certainly sold me."

"Just don't get too attached to it," I said. "It's still doesn't compare to the delicate touch of a real live, sensuous woman."

"But you said I can *combine* both sensations, with the right kind of vibrator. I might buy me one of those two-sided dildos while I'm at the store, just in case the opportunity ever arises with my roommate..."

With that image dancing around my head, I shoved the vibrator deep inside me and tapped on the rabbit ears button. As the ears began flapping against my burning clit, I humped my hips forward and back, pressing the dildo in and out of me.

"That's a sight I'd love to see," I panted, feeling the vibrations emanating throughout my body.

"I'll see if it can be arranged," Holly said, suddenly picking up her plastic vibrator and thrusting it inside her. "That is, if I can ever get past first base with her. I bet she'd enjoy watching you as much as I do. Maybe we can arrange our own little ménage à trois."

"Without her boyfriend, you mean?"

"*Definitely* without him," Holly moaned. "No boys allowed."

Holly and I watched each other holding our dildos with two hands as we fucked ourselves with increasing urgency.

"I'd like that," I panted. "But not nearly as much as being there for real. I want to feel your body pressed up against mine and make you scream in pleasure."

"You're getting pretty close to making me do that right now," Holly moaned, rolling her hips while she stared at her screen. "I'm getting close. Do you think you can cum with me?"

"Fuck yes," I grunted. "Any time. Just tell me when."

"First tell me what you want to do with me. When we get together."

"Oh Holly," I moaned, daring myself to think the unthinkable. "Everything. I want to kiss you and suck you and fuck you with every ounce of my being. We'll take our time and make it last. I'd make love to you all day long if I could."

"How do you want to fuck me, Jade?" Holly panted as her body began tensing up. The pupils in her eyes had become large and dark, signaling that she was nearing her peak. "Will you fuck me with your strap-on dildo or two-headed prick?"

"Yes," I moaned, getting even more turned on by her dirty talk. "I'll fuck you until you come all over my big dildo. I'll make you gush all over my cock while I fuck you in every imaginable way—"

"Yes, Jade," Holly groaned. "I want to feel you inside me. Make me cum all over your big dildo."

Holly was humping her hips wildly now against her plastic dildo, pumping it in and out of her pussy as her breathing became more jagged. I pressed the vibrating rabbit ears hard up against my clit and thrust my vibrator as deep inside me as I could. Within seconds, I could feel the insides of my pussy beginning to expand in preparation for a hard orgasm.

"Cum for me, baby," I groaned, feeling the first waves of passion roll over me. "Press your pussy against me and cum with me. I feel you Holly—"

"Jade!" Holly suddenly screamed, as her hips started shaking in spastic spasms. "I'm cumming!"

Her whole body began convulsing as her pointy breasts shook in tiny tremors.

"Oh baby," I growled, extending my tongue trying to reach her jiggling tits. "Mummy's coming with you. Feel me filling you up. Cum all over my big cock. Let me feel your tight pussy clamping down on me."

"Fuck yes," Holly hissed, holding her spear tightly inside her while her hips convulsed on the bed in front of her computer screen. "I'm still cumming. Oh Jade—"

Suddenly I heard the sound of a door swinging open and another girl's voice.

"What the fuck?" the girl's voice said. "I'm so sorry, Holly. I'll come back later—"

"No," Holly pleaded, peering up from the screen. "Don't leave, Jen. I've been thinking of you..."

Holly glanced down at her screen and gave me a sweet smile, then her video suddenly went blank.

Maybe she'll be getting her wish sooner than she hoped, I thought, pulling the still-throbbing vibrator out of my pussy.

3

THREE'S A CROWD

For the longest time, I stared at the empty screen, imagining what was happening in Holly's dorm room. Her roommate had surprised her in the throes of orgasm, with her naked body splayed in front of her computer and a vibrator deeply embedded in her pussy. How could anyone respond to such a sight?

There were only three possible scenarios. Either her roommate had turned tail and quickly exited the room, closing the door behind her. Or she'd continued into the dorm and gone about her usual business, pretending nothing unusual had happened. Or she'd engaged Holly directly in some way, acknowledging what she'd witnessed. It couldn't be that unusual to discover your roommate masturbating privately in the small confines of the same room. These were young women in the sexual prime of their lives. Where else could they act on their private passions but in the relative seclusion of their own room?

Holly had reached out to her friend in a vulnerable moment. Had her roommate simply brushed it off as a common practice among people their age and told Holly not to worry about it? Or had they begun a meaningful dialogue about Holly's attraction to Jen and discussed whether the feeling was mutual? Or had Jen torn off her *own* clothes and jumped into bed with Holly to begin a torrid affair?

Either way, I couldn't stop thinking about it all night. I came over and over again imagining Jen sucking on Holly's pointy nipples and probing every recess of her with her body. I wondered if Holly had been serious about running out to her local sex shop and stocking up on the latest generation of toys. The thought of she and Jen twisting their bodies together while connected by a two-sided dildo was too much. I plunged my rabbit vibrator back inside my pussy and held it tightly against my mound as I gushed all over the animated phallus.

The following night, I didn't know what to expect. If Jen had responded positively to her outreach, Holly could quickly lose interest in further contact with me. And if her roommate had shunned her advances, she might be reluctant to go back online for fear of being caught in the act again. She might even have trouble finding alone time this late at night. Her roommate couldn't be spending *all* of her free time with her boyfriend. She'd still need time to study and get caught up on her private affairs.

But there was one thing Holly said that kept me coming back. She'd alluded to the possibility of including her roommate in our online games if she got that far. *I'll see if that can be arranged,* she said. I wondered if she meant to go so far as to arrange an in-the-flesh get-together. *Maybe we can arrange our own little ménage à trois.* I'd never been with two girls at the same time, and the possibilities with three women made my head spin.

Around the same time the following evening, I logged back onto SapphicChat to see if she was still available. For over an hour, I toggled through the gallery of online visitors, but there was no sign of Holly. As sexy as some of the other candidates seemed, I had no interest in engaging with anyone else right now. There was only one person I was interested in, and my pretty college girl from UC was nowhere to be found.

I was just about to close my laptop for the night when it suddenly struck me. Maybe Holly had the same idea as me. Maybe she had no interest in wading through another collection of online strangers until she found me again. There was a good chance she was waiting for me to reconnect on our private line, via Skype. I quickly logged out of the public chatroom and launched the private app. When I logged back in, I filtered my list of contacts to display only those who were *Active Now.* Holly's familiar thumbnail appeared with a green dot beside it to indicate that she was online.

Oh my God! I thought. *She's been waiting for me!*

As my pussy fluttered in excitement, I hesitated before sending her a note.

What should I wear for this chat? What if she was with her roommate this time?

I didn't want to be too presumptuous by wearing something too skimpy and come off as some kind of floozy. What if she just wanted to chat to tell me she'd found a new outlet for her lesbian affections?

I went into my wardrobe and wrapped a silk robe over my camisole, then carried my laptop to my bed and made myself comfortable against the headboard. I paused with my hands over my keyboard, wondering how I should proceed after our last embarrassing incident. I decided to send her a text message this time, just to make sure she was free to talk.

Hi Holly, I typed. It's Jade. *Are you alone?*

Within seconds, a video call request came warbling over the line, indicating that she wanted to chat live.

Maybe I didn't scare her off so badly last time after all, I thought, clicking the Accept button.

When the call connected and our video windows went live, this time I saw Holly sitting on the bed next to another young girl wearing a UC T-shirt and skimpy panties.

My heart skipped a beat when I realized what was happening.

Could it really be? I thought. *Had she connected that quickly with her roomie and persuaded her to pull me into their affair?*

"I see you've made a new friend," I spoke into the mic, trying to conceal the excitement in my voice.

"Hi Jade," the other girl said. She appeared to be about Holly's age, and almost as pretty. With long blond hair, penetrating blue eyes, and plump rosebud lips, the pair of them looked like models straight out of an Abercrombie & Fitch commercial. "Holly's told me so much about you."

"Oh?" I said, still dumbfounded at the situation I found myself in.

"This is my roommate Jen that I was telling you about," Holly said. "I told her how you've been helping me connect with my—*feminine instincts.*"

"Um, yes," I stammered, unsure how much Holly had shared with her roommate. "We've been exploring some mutual interests."

"That's not the *only* thing she's been exploring," Jen said, leaning over to give Holly a long passionate kiss on her lips.

"I'm glad to see you two have finally connected," I said. "It sounded as if Holly might never break you away from your boyfriend, Jen."

"He wasn't really my boyfriend. More of a *boy-toy* to mess around with occasionally. I've had my eye on Holly ever since we became roommates. If it wasn't for you, I might never have known she was also interested in girls."

"Not just *any* girl," Holly said, reaching out her hand to intertwine her fingers with Jen's. "Only you."

"And *Jade* apparently," Jen said, nodding toward the screen.

"We found each other by accident," I interjected, not wanting to create a barrier between the two lovers. "Holly was just trying to find an outlet for her emerging feelings, to see if they were real."

"I can see why," Jen said, leaning toward the screen. "You're just as pretty and sexy as Holly said. I think she needed a more experienced lover to help her find her path."

"Not to mention how to learn how to make love to another woman," Holly winked at me.

"Yes," Jen said, tilting an eyebrow. "She's been trying out some of her new moves on me. I should thank you for your mentoring. It might have taken us *months* to figure out all the special things we girls can do with one another."

My pussy fluttered at the thought of the two girls making out all night long.

"Oh? You've been practicing?" I teased, fishing for more details.

Jen suddenly lifted herself up and straddled Holly's hips, facing away from the camera.

"To say the least," she said. "Would you like to see? Maybe you can show us a few new moves."

I squirmed on my bed, suddenly aware of the wet spot forming in the seat of my robe.

"I'd love to watch you ravish each other. Do you mind if this old lady has a little fun while you two go at it?"

"We were kind of hoping you would," Jen said. "And you're far from an old lady. Can we see a bit more of your body? Holly said you have an amazing figure."

"Absolutely," I said, scarcely believing my luck having the opportunity to have online sex with two gorgeous young co-eds. I quickly tore off my robe and pulled down my panties, feeling the torrent of fluid between my legs soaking into my bedsheets.

"Can we see your tits, too?" Jen said. "Those are some pretty fine looking hooters."

I hesitated for a moment revealing any more of my body, out of concern this was shaping up to be a one-sided show, rather than the two-way exchange I'd enjoyed with Holly so far. It was obvious that Jen was the more aggressive partner in their relationship, and I didn't want Holly feeling embarrassed or left out.

"Am I the *only* one getting undressed?" I asked.

"No way," Holly said, pulling her T-shirt over her head. Jen quickly followed suit, and the two girls pressed their bare breasts together while they kissed passionately.

As I watched the girls rubbing their bodies together, I pulled my camisole over my head and began pinching my nipples. Jen pressed her body forward, tilting Holly down onto the bed, then they twisted their bodies so they could watch the screen from the side.

"Damn, Jade," Jen said. "Holly wasn't kidding. You have a gorgeous body. I can see how she got off so easily watching you."

"I can't hold a candle to you guys," I said, admiring the two girls' smooth, flexible bodies. "I wish everything stood as firm and perky on me as it does on you. You've got a very sexy body too, Jen."

"Talk dirty to us," she said. "Tell us what you want us to do. Holly was telling me about some of the things you like."

I guess all pretenses are off at this point, I thought. *It's time to get down and dirty.* I spread my legs and placed my fingers over my slick opening.

"I want to watch you suck on Holly's pretty nipples. Make them hard and long again, like I saw them yesterday."

Jen leaned forward and took Holly's left breast into her mouth, then turned her head to glance into the camera. I pushed my laptop away from me a few inches so they could see my pussy and hips displayed in front of the screen. As I circled my clit with the tip of my fingers, I squeezed my breast with my other hand and moaned at the sight of Holly's teat in her roommate's mouth.

"Mmm," Jen hummed, as she tickled and teased Holly's tips.

"You are one sexy momma," Jen said, popping her mouth off Holly's nipple with a smack. "No wonder I caught her coming when I walked in the door yesterday. You could put any girl over the edge with a body like that."

"Happy to oblige anytime," I panted, feeling my juices running down my thighs.

"We might have to arrange that," Jen said, smiling at the camera. "But right now, I just want to fuck my girl while you get off watching us. What would you like us to do now?"

I couldn't believe they were letting me direct the action like some kind of erotic movie director. I moved my laptop a little closer toward my body and leaned closer to the screen.

"I want to watch you *taste* her," I said. "I want to watch Holly twisting all over your face while you make her cum with your tongue."

"My pleasure," Jen said. "She *does* taste so sweet. I can't get enough of her sex in my mouth."

As Jen slithered down Holly's body toward her hips, Holly turned the laptop with her hand to allow me to take in all the action.

"You're so sexy, Jade," she purred as Jen placed her head between her legs. "Thanks for joining us tonight. I wanted to share this with you."

"*I'm* the lucky one," I said. "I'm just glad you finally connected with Jen. It's so great to see you together this way."

"You have no idea," Jen said, placing her hands beside Holly's hips and pulling her toward her. Holly gasped and arched her back when Jen's lips found her pearl.

"Yes, Jen," she panted. "Suck me right there. Lick my clit while Jade watches us.

When I saw the look on Holly's face from Jen's touch, I buried my fingers in my pussy and began rubbing my clit with the palm of my hand. By now I was soaking wet, and a huge stain had begun to spread over my sheets between my legs.

"Yes—finger your pussy," Holly moaned as she watched me jilling myself. Jen turned her face to see what I was doing then began lapping her tongue up and down Holly's slit.

"Suck me Jen," Holly moaned. "Make me cum all over your face."

"Fuck, Holly," I groaned, watching my fantasy come true. "That is so hot! You're going to make me cum soon too."

"Cum with me, Jade," Holly said. "Let me watch you squirt while I cum in Jen's mouth. I'm close—"

"Oh God," I suddenly hissed, clamping down on my fingers. As the insides of my pussy began contracting in a powerful orgasm, I pulled my fingers out of my hole and began spraying all over the computer screen. I was so lost in the throes of pleasure, I didn't care that I might be ruining my computer. Right now, I just wanted to show Holly the effect she was having on me.

"Holy fuck, Jade," Holly groaned. "I'm cumming! Spray your juices all over me!"

Holly lifted her hips off the mattress then slammed her body back down onto the bed as she grabbed the back of Jen's head. She pulled her tightly against her pussy while she jerked and thrashed on the sheets. Jen glanced out the corner of her eye toward their computer as her eyes widened watching me gush all over my camera. My image must have been blurry from the juices running over the lens, but this just seemed to get Holly even more excited.

"God, how I'd love you feel you cumming on me like that," she panted, slowly coming down from her long and intense orgasm. When her thighs finally stopped quaking, Jen lifted her head and smiled toward the camera.

"You are one hot momma, Jade," she said, wiping the back of her hand over her lips to clear some of Holly's juices off her face. "I can see why Holly wanted to see you again. This is even *more* fun with a sexy spectator."

"Sorry," I said, lifting my camisole off the bed to wipe my screen and keyboard. "I made quite a mess."

"Are you kidding me?" Jen said. "That might be the sexiest thing I've ever seen. I never even knew a woman could squirt like that."

"Only when I'm really worked up," I said. "I guess I lubricate a bit more than some women. When I come really hard, my muscles just push it out of me. I got pretty turned on watching Holly cum on your face."

"You weren't the only ones getting turned on by that," Jen said. "I'm about to burst at the seams myself."

I smiled at Jen and raised my finger to request a short break.

"Can you give me just one minute to clean up this mess before we continue? I'm afraid all this fluid might get inside my computer and short it or something. The last thing I need right now is to lose the ability to see both of you getting off together. I'll be right back."

4

JOINING FORCES

I got up and scurried to the bathroom and ran some water over a facecloth, then wrung it out and came back to the bed. I wiped the screen, camera, and keyboard with the wet cloth, then dried all the surfaces with another dry cloth. When I peered back at the screen, I saw that Holly and Jen were lying sideways on the bed, kissing one another.

"Can you guys see me clearly?" I said, hesitating to interrupt up their embrace.

They turned toward their screen and nodded.

"Perfect," Jen said. "What would you like to see us do now? Hopefully something with a little *together* action."

"Definitely," I said. "I think it's time you got some direct stimulation too, Jen." It was obvious to me that Jen was the dominant one, and I was eager to watch her fuck Holly. "Can you get on top of Holly and place your hips over hers so you're scissoring your pussies together?"

She raised herself up and straddled Holly's hips diagonally, with one knee on the outside of her hips and the other one resting just inside her thighs.

"You mean like this?" Jen said.

"Yes. Now lift Holly's right leg up so you can get more direct contact between your vulvas."

Holly lifted her leg straight up in the air then Jen placed it over her right shoulder, twisting Holly's hips sideways. Now the two girls were locked in a tight scissor position, with their pussies tightly clamped together.

"Mmm, that feels good, Jen," Holly purred.

"We haven't tried it *this* way yet," Jen nodded. "You're quite a sex coach, Jade. We'll have to do this more often."

"Any place, any time," I smiled. "But I think you two can take it from here. You're in charge now, Jen. You should be able to get plenty of direct stimulation this way."

As Jen began to swing her hips forward and back against Holly's pussy, she let out a low moan.

"Fuck, yes," she purred. "I can feel your clit rubbing against mine, Holly."

"Fuck me, Jen," Holly panted. "Fuck my cunt with your sweet pussy."

"Damn straight I will," Jen said, pulling Holly's raised leg tightly between her tits, increasing the speed of her hip movement between Holly's flared legs.

As the two girls began humping each other, I mimicked Jen's position by lifting myself up and kneeling on my bed. Then I reached over to my side table and pulled out a dome-shaped silicone cushion with a vulva impression carved in the top. I positioned the device between my legs, then I lowered myself onto it and began grinding my pussy into the artificial vulva.

"Damn, girl," Jen panted. "You've got all the toys. What *is* that thing?"

"It's just a little something I use on lonely nights to imagine I'm doing what you're doing right now to Holly. Sometimes I like to fantasize that I'm tribbing another woman instead of just using my hands or a vibrator."

"That's pretty hot," Jen moaned. "Are you fantasizing about rubbing *us* that way right now?"

"Definitely," I panted, spreading my legs wider and pressing myself harder against the cushion.

"Does that thing *vibrate* by any chance?" Holly said, winking at me.

"It does, as a matter of fact."

"Show me."

I flicked a switch on the side of the cushion, and the vulva began vibrating between my legs.

"Uhnn," I groaned, throwing my head back in pleasure.

"Yes, Jade," Holly panted as she watched me. "Fuck her like you'd fuck me. I want to watch you cum all over my pussy like you did on the screen a few minutes ago."

"I think that can be arranged," I smiled, feeling my wetness spreading over the cushion.

"God, that's hot," Jen panted, watching me fuck my artificial lover on the screen. "My pussy's on fire, Holl. I'm going to cum for you soon."

"I feel you, Jen," Holly moaned. "Caress me with your sweet lips. Spread your love all over me."

Jen wrapped her arms tightly around Holly's upturned leg and suddenly began convulsing against her hips.

"It's happening, Holl! I'm cumming! Your pussy feels so good against mine."

"I'm cumming with you, Jen!" Holly grunted. "Press your pussy against me. Feel me cumming inside you."

As I watched the two girls twisting their bodies in simultaneous orgasm, I lost all control and began spurting all over my domed lover. While the girls thrashed their bodies together, we watched each other as we screamed in one powerful, collective climax. After what seemed like an eternity at the peak of pleasure, we all collapsed onto our respective beds, panting as we peered into our screens.

"You guys seemed to enjoy that," I said. "I told you there's lots of different ways we girls can have fun, Holly."

"You weren't kidding," Holly said, trying to catch her breath.

"The possibilities become endless with such an interesting collection of toys," Jen said. "What *other* interesting devices have you got to share with us?"

I leaned over and reached into my nightstand and pulled another toy out of the drawer, being careful to hide it from their view.

"I've already shown Holly how to use my special rabbit vibrator," I said. "But my real favorite is one *two* women can enjoy at the same time."

I held up the twelve-inch-long two-sided silicone phallus and bent it playfully between my two hands.

"Scissoring is even more fun when you've got something filling you up inside."

"Holy fuck!" Jen exclaimed, with wide eyes. "That think is huge! How do you fit that inside you? I could never—"

"You don't. It's meant to be shared with your lover. Each of you takes a separate end while you fuck each other, kind of like a man. There's nothing quite like it."

"I can imagine," Jen said. "I wish we had one of those things to play with right now."

"Well, *actually*—" Holly said, reaching over her head to remove something from underneath her pillow. She held a big purple dildo up in the air and waved it sexily from side to side. "I took the liberty today when you went out for a while to get one myself. After Jade explained how these things could be used, I thought you might like to give it a try..."

"*Hell* yes!" Jen said, raising herself back onto her knees excitedly. "Show me how to use it, Holly. Maybe Jade can play along with us on her end at the same time."

"It'll be my pleasure," I said, feeling another rivulet of juices running down the inside of my thighs. "I just wish we had a *three-sided* version so we could all do it together for real."

"I didn't see one of those at the sex shop," Holly said.

"Don't worry about me. I'll improvise. I'm just happy to watch you two enjoying yourselves. Now let me see you join together using that big snake."

"Lie down on the bed," Holly instructed to Jen. "This time it's my turn to fuck you."

Jen lay down with her hips about a foot away from Holly's, while Holly inserted one end of the long dildo into her pussy. Then she pushed closer to Jen and placed the other end at her opening. As they pressed their hips together, the giant dildo slowly disappeared into Jen's cavity as she uttered a low guttural moan.

"Yes—just like that," I purred, watching the two girls begin to hump their hips together.

"What about you?" Holly said, tilting her head back toward the camera. "What are you going to do while we're having all the fun?"

"I need something moving inside me too," I said.

I reached back into my nightstand and pulled out my rabbit vibrator and leaned back against my headboard. It made a loud slurping sound as I inserted it inside me.

"Sounds like *somebody's* still wet," Holly smiled.

"It looks that way. I hope you won't be distracted if I make a little noise while you two fuck each other."

"Not at all," Jen said, pressing her pussy closer to Holly's. "We intend to make some rude sounds of our own."

"Mmm," Holly moaned. "I like the feeling of you moving inside me, Jen. Fuck me with your big cock."

"This is way better than a real cock," Jen purred, smiling at Holly. "It's double the pleasure. I can fuck my partner at the same time I'm getting filled up by her. Who needs a man when you've got so many fun ways to play with a girl?"

"Exactly," I said. "I told you there was no going back once you experienced real lesbian loving, Holly."

"I'm *never* going back," Holly moaned as Jen picked up the pace of her hip movements. "Everything I need is right here on this bed with me."

"Normally I'd agree," Jen panted, watching the fluttering rabbit ears of my vibrator rubbing up against my clit. "But I think Jade has a slight advantage with that dual-purpose vibrator. How can we get direct clitoral stimulation like you in this position?"

"No one said you can't *touch* yourselves," I said. "Half the fun of using a double-sided dildo with your partner is watching them stimulate themselves while you fuck each other. Go ahead and rub your clits with your hands."

The two girls slid their right hand over each of their mounds, then reached down their other side and clasped hands.

"That's the idea," I said. "Does that feel better?"

"Better," Jen panted, as the girls pulled themselves closer together with their interlocking hands.

As I watched them twist and roll their bodies together, I leaned forward and kneeled on the bed. I placed my rabbit vibrator underneath me then I lowered my hips, letting the pressure of the mattress insert it inside me.

"You guys look so hot together," I moaned. "Now I'm thinking about that three-sided dildo again. I'm going to have to see if I can find one of those."

"If you do, you'll have to let us know," Holly groaned, watching me hump my dildo. "I'd love to try a three-way for real someday."

"What about you, Jen?" I said. "Would you be up for that too?"

"Fuck, yes," she purred. "I'd love to squeeze those big melons of yours while we all fuck each other silly."

"I'll look into it," I said. "Right now, I want to imagine I'm there with you girls. Can you see me? I'm imagining myself fucking you both over top."

"Yes," Holly panted. "Fuck us, Jade. Press your wet pussy against our hips and gush all over our stomachs. I want to see you cum again."

"Fuck," I moaned, imagining the movement of the animated vibrator inside me as if it were two girls underneath me creating the action. "I can't hold it much longer. I'm going to cum all over both of you soon!"

The two girls clasped their hands together on both sides and pulled themselves together. As they gnashed their clits together, the dildo disappeared completely inside their pussies.

"Oh God, Holly," Jen grunted. "I'm going to cum too. Are you almost there?"

"Yes, Jen," Holly moaned, twisting her head to watch me jackrabbiting on the vibrator deeply embedded in my pussy. "Cum Jade!"

As the two girls began to pull their torsos off the mattress and look at each other with wild eyes, I felt the first wave of passion roll over me.

"It's happening!" I shouted, holding the base of my vibrator with two hands. "Cum for me, Holly!"

The two girls' mouths gaped opened in a wide yaw, then they screamed out loud as their bodies writhed against one another in mutual ecstasy.

"Fuckk," Jen growled. "I feel you, Holly! I feel you cumming against me. Cum for me baby!"

"Yes Jen!" Holly screamed as her whole body quaked in an intense orgasm, her pointy tits shaking like two trembling pyramids over her quivering tummy while the girls held each other with tensed outstretched arms.

As each of us quivered and moaned over our embedded phalluses, I couldn't stop fantasizing about what it would be like to merge together in a true ménage à trois.

If they don't have a three-sided dildo, I'll have to make one for myself, I thought, peering down at the giant puddle between my legs.

VOLUME FOUR

THE HITCHHIKER

1

———

I'd been looking forward to this trip for weeks. Normally, I flew to client meetings this far from home, but Des Moines was only four hours away by car. Factoring in check-in time at the airport, going through security, and taking taxis on both ends, it would take at least that long to travel there by plane. Plus, driving was infinitely less hassle. All I had to do was jump in my SUV, turn on the nav system, and point my way to my destination. All while soaking up the pretty midwestern scenery and listening to my favorite tunes on the radio.

Besides, I hadn't been on a road trip in years, and I was looking forward to feeling the sun on my face and the wind in my hair. There was something strangely romantic and liberating about the call of the open road. Being able to stop whenever you wanted, take a little detour if the mood struck, and watching the intoxicating flow of traffic like so many ants scurrying over their anthill.

After packing up a few days' worth of provisions and locking up my house, I turned out of my subdivision onto Route 30, heading west. This part of the trip was still familiar from my childhood forays into the lake district of northern Wisconsin, and I smiled as I breathed in the pastoral landscape of the passing farms. The countryside was a brilliant patchwork of yellows and greens, and my head lolled from side to side as I followed the neatly arranged rows of corn, soybeans, and wheat while my car glided down the two-lane highway.

After glancing down to dial in my favorite country music station, I looked up to see an unusual sight on the side of the road a few hundred feet ahead. It was something I hadn't seen for a long time–a hitchhiker. Curious to see who was still daring enough to catch a ride from a stranger in these troubling times, I squinted as the traveler came into focus. As the distance between us closed, my eyes widened when I realized it was a girl.

A young, scantily clad girl.

I could hardly believe my eyes as my car rushed past her. She couldn't have been more than eighteen years old, if that. Wearing tight, cut-off jean shorts and a white tank top, she had the young, nubile figure of a high-school teenager. My first reaction was one of shock and disbelief.

What in God's name is a girl like that doing thumbing a ride on the highway? Doesn't she realize how many predators are out there looking for an easy mark just like her?

As I watched her get smaller and smaller in my rear-view mirror, I shook my head disapprovingly, then suddenly screeched on the brakes and pulled over onto the shoulder. Normally I wouldn't give a second thought to taking on a hitchhiker knowing there was just as much risk for the driver, especially for a single woman like me. But there was something about this girl that I couldn't resist. Whether it was her naïve vulnerability or the appearance of her slender brown legs, I wasn't sure. Either way, the little twitch in my pussy told me this was an opportunity I couldn't pass up.

At first, she didn't notice that I'd pulled over, since I was so far ahead of her. I honked my horn and flashed my lights and she turned her head in my direction, then she picked up her small suitcase and began jogging toward me. Feeling sorry for her, I put my car in reverse and slowly backed up along the shoulder until we closed the gap. When she came up on my right side, I rolled down the passenger window and peered out at her.

"Where are you headed?" I smiled.

"California," she said, catching her breath.

"I'm only going as far as Des Moines, but I'm happy to point you in the right direction."

"Thanks," she nodded.

I unlocked my doors and tilted my head toward the back seat.

"You can throw your bag in the back if you want. But there's a lot more room up front to stretch your legs."

The girl opened the rear door and threw her carry-on-size roller bag on the back seat then climbed in the front next to me.

I smiled at her and checked my driver's mirror, then slowly pulled back onto the highway.

"I'm Jade," I said, introducing myself.

"Brooklyn," the girl replied.

"That's a pretty name. Do you go by Brooke, or Lynn, or do you like to be called by your full name?"

"Either way is fine. But most of my friends call me Brooke."

"Brooke it is," I nodded, interested to learn more about this mysterious stranger. "So, *California*? What's taking a pretty girl like you so far away from home?"

"I dunno," she said. "Just spreading my wings, I guess. Now that I've finished high school, I figured I might as well try my luck in La-La Land."

"Are you looking to be a movie star?" I laughed.

"Probably not. I thought I'd get a job as a waitress and check things out. But you never know, right? Wasn't that how Marilyn Monroe got discovered?"

I glanced over at the girl and smiled. With her curly blonde hair and piercing blue eyes, she could easily pass for a younger version of the matinee idol.

"Actually, I think she was working in a factory. But with those all-American looks, you've got as good a chance as any."

"Thanks," the girl said.

For the next couple of minutes, awkward silence filled the car as Brooke peered out her side of the window at the passing fields.

"It's pretty this time of the year, isn't it?" I said, making small talk. "I always like going for a drive as we approach harvest time. The crops are nearing full bloom, and you can smell the perfume in the air. Do you mind if I open the sunroof a bit so we can soak up the sunshine?"

"By all means," she said. "I probably should start working on my tan so I can keep up with all those California golden girls."

"I don't think you've got much to worry about," I said, glancing at her tawny thighs poking out of her cut-off jeans. There were so many questions I still had about this shy beauty. "But you're awfully young to be pulling up stakes and heading to the other side of the country. What do your parents think of this idea?"

"I'm not sure they much *care*," she shrugged. "My father lives in New York and my mother shacked up with an alcoholic who only seems to care where his next drink is coming from."

"I'm sorry to hear," I said, wincing at the thought of this pretty girl being neglected by uncaring parents.

"It's cool," she said. "I'm free as a bird now and the world is my oyster."

I peered over at Brooke, noticing her body language didn't match her cavalier attitude. She had her arms crossed tightly over her chest while her foot tapped nervously against the floorboard.

"Do they even *know* where you're headed?" I said. "I'm sorry to sound like an overbearing mother, but I'd hate for them to worry what happened to you."

"We had a fight earlier in the week when I told them I was thinking of leaving. My mother wanted me to go to college and my step-father just sees me as his meal ticket. I think he was afraid if I left that my mother wouldn't have any reason to keep him around."

I glanced over at Brooke and noticed a faint bruise around the base of her neck.

"But you *are* eighteen though? I mean, I wouldn't want to get either one of us in trouble..."

"Yes," she huffed sarcastically. "Just turned. I got the hell out of there just in time."

"Do you mind my asking why you weren't interested in going to college? You seem like a smart, well-spoken girl. Weren't your grades good enough?"

"I did well enough in high school," she said. "I just wanted to spread my wings before I get locked into another four years of school and a boring, dead-end job."

I couldn't help admire her free spirit and sense of adventure. But I wondered if there was another reason for her sudden uprooting.

"And there's nothing *else* keeping you close to home? Boyfriends, a steady job..."

"I've been saving up from my weekend job at Applebee's these last two years. Now I've finally got enough to start over on the west coast. I've had plenty enough of boys. They're only interested in one thing anyhow."

I felt my heart racing, seeing a window of opportunity opening. While I was in no hurry to take advantage of her, I felt like I'd found a kindred spirit. Even though there was fifteen years separating us in age, we shared a similar view on life with neither of us wanting to be held back by society's norms.

"Yeah, I know what you mean. My first husband wasn't exactly Mr. Perfect either. I'm in no hurry to jump into bed with another guy anytime soon."

I noticed Brooke's body language beginning to relax as she placed her arm on the door rest for support, hunching down a few inches in her seat.

"What are you headed to Des Moines for?" she asked.

"A meeting with a client. I'm a graphic designer and I'm going to review some ideas he had for updating his corporate identity."

"Corporate identity?"

"He operates a chain of restaurants. He wants to refresh his logo, menus, signage, and so on. It's a branding thing."

"Mmm," Brooke nodded. "Will you be staying long?"

"It's just a one-day meeting. But I've booked a hotel overnight so I'll be fresh for the drive back tomorrow."

Brooke peered back out the side of her window as we listened to the sound of the wind whistling through the overhead sunroof and soft country music on the radio. Periodically, I'd catch her stealing glimpses out the side of her eyes at my legs in my tight jeans and my loose blouse flapping in the breeze.

"Do you like your job?" she asked after a few minutes.

"It's a living," I said. "At least I'm my own boss and I get to exercise my creative juices. Each commission is different and I meet some interesting people along the way. How about you? Do you have any special passions or talents?"

"Not really. I was pretty good at science and math at school, but I can't think of a job in either of those fields that interests me."

I nodded my head, trying to think of a way to get her to open up a little more. So far, she'd played her cards pretty close to the vest, and I was beginning to wonder if there was any way I could draw her out of her shell.

"There's a lot you can do with those skills," I said. "Especially if you go on to college. Quite a few math majors move into finance. Quants make some big bucks on Wall Street. Trading, risk management, investment banking–maybe it would be an opportunity for you to reconnect with your father in New York?"

"He's got his own life now with a new bride and two toddlers. I'm not sure there's much room for me in his picture any longer."

"What about science?" I frowned. "There's so many interesting careers you could explore in that area. Marine biology, space exploration, you could even be a doctor."

"I'm too young to be thinking about all that mature stuff," Brooke said. "I've got my whole life ahead of me. There'll be plenty of time to explore my options when I settle down."

I peered over at Brooke, watching the breeze from the open sunroof swirling her blonde locks against her pretty face as she leaned back, closing her eyes.

"Sorry, I'm sure the last thing you want right now is to be stuck on a four-hour road trip with someone who sounds like your mother. No more career counseling, I promise. Let's just enjoy the open road and the wind in our hair!"

She issued a smile of relief, then I noticed her tapping her fingers on the edge of the door as she peered outside.

"Do you like Blake Shelton?" I said, seeing her foot tapping in rhythm to the music on the radio.

"He's fun to watch on The Voice. But I like this song. He and Gwen look like they really love each other in the video version."

"It sure is dreamy," I said, turning up the volume. "I'm not sure I'll ever find that kind of love."

While we listened to the song, Brooke began to hum the melody quietly under her breath.

"*I don't wanna look back in thirty years,*" I sang along to the lyrics, trying to get her to open up. "And wonder who I'm married to..."

"*Wanna say it now, wanna make it clear,*" Brooke joined in softly. "*For only you and God to hear...*"

"*When you love someone,*" we joined in together, "*they say you set 'em free. But that ain't gonna work for me...*"

As the drumbeat introduced the chorus, I turned the volume up higher.

"*I don't wanna live without you,*" we both belted. "*I don't wanna even breathe, don't wanna dream about you, wanna wake up with you next to me.*"

Brooke had a sweet, lilting tone, but I could see sadness in her eyes as she sang along with me. I smiled at her as I cranked the volume up until the beat surrounded us in the pounding cabin.

"*I don't wanna go down any other road now,*" she sang, looking back at me. "*I don't wanna love nobody but you.*"

"*Looking in your eyes now,*" we sang together. "*If I had to die now, I don't wanna love nobody but you...*"

As the song drifted off to the second verse, Brooke peered out her window, singing the rest of the song to herself. When I glanced over at her, I realized how vulnerable and alone she must have felt. I had no idea what kind of hardships she'd experienced in her young life, but from the pining sound of her voice, she looked broken and lost.

I peered ahead and saw a sign for a roadside rest area and looked over at her.

"Are you hungry?" I said. "There's an A&W restaurant at the pull-off. Nothing like a burger and fries with a down-home root beer to drown out your sorrows. My treat."

"Sure," Brooke said, smiling back at me. "I could go for a root beer right about now."

As I pulled off into the rest area, my heart skipped a beat. Somehow I knew this trip was going to have a lot more twists and turns than I planned.

2

Brooke and I went inside the restaurant and waited in line while we decided what we wanted from the display menu behind the counter. I noticed a group of teenage boys in an adjacent line ogling her figure while they snickered and elbowed each other playfully. Whether they chose to keep their distance because they were too afraid to approach her or because they thought I was her mother, I wasn't sure.

But for the first time since I'd met her, I saw her up close from head to toe. Her ass was firm and well rounded, with the tight seam of her cut-off shorts separating her buttocks into two perfect circular globes. Her breasts weren't large, but they sat up prominently on her chest, pointing out like two snow cones under her form-fitting tank top. Her skin was soft and dewy like a teenager's, and golden brown with not a blemish to be found anywhere on her slender arms and legs.

As I admired her youthful, girl-next-door good looks, I understood why half the eyes in the room were checking her out.

If I was a teenage boy, I'd want a piece of that ass too.

I moved protectively beside her, and after we placed our order and collected our food trays, I found a booth in the far corner of the room. As she dug into her bacon and cheese burger, I watched the movement of her face while she peered back at me.

"What?" she said, gulping down her first mouthful. "Have I got mustard on my face or something?"

"No," I chuckled. "I was just thinking how a pretty girl dressed in such a skimpy outfit figured she could safely hitchhike her way all across the country."

"I don't know," she shrugged. "I've never done it before. But I figured the more skin I showed, the quicker I'd get picked up."

"That's for sure," I said, noticing the boys seated on the other side of the restaurant still stealing glances at her. "But you must know how attractive you are and how vulnerable you'd be to somebody who might have ulterior motives."

"I never really thought much about it, I guess," she said, dipping one of her fries in the cup of ketchup. "I was in such a hurry to get the hell out of my current abusive home, I just packed my bag and left."

"Is that what happened to your neck?" I said, glancing down at her bruise.

Brooke sat back on the bench and peered out the window pensively.

"My mom's boyfriend grabbed me there when I threatened to leave. Par for the course with that asshole."

I glanced at her and furrowed my brow, wondering what other indignities she'd suffered at the hands of the abusive lush.

"Did he abuse you in any *other* ways?"

"He tried often enough, but I got pretty good at reading the signs when he had too much to drink. I just made myself scarce until he sobered up."

"Now I see why you were so eager to leave," I nodded. "But you have to be careful that you don't trade one dangerous caretaker for another. There are a lot of ill-intentioned people out there just looking for an easy mark like yourself."

"I can take care of myself," she said. "I've made it this far on my own."

"Well, technically, you're less than one tenth of the way to Shangri La Land," I chuckled. "You've still got a long road ahead of you."

Brooke dipped another french fry into her ketchup, drawing some circles on the paper placemat lining her tray.

"As long as I'm careful whose car I get into, everything should be okay, right? There must be *lots* of other nice people like you out there willing to help a girl out."

"I suppose so, but you're rolling the dice with every new pick-up. It's unlikely you're going to find one person who'll take you the entire way."

"Maybe," she said, noisily sipping her root beer through her straw to distract attention from the conversation. "But tell me more about you. Do you have kids? Where do you live? Do you have any special plans for the future?"

"No kids," I laughed. "We barely had enough time to get started before our marriage disintegrated. I live in Naperville, just outside Chicago. As for the future, I'm just taking it day by day."

"You're not far from where *I* used to live in Aurora," Brooke said. "We're almost neighbors. What happened to your marriage, if you don't mind my asking. Why was it so short?"

"He wasn't very–*attentive*–to my needs," I said. "I guess it just wasn't everything I thought it was cracked up to be. You know, the knight in shining armor and all that."

"Like in that movie Pretty Woman?"

"Ha," I laughed, almost choking on my drink. "It was slightly different circumstances, but yeah, I guess I was expecting someone to sweep me off my feet and take me away to his castle to live happily ever after."

"No *other* worthy candidates since then?"

"I'm not really looking for that kind of relationship anymore. Like you said–I've had my fill of boys."

"Mmm," Brooke nodded, glancing down at the cleavage in my open blouse as she took another sip of her root beer.

For the rest of our lunch date, we teased each other about our inept experiences with men, giggling amongst ourselves at the juvenile attempts of the boys across the room trying to attract her attention. When we finished our meal, we skipped out into the parking lot holding hands, then we jumped in the car and cranked up the music, wailing together over the corny country songs. The time passed quickly, and before I knew it, I saw the interchange approaching to exit into Des Moines.

"Listen," I said, glancing at the clock on my dashboard. "I don't feel right about just dropping you off at the side of the highway. Why don't you come with me while I check into my hotel before I head off to see my client? You can freshen up and watch a movie until I get back. Then we can have dinner and you're welcome to stay with me overnight before heading back out on the road tomorrow."

"Okay," Brooke said, nodding her head gently. "Thank you for everything. For lunch, for picking me up–and for being such a good listener. I can't imagine I'll find anyone who's half as much fun as you to spend the rest of my trip with."

"Don't give it a second thought," I said, smiling back at her warmly. "This has been an unexpected surprise for me too. You've made my boring trip to Des Moines so much more interesting."

I took the second exit and drove to the downtown Marriott, then I ordered a room with two double beds, and we carried our light bags inside. After changing into my business clothes and straightening up my lipstick and mascara, I handed Brooke one of the two room keys I'd been given at the front desk.

"I shouldn't be more than a couple of hours," I said. "Why don't you make yourself comfortable while I'm away. Feel free to order a movie and charge any meals to the room. But whatever you do, stay far away from the single men you find in the hotel. You'd be the perfect distraction while they're away from their wives back home."

"Don't worry," Brooke laughed. "I'll stay right here until you get back. Good luck at your meeting."

"Thanks, hun," I smiled. "See you soon."

For the rest of the afternoon, I had a hard time concentrating at my meeting with my client. All I could think about was Brooke's pretty face and the look she gave me when I left the room. Even though there was a wide gulf in age between the two of us, I found myself strangely attracted to the free-spirited girl and I was eager to get back to her as quickly as I could. I felt much more than a mother-and-daughter-type bond; my head was spinning and my stomach had butterflies, like I had a teenage crush. Which I suppose it *was*, in a strangely perverted way. Although the periodic twitching in my pussy told me this was a decidedly *grown-up* infatuation.

When my client invited me out for dinner at the close of our meeting, I politely declined, using the excuse of wanting to visit family members in town. I rushed back to my hotel, hoping Brooke hadn't gotten second thoughts about staying with me for the evening, as I fumbled awkwardly with my room key outside the hotel room door. When I swung it open, I was relieved to see her sitting upright on one of the beds, watching the movie Pretty Woman while munching on a large bag of Cheesies.

"I was afraid maybe you wouldn't *be* here when I got back," I said, throwing my briefcase on the opposite bed.

"Of course I'd be here," she said. "Why would I throw away this free meal ticket?"

I glanced at the TV and smiled.

"I see you've made yourself comfortable. Have you been fantasizing about finding your knight in shining armor?"

"Maybe," she said. "Although Richard Gere isn't exactly my type."

"Oh?" I said, hoping to get more hints about her sexual persuasion. "Who *is* your type?"

"I dunno," she said. "I'm still figuring it out. But it seems to be rapidly morphing away from the Tom Cruise leading man prototype."

"He's too short for you anyhow," I laughed, recognizing a familiar scene in her movie. "I love this part when Richard Gere's character pulls up in his stretch limousine and begs Julia Roberts to run away with him."

Brooke peered up at me then patted the bed beside her.

"Why don't you come join me while we finish the movie together? Do you like Cheesies?"

I laughed as I kicked off my leather pumps and threw my suit jacket on the bed.

"I haven't had them in ages, but yeah, they used to be one of my favorite guilty pleasures."

I plopped myself down on the bed beside Brooke, and we watched the rest of the movie side-by-side as we noisily crunched on the cheesy snack. When it was finally over, we looked at our orange-crusted fingers and giggled.

"*Ew,*" Brooke said, scrunching up her face. "I can't believe we ate that whole bag in one sitting. I've got to wash myself up before I get this all over everything."

While Brooke disappeared into the washroom, I cleaned my hands with wet wipes from my purse, then I changed out of my work clothes back into my jeans. When she emerged a few minutes later, she peered at my new ensemble and smiled.

"I like this look better on you," she said. "You look less like my mother and more like my partner-in-crime."

"Like *Thelma and Louise*?" I smiled. "God forbid that I'd remind you of your mother."

"I don't think there's any danger of that," she said, checking my figure out like I was with her at the restaurant.

"Are you up for a proper dinner after eating all that junk food?" I said, changing the subject. "I could go for a nice steak and a glass of wine right about now."

"Absolutely," Brooke said. "Although I'll have to pass on the wine, unless Iowa has a lower drinking age than Illinois."

"Oh yeah," I said. "I keep forgetting how young you are. I'm sure we can find something else to keep you amused. Maybe they can scare up a Shirley Temple or something like that."

"Ha!" Brooke said, placing her hands on her hips in mock protest. "I'm not *that* young!"

We took the elevator down to the lobby, then I asked at the front desk for the location of some good nearby restaurants. After enquiring about Brooke's food preferences, we decided on the Outback Steakhouse. When we were seated at the restaurant, I ordered a top sirloin steak with a glass of cabernet and Brooke ordered the pork ribs and a Coke. As we dug into our meals and talked about our favorite movies, I kept staring at Brooke's pretty face smeared with BBQ sauce, imagining it was my pussy juices instead of the tangy marinade.

"You're giving me that *look* again," she said, noticing me staring at her lips.

"It's just that you seem to have a propensity for finger food and getting your fingers messy while you eat."

"Hey, I'm a *teenager!*" she protested. "You can go ahead and eat your old-people food all prim and proper with a knife and fork. I'm gonna enjoy my pizza and burgers and fried food all I like."

"Who are you calling *old*?" I said, raising an eyebrow.

"Well you're older than *me*, aren't you? You've already been married and divorced, holding down a boring day job, driving an old person car–"

"It's not an *old person's* car," I said. "And I'm not boring, I'm just–*responsible*. Something you'd do well to learn before you end up living in the streets or get picked up by some sugar daddy."

"I didn't *ask* for all this," she said, twirling her finger sarcastically in the air while peering around the restaurant. "I was doing just *fine* before you plucked me off the highway."

I swallowed my mouthful with a lump in my throat as I digested what had just happened. Somehow, we'd gone from laughing about our favorite movies to disparaging each other's life choices. My heart began racing a million miles an hour, shocked that we'd had our first fight after barely knowing each other for one day.

For the rest of the meal and the drive back to the hotel, we hardly said a word to one another as we stared out our windows, fuming. But the tightness in my stomach told me this was more than just a minor quarrel. People didn't get this passionate about issues and this angry at one another unless there was already some strong feelings between them. But mostly, I was afraid that I'd lost Brooke and that she'd use this as an excuse to run away again.

When we got back to the hotel, we took the elevator silently back up to our room then Brooke kicked off her sneakers, pulled her bra out from under her tank top and she climbed under the covers of her bed, sulking. I took a few minutes to brush my teeth and remove my makeup, then I pulled on a t-shirt and got into my bed wearing only my panties. As we both lay on the bed staring up at the ceiling, we could hear each other breathing mere inches away.

My mind raced thinking about what I should do with this young girl who'd I'd grown so close to in such a short period of time. I dreaded the idea of driving back home tomorrow without her, but I was far more worried about her continuing on her way by herself. After this new flare-up, I began to wonder if it wasn't for the best for the two of us to part company cleanly.

After a long pause, Brooke was the first to break the silence.

"I'm sorry, Jade, she said. "I didn't mean what I said about you being old and boring. I actually think you're one of the coolest, prettiest, and smartest persons I've met in a long time."

I paused for a long moment, feeling my heartbeat returning to normal.

"And I didn't mean what I said about your being irresponsible. I admire your free spirit and independence. I wish I were as courageous as you when I was your age."

For the next two hours, we talked about our dreams and aspirations, joking about our lost loves and missed opportunities. By the time I drifted off to sleep, I felt much more comfortable about the strength of our fledgling relationship. But a few hours later, I woke to the sound of rustling next to me in the pitch black. Brooke was shifting her weight erratically under her bedsheets, and I held my breath trying to listen to what she was doing.

After a few minutes, it became apparent from her raspy breathing and the rhythmic rustling of her sheets that she was masturbating under the covers. I could hardly believe what I was hearing, and my panties filled with moistness as I got more and more turned on listening to her pleasuring herself. She tried to be as quiet as she could, but the unmistakable ratcheting of her breath and the faster rustling of her sheets left little doubt that she was nearing climax. Suddenly, I could see her lifting her hips off the bed in the soft moonlight filtering through the crack in our curtains while she gasped in staccato succession.

Fuck me, I thought, squeezing my thighs together quietly under my covers. *That is the hottest thing I've ever heard in my life.*

I wasn't sure if her sudden arousal was because she was lying next to me in the quiet hotel room and she felt attracted to me, or if it was simply her teenage hormones taking control. Either way, there was no way I was going to be able to get back to sleep after that, and I waited until I heard her breathing returning to normal and she rolled over in her bed.

When I was sure she'd fallen back to sleep, I pulled down my panties and began jilling myself in furious circles over my burning clit. After getting so worked up listening to her touching herself, it didn't long for me to reach the peak of my pleasure. I bit my lip trying to stifle my groans as my body began convulsing in rhythmic contractions with my hand pressed tightly between my legs. When I finally stopped coming, I tried to control my breathing so as not to wake Brooke up. But when she suddenly rolled over again, I wondered if it was because she was restless or because she'd been listening to me the whole time.

Either way, I knew we'd both passed an important milestone in our mutual journey of discovery.

3

———

In the morning, Brooke woke up before me and went into the washroom to brush her teeth. My panties were still damp from my late-night masturbation session, and I was eager to get myself cleaned up before heading out. I sat up on the edge of my bed to check my messages, but it was all a blur as my mind raced thinking about what to do next. I couldn't bear the idea of leaving Brooke, but I had my life in Chicago and she was dead-set on traveling to LA. As I contemplated how to reconcile my conflicting urges, she stepped out of the washroom and paused in the doorway.

"Did you sleep well?" she asked.

I peered up, seeing the raised bumps of her areolas protruding atop her perky breasts under her braless tank top.

"Um, yes thank you," I stammered, momentarily taken aback by her sexy Elizabeth Taylor pose. "How about you?"

"Better than I have in a long time. Must be all this fresh midwestern air."

"That, or us staying up so late. What time do you figure we nodded off?"

"I dunno, but I enjoyed chatting with you into the wee hours. I haven't had that much fun since my grade school sleepovers."

"Everything but the pillow fight," I chuckled, alluding to our silent late-night tryst.

"Mmm," she nodded, flushing slightly.

I stood up and picked my toiletry bag out of my suitcase lying on the bench at the base of my bed.

"I need a shower. You'll probably want one too before heading back out on the road. You don't know when you might have the next opportunity. Do you want to go first?"

Brooke peered at my full breasts pressing against the flimsy cotton of my t-shirt. They were bigger than hers, and my erect nipples poked two sensuous darts in the light fabric. As I approached her near the entrance to the bathroom, she peered into my eyes and we hesitated for a moment. I was tempted to lean in and kiss her, but it still felt too soon. Besides, I didn't know if I was ever going to see her again. The last thing I needed was to get my pheromones all worked up again, only to be dashed when she sailed off into the sunset.

"No," she said, feeling our breasts only inches apart in the narrow doorway. "You go first. I'm going to check the highway route map to see the best place to pick up on my journey."

"Mmm," I nodded, not wanting to broach the subject that was on both of our minds. I could tell that neither of us was in any hurry to separate, but we were both painfully aware of the reality of the situation.

I continued into the washroom, closing the door partway behind me. Then I stepped out of my panties and pulled off my t-shirt, bending over to adjust the shower temperature. When I stood up to step into the tub, I caught Brooke peeking at me through the narrow crack, and she quickly turned away, pretending to thumb through her phone.

As I stepped into the warm shower feeling the soft spray caressing my bare tits and stomach, I flashed back to the scene from last night. Remembering the way Brooke raised her hips off the mattress and mewed when she came made my pussy tingle, and I snaked my hand between my legs and began to play with my nub. Within seconds, I had another powerful orgasm as I jerked and panted, trying to support myself with one hand against the slippery wall. When I finished washing my hair and cleaning my body, I stepped out of the tub and wrapped a towel around my torso and another around my wet hair. Then I opened the door as a rush of warm humid air spilled into the bedroom.

"Your turn," I said, smiling at Brooke. "I hope you don't mind that I took a couple of towels. There's still one large bath towel and a hand towel for you to use. You can borrow my hair dryer if you forgot to pack one."

"Thanks," Brooke said, slipping past me into the washroom. "Do you mind if I leave the door slightly ajar so as not to steam up the mirror?"

"I was thinking exactly the same thing," I smiled back at her.

Brooke closed the door partway then I heard the rustling of clothes as she disrobed, followed by the sound of the shower curtain being pulled back. When I heard the spray turn on, I peered up and saw her naked body briefly exposed in the mirror over the sink from my angle on the bed. Her tits were soft and round, like two bowls of Jello resting high on her chest, with pointy nipples that danced in the warm spray.

Oh, to be eighteen years old again, I thought as my pussy pulsed in unconscious spasms.

When she got out of the shower, she wrapped the bath sheet around her body and we took turns drying our hair with my blow dryer. Brooke left hers purposely damp to let it dry with a natural curl, and when she emerged from the bathroom, she reminded me of Kristen Stewart in the famous river scene from the finale of the Breaking Dawn Twilight movie. We got dressed separately in the privacy of the washroom, then we headed downstairs for a quick breakfast in the hotel restaurant before checking out.

After collecting a plateful of bacon and eggs from the breakfast bar, we sat down at our table and ate quietly together. Neither one of us wanted to acknowledge the elephant in the room. After a couple of minutes of awkward silence, I put my fork down on my plate and peered up at Brooke.

"Listen," I said. "I've been thinking. There's nothing urgent I need to rush home to for a few more days. Why don't I take you a little further along the way toward your destination? We can make a little adventure of it. Stop at Mount Rushmore, see the Grand Canyon, stuff like that."

"Like *Thelma and Louise*?!" she said, her eyes suddenly widening in excitement.

"Yes, everything except the driving over the cliff part at the end. That is, if you don't mind being seen in an *old person* car."

"I dunno," Brooke grinned. "It's a far cry from the Thunderbird convertible that Louise drove. But hey, beggars can't be choosers."

I lifted my glass of orange juice off the table and pointed it toward Brooke.

"Here's to new adventures," I said.

"To new adventures," she nodded, clinking her glass against mine.

***

After we packed our bags in the back of my SUV, Brooke turned toward me and wrapped her arms around my neck, giving me a bear hug.

"Thanks, Jade," she said. "I couldn't bear the idea of going the rest of the way without you. I feel like I've known you my whole life after being with you for only one day."

"Don't get your hopes up *too* far, young lady," I smiled. "I didn't promise to drive you the whole way. We'll take it day by day and see how far we can make it without getting into another fight."

"*Deal*," Brooke said, clapping her hands together excitedly.

We jumped in the car and after reaching the outskirts of Des Moines, I pulled back onto I-80 West, before angling northward toward Sioux Falls in South Dakota. We marveled at the passing landscape as the highway wound its way along the banks of the

Missouri River, singing country songs the entire way while our hair flapped in the wind outside our open windows.

When we got to Mount Rushmore, we picnicked in the grass at the base of the mountain, then took selfies with the four presidents peering over our shoulder. I mimicked the serious expressions of Lincoln, Jefferson, Washington, and Roosevelt, while Brooke made funny faces, sticking her tongue out the side of her mouth as she rolled her eyes. I hadn't laughed and had so much fun for as long as I could remember, and for the first time in ages, I lost track of what day of the week it was. We were just following our noses, letting the car take us wherever it wanted as we pointed west.

I felt my heart soaring with every new mile we traveled, feeling closer and closer to this free-spirited girl. But it was more than just a strong friendship. I lusted to be in Brooke's arms, to feel her body pressed against mine as I ravished her and we pleasured each other to new heights. After our silent tryst the night before, I was afraid to make the next move, not knowing if she was ready for an intimate relationship with a woman.

As we continued across the midwestern plains into Wyoming, Brooke seemed to become more and more restless and she began to shift in her seat distractedly. Suddenly, she popped open the glove box and reached inside.

"Have you got any *good reading* material in here?" she said. "There's only so many cornfields a girl can watch before she needs a diversion."

"Um—not really," I hesitated, remembering something *else* I kept stored in the stowage compartment.

Brooke felt something hard with her hand and began pulling it out of the box.

"What's this?" she said. "Do you keep a gun in here, just like Louise? Were you planning on running into some dangerous characters along the way?"

"Ah—" I stammered, unsure how to stop her.

"*Holy shit!*" she said, holding up my special vibrator that I carried to keep me amused on long trips. "Is this what I *think* it is?"

"Um..."

"It *is!*" Brooke squealed, squeezing the soft silicone covering. "But I've never seen one like this before. Why is it shaped like a horseshoe?"

"It's a special type of vibrator," I smiled. "One that stimulates you on the inside and the outside at the same time."

"Really?" Brooke hummed. "You actually *use* this thing sometimes when you're driving?"

"Only when I'm especially bored or I feel drowsy on long trips. It certainly keeps me awake."

"I can imagine," Brooke said, gently flexing the two sides of the U-shaped device. "I've never used one like this before."

I smiled, happy to know she'd had a little experience using vibrators.

"You haven't *lived* until you've tried this one. You said you were looking for a distraction. Why don't you give it a try?"

"What–right *here*? Right *now*?"

"Why not? It's just us girls. No one will be able to see what you're doing this far under the windowsill."

"Except *you*. You're sitting right next to me."

"I promise not to look if you don't want me to. Besides, I need to keep my eyes on the road."

"Um," Brooke hesitated, beginning to squirm in her seat.

I could tell she was curious about giving it a try, but her modesty was holding her back.

"Here," I said, reaching into the back seat to retrieve her small travel bag. "Why don't you rest this on the console between the two of us. That will give you a certain degree of privacy. I won't be able to see much below your upper body that way. If you insist on being discreet."

Brooke hesitated for a moment, then peered over her shoulder into the back seat.

"I can't believe I'm actually thinking of doing this. But now you've piqued my curiosity."

"You could always wait until later tonight when the lights are out in our hotel room," I smiled.

"Very funny," Brooke grinned back at me. "I think I'll try it here. I'm going to enjoy teasing you while your hands are tied up on the wheel. No peeking though, okay?

"I promise," I said. "Not unless you want me to."

Brooke lifted her travel bag between the two front seats and placed it on the dividing console. It wedged snugly between the two seats, and the gearshift kept it from sliding forward.

"Okay," Brooke said, peering over the top of the bag at me. "No cheating."

"Yes ma'am," I said, squeezing the steering wheel so tightly in anticipation that my fingers began to turn red.

Brooke reached down with her hands and wiggled her hips as she pulled her cut-off shorts and panties down around her ankles. Then she lifted up the U-shaped vibrator and peered at it curiously.

"Which end goes *inside*?"

"The fat end that's curved like a finger. I think you'll find it does quite a nice job of stimulating your G-spot. Then you place the narrower, flat end against your mound and push it all the way inside until it rests against your vulva. Do you need some *lube*? There's a small jar inside the glove–"

"No need," Brooke smiled. "I'm plenty lubricated already."

She spread her legs, and I saw the muscles of her arms tense as she pressed the device slowly inside her with two hands. She purred softly, then gasped when the soft outer tip rolled over her clitoris.

"Mmm–it feels heavenly," she purred. "But how do I turn it on?"

"That's the most fun part," I said, grinning back at her. "If you reach into the glove box, you'll find a separate attachment in the shape of a pink disk. It's a remote controller–so you can use it completely hands free."

Brooke placed her hand into the glove box and pulled out the strange-looking device, rubbing her fingers over the various indentations.

"There's a lot of buttons and switches on this thing," she said. "Which button controls which part?"

"You know what would be even *more* fun," I grinned. "Is if you let *me* operate the controls. That way, you can just put your head back and enjoy the ride."

"But I thought you said you needed to keep your eyes on the road?!"

"Oh, I can operate these controls entirely by *feel*, believe me. I've had plenty of practice."

"Okay," Brooke said, slowly handing me the controller overtop of the console. "But if I tell you to slow down or stop, you have to follow my instructions. I don't want you giving me a seizure or something."

"I wouldn't think of it," I smiled. "Are you ready?"

"I guess so," she said, tilting the back of her seat down a few inches and closing her eyes.

I tapped the lower control button once and I heard the vibrator begin to hum inside Brooke's pussy. She groaned as she wedged her body further down the seat, spreading her legs wider apart. I smiled, knowing the internal finger had begun to move slowly inside her.

"Good so far?" I said.

"Mmm, yes," she said, squirming in her seat. "More, please."

I tapped the lower button two more times, and the speed and motion of the internal wand ramped up in intensity.

Brooke groaned softly as her right hand gripped the handle on the side of her door.

"You *like*?" I said.

"Oh yes–very much," she mewed, beginning to move her hips in rhythmic circles on the leather seat. "But what about the *outside* part? I can't feel it moving yet."

"Are you sure you can handle it?" I teased.

"*Fuck* yes," she groaned. "I need you to stimulate my clit."

I squeezed my legs together in my tight jeans, getting increasingly turned on by the sights and sounds of Brooke's mounting arousal. I gripped the disk tightly in my right hand while trying to keep my eyes glued ahead, but my vision kept drifting to my right the more worked up Brooke became.

"Okay," I said. "Here goes."

I tapped the upper button on the controller, then I heard a higher-pitched sound as the clitoral vibrator began to buzz against Brooke's mound.

"Oh *God*," Brooke moaned, gripping the door handle more tightly. "That feels incredible."

I glanced over at her upper body and saw her chest beginning to rise and fall as her breathing became more ragged. Suddenly I wished she'd chosen to go braless again under her tight tank top as I flashed back to the memory of her pretty tits pressing against the soft fabric.

"Mmm," I encouraged her, rubbing my thighs tighter together, feeling the seam of my crotch pulling up harder against my throbbing button.

"Do you want more?" I asked, peering over at her.

"There's *more*?" she said, looking at me incredulously.

"I can turn up the speed a bit higher if you think you can take it."

"Oh, I can *take* it, alright," Brooke panted.

I tapped the upper button twice more, and the clitoral vibrator began buzzing at a higher pitch and faster intensity.

"*Uhnn*," Brooke groaned, shifting further down in her seat and spreading her legs further apart until her knees pressed against the sides of the footwell.

"Damn," she grunted. "I can't take this much longer. You're enjoying tormenting me, aren't you?"

"You have *no* idea," I purred, feeling my own pleasure rising from the friction of my seam against my burning clit.

"Oh God," she suddenly panted. "I'm gonna cum. I'm gonna come so hard–"

She lurched forward, jerking her torso in rhythmic movements as her legs flapped rapidly in and out.

"Oh *fuckkk*!" she hissed. "I'm cumming, Jade! *Uhnnn...*"

As I watched Brooke spasming in her seat from her powerful

climax, a switch suddenly flipped in my body, and I grunted softly as my own silent orgasm washed over me. I was oblivious to the traffic rolling past us in both directions as my vision blurred from the intense pleasure I was feeling, knowing the two of us had achieved a new level of intimacy in our rapidly blossoming relationship.

I smiled, realizing this was another unexpected turn in our open-ended adventure.

4

____

After Brooke came down from her climax, she wiped down the vibrator then placed it back in the glove box. I was hoping she'd play with it a little longer or dare me to use it while I was driving, but it was starting to get late and we needed to find a place to put in for the night. Hotels were scarce in the eastern part of Wyoming, so we pulled into a run-down motel and I booked another room with two double beds.

After checking for any sign of bedbugs, I told Brooke to make herself comfortable while I searched for some takeout food. I had to drive ten more miles to find a fast-food outlet in the nearest town, and after picking up a bucket of fried chicken, I stopped off at the liquor store to buy a bottle of wine. I hoped that one or two glasses in the privacy of our own room might loosen Brooke's inhibitions about taking our relationship to the next level.

But when I stepped into the store, I immediately felt uncomfortable, surrounded by a bunch of middle-aged truckers and noisy rednecks wearing dirty baseball caps and greasy mullets. They leered at me as I stepped into the checkout line, and I was happy to get out of there and back to the relative safety of our little motor hotel.

But when I pulled into the parking lot, I saw Brooke standing outside our door flanked by two young men who were pushing her against the wall, trying to grope her. I could tell from the look in her eyes that she was frightened, and I screeched the brakes, pulling up directly in front of them.

"*Hey!*" I yelled, swinging my car door open and grabbing the paper bag with the bottle of wine. "*Get away from her!*"

"Who's this?" one of the punks said, gripping Brooke's arm while he pressed his face closer to hers. "Is this your Mommy coming to save you from the big bad wolf?"

Brooke shook her head apprehensively while pressing herself further back against the wall.

"What do you want, *bitch*?" the boy said, teetering unsteadily and obviously drunk. "Can't you see I'm busy? Why don't you mind your own business and lose yourself in your bottle of wine? Or better yet, share it with *us*."

As he lurched toward me, without thinking, I coiled back and gave him a hard kick to the side of his knee. He howled in pain from the torn ligament and crumpled to the ground. His friend stepped toward me threateningly, and I crashed the end of the bottle against my side mirror as wine spilled out onto the pavement and jagged glass jutted out the end of the torn bag.

"You want some of this too?" I scowled, pressing the sharp glass up close to his face. "I won't hesitate to cut you up like a tree chipper if you get any closer."

The boy looked at me for a moment, then peered down at his fallen comrade, still squirming in pain on the ground.

"Come on, Bo," he said, reaching down to help him off the pavement. "This bitch is bat-shit crazy, and that tramp ain't worth it. Let's get the hell out of here before someone calls the cops."

The boy on the ground staggered to his feet and began limping away, when I noticed a bulge in the back pocket of his jeans. I reached in and pulled out his wallet, flipping through the contents.

"What the *fuck*?" the boy said. "Give me back my wallet or I'll call the cops!"

I pulled out his driver's license, then threw his wallet back down on the ground.

"You can *have* your wallet," I said. "But I'm keeping your ID in case you two get any ideas about coming back here anytime soon. Feel free to call the police. We'll see who gets taken to the station house. I'll leave your license at the front desk when I check-out. Now get the fuck out of here!"

The injured boy placed his arm over his friend's shoulder then they limped to the other side of the parking lot and got into an old Camaro, squealing their tires out of the compound.

Brooke peeled herself off the wall and looked at me incredulously.

"Holy shit, Jade!" she said. "That was *bad-ass!* Where did you learn those moves?"

"Just reflex, I guess. The adrenaline was pumping pretty hard when I saw what they were doing to you. Are you alright?"

"Yes," she said. "It's mostly just my pride that was injured." She peered down at the broken bag of wine, still dripping onto the black-top. "It's a good thing you brought that bottle of wine. That scared them away right quick!"

"Sorry," I said, throwing the bag into a trash receptacle near our door. "I was hoping we could share a little together to celebrate reaching your halfway point."

"No worries," Brooke said. "There'll be plenty more opportunities along the way. Did you pick up some food? I've been starved since our picnic earlier in the day."

I opened the rear driver's side door and pulled out the bag of KFC.

"Fried chicken," I smiled. "Your favorite!"

We went inside the cabin and spread a towel over one of the beds, then we sat cross-legged on the mattress facing one another while Brooke replayed the scene outside.

"What were you *thinking*?" I said, peering at her with pinched eyebrows. "What prompted you to leave the room?"

"I just wanted to get a soda from the pop machine near the lobby. I didn't see the two goons until it was too late."

"It's okay, babe," I said, placing my hand on her still-quivering shoulder. "You've got to be careful out there. Like I said, there's a lot of scary people just waiting to take advantage of a single girl like you."

"Don't worry," she smiled guiltily. "I'm not going *anywhere* without you from now on."

After we finished eating and cleaning up in the washroom, I peered at Brooke and smiled.

"Are you ready to turn in? It's getting pretty late. Do you think you'll be able to sleep after all this?"

Brooke stood next to her bed with her arms crossed tightly over her chest, still shaking visibly.

"Do you mind if I sleep with you tonight?" she said. "I'll feel safer having a warm body next to me."

"Of course," I smiled, turning down the covers of my bed. "There should be enough room for the two of us."

As I pulled off my jeans and draped them over the back of the chair, Brooke stepped out of her cut-off shorts and threw them on top of the opposite bed.

"You might want to put those somewhere *else*," I said. "I'm guessing that bedspread hasn't been washed in months. You never know what kind of germs might be lurking in this place."

"Right," she said, lifting her shorts off the bed and placing them atop my jeans on the back of the chair. Then she pulled her bra down under her shirt and placed it cup-side-up on top of her shorts. I followed suit, then we both lay down on the bed wearing only our cotton shirts and panties.

After I turned out the night table lamp, Brooke nestled in closer to me, squeezing her body against mine.

"Thanks, Jade," she whispered in my ear. "I feel so lucky to have found you. And not just because you saved me today. There's something else. I've never felt this way with–"

I placed my hand at the side of her head and pulled her face into mine, kissing her gently. She mewed like a kitten while pressing her hips against me, grinding her mound against mine. I pulled her head harder toward me and slipped my tongue into her mouth, teasing the inside of her lips. She moaned as she wrapped her arms around my back, pressing her tits against mine.

I pulled back for a second and peered into her eyes in the faint light projected by the digital clock on the desk.

"Are you sure you want to do this?" I asked. "I don't want to take advantage–"

"I've been wanting you to make love to me ever since we had that fight in the restaurant. Haven't you felt the sexual tension too?"

"Yes," I said, kissing her softly. "I've just been looking for the right moment–"

Brooke leaned back a few inches and pulled off her tank top then threw it over her shoulder onto the opposite bed.

"Aren't you worried about the *germs*?" I said.

"Not *those* ones," she smiled. "I'm looking forward to intermingling with some *other* organisms."

"Mmm," I said, pulling off my t-shirt and throwing it on top of hers.

Brooke threw her arms around me, mashing her tits against mine as we moaned into each other's mouths. I could tell from her awkward movements that this was her first time with a woman, and I decided to go slow so as not to scare her away. Normally, I'd have started kissing my way down her body by now, sucking her teats and clit into my mouth as I indulged her with my more experienced skills. But right now, I just wanted to feel her body against mine while I kissed her sweet face. There'd be plenty more time to get down and dirty after a good night's sleep.

As the two of us intertwined our legs and began rubbing our pussies together, I could feel my panties getting wetter and wetter as the lacy fabric pulled and scratched against my skin. I reached down under the covers and began pulling Brooke's panties down over her hips, and she lifted her knees up and kicked them off her feet. I raised my hips off the mattress and did the same thing, pushing the two pairs of panties out of our way down toward the base of the bed.

Then I pressed my knee between her legs and pulled my thigh up toward her crotch. I was surprised how wet she was already, and I groaned when I felt her warm pussy against the soft skin of my upper leg. As I began rocking my thigh over her dripping vulva, she sighed in my ear while nibbling my earlobe.

"Make love to me, Jade," she whispered. "I want to feel your body against mine while I listen to you in the dark again."

I pulled away and smiled into her eyes.

"So you *did* hear me last night after all?" I said, flaring my eyes in mock surprise.

"Of course," she said. "Did you hear me?"

"How could I *not*? With all that shuffling and heavy breathing, I knew immediately what you were up to."

"Did that turn you on?" she said.

"Damn straight," I said, rolling on top of her. "You have no idea how much I've fantasized about fucking you since then."

"Mmm," Brooke groaned, feeling my bare mound rubbing up against her soft muff. "Fuck me, Jade. I want to feel your juices dripping over my pussy."

"*God* yes," I panted, pressing her legs apart with my knees and positioning myself over her upper body as our sweaty tits slid effortlessly over one another.

Brooke tilted her hips up a few degrees until her clit made contact with the base of my mound, then she thrust her tongue into my mouth, groaning loudly as I rubbed her wet vulva. I loved the feel of her downy pubic hair against my belly, and as much as I wanted to bury my face in her pussy, there was something sweet and romantic about pressing our bodies together in the missionary style.

As I began rocking my hips back and forth against hers, I felt her hard button flapping against mine while I coated the insides of her thighs with my juices. Brooke dug her fingernails into my back as she pressed her pussy harder against mine with her breathing slowly ratcheting up in intensity.

"Yes, Jade," she grunted. "You feel so good."

"Even better than my vibrator?" I teased.

"Fuck, yes," she panted. "You're warm and soft, and *much more* responsive. *Come* with me, Jade. I'm getting close...."

"*Brooke,*" I panted in her ear, feeling my pleasure rapidly spreading inside me. "I feel so close to you..."

"Uhnn," Brooke groaned, wrapping her legs tightly around my ass. "I'm cumming, Jade! Cum with me!"

Suddenly I felt the floodgates open as my hips began shaking over Brooke's steaming pussy. For the next thirty seconds, we bucked our hips wildly together, holding each other close and kissing each other passionately. My mind was swimming in delirious pleasure, not only because of the intense contractions emanating from between my legs, but because I knew Brooke and I had reached a new level of intimacy. I hadn't felt this close to anyone in a long time, and as we held each other tightly in the pitch dark, Brooke whispered in my ear that she loved me too.

5

———————

Brooke and I fell asleep in each other's arms not long after, and when I awoke she was nestled with her back against my tummy. I reached around and caressed her breasts, and she purred softly. Then she turned her face toward me, and I kissed her gently.

"Mmm," she purred. "I could get used to this."

"Me too," I said, wrinkling my forehead as I peered into her eyes. "But I don't know how much longer we'll have a chance to be together like this."

She flipped over to face me and smiled, ignoring the black cloud that seemed poised to burst our bubble.

"We better get *busy* then," she said, rubbing her breasts playfully against mine. "You seem to have more experience with this sort of thing than I do. Teach me how to make love to a woman. I want to learn *everything* about you."

"It's not so different than you might expect," I said, temporarily forgetting my troubles as I nibbled my way down her neck. "Just do what comes naturally. You'll know when you're hitting the right buttons."

Brooke arched her back, lifting her chest to meet my face.

"Yes, Jade," she mewed. "Kiss my body all over. I want to learn how to please you like your other partners."

"*You're* the only partner I want right now," I said, rolling my tongue over her raised areolas, wondering how much sexual experience she'd actually had. "I love your pretty breasts. Have you ever been kissed like this before?"

"Never like *that*," she groaned. "Boys just go straight for my nipples and suck on them like they're inhaling a milkshake."

"The key is to go slow and *worship* a woman's body," I chuckled. "Girls are different from boys in the way they get aroused and experience sexual pleasure. It's not just about sticking it in and getting off. You have to *tease* your partner, build up her excitement, and let her enjoy the journey instead of focusing on the destination."

"Mmm, I like that metaphor," Brooke sighed as I squeezed her breasts while teasing the base of her nipples with little circles of my tongue. "This trip has exceeded my expectations in *so* many ways. I never expected to find my soulmate in the middle of the desert."

I could feel my heart beating faster and faster the more Brooke talked about how she felt about me, but I wasn't sure if it was because I shared similar feelings, or because I knew she'd soon be wrenched away from me. But at this moment, that was the last thing I wanted to think about. I just wanted to revel in her body and bring her to new heights of pleasure.

I pinched her nipples, feeling them harden between my fingers, then I placed my lips over one of her teats and sucked it like a lollypop, swirling my tongue around the edges as Brooke groaned in pleasure.

"*Jade*," she whispered. "I love the way you make love to me. I want to feel you caress *every* part of my body."

I smiled as Brooke's hips began to undulate in expectation against my belly while I kissed my way down the center of her stomach. When I reached her navel, I pressed my tongue inside her cavity and swirled it around the perimeter, foreshadowing what we both knew was soon to come.

"Uhnn," she moaned, lifting her hips off the bed and grinding her wet pussy against my breasts nestled between her thighs. I rocked my tits against her opening, feeling her juices coat me like maple syrup.

I nibbled my way further down her abdomen until I reached her soft muff, rolling my face over her downy fur. As much as I enjoyed a bare pussy, it was always a delight whenever I encountered a full patch of pubic hair, since it reminded me of my partner's innocence. Brooke was still too young and inexperienced to succumb to the societal pressure to trim her bush. I could taste her dewy sweetness on the tips of her hair, and as she rocked her pussy against the front of my neck, I smiled, knowing how much I was turning her on.

"*Lick me*, Jade," she begged. "I want to feel you kissing me the way you did last night."

"Mmm," I purred, lowering my face to her fragrant pussy, licking the sides of her slit while I tasted her honey.

The closer my tongue came to her opening, the wider she spread her knees, pulling my face closer to her snatch. I extended my tongue and pressed it inside her hole, and she groaned, gripping the sheets on either side of her hips.

"Oh God, Jade," she sighed. "Fuck me with your tongue. That feels so good."

I grinned, realizing this was a whole new experience for her, so different from the feeling of the plastic vibrator buzzing inside her yesterday. There was no substitute for a warm body lying next to a woman–licking, sucking, and caressing her body with her soft skin.

I gripped the sides of Brooke's hips with my hands and pulled her closer to me, burying my face in her sopping pussy. She began rocking her vulva faster and faster against my face, and I could tell from the pace of her breathing that she was going to come soon. But I wanted to feel her in my mouth when she came, and I pulled out of her hole and swiped my tongue up towards her apex like I was licking an ice cream cone. When I reached her flaring jewel, she gasped and threw her head back against the pillow.

"*Oh my God!*" she gasped. "This is *so* much better than a vibrator. I had no idea it could be this good."

"You've never been kissed down here before?" I said, peering up at her from under the covers.

"Nothing like this. The few boys I've been with never seem to be able to *find* it, let alone spend time pleasuring me there. They only seem interested in one thing. I had no idea how good this could feel."

"We've hardly just begun, baby," I said, encircling her gland with my lips, rolling my tongue over it gently.

"*Fuckkk,*" Brooke hissed, pulling the undersheet up harder toward her. "Suck me, Jade. I want to come in your mouth."

"Mmm," I nodded, too busy teasing her clit to come up for air.

While Brooke slowly titled her hips toward me, I felt her buttock muscles clenching in my palms as I gripped her ass tightly. With her chest rising and falling in erratic gasps, her legs began to quiver, and I buried my nose in her dripping pubic hair as she began to lift her hips off the mattress.

"Jade," she squealed. "I'm going to cum. Oh God, I'm going to cum in your sweet mouth. Feel me Jade! Feel me–"

Suddenly, Brooke grabbed the back of my head and pulled me hard against her pussy while her hips began quaking against my face. I could feel her juices running down over my neck and tits as her pussy began spasming in powerful contractions.

"*Jade, Jade, Jade...*" she panted with each contraction. "I'm cumming. I'm cumming in your beautiful mouth."

Up to this point, I'd hardly paid any attention to my own pleasure while I concentrated on pleasing Brooke. But when I felt her shaking against my face and she began wailing in ecstasy, suddenly my own pussy pulsed in sympathy as I began gushing all over the sheets between my legs. I held her softly in my mouth until she stopped quivering, then I lifted my head and kissed her soft pubic patch, inhaling her heavenly aroma. Then I pulled myself up next to her and kissed her as we intermingled our tongues.

"Oh my God," she said when we finally pulled ourselves apart. "I've never been made love to like that before. That was the most beautiful, erotic, tender thing I've ever experienced."

"I'm glad you liked it baby," I smiled. "I felt exactly the same way. I like making love to you."

"What about *you* now?" she said, propping herself up on an elbow. "I want to learn how to please you the same way. I've been dreaming about licking you down there for two days..."

"There's still plenty of time for that," I said, pinning her back down onto the bed. "But this time I want to *see* you while I make love to you. No more hiding under the covers and rubbing our bodies together in the dark."

"I like the sound of that," Brooke smiled. "But when do *I* get to be on top?"

"Maybe next time," I grinned, placing my ass over her pelvis. "You said you wanted me to teach you how to make love to a woman. Well this time, I'm gonna *fuck* you. Sometimes you want it soft and sometimes you want it hard. This time I want it *hard*."

"Fuck yes," Brooke hissed. "Fuck me, Jade. I want to look into your eyes while you fuck me."

"You're reading my mind, girl," I said. "Now lift up one knee and spread your legs."

"That sounds dirty–"

"Sometimes dirty is *good*," I smiled, straddling her extended leg and lowering my pussy toward her crotch.

When our vulvas touched, Brooke groaned and reached up to squeeze my tits.

"Mmm, yes," she purred. "I'm going to enjoy watching you fuck me. Plus, I get to play with *other* parts of you while we watch each other."

"Exactly," I said, pulling the underside of her raised leg against my stomach as I pressed my cunt hard against hers.

"Uhnn," Brooke whinnied, squeezing my tits tighter. "Your pussy's so wet."

"That's at least half *you*, girl," I grunted, pulling her tighter against me.

As we began to rock our hips together, Brooke reached out her hands to me, and I intertwined my fingers with hers, clasping her hands tightly.

"You're so beautiful," she said, peering at me with a sad expression. "I love watching you make love to me."

"You too, babe," I smiled, happy she was recognizing the distinction. Although I was fucking her in every sense of the word, at this moment, I felt closer to her than I ever had.

"I'm going to come soon, hun," I said, suddenly feeling overwhelmed with the sights and sounds of this sweet angel lying prone underneath me.

"Yes, Jade," Brooke said. "Let me watch you come while we're connected together."

I was surprised how quickly I'd reached the height of my passion, but there was something about the sight of my new lover peering up at me bittersweetly while squeezing my hands that put me over the edge. We both knew that we'd soon have to part company, and the thought of it tore us both apart.

As my body began quivering atop hers, a small tear streamed out of my eye and rolled down my cheek. No words were necessary between us as our bodies began shaking together and we peered into each other's eyes. After we came down from our climaxes, I slumped over onto her body, feeling her soft breath caressing the side of my ear. I didn't know how much longer I'd be with Brooke, but in this moment, I just wanted to hold her forever.

6

———————

Brooke and I made love for the rest of the morning, then we got back in the car and headed south along I-25 toward Colorado and the Grand Canyon. As we marveled at the spectacular scenery of the snow-capped Rocky Mountains, neither of us was very talkative knowing we were getting ever-closer to the west coast where we'd have to part company. But after a half hour of pensively looking out her side window, Brooke suddenly laughed.

"What?" I asked.

"I was just thinking back to the incident outside our motel yesterday..."

"What was so funny about that?"

"*Wood chipper?*" she said, looking at me with a raised eyebrow.

"Huh?"

"When you said to that guy that was threatening you that you'd cut him up like a wood chipper if he got any closer."

I chuckled, realizing how ridiculous that sounded after the fact.

"It was the best I could think of in the heat of the moment."

"Well it sure worked," she said. "You scared the crap out of both of those guys."

"Well, good riddance," I said, peering over at Brooke. "Who needs *boys* anyway, right?"

"After last night," she smiled, "I can't imagine I'll ever want to turn back."

I gazed out my windscreen for the next few minutes, thinking about Brooke's future life. Was it really fair of me to steal her affections when she'd be leaving so soon? Was it even fair for me to try to turn her against boys her own age? She had her whole life ahead of her and there'd be so many new and exciting opportunities in California.

"Have you been thinking much about L.A. these past few days?" I said.

"A little bit," she said. "I'm a bit worried, to be honest. Being all alone, competing with all those beautiful people in Hollywood. Do you think I'll be able to make a go of it?"

I reached over the console and squeezed her hand gently.

"Well, since I met you, you've reminded me at different moments of Marilyn Monroe, Elizabeth Taylor, Geena Davis, and Kristen Stewart. I think you can hold your own against *anyone*. I wouldn't be surprised to see you on the big screen one day."

"Opposite *Robert Pattinson* maybe?" she said.

"Is that your leading man type?"

"Well, he *is* kind of dreamy," Brooke said. "Or maybe it was just that whole romantic premise of the Twilight story line."

"So you're saying you dig *vampires*?"

Brooke chuckled softly, then peered back outside her window at the passing landscape. The road was almost devoid of cars as we rolled by the broad ranches of southern Wyoming. Suddenly, a lone figure appeared on the horizon, about a half a mile ahead of us on the side of the road. It appeared to be another hitchhiker. As we got closer, we saw that it was a young man wearing a cowboy hat and faded jeans. Brooke suddenly perked up, squinting through the windshield. When we passed by, we couldn't help noticing how handsome he was.

Brooke turned to look at me with wide eyes.

"Did you *see* that?" she said.

"Uh-huh. He was kind of cute, wasn't he?"

"Cute?" she said. "That was one sexy-ass cowboy."

"Well he's no Brad Pitt. But I suppose he'd do in a pinch."

"Aren't you going to *stop*?" she said, furrowing her brow like a sad puppy dog.

I took my foot off the gas pedal for a moment, considering her request. As much as I wanted to have Brooke for myself the rest of the trip, I knew this would be the perfect opportunity to wean her off me and begin making some new friends with people her own age.

I peered back at her and smiled as I pulled off the road. Then I honked my horn twice and began to back up along the shoulder. I had no idea where the boy was headed or how long he'd stay with us, but something told me the sparks were about to fly once again with my pretty, young wayfarer.

VOLUME FIVE

POLYNESIAN PLEASURE

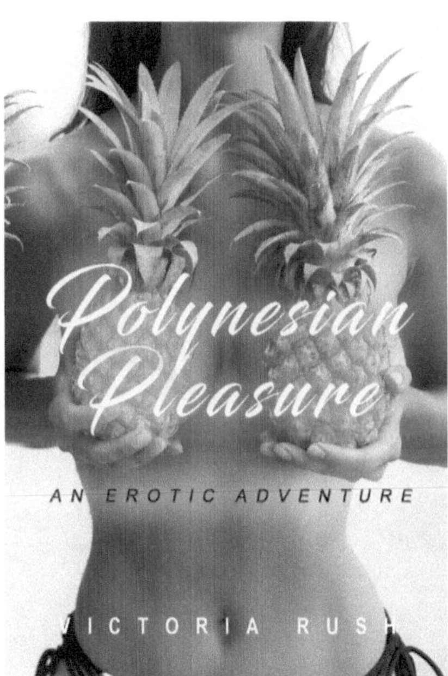

1

———

Peering over the prow of our fifty-foot schooner at the rising sun on the horizon, I closed my eyes and breathed in the fresh scent of the ocean breeze. After a series of short but intense one-night stands, I was beginning to feel cheap and demoralized. Even though I'd taken the initiative in most of the flings, at the end of the day I'd always come home alone feeling shallow and empty.

The affairs had helped free me from the bonds of my passionless marriage and opened my eyes to the pleasures of lesbian love, but somehow I'd never been able to make any of the relationships stick. Even calling them relationships was laughable, given the longest ones never lasted beyond the occasional overnight stay. I needed to clear my mind and get away from all the distractions and temptations of the big city.

This chartered cruise was the perfect balm for my aching heart. With a tiny crew of three sailors and eleven passengers, I had plenty of time and space to collect my thoughts and recharge my batteries. In the absence of the usual big ship amenities, our private yacht provided a much-needed respite from the hectic bustle of the urban jungle. The only sound I could hear was the rhythmic flapping of the boat's sails in the gentle breeze and the peaceful slapping of the waves against the hull as our sloop pierced through the cobalt-blue water.

As the sole uncoupled passenger on our month-long tour of the South Pacific Islands, I was happy to curl up with a good book on the forward deck and feel the wind flowing through my hair. Although everybody went out of their way trying to keep me engaged, I made it clear I was content to be left to my own devices. I'd paid a hefty sum for this cozy cruise, and I just wanted to have some alone time to cleanse my soul.

"Another beautiful day in paradise?" the ship's captain Ben said as he leaned his arms on the rail beside me.

"Yes," I said, gazing off into the distance. "It's so quiet and peaceful I can actually hear myself think."

Ben pinched his eyebrows as he glanced over at me briefly.

"Is that what you've been doing up here? I thought most people came on these cruises to get away from all those distractions. You know, to free their minds and commune with nature and all that."

I turned my head and peered into Ben's weathered eyes. His dark skin was prematurely wrinkled, but his salt-and-pepper beard and chiseled jaw revealed a handsome, sea-worn face. I wasn't sure if he was making a veiled pass or if he was genuinely concerned for my emotional state of mind.

"Never fear, Captain. I'm feeling the weight of the world fall off my shoulders with each new nautical mile we pass through these azure waters."

"Happy to hear," he said, straightening his arms on the handrail. "Is there anything I can get for you? Are you hungry? I've got some fresh halibut or pineapple if you're in the mood for a snack."

"Thanks," I said, shaking my head. "I'm still feeling pretty full from that full-course breakfast your chef prepared for us this morning. But in another hour or two, some fresh fruit and seafood will be just what I'm looking for."

"I'll see what we can scare up. You're going to need a little extra energy for our planned excursion later today."

He pointed toward the horizon on the port side of the ship.

"We'll be dropping anchor in another hour or so at that small island. There'll be lots of hiking trails with plenty of local flora and fauna to explore."

I squinted my eyes in the direction he was pointing and saw a tall green patch rising over the blue expanse of ocean. Up to this point in our cruise, most of the islands we'd visited had been little more than shallow reefs and sandy atolls.

"Judging by its elevation above sea level, it doesn't look so tiny from here. Is this another uninhabited island?"

"Actually, this is the first inhabited island we'll be visiting on our tour. But we're unlikely to encounter any natives. There's a small tribe on the opposite side of the island, but they're not very accommodating to visitors. They like their privacy. In fact, they're among the most isolated people you'll find anywhere on earth. With hundreds of miles to the next nearest inhabited island, they've learned to become quite self-sufficient."

I stared at the island as it slowly grew larger the nearer our vessel passed. It looked dense and lush, with thin silver waterfalls cascading through the thick jungle foliage.

"As long as they don't feed on *foreigners* to mix up their diet," I laughed nervously. "Are you sure we'll be safe there?"

The captain chuckled as he wiped a wash of sea spray from the bow of the boat off his forehead.

"Not to worry, m'lady. The whole cannibal myth is overblown. There are very few tribes that still practice that custom anywhere in the world. These people are reasonably enlightened, considering their remote location. Missionaries passed through here centuries ago, instilling a modicum of Western values. Some of them even speak English. But we'll be putting in on an isolated section of the island. In the unlikely event we encounter any natives, they shouldn't give us any trouble. Just be sure to stay close together and not stray off the beaten path."

"I wouldn't dream of going off on my own, Captain. My jungle survival skills are nonexistent—cannibals or no. I'll be happy to join up with the group for this expedition."

As Ben returned to the rear of the ship to navigate us around the encroaching shoals, I watched the beautiful island as we sailed closer. The lush foliage and turquoise water surrounding the sandy beaches reminded me of the stories of my youth. I fantasized about being marooned on the isle like Robinson Crusoe, building a fanciful fort in the trees and catching live fish to feed myself. Of course, having a hunky partner like Mel Gibson or Brooke Shields to keep me company in my little blue lagoon would make it even dreamier.

Suddenly I felt a stirring in my loins that reminded me how long it had been since I'd felt the tender touch of a lover.

2

———————

When we put in on the secluded beach and carried our provisions onto dry land, I marveled at the surrounding landscape. Unlike the other remote islands we'd visited so far, this one looked tall and imposing. A dense blanket of trees carpeted the steeply sloped mountains, rising to a flat crater hundreds of feet above sea level. I could hear the harsh trill of birds screeching from behind the blind as thick, shiny leaves rustled in the distance. A small reef encapsulated our lagoon in a little crescent, creating a shallow pool to wade through. It would be the perfect spot to cool off after lunch and a hike through the humid jungle.

I watched with fascination as the captain and his crew caught some fish in the lagoon then cleaned and prepared the catch on a wooden plank on the beach. I don't think I'd enjoyed a seafood meal so much in my entire life. Whether it was simply the succulent taste of the freshly caught snapper or the exquisite scenery, I savored every bite as I soaked up the spectacular view.

I'd brought with me a minimum of provisions—just enough to fortify me for our planned excursions. Foam sandals for walking on the beach, hiking shoes for the trail hike, and a cloth handbag with a few bare essentials: a bikini for a swim in the lagoon, some sunscreen and lip balm to protect me against the sun, and my smartphone to read romance novels during quiet moments. After we all finished lunch, the captain stood up to address the group.

"I hope you all enjoyed our impromptu picnic lunch. We'll be spending the rest of the day on the island and setting anchor for the night. For those of you still finding your sea legs, a calm sleep in the lagoon under the stars should help quiet your stomach. In a few minutes, we're going to organize a little inland hike. If you prefer to stay on the beach and have a swim or collect shells, our first mate Mike will stay behind to keep watch on our belongings. The rest of you can join Will and me as we explore the amazing landscape of this island. There's some beautiful wildlife and waterfalls, and at the top of the island there's a dormant volcano from which you can see a spectacular view of the Pacific for miles around. Before we head out, does anyone have any questions?"

One of the young couples raised their hand.

"Yes, Tricia," Ben said, nodding at the couple.

"Do we need to bring any special protection with us? I mean, are there any dangerous animals like monkeys or bears? I heard there are some tribespeople on the island. What should we do if we encounter someone?"

Ben chuckled at the familiar question. It never failed to amuse him how ignorant city slickers were of local customs.

"The islands of the South Pacific are actually some of the safest places in the world in terms of wildlife. There are no mammals other than harmless fruit bats and the local tribespeople, who are far away on the other side of the island. The only creatures that might harm you are brown tree snakes and mosquitoes. Just keep your head away from overhanging branches and wear lots of insect repellant and you should be fine."

Ben and Will passed out some silver whistles connected to a key chain.

"In the unlikely event that we should encounter a native person in our travels, do not approach them unless they approach you. They generally like to keep to themselves and won't engage unless provoked. Keep us in sight at all times and don't stray too far off the path. If anybody should get separated from the group, just give us a tweet using these whistles so we can find you. If for whatever reason you get lost, just follow the trail down to the shore. We plan to be back to the boat around five p.m. local time."

After collecting our gear and fastening our whistles to our belt loops, we followed single-file behind Ben along a narrow trail into the woods, with Will taking up the rear. It didn't take long for the brush to thicken, and as I swatted the thick leaves aside, I kept glancing upward for any sign of slithering reptiles. The one thing I feared more than anything was snakes, and I could feel my heart beating in my chest as much from the fear of being bitten as from the exertion of the steep climb. I was glad when our path crossed the occasional stream, giving me a chance to soothe my hot and aching feet in the cool running water. After an hour or so, we passed another creek and I sat down on the bank to tighten a loose shoelace.

"Everything okay?" Will asked, pulling up behind me.

"Just a loose string," I said. "You go ahead, I'll catch up in a few seconds."

Will peered ahead, noticing our group turning a corner in the dense forest.

"Are you sure you'll just be a moment? We don't want to get too separated from the rest of the group."

"Yes, I'll be fine—I promise." I patted the whistle hanging from the belt loop on my cargo shorts. "Besides, I can always give you a ring if I can't find you, right?"

"Yes," he said. "But it's always best to maintain line-of-sight. The terrain up here is pretty steep and treacherous. We've had people fall and twist an ankle. Just be careful. I'll be walking slowly ahead."

As Will continued up the trail and turned around the corner out of sight, I paused to take in the peaceful sound of the forest. Besides the occasional call of a distant bird, the only sound I could hear was the soft gurgling of the water as it tumbled over the mossy rocks. After I finished tying my lace, I hesitated when I heard an unusual sound emanating from the forest a few hundred feet upstream. I turned my head and strained to listen, then my eyes widened in recognition.

It was the sound of a woman's voice. A sweet, lilting sound, like she was singing. I squinted through the dense thicket of trees, then my eyes grew wider as I recognized the familiar figure. She was standing under a waterfall, stark naked and rubbing her body like she was taking a shower. It was hard to tell how old she was from my distant location, but she had the slender, lithe figure of a young girl. I glanced up the path in the direction Will had headed then back toward the girl.

What the hell, I thought. *I'm on vacation. Everyone says the best way to enjoy a different culture is to go native. I can always catch up with the group later. If Will is really worried about me, he'll double back to find me. Worst-case scenario, I'll have to wait for them to return along the same path on their way down, or I return to our cove. But this is some local fauna definitely worth exploring.*

I followed the tributary upstream, picking my way carefully over the slippery rocks and boulders. As I got closer to the girl, her voice became louder and I found myself humming softly, mimicking her lilting tune. She was speaking a language I'd never heard before, but the melody was simple and rhythmic. I flashed back to another one of my favorite fairy tales from my youth, when the English explorer John Smith stumbled across Pocahontas by a waterfall in the forest. The closer I got to the girl, the more mesmerized I was by her. I could only catch fleeting glimpses of her through the breaks in the heavy brush, but it was quickly becoming apparent that she had the body of a goddess.

When I reached a clearing about fifty feet away from the waterfall, I stopped next to a tree and gently parted the branches blocking my vision. When I finally saw the girl close-up, I gasped. She couldn't have been much beyond her teens, but she was stunning. With thick, shiny black hair cascading over her shoulders and breasts, her pouty lips and high cheekbones reminded me of a young Halle Berry. Her body had all the same curves and swells of her Catwoman avatar, except in this case, she was completely naked.

As I watched the water splash over her full breasts and hourglass-shaped hips, I couldn't stop gawking at her like some kind of creepy peeping Tom. I didn't even know if she was of legal age, if that even mattered out here in the remote stretches of the Pacific Ocean. But when I saw her hand disappear under the triangle-shaped patch between her legs and she began moaning under the torrent of water, I couldn't help myself. It had been far too long since I'd had any kind of sexual contact, and here was the girl of my dreams putting on the sexiest live show I'd ever seen.

I thrust my hand down the front of my cargo shorts and began circling my slippery pearl, trying to stifle my own moans of pleasure. Within moments, I felt the rising swell of my passion beginning to overtake me and I rested my left arm on the tree trunk to support my quivering legs. Just as I was about to be overtaken by my climax, I felt a strange object slithering up my arm. As I turned my face in shock to see what was crawling on me, I stared directly into the eyes of a long brown tree snake.

I had just a moment to scream and flinch my arm away before the snake lunged forward and embedded its fangs deep into the flesh of my neck. Within seconds, I began to feel faint and numb as my legs suddenly collapsed beneath me. As I crumpled to the ground beside the tree, the last thing I remembered was the shocked look on the face of the pretty native girl as she watched me lose consciousness on the moss-covered ground.

3

———

I woke up on the hard floor of a stick-frame hut, peering through bleary eyes at the interwoven leaves covering its thatched roof. An old native woman sat cross-legged beside me, holding a smoky bowl under my nose. The aroma was pungent, and I instinctively flinched my head to the side. The pretty girl I'd seen at the waterfall kneeled by my other side, holding a wet compress against my neck. I felt dizzy and weak, and my head throbbed with pain. When I tried to speak, I realized that the left side of my face was numb.

"Wh—where am I?" I said in a slurred drawl, trying to lift myself up on my elbows.

The girl smiled at me as she removed her hand from the side of my neck. I noticed a green paste on her palm, which she wiped off with a heavy cloth next to a wooden bowl containing what appeared to be a long animal bone.

"You're in our village," she said in a strange accent I'd never heard before. "You're safe now, but you need to rest. You're still weak from the after-effects of the *gata* bite."

She placed her other hand on my chest and gently pressed me down on top of a scratchy mat.

"Gata?" I said, pinching my eyebrows in confusion. "How did I get here?"

"It's our native snake. Normally, it doesn't cause this much trouble, but it struck you in the neck and the poison traveled quickly to your head. I had to carry you back to our village."

"*Carry me?*" I said, wondering how her small frame could support my weight. "How far?"

"I guess it would be more accurate to say I dragged you. I built a rough stretcher out of tree branches and vines. It took almost a full day to bring you back to our village."

I paused as I looked at the girl quizzically.

"Where are my travel mates? I came with a dozen other people—"

"If you're referring to the people on the sailboat, they stopped by our bay a few hours before we arrived asking if anyone had seen a yellow-haired European woman. The chief wasn't very happy with their intrusion, and when he said he hadn't seen any other foreigners, they sailed away."

"Away?" I said, shaking my head in dismay that they would abandon me so quickly. "Does that mean I'm *alone* on this island?"

The girl reached out and clasped my hand in hers as she smiled at me warmly. A group of young naked children suddenly rushed into the hut giggling, and the old lady shooed them away.

"You're hardly alone here," she said, glancing up at the woman who was still holding the smoking cup under my chin. "My family and tribe will care for you until your friends return."

The old woman said something to the girl in their native tongue and I flinched again, smelling the strong vapor rising from the bowl.

"What's this strange smoke you're having me inhale? It smells like incense—"

"It's burning hibiscus leaves. We've found that it helps neutralize the effects of the toxin. Since you were unconscious, it was the only way we could get the medicine inside you. But now that you're awake, there are some more potent herbs you can take internally."

The old woman reached down beside her and lifted a coconut

shell filled with a milky substance and raised it to my lips. She smiled at me softly and nodded for me to drink the elixir.

"What is that?" I said, frowning from the pungent smell of the mixture. "It smells like something died in there."

The girl chuckled as she squeezed my hand.

"It's made from the same natural ingredients that I've been using to neutralize the pain and swelling on the side of your neck. It's a mixture of plantain leaves, papaya bark, and turmeric, dissolved in coconut milk. You have to trust us. We've been administering this medicine for hundreds of years, and we know it works. I think you'll find the taste quite pleasant."

I reluctantly lifted my head and parted my lips as the old lady tilted the bowl toward my mouth. The potion was thick and grainy, like a soup broth, but it tasted more like chocolate milk. I swished it around in my mouth for a few seconds, then gulped it down nervously. The old lady looked into my eyes and nodded as she tilted the cup higher.

"*Sila atu*," she said in a heavy accent.

"Drink the rest," the native girl said. "It will help settle your stomach and ease the pain."

I slowly emptied the bowl, then the old lady got up and said something to the girl before she stepped out of the hut.

For the first time since I'd woken up, I began to feel a little less anxious about my situation, and I gazed up at the native girl, studying her face. She was even more breathtaking close-up than I'd remembered. Her large brown doe eyes, small slender nose, and spongy cheeks gave her the appearance of a girl far younger than her sexy figure would suggest. I glanced at her chest and was disappointed to see that she was fully covered with some kind of dyed dress. The cloth looked thick and dense, more like a mat than the woven cloth used to make our Western garments. I glanced down my own body and was relieved to see that I was still wearing the same clothes I'd left the boat with.

"How long have you and your family lived here?" I asked, interested as much to learn about the history of her culture as her actual age.

"Our family and those of our tribe have lived on this island for centuries. As best we can tell from the oral traditions passed down from our ancestors, the island was settled by Polynesians traveling from the larger islands around 300 AD. I myself have lived in this little hamlet my entire life, which I'm told is eighteen rainy seasons."

So young, I sighed. With her flawless brown skin and soft cheeks, she looked even younger than her chronological age. I flashed back and remembered what she looked like naked under the waterfall, and shifted uncomfortably on the mat beneath me. I could feel the wetness building between my legs and blushed suddenly, realizing how attracted I was to this island goddess.

"You look even younger than that," I said, glancing at her tight-fitting frock. "At least, from the neck up. You're very pretty."

The girl smiled at me as she leaned in closer and lowered her voice.

"I saw you watching me," she said. "And I saw what you were doing behind that tree."

"Um..." I stumbled, not knowing how to react at being found out.

"It's okay," she said. "We're very open about our sexuality in our tribe. It's perfectly healthy and normal. I'm glad that you saw me. I think you're very beautiful also."

I felt a sudden tingle between my legs as I squeezed my thighs together, unconsciously rubbing myself against my tight cargo shorts.

"Oh?" I said, fishing for more details. "Have you had a lot of experience in that area? Where I come from, girls don't usually become active until your age or later."

"Most of the boys and girls in our tribe become sexually active soon after they reach maturity. But since I'm the daughter of the chief, he expects me to save myself until marriage."

"Now I see why you needed to find another form of release under the waterfall."

The girl smiled at me as I began to feel the perspiration building between our palms.

"A woman can only go so long with unsatisfied needs—"

"I know the feeling all too well," I nodded. "It's been a long time for me too."

The girl's eyes widened in surprise as she rubbed my ring finger with her fingers.

"You're not married? I would have thought a pretty woman of your age would have plenty of suitors..."

"I was, once. But my interests seem to have gravitated more toward women these last few years..."

The girl shifted her weight off her knees and sat cross-legged beside me, pulling the heel of her foot under her dress against her crotch.

"So have mine lately."

I paused for a moment, wondering how far I should take our little flirtation.

"You've never even been *kissed*?" I said.

The girl chuckled as she looked towards the front door of her hut.

"Not unless you count all the pecks on my cheek by my *matua*. I'm expected to remain chaste until the day I'm given away."

"Given away?" I said, shaking my head in confusion.

"Any potential mate must first be approved by my father. Not many suitors have stepped forward in deference to his authority."

"How many men are there in your tribe of marrying age?" I asked. "I can't imagine *any* young man or woman not being attracted to your physical beauty."

"It would have to be a man," the girl frowned. "It's considered *tapu* for a woman to sleep with another woman after she's reached child-bearing age.

"That's a shame, because it's a singular pleasure to be properly kissed by a girl."

She paused for a moment as she looked longingly into my eyes.

"I suppose it wouldn't be a sin if we were to kiss briefly. My grandmother says the exchange of saliva acts as a potion in the case of snakebite. Something about the built-in immunity I've acquired from so many of my own snake bites. In this case, it would be more medicinal—"

I pulled the girl's hand toward me as I lifted my head up to her face.

"What's your name?" I whispered in her ear.

"Teuila. It means red flower in our native language."

"My name's Jade. It means pretty green stone in my language. Kiss me, Teuila."

The girl leaned forward, and when our lips touched, it was like a lightning bolt passed through me. I could feel goose bumps on my arms as my heart pounded in my chest. As she pursed her lips awkwardly against mine, I felt the sweet taste of her wetness filling my mouth. But as I reached up with my hands to cradle her head, I heard the loud flap of the blanket covering the front door sweep aside and the thud of heavy footsteps on the wood lattice floor.

"*O le a lea?*" a gruff middle-aged man shouted in front of the doorway, flanked by the older woman who'd treated me earlier.

Teuila shot up into an erect position and said something in her native language to the man. He looked at me with an angry expression and continued talking to her in an agitated manner. It was apparent from her submissive body language that the man was her father and the chief of the village. He obviously disapproved of a foreigner in his house as he pointed at me and motioned with his finger in the direction of the beach. He continued berating Teuila for many minutes before storming out of the hut and down the front steps. The older woman said some gentle words, then followed the man out of the hut as I heard them talking some distance away.

"I'm guessing that was your father?" I said.

"Yes," the girl said. "I suppose it was a bit of a surprise to find a strange European woman lying in his house after he'd been out fishing all day."

"He seemed a little angry," I said. "Was it because of our kiss?"

"I explained to him that I was trying to administer *pulu*, but I don't think he was very convinced."

"What was all that gesturing about when he pointed at me and then toward the sea?"

Teuila exhaled heavily as her lips tightened into a frown.

"He said that he wants you off the island as soon as possible. If your friends don't return soon, there's a cargo ship that passes by here every month or so, where we exchange goods. He insists on your being on that ship by the latest."

I glanced up at Teuila, grunting as I tried to sit up.

"In the meantime, where do you want me to stay?"

"You're still weak and sore," she said, easing me back down onto the mat. "You're welcome to stay with us until you're fully recovered. I'm sorry to have put you through all this. My father can be a little hard-headed sometimes. I'm sure he'll come around once we explain the situation. How are you feeling?"

I smiled at the native girl and reached back out for her hand.

"I was feeling much better when you were administering your magic elixir. If the coast is clear, can I have another one of your healing kisses?"

Teuila turned her head as she watched her father and grandmother walking slowly toward the other end of the village.

"Maybe for just a few more minutes..."

She leaned down to kiss me, and I reached up and ran my fingers through her soft hair. When our lips touched, I gently probed her mouth and played with her tongue, tasting her sweet salve. Teuila moaned softly, as she rolled her hips over her splayed skirt on the floor.

This won't be the only waterfall we'll soon be experiencing, I thought, feeling my panties begin to rapidly moisten.

4

———

Later that day, the chief returned to the hut, and he and Teuila had a calmer discussion. His countenance seemed to have changed completely toward both of us, and he nodded as he made eye contact with me before leaving to attend to other business. Not long after, the old lady entered the cabin carrying a platter of food and some fresh water. She spoke with Teuila briefly, then she kneeled down beside me and felt my forehead, encouraging me to drink the cool water. I was beginning to feel stronger, and I was able to sit up as the two women tended to me.

"Your father seems less angry," I said. "Should I thank your grandmother for that?"

"Probably," Teuila nodded. "When she explained the circumstances of your arrival and reminded him of our longstanding tradition of giving refuge to wayward travelers, he softened up. In fact, he insisted on holding a ceremony this evening to celebrate the rapid recovery of our honored guest. Do you think you'll feel well enough to attend the festivities?"

"Will it require my active participation?" I said, still feeling a bit sore and lightheaded.

"Not unless you want to. It mostly involves a lot of singing and dancing. My father has asked that we prepare a special feast for the occasion. There will be lots of local dishes for you to sample. All you really have to do is watch and eat. You haven't had anything in over twenty-four hours. It will be good for you to regain your strength."

I looked at the large platter of food that the old woman had placed on the floor beside me and smiled at her.

"I'm beginning to feel my appetite coming back. Is this all for me?"

"*Ai meaai,*" the woman nodded, holding the platter up and motioning with her hand toward her mouth.

The tray was filled with pieces of sliced banana, papaya, fresh fish, and some kind of shaved gourd. In the corner of the board sat a hollowed out half-coconut shell filled with the same creamy brown fluid the woman had administered to me earlier.

I looked at the plate, inhaling the rich fragrance of aromas, then peered up at Teuila.

"Is it okay to eat it with my hands?" I asked, not seeing any utensils.

"Of course," she said. "That's the only proper way to enjoy good food. Dig in!"

I picked up a slice of papaya, and when I bit into it, I closed my eyes, humming in appreciation.

"Oh my God," I said. "That is *so* good. It's so much more flavorful than the fruit I buy at my local grocery store. Do you grow all of your food on the island?"

"Absolutely. We have a great variety of fruit, vegetables, and seafood. The gods have blessed us with an abundance of natural resources to allow us to be self-sufficient."

I picked up a piece of white fish and sucked it slowly into my mouth. It appeared to be raw and marinated in some kind of citrus seasoning. Unlike the fresh snapper our charter chef had cooked up on the beach yesterday, this seafood was far more tender and juicy.

"You're spoiling me," I said, purring as I savored the succulent flesh. "This is the most tender seafood I've ever tasted. What kind of fish is it? And what's the seasoning? It tastes so simple and pure."

"We call it *fa'aipoipo,* but I think you call it halibut. It was fresh-caught today by my father and his fishing crew. We've added nothing but fresh lime juice to season it."

I shook my head at the simplicity of the native diet. I'd always felt that the best food needed little extra embellishment if it was truly fresh. And you couldn't get much fresher than this—from sea to plate in a matter of hours.

I took a sip of the coconut milk, then picked up the large pear-shaped tuber and took a small bite off the tip. It tasted a bit like sweet potato, but I also detected traces of the fresh seafood and papaya juices that covered the wooden board.

"What's this interesting fruit? It's got a delicious texture and flavor. I've never seen it before."

"It's one of our staples," Teuila said. "The taro root is actually a vegetable, not a fruit. We use it in much the same way that Westerners use potatoes. It's a very nutritious side dish that soaks up the flavors of other foods it's paired with. Do you like it?"

Holding the curved tubular vegetable in my hand, it reminded me of one of my favorite sex toys that I'd use on lonely nights to stimulate my G-spot.

"Mmm," I said, sucking the rich seafood juice from the tip of the bulb while raising a suggestive eyebrow at Teuila. "I'll definitely have to try more of this. I can imagine *all sorts* of ways it can be paired with other delectable dishes."

After I devoured the rest of the food on the serving plate, the old lady smiled at me and said something to Teuila.

"We should probably start getting you ready for the celebration tonight," she said, glancing at my soiled hiking clothes. "You must be looking forward to a bath. Let's get you cleaned up and into some fresh clothes. There's a private section of the lagoon where I can take you if you're strong enough to walk. Then my matua and I will prepare you with our local costume for the festival."

My pussy suddenly pulsed at the thought of bathing privately with Teuila.

"You're really having me go native, aren't you?" I said. "I think a swim in the lagoon would be very refreshing. I shouldn't have any trouble walking as long as you stay close by my side."

"I wouldn't think of leaving you," Teuila smiled. "Besides, I saw the way some of our young tribesmen looked at you when you came into our village. I need to make sure they don't get any ideas about the sexy white girl in their midst."

5

———

As Teuila escorted me toward the bathing lagoon, women and children smiled at me from the open verandas of their huts flanking the main thoroughfare of the village. But a group of men carving a dugout canoe on the main beach eyed me suspiciously when we veered off onto a flagstone-lined path leading into the woods. When we reached the secluded lagoon, I peered around me at the natural splendor of the landscape.

"Your island is so beautiful," I said, inhaling the fresh onshore sea breeze. "Where I come from, people pay a small fortune to visit these tropical paradises. And here I am, being feted by my native hosts, with never a thought to any kind of compensation."

"At least for a few more weeks," Teuila frowned, reminding me of the cargo ship pickup that was scheduled to pick me up later this month.

"If not earlier, if my shipmates return before then." I glanced toward the thick canopy of trees lining the lagoon. "If I hide in the forest, will you tell them I'm still lost? I'm in no hurry to leave this Shangri-La."

"I'd be happy to, but I think my father will have other ideas. We have to be careful not to test his patience too much. He's very suspicious of European visitors overstaying their welcome. He's heard stories of the destruction they brought to some of the other Polynesian islands."

I nodded, recalling how the indigenous people of Easter Island were nearly wiped out by disease and infighting after Dutch settlers arrived.

"I can appreciate why he'd want your people to be left alone. But you'll have to stop referring to me as *European*. I'm actually from the United States. I'm technically an American."

Teuila chuckled as she shook her head.

"They're just another colonial oppressor as far as he's concerned. He doesn't trust anybody who travels to these islands on fancy boats and planes. He thinks you'll corrupt our simple and natural way of life."

"He's probably right," I said. "Lord knows, our so-called advanced civilization has plenty of shortcomings."

I looked at Teuila's simple one-piece toga and motioned to my soiled clothing.

"Shall I take these off and leave them on the beach? Will you be offended if I swim in the nude?"

"Not at all," Teuila smiled. "It will give me a chance to clean your garments while you cool off. We all swim naked when we're bathing in the lagoon."

I glanced around me to see if anyone else was stealing glances from the surrounding brush and slowly began to disrobe. I knew that if anyone wanted to gawk at the white woman while she bathed that they could easily hide undetected behind the thick blanket of foliage, but I didn't really care. There was something about this remote island that seemed so natural and carefree to me. I was far more mindful of the impression I'd leave with the pretty native girl.

I turned my back toward Teuila, then pulled down my cargo shorts and panties, and slipped off my sweaty t-shirt and bra. It felt good to be liberated from the vestiges of Western civilization, and for the first time in my week-long tour of the South Pacific, I slipped into the warm waters of the tropical lagoon completely naked. It felt exquisite to be immersed in the buoyant salt water, and for the longest time I just floated on the surface, watching the wispy white clouds pass slowly over the sky. When I caught sight of the thin contrails of a jet aircraft high up in the atmosphere, I couldn't help smiling.

Those suckers have no idea what they're missing down here, I thought. *They probably can only imagine what it must be like to be untethered from society, living on these remote islands.*

I hadn't even once thought of picking up my smartphone since I'd left the boat. Not that I could do much with it, hundreds of miles away from the nearest wi-fi signal. I glanced over at Teuila, who was rubbing my cargo shorts with a taro root amid a froth of white foam in the shallows near the beach. She looked up at me and smiled in my direction.

"Are you starting to feel better?" she called. "Don't stray too far from the beach. There are treacherous currents near the reef. The last thing we need is for you to drown after nursing you back to health."

"Not to worry," I shouted. "I'm just enjoying this little moment of bliss."

After five minutes or so, I began to walk out of the water in Teuila's direction. As I emerged from the surf, she eyed my body from top to bottom. She seemed particularly interested in my bare mound as her eyes danced over my pale white hips. As I approached her, she held open a painted native dress, and I stepped into it while she pulled it up over my breasts and fastened it with loose strings behind my shoulders.

"Do you mind my asking," she said, as I turned around to face her. "Why your *agava* is smooth like a young girl's? It seems strange to see a full-grown woman without any hair down there. Is this a particular custom of Euro—I mean *American*—women?"

"As a matter of fact," I chuckled. "It is. "It's become the norm for Western women to shave themselves down there. I'm not exactly sure how the practice started. Maybe it's because it makes us seem younger and more alluring to our sexual partners. Or maybe it's just easier to navigate around down there. I find it heightens the sensation when I'm touched in that delicate area. But I can see how strange that must seem to someone who's used to living a natural lifestyle."

"Actually," Teuila said, thinning her eyelids as she peered at my deep cleavage atop the tight-fitting tunic. "I find it quite sexy. You look like a doll. A very curvy and *sexy* doll."

"I've never been called that before, but I'll take it as a compliment." I glanced in the direction of the village. "When does the festival start? What can I do to help you prepare?"

"First of all, we need to get you properly dressed for the festivities. The ceremony will start at dusk. Let's go back to my hut and see if we can make you look like a proper Anutian girl."

I paused for a moment, raising my eyebrows in curiosity.

"Is that the name of your island—*Anuta*?"

"Yes. It means slippery shore. Because our island is so small and far away from anybody, everything seems to just slide by us."

That's not the only thing that's slippery right now, I thought, feeling the cool sea breeze wafting over my bare vulva as I watched Teuila's sexy lips moving.

When we got back to her hut, Teuila and her grandmother fitted me with a grass skirt and decorated my hair with a garland of native flowers. The old lady pinched her eyebrows when she saw my bare pubis and she ran the back of her hand over my mound, making a comment to Teuila about my lack of *lauulu*. I wished it had been the young girl who had caressed me instead, but I hoped we'd soon have an opportunity to explore each other when we alone later.

I found it interesting that they left the upper half of my body exposed, draping it simply with the long floral lei that her grandmother had brought into the hut earlier. The flower petals were bright and soft, and they tickled my nipples as they fell over the fullness of my breasts. I smiled at the old woman and nodded in appreciation as she pulled it over my neck.

"What's your grandmother's name?" I asked Teuila.

"Her given name is *Tausa'afia*, meaning kind one, but we all call her Nona."

"You Anutians seem to prefer long and difficult-to-pronounce names. Does your grandmother have a pet name for you?"

"She calls me Te', like the French word for tea."

"That's perfect," I said, "because you're both so kind and calming."

I looked at the old woman and smiled, caressing the floral lei gently between my fingers.

"Thank you, Nona," I said, "for this lovely gift. You've both made me feel so welcome in your home. I'm looking forward to tonight's celebration."

6

———

Shortly after dusk, Teuila and her grandmother escorted me out to the main promenade of their village. A huge bonfire was burning at one end while her father sat on an elevated platform at the opposite end. Nona sat on the right side of the chief's platform along with his younger sons, while Te' and I sat on his left side with her sisters. This was the first time I'd seen her entire family assembled in one place, and I counted a grand total of eight siblings, all considerably younger than Teuila. Arrayed in front of us on a long serving plank were huge bowls and plates made of seashells festooned with a variety of fragrant foods. The rest of the villagers sat in family units on opposite rows lining the central esplanade, eyeing me curiously.

Further to the side of the chief's platform stood two men dressed in grass skirts with woven mats on their chests, wearing what looked to be war paint on the sides of their cheeks. In front of them rested hollowed-out logs with an animal skin pulled tightly over the top, while they held two large bones in each of their hands. When all the families had taken their designated seats, the chief raised his arm and a hush fell over the assembly.

"*Amata le pati!*" he hollered, nodding toward the two drummers flanking his platform.

The drummers started beating their drums rhythmically, and everyone began singing and chanting in their native dialect while the young women of each family stood to assemble in the central square. Teuila squeezed my hand, then stood up to join the other girls in the pit. As the older women began singing in their heavily accented intonation, the girls in the square began swinging and shaking their hips in rhythm with the beat. I watched in fascination as they swiveled their perfectly toned bodies to the music. Their grass skirts shimmied suggestively as their bare stomachs and breasts writhed under the skimpy covering of their flowery leis.

This was the first time I'd seen Teuila's pretty figure partially unclothed since the waterfall, and my eyes widened as I watched her sexy hips swaying to the music. She had virtually no fat on her immaculately toned stomach, and my mouth watered watching her abdominal muscles twitching and flexing on her tanned midriff. Knowing she was naked under her heavy straw skirt made the display all the more intoxicating, and I began to shake my own hips on the ground, as much in sympathy with the dancers as to produce some much-needed friction on my acting clit.

After a few minutes, Te' pointed at me and curled her finger in a come-hither manner, motioning for me to join the girls in their hula dance. I looked at her with a quizzical expression shaking my head, but she danced closer to me and held out her hand for me to stand up. I looked at the other women sitting around the square as they continued singing, and they smiled and nodded at me, encouraging me to join the group. I was still feeling a bit dizzy and sore, but I knew this was an opportunity I'd regret if I didn't take part.

I clasped Te's hand and walked with her toward the other dancers, trying to mimic the shaking of their hips like I did when I was a little girl trying to balance a hula hoop. It felt awkward trying to match the vigor and pace of their movements, and as I joined the line, the older women around the camp smiled at me with big grins. Whether they were simply trying to contain their mirth at the awkward attempts of the European woman attempting to mimic their native dance technique, or they were just happy to see me joining in with the rest of the locals in the celebration, was unclear. I looked up at the chief resting on the platform, and he nodded approvingly at my awkward attempt to dance an authentic tribal hula.

At least I can blame my rubbery legs on the after-effects of the snake venom, I thought.

After ten minutes or so, I began to feel wobbly, and I motioned to Teuila that I needed to sit down. She nodded and escorted me back to our resting position, holding my hand as she continued shimmying her hips to the music. When the song ended, the hula girls sat down with their families, and a group of young men carrying long spears stood to take opposite positions in two straight lines facing one another about five feet apart.

As the drummers began beating their drums more vigorously, the two men at the far end of the line moved into the center row and began dancing in a side-step fashion toward the front of the line, thrusting their spears forward and back in a menacing fashion. The combination of their fierce expressions and scary war paint, along with the waving of their stone-tipped spears, certainly looked convincing to me. I wondered what purpose these warrior actors could find for their threatening weapons in what appeared to be an otherwise peace-loving culture.

When the two men from the back of the line reached the front, they took positions beside their compatriots in the straight lines, stomping the bottom of their spears on the ground as the next pair at the end of the line copied their routine. In this manner, the line of warriors slowly but steadily approached closer to the chief's platform and our own position. As the drumming and chanting slowly built toward a crescendo, Teuila squeezed my hand as if to assure me that the spectacle was all for fun.

But I noticed as the final pair of dancers approached the front of the line that the tallest and most imposing one kept his eyes locked on Teuila the whole time. When he reached the end of the line, he bellowed some kind of war chant and glanced down at the two of us holding hands, then he took his position at the front of the formation, closest to the chief.

"That one seems to have a special interest in you," I whispered to Teuila, trying not to stare at his scary expression.

"I think he has designs on me," Te' nodded. "Manaia's been following me around the village the last few months. I've caught him and my father having private chats whenever I return from the women's lagoon."

"Well he certainly looks like a *capable* mate," I said, noticing the young man flexing his arm and leg muscles as he stared at us.

"That's exactly what I'm afraid of," Teuila said as she passed me some fresh plates of fish and manioc from the buffet table in front of us. "But for now, let's not fret about what may be. Let's enjoy the moment and savor all the good food and dancing."

After the ceremony ended, Teuila's family returned to their small hut, where we all slept shoulder-to-shoulder on the dusty floor. I wanted to reach out and touch her lying next to me, but her father's heavy breathing so close by soon squelched my desire. In the morning, we all shared a hearty breakfast of frigate eggs, yams, and fermented breadfruit paste on the porch overlooking the courtyard. As I gobbled up the savory mix of yolk-stained starch and sour mash, I marveled at how tasty the local cuisine was in the absence of our typical Western condiments.

Later that morning, Teuila led me on a private tour of the island. As we traipsed into the heavy brush along a stony path, I shook my head wondering how she could cover such rough ground in bare feet. The only thing she carried with her was a stone adze which she used to hack away the overhanging leaves, and the one-piece dress on her back made from pressed bark.

"Be careful with that thing," I said, following her a few feet behind. "We don't want to antagonize another one of those tree snakes. I'm not sure I could carry you back to the village like you did for me if you get bitten."

"Don't worry about me," Teuila said. "I've acquired a certain degree of immunity. Our people believe that all living things are endowed with supernatural powers—what we call *mana*. We've learned to live in harmony with our fellow island dwellers. As long as we leave them alone, they shouldn't cause us too much trouble."

"Tell that to the critter who bit me by the waterfall. I don't think he's recognized my mana yet."

"Never fear," Te' chuckled, "Worst-case scenario, I can always resuscitate you with my special potion."

"Mmm, yes," I said, remembering our last kiss. "In that case, bring on all the angry serpents you can find."

As I watched her scamper over the jagged rocks and thick brush lining the trail, I glanced at her soiled feet.

"How can you walk over all this rough terrain in bare feet?" I asked. "I'm wearing heavy hiking shoes, and I'm already feeling sore and all scratched up."

"The soles of our feet get pretty toughened up from all the coarse surfaces we walk on from the moment we're born. Between the sandy beaches, the rocks in the lagoon, and rough brush in the jungle, we soon develop a thick skin to protect us against most obstacles. But if you need to rest for a moment, there's a clearing up ahead where we can stop for a bite to eat."

"I could use a little respite," I nodded, breathing heavily from the steep uphill climb. "I'm a little out of shape from all the lounging around I've been doing since I began my tour of these Pacific islands."

We stopped at a small clearing surrounded by a copse of tall palm trees.

"Are you hungry?" Te' asked.

"I could do with a bite, but we didn't bring anything. What did you have in mind?"

"The island provides everything we need," she said, glancing up toward the canopy of trees. "How about some fresh pineapple?"

I looked up and saw a clump of spiny pods bunched together under the leafy umbrella of long green fronds at the top of the tree.

"I'd love some, but how can we get those down?"

Teuila smiled, as she rubbed the bottom of her feet.

"These tough soles are good for more than just *walking* over rough surfaces," she said.

She placed her adze on the ground, then approached one of the palm trees and grasped its cracked bark with two hands, placing the soles of her feet in perpendicular positions against the sides of the trunk. She pulled her body toward the trunk and lifted her feet a few inches higher, pointing her knees outward. Then she pressed upward with her legs, taking a higher handhold on the stem. After a series of similar shimmying maneuvers, it didn't take long for her to ascend halfway up the tree.

I shook my head, dumbfounded at how easily she could scale the timber using just her arms and legs. With her legs splayed apart, I could clearly see under her tunic, and my pussy began to water as I watched her buttocks and vulva flexing with each leapfrog up the tree. When she neared the crown, she looked down and called out to me.

"You might want to stand back a bit. I'm going to shake the tree now, which should drop a few pineapples. They're pretty sharp and prickly, so make sure you stay out of the way."

I nodded as I looked up at her, taking a few steps back. As she started shaking her body against the tree, the leaves began rustling and a few seconds later four or five pineapples plopped to the ground beside me. She descended the tree just as easily as she'd climbed it, and when she got to the bottom, she rubbed the loose bark off her hands then brushed the debris covering the front of her gown.

"Now I see why you native girls wear such thick clothing," I said, pinching her cloth between my fingers. It felt a bit like thin cardboard, though it clung to her curvy figure like a cotton dress.

"The bark of the mulberry tree is like papyrus," she said. "And it's easy to decorate using turmeric dye and volcanic mud. Nothing goes to waste on our island."

I picked up one of the spiny pineapples off the ground and held it in my hand, feeling its heavy weight.

"These look pretty nutritious. But how will we get to the flesh inside?"

"It's simple with the right tools," Teuila said, taking the fruit from my hand.

She placed the husk against the side of the tree, then deftly hacked the two ends off with her sharp adze. Then she chopped the shell in half across the middle and placed the two hollow rings against the trunk and cut each section into two semi-circular crescents. We sat down, leaning our backs against the tree, and bit into the juicy pulp like watermelon pieces. The yellow juice squirted all over my face as I bit into it, running down my chin. I drew the back of my hand across my mouth, then wiped the sticky juice on the blanket of leaves lining the forest floor.

"Be careful there," Teuila said, noticing the juice dribbling down my neck toward my T-shirt. "Or we'll have to do another load of wash."

She rubbed her fingers over my chest just above my cleavage then sucked her fingers into her mouth.

"Anything to get me out of my clothes again near you," I said, feeling my pussy throb from her seductive gesture. "Besides, I can always change into my new native garb," remembering how sexy I felt wearing just a grass skirt and floral lei around my neck.

"We might be able to get you out of those clothes and cleaned up sooner than you think," Te' said, motioning further up the trail. "There's another waterfall about twenty minutes up the slope, with a secluded swimming hole. It's one of my favorite places to go when I want to be alone."

"To convene with nature or to find some private play time?" I said, raising an eyebrow.

"Both. But this time, we won't just have to *watch* each other."

"Mmm, yes," I said, feeling my panties moistening with a different kind of juice. "I've been dreaming of touching you ever since I laid eyes on you two days ago."

"We better get a move on then," Te' said. "Because I'm definitely starting to feel hot under the collar."

Teuila and I quickly finished eating our pineapple slices, then we continued walking up the trail. As I watched her sexy hips rocking back and forth in her tight native smock, I reflected back to the ceremony last night and her extended family sleeping on the floor of their straw hut.

"Do you mind my asking," I said. "Whatever happened to your mother? Your grandmother is so sweet and helpful, but with such a large family, how do you and your father manage?"

"She died many years ago when she stepped on a rusty knife a European traveler had left on the beach and her foot became septic. The infection spread rapidly, and we had no way of saving her. I think this is one of the reasons why my father is so suspicious of Western visitors."

"I'm so sorry to hear that. Did your father ever remarry? I noticed that most of your siblings are quite a bit younger than you."

"He never quite recovered emotionally from her loss. But our tribe has a culture of sharing between families, and he's adopted many children whose mothers and fathers died during fishing expeditions and other natural disasters."

"So your Nona raised you from the time you were young? Where did you learn to speak such good English?"

"There was a period when my father welcomed the presence of Western visitors. We had a missionary school set up for many years where other children of my age studied many of the same subjects you learn in primary school. But my father became suspicious of their motivation after a period of time and banished them from our island, fearful they were stealing his *mana*. Ironically, they might have been able to save my mother if he'd allowed them to stay."

"It's a difficult proposition," I nodded, "melding two disparate cultures. Many other native people around the world have rejected Western help for the same reasons. It's never easy for men to relinquish the reins of power, no matter how much his subjects may welcome the change."

"My father can be a stubborn man," Te' said. "But his heart's in the right place. Even though our tribespeople defer to him, our culture of *aropa* dictates that all of our natural spoils be shared equally by the community. He's never tried to hoard resources or oppress our people in any direct way."

"What about this cargo ship that visits the island from time to time?" I said, reflecting back on his order that I leave the island as soon as practicable. "Why does he still permit the occasional outside intrusion?"

"We only exchange *goods* when the ship comes around," Teuila explained. "The markets in Honiara on the Solomon Islands are willing to pay a high price for the shark fins we harvest. We barter their equivalent value for things like nylon fishing line, cloth sails, and nets for catching fish in the lagoon."

"*Shark fins?*" I said, cringing at the thought of sharks flapping help-lessly in the sea without their essential means of navigation.

"Don't worry," Te' said. "We use every part of the fish we catch. Shark flesh is considered a delicacy in our tribe. We even use their teeth as cutting blades."

"Nothing goes to waste," I nodded, breathing a sigh of relief.

After another twenty more minutes of hiking, I began to hear the sound of a cataract in the distance, and before long we came upon a break in the forest with a small waterfall cascading into a shallow pool.

"Do you feel like cooling off?" Teuila said, smiling toward me.

"Do I ever," I said, practically tearing my clothes off.

As I watched Te' step out of her one-piece tunic, I studied her body carefully. I hadn't seen her fully naked since the last time we were near a waterfall, and I could feel my nipples hardening as I ran my eyes all over her athletic figure. Her breasts sat up firm and high on her chest, and her dark teats stood out prominently on her caramel-colored skin. As she wiggled out of her tight dress, I couldn't help staring at the triangle-shaped patch of dark pubic hair nestled between her exquisitely carved hips.

"You look like you've never seen a naked woman before," Te' laughed, noticing me soaking up her body.

"Just not one so naturally pretty," I said.

"Come on," she said, standing on the edge of an abutment overlooking the aquamarine pool. "How do you Americans say it? Last one in is a rotten egg!"

Teuila placed her arms over her head then executed a perfectly clean dive into the murky water. Before she could surface, I chickened out and jumped off the cliff, placing my hands between my legs to protect the slap of water against my private parts. When we both surfaced, we splashed and squirted water towards each other's faces, giggling like little girls. I swam toward her and wrapped my arms around her back, pressing our chests together as our mouths joined in blissful union. As we kicked our legs together under the surface to stay afloat, our hips bumped together and I could feel her bush rubbing against my bare mound. The more passionate our kiss became, the harder it became for the two of us to stay above the water.

"Come," Teuila smiled, motioning toward the waterfall. "Let's go somewhere more comfortable. I bet you've never experienced a true Anutian shower before."

We swam to the base of the waterfall, then climbed up over the slippery rocks and ducked our heads under the chute. As we pressed our bodies together under the torrent, I leaned down and sucked Te's nipples into my mouth. She placed her hands behind my head and pulled me closer, purring under the falling water. I slowly kissed my way back up her chest and thrust my tongue deep into her mouth, kissing her passionately.

As our tongues danced in each other's mouths, we ran our hands over each other's bodies. I reached behind Te's back and cupped her firm buttocks in my palms, and she pressed her mound tightly against mine. I pulled away just far enough to slip my hand between the front of her thighs and began to stroke her slippery lips, pressing my fingers gently inside her. She spread her legs further apart and I drew my hand over her soft bush, pinching her clit softly between my two fingers.

As Teuila began moaning in my mouth, I rubbed my fingers in gentle circles around her nub. It only took a few moments before her hips to begin shaking as she gasped into my ear. I held her tightly against me, rubbing our nipples together, as she experienced her first orgasm at the hand of another woman.

8

———————

Teuila and I made love on the grassy knoll overlooking the waterfall then slept under the late afternoon sun to dry off. By the time we woke up, it was already starting to get dark and we headed back to the village, walking hand-in-hand along a moonlit beach. It felt sublime to take my shoes off and feel the warm seawater lapping at our feet as we talked about our past experiences and future plans. But as we neared her village, Te' suddenly became quiet.

"Is everything alright?" I asked, fearing she was having second thoughts about our making love. "Are you angry with me for taking advantage of you at the waterfall?"

"No, Jade," she said, smiling warmly into my eyes. "It was beautiful. I'm so glad you were my first. I can't imagine a more tender and giving lover."

"You seem a little pensive. Was there something on your mind?"

"It's just—", Te' paused, as she looked out over the moonlight reflecting off the ocean. "I know you'll be leaving soon. I've grown fond of you in the short time we've been together. I can't imagine being alone on this island without you."

I paused and ran my hand softly through her hair.

"As you said earlier, you're hardly alone here. You've got a loving family and the support of your entire community. I've rarely seen the kind of mutual love and generosity practiced by your tribe. Your tradition of aropa is a rare and wonderful thing."

"It's true that we all get along and share everything communally," Teuila said. "But what you and I have is something personal and special. I've never felt this way with someone else before. You make my heart dance."

I placed my arms around Te's shoulders and held her gently as I watched the surf crash softly against the shore. I was surprised by how close I'd grown to her in the three days we'd been together. But I worried that her feelings were being influenced by her youth and inexperience. I remembered what it felt like to fall in love the first time and how fragile our relationship was as my high school sweetheart and I took our first steps into the adult world.

"Oh Te'," I said, cradling her face in my hands. "I feel the same way about you. But we have to be careful about letting our emotions get carried away. We have such a short time together. I think we should just live in the moment and enjoy this while it lasts."

Teuila looked at me with a pained expression as a tear rolled down her cheek.

"Why can't you take me *with* you?" she pleaded. "The missionaries have taught me so much about the outside world. I think it would be so exciting to live with you in America."

I paused for a long moment as my eyes traced back and forth across her pretty face. She'd broached a subject both of us had fantasized about, but up until now neither of us had had the courage to express.

"How would that work?" I said. "America is thousands of miles away, both geographically and culturally. It would be a huge adjustment for you. And besides—I'm not sure your father would allow it. You're his only natural child, and you've already told me how suspicious he is of Western people."

Even though I was trying to talk her out of the crazy idea, I was already thinking about how I might arrange her landed immigrant status. The island of Anuta had no sovereign status as an independent nation and there were no embassies or consulates to help prepare the necessary paperwork. How could I even prove that she'd reached the age of majority?

"I'm a grown woman!" Teuila shouted. "I'm old enough to make my own decisions. Some of the young men from our island have traveled aboard the cargo ship in the past to pick up provisions in Honiara. My father can't stop me if I want to explore the world. And there's no one I'd rather do it with than you."

I pulled her close to me and held her tightly, feeling her heart beating against mine. It was an audacious idea, but not an insurmountable one. Surely there must be a protocol in place for allowing people from unrecognized jurisdictions into the United States. Even if I had to *marry* her—"

I pulled myself back and placed my hands on Te's shoulders. I couldn't believe I was thinking the unthinkable.

"Let's sleep on this tonight and talk about it in the morning, okay? This is all happening so fast. I don't want you to do something you'll regret later. We've still got a couple of weeks to explore our feelings for one another and talk to your father to test his receptivity to this idea."

I glanced over in the direction of the village and noticed a billow of white smoke rising into the night sky.

"Let's head back to your hut. He's probably worried about you. Like you said, we shouldn't test his patience too quickly."

"Yes," Te' sighed. "He's probably thinking about sending out a search party if we don't return soon." She clasped my arms firmly, furrowing her brow. "Promise me that you'll think about this. I want to be with you forever."

I looked into her limpid brown eyes and smiled.

"I promise," I nodded.

As we continued strolling through the foamy surf, I suddenly felt my own heartbeat pounding strongly in my chest.

Forever's a long time, I thought.

When we returned to Te's village, everyone was already lying asleep on the floor of her hut. Her father was reclining in a rocking chair on the front veranda with his eyes closed, snoring loudly. We crept up the front stairs and passed by him as he snorted, then we took off our clothes and pulled a taro blanket over us, reclining in the far corner next to some of the young children. We tried to sleep, but we were both still too excited about what had happened at the waterfall and about our discussion on the beach.

Te' rolled over on her side and pressed her hips against mine, and we mashed our mounds together, sighing quietly in each other's mouths. It was difficult to remain quiet with the sound of our moving bodies on the crunchy mats underneath us, but once our clits joined together, we couldn't stop tribbing one another until we both reached a powerful climax together. Five minutes later, Te's father rose from his chair on the porch and paused in the doorway for a long time, watching the two of us lying peacefully next to one another. When he finally lay down on the other side of the cabin and began snoring, we giggled under the covers and fell asleep in each other's arms.

We woke up to the sound of Te's siblings chattering on the front porch and got dressed, finding Nona preparing breakfast. The chief was nowhere to be found, but a few minutes later I noticed him talking privately at the far end of the courtyard with the young man who'd shown such an intense interest in Te' at the feast two nights ago. When her father approached the hut, he looked at Te' with a serious expression and motioned with his head for her to join him in the courtyard.

I watched the two of them walk down the sandy esplanade together, then Teuila suddenly stopped as she confronted her father with a raised voice. I heard the chief mention something about Manaia, and Te' shook her head violently, gesturing wildly with her hands. Shortly after, she stomped up the path and grabbed my hand, leading me into the woods.

"What is it, Te'?" I asked. "Was your father angry that we returned so late last night?"

"Worse," she said as tears streamed down her cheeks. "Much worse. He heard us making love last night and disapproves of how close we've become. He intends to marry me to Manaia in a ceremony tomorrow night."

9

That night, neither one of us slept well. I kept replaying the image of Teuila being violated by her groom as she fought to resist his advances. I could feel her tossing and turning next to me, and whenever she cried out or whimpered in her sleep, I cradled her gently in my arms. My mind raced with crazy ideas of stealing one of the tribe's canoes and sailing to safety to the nearest neighboring island. But I no idea in which direction that might be, and neither Teuila nor I had any way of navigating our way through the open seas. Even if the charter boat crew returned for me, it wouldn't be easy to kidnap the chief's daughter from the clutches of her heavily armed tribe. After running every possible scenario through my head, I eventually fell asleep resigned to the idea that my precious island girl would soon be wrenched away from me.

In the morning, Nona began preparing a special meal for the evening's ceremony while some of Te's sisters braided her hair under the watchful eye of her father. We were both under virtual house arrest, with the chief posting an armed guard outside the front door of their hut. He wasn't taking any chances that the two of us might steal away again before his daughter was betrothed to Manaia. Te' put on a brave face as her sisters talked excitedly with her, but she kept glancing toward me with sad eyes. Fortunately, we were the only ones in her family who spoke English, so at least we were able to carry on a limited discussion.

"You look beautiful," I said, peering at her pretty face with her hair pulled back behind her head. "I like you in braids."

"The girls have lots of practice," Te' frowned. "With all the mats and baskets they've woven, they could probably do this with their eyes closed." She looked at her grandmother scraping some manioc shavings into a large wooden bowl. "That and cooking is pretty much all we women do around here."

I glanced at Teuila's father, who was sitting cross-legged on the other side of the hut, watching us with a stern expression.

"What about raising a *family*?" I said. "Isn't that something you're looking forward to? You and your sisters seem to have a close relationship."

"Jade," Te' said, shaking her head slowly. "I know you're trying to make me feel better, but it's no use. You're the only one I want. There's nothing else in the world that I need as long as I'm with you."

I tightened my lips, trying to hold back my emotions.

"It won't be so bad," I said. "Lots of marriages are arranged. Over time, I'm sure you'll grow to love your new husband. After I'm gone, you'll soon forget about me—"

"I could *never* forget you," she said, her eyes flaring. "And I'll never love that brute. As long as we're apart, I'll never be happy."

"Te'," I said, glancing in her father's direction. "We have to accept the reality of the situation. It's out of our hands now. You'll soon be married, we'll be separated from each other, and I'll be banished from the island. It's best that you get on with your life..."

"I've been thinking," she said. "There might be another way. All we have to do is find a way to get the two of us away from the clutches of my father for a few moments. Then we can slip into the forest and hide away until one of the boats comes to pick you up."

I glanced at the two burly men standing opposite the front steps of their hut holding sharp spears in their hands.

"How could we do that? Your father doesn't seem to want either one of us out of his sight, much less *both* of us at the same time."

"It shouldn't be too difficult to stretch your legs for a moment. It's me that he's primarily worried about. He knows you couldn't fend for yourself very long if you ran away. He'd probably be *happy* if something were to happen to you, so I'd stop pining for you. We just need to find a way to get you out of the hut. Then all I'd need to do is create a distraction and slip away. I know this island better than anyone. There are lots of places where we could hide out for a few weeks."

"I don't know, Te'," I said. "It sounds risky. What if we get caught? Your father doesn't seem like the kind of man to let that sort of challenge to his authority go unpunished. There's no rule of law on this island. It wouldn't take much for him to have me put down. I have a feeling he's already at the end of his patience."

Teuila paused for a long moment as her eyes studied my face. As much as I was concerned for my own safety, I was far more worried about the consequences to *her* if we got caught. The worst thing would be for her to see me tortured or killed for disrespecting the chief's power.

"Do you think you could find your way back to the waterfall we visited yesterday?" she asked.

"I don't know, maybe. I suppose if I followed the same path—"

"If you can find your way there, I'll meet you in a couple of hours. Worst-case scenario, you can hide out in the jungle and live off pineapples and taro root until your ship arrives. My father won't harm you with other Westerners around. He knows it would just bring more visitors to the island and threaten his position as chief."

I shook my head and sighed heavily.

"But on what pretense would he let me out of the hut? And what if he sends an armed guard with me? How would I escape?"

Te' paused as her eyes darted from side to side.

"We'll need to relieve ourselves eventually. My father isn't such a brute that he'd insist on our doing our business right here on the floor of the hut. You can ask to be escorted to the women's bathing lagoon, then ask the guard to let you take care of business behind a clump of palm trees. When his back is turned, do you think you could climb to the top of one of those trees like I showed you? He'll never expect you to do that, searching the trails and beach for your footprints, not looking up."

I closed my eyes, reflecting back on Te's technique climbing the pineapple tree. She'd made it look remarkably easy, and I was still in decent shape from my regular trips to the gym.

"I think so. But how long will I have to stay up there before it's safe to come down?"

"My guess is that if the guard can't find you within a few minutes, my father will tell everyone to forget about you. He'll be far more concerned about letting me out of his sight."

"And how will you manage that?"

"Let *me* worry about that," Te' smiled. "I'm very resourceful. Just make sure you find your way back to the waterfall. It's a big island, and it will be very difficult to find each other again if you get lost."

"I can't believe I'm considering this," I said, feeling my heart beginning to pound in my chest.

For the first time in many years, I'd never felt so alive. The idea of running away from an angry tribe on an isolated island with the girl of my dreams was beyond any fantasy I'd ever imagined. I could feel the adrenaline coursing through my veins and the hairs on the sides of my arms standing on end.

"I'm in," I said.

Teuila turned to speak with her father for a few moments, then he paused as he appraised my demeanor. I tried to remain as calm as possible, but I could feel the veins in my neck pulsing like crazy as he glared at me. Eventually, he gave a single nod of his head, then rose to give instructions to one of the guards standing outside the front door.

"*Alu*," he said to me, jerking his head towards the open door. "*Le maua manatu.*"

"What did he say?" I asked Teuila.

"Pretty much what we expected. He's going to send a guard with you who won't give you a lot of space to maneuver, so you'll have to choose your position carefully. Find one with enough cover to protect your modesty, but also close enough to a tree so that you can climb it without him noticing you. I'll come for you as soon as I can."

"Be careful," I said, standing to exit the cabin.

"You too."

I paused at the door of her hut and looked back at Teuila one last time. I didn't know if or when I'd see her again.

When I got to the base of the front steps, one of the guards looked sternly at me then motioned with his spear in the direction of the women's lagoon. As I walked down the same sandy path where all the tribespeople had welcomed me so warmly two nights ago, I noticed the women and children tracing my movement with vacant expressions.

It looks like I'm on my own again, I thought.

When we reached the edge of the lagoon, the guard motioned to a shallow depression at the edge of the brush.

"*Oe alu ai*," he ordered, pointing to the basin with his spear.

I glanced around the area, noticing there was little surrounding vegetation to provide privacy for someone taking care of such intimate business.

I shook my head as I pulled on my shorts, indicating that I needed more privacy. He looked around the edge of the lagoon and pointed to a more secluded spot about a hundred feet up the beach, next to a small clump of coconut trees. When we reached the spot, I climbed behind a small bush and began to squat, noticing the guard still watching me.

I motioned with my hand for him to look away, and he turned his back briefly. Knowing I'd only have a few seconds to act, I removed my hiking shoes and hid them in the brush. Then I crawled behind the sandy embankment toward the nearby palm trees. When I reached the furthest one, I stood and peered around the side of the trunk. The guard had turned around and was glancing curiously in the direction of the pit, tilting his head high in the air as he lifted his heels off the ground. He shouted something in his native language, and when I didn't respond, he rushed forward with a look of alarm, finding the pit empty.

He swiveled his head quickly from side to side, then peered at the stand of trees. As he began walking in my direction, I placed the soles of my feet against the side of the trunk as Teuila had shown me, then I grasped the crusty bark and pulled myself upward. As I heard the guard's footsteps nearing the stand, I began slowly shimming myself up the tree. With most of my weight borne by the inward pressure of my feet pressed against the trunk, it was easier than I expected to scale the thick stem. But as I pulled my knees inward, worrying he'd see them sticking out from the side of the tree, I ended up using more arm strength than I intended to move upward.

By the time I reached the crown of the tree and glanced down, I was sweating profusely. My feet were bleeding from the sharp crust pressing into my tender skin, but I was able to leverage my weight with tight handholds against the layered bark. As the guard peered frantically from side to side looking for me, I noticed the pod of coconuts under the palm fronds shaking precariously. Just as one of them snapped from its stem, I reached out and caught the husk as it fell into my open palm.

The guard cocked his head hearing the sound and started to look up. I threw the nut as far as I could in the direction of the bush, and when he heard it land in the dense thicket, he took chase into the forest. I sat in my cramped position breathing heavily as sweat poured down the front of my T-shirt, listening carefully for the sound of the guard's footsteps in the jungle. When the footfalls diminished into the distance, I quickly descended the tree, falling sharply to the ground. I looked around to make sure the way was clear, then I hobbled toward the far end of the beach and disappeared into the thick brush.

Half a mile away, Teuila sat patiently on the floor of her hut as her sisters finished decorating her hair with scented frangipani blossoms. She glanced toward her grandmother preparing the wedding ceremony dishes on the front veranda and asked her father if she could help. The chief nodded and followed Te' out onto the porch, taking a position in the rocking chair as he nodded toward the remaining guard.

Teuila sat next to her grandmother and Nona smiled, handing her a knife and a taro root to peel. Suddenly, the other guard came running up to the front of the hut, and when he told the chief that the white woman had escaped, her father summoned a group of young tribesmen and they ran off in the direction of the lagoon. Nona glanced at Teuila, pinching her eyebrows in suspicion, wondering what kind of trouble the girls were getting into now.

Te' picked up the taro root and smiled, remembering how Jade had teased her when she first bit into it. Suddenly, the vegetable slipped in her hand and the knife cut a deep diagonal gash along the side of her index finger. As her hand began spurting blood all over the white gourd, Nona dropped what she was doing and motioned for the guard to summon the village's medicine man. When the guard hesitated remembering the chief's orders to keep a close watch on his daughter, Nona screamed at him, warning that if Teuila was not attended to soon, she could suffer the same fate as her mother.

"Do you want to be responsible for the death of the chief's daughter on the eve of her wedding?" she shouted in their native language.

The guard mumbled something and took off scurrying down the path. Nona looked at Te's cut shaking her head, then she wrapped a banana leaf around the wound and peered into her granddaughter's eyes.

"This wasn't an accident, was it?" she said.

"Forgive me, Nona," Te' said. "I love her. This is the only way I can be with her. Can you help me?"

Nona glanced down the sandy courtyard, then escorted Teuila

toward the rear of their cabin, where she lifted a flap of leaves and pointed into the forest.

"*Lau manamea*," she said. "Be with your lover. I'll pray that you both find happiness. Go quickly now, before your father returns."

As Teuila scampered into the forest holding the green bandage tightly against her swollen finger, she yelped in glee, knowing she'd soon be in the arms of the only person she ever truly loved.

10

———

When I got far enough away from the cluster of palm trees, I ducked into the bush and paused to get my bearings. From my new location, it would be difficult to find my way back to the waterfall. All I could remember was that it was about an hour's hike uphill in a roughly forty-five-degree angle from the village. But from my vantage point in the women's lagoon, it would be almost impossible to pick up the trail through the thick jungle. My only chance would be to double-back towards the village and hope that nobody saw me.

To make matters worse, my feet were sore and bleeding from climbing the rough palm tree. I thought taking my shoes off would help me to climb the trunk more quietly, but I hadn't counted on puncturing my skin in multiple places. And it would be too risky to try to return to the pit to retrieve them. Like it or not, I'd have to make my way back up to the waterfall in bare feet.

I shook my head at the irony of my predicament.

The only way to truly appreciate another culture is to immerse yourself in it, I reminded myself. *Well now I'm really going native. Let's see how quickly I can develop tough Anutian soles.*

I peered over the top of my sand dune to see if the coast was clear.

I hadn't heard from the guard since he ran off into the jungle, but I knew it would be too risky to use the cover of the thick brush to find my way back to the village. The carpet of broken twigs and sharp rocks on the forest floor would just make my feet worse, and the rustling of leaves could draw attention to my position. My only chance would be to backtrack along the beach before he returned.

But just as I prepared to sprint down the beach, I noticed my guard running toward me from the direction of the village, along with the chief and a group of other young tribesmen. They paused at the location where I'd squatted, and it didn't take long for the chief to find my hiking shoes.

"*O a nei?*" he shouted, holding my shoes up in the air.

The guard shook his head in bewilderment, then pointed into the jungle in the direction where I'd thrown the coconut.

"*Ona mamao,*" the chief said, throwing my shoes far into the lagoon. "*Salalau solo!*" he said, gesturing into the jungle in multiple directions.

As the group fanned out into the thick brush, I waited for a few moments then dashed back along the beach in the direction of the village. Feeling my blistered feet burning in the hot sand, I hobbled my way across the lagoon, glancing into the bush for any sign of the tribesmen.

Maybe it wasn't such a bad idea taking my shoes off after all, I thought, watching the impressions my feet left in the sand. I'm the only one on this island with Western shoes. It would be a whole lot easier to track me from the unique tread they'd leave on the ground than with my bare feet.

I just hoped the blood from my soles wouldn't leave another type of trail.

When I got to the edge of the village, I crouched low behind the back of the huts lining the central promenade, trying to stay out of sight. Small children giggled as they ran across the courtyard, playing a game of tag. One of the boys ducked under the crawlspace of the cabin I was hiding behind, and I pulled myself up on the side of the hut, trying to conceal my legs. He glanced in both directions to see if the coast was clear, then scampered back across the courtyard behind another hut.

Great, I thought. *Just what I need right now. A bunch of kids playing hide and seek. At least they're showing me some good hiding spots.*

As I slowly made my way toward the far end of the courtyard, I paused when I saw the chief's hut. There was no armed guard outside the front door, and I peered inside the darkened interior for any sign of Teuila. Her grandmother was peeling vegetables on the front porch, and she glanced in my direction, noticing movement across the lane. We locked eyes and for a moment and I was afraid she'd call out. But instead, she placed her finger to her lips, then motioned with an open hand toward the trailhead at the end of the square.

She made it! I breathed a sigh of relief. *God bless that woman.* Maybe I had a friend in the village after all.

I crept past the remaining huts lining the square then dashed onto the trail and scampered up the familiar path leading to the waterfall. Once I was on the path, I recognized the familiar land-marks and made good time picking my way up the slope. Even though the brush was thick, I was far more worried about bumping into one of the chief's chase team than I was about encountering another tree snake. When I reached the pineapple tree clearing, I knew I was on the right track and I smiled remembering the sight of Te's pretty ass climbing the tree.

Soon, I thought, *I'll have her all to myself.*

Thirty minutes later, I heard the sound of the waterfall nearby, and I breathed in the fresh scent of the misty air wafting over the trees. I didn't know if it was because all my senses were on high alert being on the run, or if it was because my heart was pounding knowing I'd soon be back with Teuila, but everything around me suddenly seemed so much more *alive.* The flowers at the side of the trail looked prettier, the air smelled sweeter, and the birds chirping in the distance sounded happier.

For the first time in many years, I was madly, deliriously in love.

When I reached the waterfall, I looked around frantically for my island girl, but there was no sign of her. I furrowed my brow, puzzled why she'd have taken longer to reach our destination than I had. She appeared to have had a head start on me, and she should have been able to scale the uneven path much quicker than me, especially with my chafed feet. But seconds later, she broke through the heavy brush on the opposite side of the waterfall and rushed toward me.

"Thank God you made it!" she said, throwing her arms around me. "I was so worried about you."

"Our little trick worked," I nodded, tilting the underside of one foot up toward her. "Although it looks like it's going to take a little longer than we hoped for the soles of my feet to get properly toughened up."

Teuila looked at my scarred soles and shook her head.

"What happened to your shoes?"

"I thought it would be safer to climb the tree without them. But it didn't take long for your father to find where I'd hidden them. I guess I'll be walking around barefoot like a real Anutian sooner than we thought."

Teuila chuckled as she squeezed my hand.

"It's probably better this way anyhow," she smiled. "Those treads would be visible a mile away."

"Why did you come up the other way?" I said, pointing to the direction of the jungle where she'd emerged.

"I wanted to throw my father off the trail," she said, pointing to the imprint of my boots on the muddy embankment. "But it won't take long for them to find us. We have to get out of here as soon as possible."

I noticed that the leaf wrapped around Te's index finger was dripping blood down her hand.

"What happened?" I said. "You're hurt!"

"It's just a flesh wound," she said. "It looks worse than it is. We'll be able to patch up our wounds when we get to safety."

Suddenly we heard the shouting of men's voices approaching our position. I looked at Teuila with terrified eyes.

"What should we do?" I said. "In which direction should we head?"

"There's no time for that," Te' said. "We have to *hide*. There's too many of them. They'll catch us too quickly."

"Where?" I said, looking around the clearing. "In the brush?"

Te' glanced around the glade, then peered into a still section of the pool furthest from the waterfall.

"How long can you hold your breath?" she said.

I looked at the surface of the pond for a moment, then back towards her.

"Not long in my present state," I said, feeling my chest heaving up and down. "Between my elevated state of adrenaline and my fear of being caught, I can hardly catch my breath as it is."

"What if we fashioned some kind of breathing tube?" she said, peering at some bulrushes at the far end of the pond. "Do you think you could remain still under the water while our tribesmen search the area?"

"I suppose so. What did you have in mind?"

"Those reeds on the other side of the pond are hollow. Follow me, but try to step as much as possible on the rocks instead of the dirt. We don't want them to be able to trace where we're hiding."

Teuila took my hand and led me to a flattened section of the embankment where we tiptoed over the scattered rocks on the edge of the shore. Then she slipped into the water and pushed herself away from the shore.

"Be careful when you step into the pond," she said. "We don't want to make too much noise or stir up the mud around the bank where they could see where we entered the water. Quickly now—I can hear them getting closer."

I lowered myself into the water then I pushed myself gently away from the shore. Teuila led me to the other side of the pond, then she pulled a pocketknife out of a pouch on her tunic and cut two four-foot lengths of reed. She tested each tube by puffing through them, then handed one to me. I could hear the sounds of the men's voices rising in volume and the rustling of the brush very close by.

"Put this in your mouth then duck under the water about three feet. Don't go any lower than that or you'll choke if the other end dips beneath the surface. Then follow me toward the waterfall. The rippling current will help camouflage us in the depths."

I looked at Teuila with frightened eyes, then placed the tube in my mouth and submerged under the water. After a brief moment of panic, I realized it wasn't so different from using a snorkel. I was scared using one of those at first too, but once I learned that I could breathe comfortably underwater, it didn't take long for me to relax. After I dropped a few feet, I opened my eyes and saw Te' submerge beside me. Then she took my hand and pulled me toward the churning undercurrent next to the waterfall.

When we reached the base of the cataract, I glanced up through the foaming water and noticed a group of half-naked tribesmen walking around the base of the swimming hole, pointing toward footprints in the ground. I looked toward Teuila fearfully, and she pumped her palm up and down, motioning for me to remain calm. Her dress was billowing underneath her, spreading out to her sides, and I worried the white sheen of the fabric would be noticeable from above. But she placed her hands between her legs in a Marilyn Monroe manner and pressed the gown downwards as her long black hair floated upwards.

I shook my head, smiling at the improbability of the situation. Only Teuila could make almost suffocating under water while a bunch of savages circled around us menacingly look sexy.

Suddenly, I noticed Manaia standing on the edge of the embankment, looking intently into the water. He walked around the edge of the pond, thrusting the dull end of his spear into the water, as if searching for something under the surface. When he reached the clump of reeds, he paused for a moment, then moved closer to the edge of the waterfall. Teuila's eyes widened as he got closer, and she motioned for us to move closer to the base of the cataract. She pinched her fingers around the base of the tube in her mouth then pulled them away quickly as she puffed her cheeks.

I glanced at her for a moment, then nodded my head in understanding. One of the first things I'd learned when using a snorkel was how to purge the water from the tube whenever I ducked under water. I took a deep breath in, then we paddled under the falling water as I felt the reed vibrating from the pressure of the deluge above us. When the we finally reached a calmer section near the embankment, I blew heavily out the tube, feeling the water passing upward through the reed, then I breathed deeply in. There was still a bit of water in the cylinder and I coughed suddenly, but after a few more frantic purges, I was able to breathe comfortably again.

As we treaded water trying to remain in a fixed position, we looked up through the gurgling surface. Manaia stared in our direction for a long moment, then he finally stepped back from the shore and joined the rest of his team on the cliff. Teuila's father motioned in the direction of the brush where she'd emerged earlier, then the group quickly dispersed. I kicked my legs toward the surface, but Te' reached out and grabbed my arm, motioning for me to stay submerged a little longer. About a minute later, Manaia reemerged at the edge of the abutment and turned his head to scan the surface of the lagoon, then he took off again into the forest. Teuila waited another five minutes, then she signaled that it was safe to resurface.

"Oh my God!" I said, looking at her with wide eyes. "That was *intense*. I was sure that Manaia had seen us. That was smart of you to wait until he'd left the second time."

"It's still not entirely safe," Teuila said. "I think we should wait here for another half hour or so. Once we know that they're not coming back, we'll have to find another place to hide. I want to put as much distance between us and the village as possible."

I circled my hands gently underwater as my eyes darted over her face.

"What about the beach where my charter boat came in? You said that was a good day's hike from your village. That should be the first place my crew will look for me if they return."

"That might work," Te' nodded. "But we'll have to be careful about staying too close to the shore. My father will probably send out another search party following the perimeter of the island by canoe. We'll scope out the area when we get there."

I kicked my legs excitedly, realizing we'd soon be alone again.

"Teuila," I said, throwing my arms around her, almost pulling both of us underwater. "I'm so happy we're together again. I could live in a *cave* with you if I had to."

"Let's hope your friends return for you soon," she said, peering nervously around the edge of the waterfall. "That might be the only safe place for us to hide soon if they don't."

11

———

Teuila dressed my wounds with the milky sap of a spongy plant, then she wrapped my feet in banana leaves to help quell the bleeding. After a few minutes, I could feel the pain and throbbing begin to subside, and I shook my head marveling at her ability to apply natural cures. But I was far more concerned about the cut on her finger, which was still dripping blood under her makeshift bandage.

"That feels better," I said, lifting her hand to take a closer look at her incision. "But your cut looks far worse. Will a couple of leaves will be enough to close that wound?"

"I missed the main artery," she said, squeezing her finger tenderly. "I just need to apply a tight compress to stem the bleeding and allow it to clot."

She glanced down at my wet T-shirt and smiled.

"Do you think you'd be willing to part with your shirt? If we tear it into strips, we can wrap it around both my finger and your feet. We've got a long walk ahead of us to get to the other side of the island and it will help keep the dirt out of your wounds."

"Why not?" I smiled. "I've done it once before already. Now that we're alone, I don't feel so self-conscious about protecting my modesty." I pulled my shirt over my head and handed it to her. "Do you want my bra too?"

Te' peered at my bosom pushed together with the constricting garment and shook her head.

"It's probably best that you keep that on for a little longer. There will be plenty of sharp objects poking out of the brush as we make our way through the jungle. We don't want to get those pretty breasts of yours all scratched up. Besides, we might be able to find a better use for it later."

She bit the bottom of my shirt to make a small incision, then tore it in half lengthwise down the front and the back before pulling off the sleeves. Then she hacked two narrow pieces of bark off a nearby tree with her adze and placed them under my feet, wrapping the long ends of my shirt around the husks and tying the ends firmly behind my ankle.

"Not quite as pretty as your Western shoes," she said, but hopefully they'll last at least until we get to the other side of the island.

I stood up and paced forward and back a few steps, testing my newly fashioned sandals.

"They're surprising comfortable," I nodded. "Especially with those leafy insoles. Maybe we can hook you up with Nike when we return to the States."

"Nike?"

"Just kidding," I laughed. "They're a big shoe manufacturer back home. You're a woman of many talents, Te'. I'm sure we can find you a more interesting job when the time comes."

Teuila looked up at me and smiled.

"I'm excited to learn all about your culture. But right now, I think we should head over to the other side of the island. We don't want to overstay our welcome here. My father may come back to search for us if he doesn't find us elsewhere."

Teuila tore up one of the sleeves into a spiral strip, then she wrapped and tied it tightly around her wounded finger.

"Come on," she said. "Let's go see if we can find a better hiding place."

It took most of the day to cross to the other side of the island. Te' wanted to stay off the marked trails to avoid running into our search party, so we walked along the side of narrow creeks and streams to stay out of sight. I was afraid the stony riverbeds would splinter my makeshift moccasins, but the flexible bark absorbed most of the brunt and the shirt-tie miraculously survived the entire trip. When we passed the same waterfall where I was bitten by the snake, I knew we were getting close to the beach.

"How can you navigate through this dense jungle so easily?" I said, amazed at how she'd found her way back to the same spot on such a large island.

"I've lived here my whole life," she said. "I know this island like the back of my hand. There's not much else to do for fun around here, so I've made lots of expeditions in my eighteen years."

"I hope your father and your boyfriend don't know the island as well as you do. Otherwise, there'll be nowhere safe to hide."

"Don't worry about that," Te' said, peering up at the darkening sky. "I've had lots of practice hiding out in the forest. It's starting to get dark, so we won't have time to build a more comfortable shelter until the morning. We'll have to make do with a camouflaged lean-to for this evening. I'm looking forward to showing you how easily we can live off the land. We'll try to make the most of our little exile until your friends return."

"I'm looking forward to it too," I said, recalling my Robinson Crusoe fantasy. "This should be quite the adventure."

When we reached the beach where our charter boat had set anchor, Teuila checked out the lagoon and nodded.

"This will work fine. It's nicely secluded, has shallow water and shoals to catch fish, and has a good lookout for approaching boats."

"Where will we sleep?" I said, wrapping my arms around my chest, feeling the cool onshore breeze.

"It's probably best not to sleep on the beach tonight. My father may be sending out a canoe patrol to search the perimeter of the island. We'll have to sleep inland this evening."

I peered into Te's brown eyes and smiled.

"As long as lying I'm next to you, I can sleep anywhere."

Teuila found a secluded spot behind a sand dune and hacked down some large palm leaves to provide cover and keep us warm. Then she harvested a few pineapples and coconuts from some nearby palm trees, and we enjoyed an impromptu dinner.

"You must be hungry after trekking all day," she said, noticing me shivering as she placed some leaves over my bare torso. "Tomorrow we'll catch and cook up some fresh fish. But it's too risky to build a fire right now. Will you be warm enough sleeping here tonight?"

We lay down in the pit and Te' snuggled up close to me, pulling the big leaves over our bodies.

"I am *now*," I said, feeling her warm skin pressed against mine.

As much as I wanted to make love to her again, after ten hours of hiking we both fell asleep within minutes. In the morning, I woke to the sound of seabirds chirping in the distance as the morning sun began to warm up our little nest of leaves. Te' rolled over when I began to stir, and I kissed her gently.

"Did you sleep well?" I asked, caressing her warm shoulders.

"Like a log. But I had a few nightmares. I dreamed that my father found us and dragged us back to the village where he tied you to a stake in the main square. As everybody celebrated my marriage to Manaia, he set you aflame while I watched helplessly from his arms."

"Jesus!" I said, flaring my eyes open. "Would he actually *do* that if he caught us?"

"Perhaps not quite so viciously. But he's had other tribespeople punished for far less an offense."

Te' began lifting herself up to get out of the pit.

"We need to begin building fortifications and a better hiding place."

"Can't it wait a few more minutes?" I said, clutching her wrist. "This is the first time we've been alone in almost two days. I was hoping we could have a little fun before we get to work. Besides, don't you need to let your finger rest a little longer to let it heal?"

Teuila lifted her hand and untied the strip of cloth around her finger then opened the leaves to peer at her cut. The bleeding had stopped, but she had a nasty inch-long scar on the side of her hand.

"It still looks tender," I said, lifting her finger to my mouth as I sucked on the tip gently. "Maybe it needs some of my special healing juices."

"I'm not sure it works that way," Te' chuckled. "But it feels good, just the same."

"Well if it feels good licking your *finger*, maybe I can make you feel even better licking you somewhere else."

I lifted Teuila's robe over her shoulders then lay her down on the leaves.

"Lie down while I give you some loving."

As I nibbled my way down the front of her chest, I cupped her firm breasts in my hands and sucked on her nipples. It felt sublime to be holding her in my arms for the first time, knowing she was truly mine. I swirled my tongue over her fleshy peaks, and she moaned in pleasure. I could feel her hips gyrating below me, and she gasped when I pressed my thigh against her opening.

While I continued to suck and nibble on her breasts, Teuila ground her pussy into my thigh, coating the front of my leg with her wetness. After a few minutes, I pulled away and drew my tongue over her quivering abdomen until I reached her furry mound. It had been eons since I'd seen or felt a full patch of pubic hair, and I paused as I caressed her soft fur.

"Mmm," I purred. "I love how soft you are down here. I could run my hands through your hair all day."

"I like the way you touch me, Jade," Te' panted. "Kiss my private areas. I want to feel your lips on my *agava*."

As I drew my face over her bush, I could feel the moisture from her pussy beading in her hairs. I closed my lips over her muff and lifted my head up a few inches, gently tugging her hair as I sucked her dew into my mouth. It might have just been my wild imagination channeling my Blue Lagoon fantasy, but her juice tasted sweeter and fresher than anything I remembered.

The closer I got to her jewel, the harder she pushed her hips up into my mouth, and when I finally encircled her clit with my lips, she gasped out loud. As she spread her thighs further apart and I began to circle my tongue around her button, she began to whimper and call my name.

"Oh Jade," she whispered. "That feels so good. Lick me with your beautiful mouth. I want to feel you kissing me everywhere."

Hearing her cry out my name in the throes of passion sent a shiver down my spine, and I began to feel my own panties sticking to my skin. I wanted to feel her trembling against my face and call out my name as the waves of pleasure rolled over her. As her hips began shaking with increasing fervor, I sucked her into my mouth, dancing my tongue over her nub. When her hips began to rise up off the ground, I cradled her buns in my hands as she pressed herself tighter against my face.

"Yes, Jade," she groaned. "I can feel it coming now. Hold me while I release my *pito*. It's coming now!"

Suddenly, Te' growled as her hips began bucking wildly against my face and her buttocks started quivering in my palms. I opened my eyes and watched her tummy cavitating as she thrashed her head from side to side. I held her tightly while she spasmed against my face, coating me with her sweet, pungent syrup. When she finally stopped shaking, I lowered her hips to the cool leaves and snuggled up next to her.

"Does my healing touch work better that way?" I smiled, grinding my hips against her wet mound.

"Yes," she purred. "But now I think there's *another* wound that needs my attention."

Te' and I made love for the rest of the morning, then our growling stomachs reminded us how little we'd eaten in the last twenty-four hours.

"Come," she said, pulling me out of the pit. "Let's catch ourselves a proper breakfast, then we need to begin preparing a safer resting place. No more sleeping on the beach. I don't want to take any chances that my father and his thugs will stumble across us while we're resting. Let me show you how to catch fish the Anutian way."

She led me into the brush until we came upon a small stand of seedlings. Te' hacked two of them off near the base with her adze, then whittled the ends of each shoot down until they had sharp pointed ends.

I looked at her quizzically, wondering what she had in mind.

"Were you planning on using those in case we get ambushed?

"No, I would never harm my own people. These are for another type of creature. We're going to use them to spear fish."

"Really?" I said with wide eyes. "You can do that too? You really are a woman of many talents."

"It's not so easy to spear a free-swimming fish," she said. "But it's a lot easier when there's a bunch of them trapped in a contained area. That's where you come in. You're going to push them toward me."

"How will I do that?"

"You're going to rake them into a trapping area."

I pinched my eyebrows with a confused expression, and she smiled at me as she began chopping down a taller seedling. After she felled it, she chopped off the top to about a fifteen-foot length, then hacked off the branches on three sides so that it looked like a giant comb.

"That's a pretty big rake," I said.

"You'll find it works remarkably well at herding schools of fish into shallow water," Teuila said.

"How am I supposed to use it? It barely looks like I'll be able to lift that thing."

"I'll help you carry it to the shore. Then all you need to do is place the branch atop the water and push it up and down to scare the fish forward. I'll look after the rest. Are you ready?"

"Lead on, Pocahontas," I chuckled. "Show me your ways."

Teuila and I carried the big branch to the edge of the water, then we floated it to the far corner of the lagoon where we saw some schools of iridescent fish darting underneath the clear water.

"Those critters sure can scamper around down there," I said. "Are you sure we'll be able to snare one of them with just a spear?"

"Watch and learn, city girl."

Te' escorted me to a spot waist deep about twenty feet from the shore.

"I'm going to wade a little closer to the shore," she said. "When I signal that I'm ready, I want you to pump the pole up and down on the surface of the water as you slowly walk toward me. The sound and motion of the spikes pointing underwater will scare the fish in my direction. As they begin accumulating in the shallow water, it will make it easier for me to catch one."

When she got into position, Te' nodded toward me and I began to churn the water as she had instructed. Sure enough, within seconds a group of fish began flapping in her direction as they twisted and turned, confused by the agitating water. Some of them slipped around the ends of the rake, but enough moved forward that they began to congregate in the shallower water. When I got to within five feet of Teuila, she pulled one of the spears high above the surface and paused for a moment, then thrust it rapidly down into the water. Seconds later, she pulled the pole out of the depths with a flapping striped fish impaled on the end of the spike.

"Holy crap!" I said, hardly believing my eyes. "Is it that easy?"

"It takes a bit of practice. But it's a whole lot easier when you've got them bunched up in a narrow space."

"Here," she said, holding out the other spear to me. "Do you want to give it a try?"

"Okay," I said, wincing momentarily at the idea of killing such a pretty fish. But I loved my seafood, and catching a fish this way looked a whole lot less messy than using a hook and bait.

"Make sure you wait until you see a bunch of fish swimming near your feet," Te' said. "You don't have to aim at a single fish necessarily. It's a bit hit and miss. It might take you a few attempts to hit one. Just be careful you don't spear your own foot."

"No," I said, peering down at my still bandaged feet. "I think I've had enough scratched up feet for a little while, thank you. Just don't laugh at me."

"I wouldn't dream of it," Te' said.

As we took up our respective positions and Te' began scaring the fish toward me, I could see them darting underwater closer and closer to me. When she got close enough, she looked up and nodded.

"Now, Jade!" she yelled, as she pumped the surface of the water into a foamy brine. "Get them before they escape around the sides of the rake."

I saw three or four striped fish darting about in front of me and I lurched back, flinging the pole into the water. It knifed into the surf and struck the sandy bottom. I pulled it out shaking my head, realizing this wasn't going to be as easy as Teuila made it look.

"Try again," she said. "You'll get it. But you have to act fast, before they escape."

I reared back and thrust the spear into the water a few more times, and on my third attempt it stopped half way underwater, shaking rapidly.

"Grab the stick!" Te' yelled. "Don't let it get away!"

The fish was twisting in a frenzy with the stick running through it, and I grabbed the pole as it slapped on top of the water, then lifted it above the surface to show my prized catch to Teuila.

"Not quite as big as yours," I said. "But not bad for a first time, what do you think?"

"You did great, Jade," Te' said, beaming at me. "Tomorrow, we'll build a retaining wall to funnel them toward us more easily. Then we'll have no trouble catching all the fish we can eat. Let's take a break to enjoy our catch."

As Teuila and I waded toward the shore, I looked around the lagoon and smiled. I knew I'd finally found my slice of paradise.

12

———

euila cleaned and filleted the fish we'd caught then we sat on the beach and enjoyed some fresh sushi marinated in pineapple juice and coconut cream. While we ate, she asked me about my life in the United States and I learned more about her culture on the island of Anuta. The more I listened to her, the more I began to envy her stress-free life in this tropical paradise. With each passing day, I was becoming less dependent on my Western comforts. For the first time in years, I didn't miss having my phone next to me.

When we finished eating, she examined our wounds and decided to keep the bandages on for one more day to let them fully heal. But there was no longer any need for me to wear my bra, and I happily threw it into the pit, symbolizing my liberation from the binds of Western civilization.

"So what's on our agenda for today?" I asked, bouncing up and down like a giddy schoolgirl. "Swimming in the crystalline waters of the lagoon and lounging on the beach?"

Te' ran her eyes over my pale breasts and smiled.

"As much as I'd like to rest and relax, I'm afraid we've got a fair amount of work to do. We don't know how long it will take for your friends to return. I want to build a more secure place for us to sleep, one that's better hidden from the lagoon and any foot patrols.

"Besides," she said, noticing the burn lines around my chest. "I think you need to be careful about getting too much sun too quickly. It's going to take a few more days for you to get a proper Anutian tan."

"Yes," I said. "Especially since I left all my sunscreen in my purse at your village. What kind of shelter did you have in mind?"

"One higher off the ground, in the trees. It might take us a couple of days to finish it. The most important material will be twine to hold the support beams in place. And that takes a bit of time to produce. But two people can do it twice as fast. Let me show you how to make organic rope."

Te' led me a few hundred feet into the forest until we came upon a clump of short, spiky bushes.

"This is the pandanus plant," she said. "Our tribe normally makes ties using bark, but the fewer trees we have to strip the better in case someone comes snooping around. The leaves of this plant are very fibrous and will be a good substitute."

"You can hold up a *house* with just a few leaves?" I said, bending the skinny stalks in my hand.

"With the right braiding, yes. Plant cellulose is an incredibly strong material, especially when it's properly twined."

She snapped one of the leaves off near the base, then ran her fingernail along its length to separate the fibers. She pulled a few of the stringy strands apart and lay them in her hand.

"Now they look even flimsier than before," I said, shaking my head. "How can those skinny fibers hold much of *anything* together?"

"For such an enlightened culture," Te' smiled, "you Americans sure lead a sheltered existence. Watch what happens when we combine the strands and weave them together."

Teuila bunched the strands together in her palm and folded them into a long U-shape, then she bent one end down, forming a small loop at the joined end. As she pinched the loop with the fingers of her left hand, she twisted the horizontal band of strands away from her with her other hand while using her middle finger to lift the end pointing down and pulling it toward her, wrapping the two shoots around one another. She repeated this process for a minute or two, until she'd formed a six-inch-long line of interlaced strands that looked just like a braided rope.

"That's pretty cool," I said, nodding at how quickly she'd fashioned a rope out of natural materials. "But that doesn't even look long enough to tie around my wrist. What do you do if we need to make a longer rope?"

"It's simple to join extra pieces together," she said. "Watch carefully."

Te' gathered another bunch of leaf strands and folded them in half, pinching them tightly together at the fold. Then she inserted the V-end of the folded shoots into the open end of the braided strands and repeated the wrapping sequence, twisting the two ends of the joined strands away from her while simultaneously pulling the other two loose ends toward her. Within seconds, the loose ends of the first set of strands disappeared into the lengthening braid until there were only the short ends of the new set of strands remaining at the end of the rope.

"Holy crap," I said, shaking my head at how easy it was to create any length of rope using just plant leaves. "But how *strong* is it? And how firmly connected are the two joined pieces?"

"Why don't you see for yourself?" Te' said, handing me the waxy twine. "Try to pull it apart."

I grasped the braid on each end and yanked it as hard as I could in opposite directions. Still not believing that a plant leaf could be so sturdy, I lifted my leg and wrapped the twine over my knee and pulled as hard as I could on each side. Still skeptical of its strength, I lifted it in front of me and bent it up and down a few times. When it began to splinter and crack, I looked up at Teuila triumphantly.

"Hold on, girl," she said, taking the leaf rope out of my hands.

"If you bend anything like that long enough, just about anything will break—even steel. But we're not going to use it that way. We're going to bend it around large poles and tie it in a fixed position. You saw how it's almost impossible to break with fixed tension. That's all we care about at this point. We're going to use it to *hold* things, not as a swing!"

"Okay," I sighed. "You've convinced me. How much of this stuff do we need to build our tree house?"

"A lot. A few hundred pieces of cord a couple of feet long should do it. If we separate the tasks and work together, it shouldn't take too long. Would you rather harvest the strands or braid them together?"

I held Te's bandaged hand and peered at the swelling around her finger.

"Which task will be easier on your hand? It looks like you still need a bit more rehabilitation time than me."

"The less twisting and bending, the better," she nodded, pinching her finger tenderly near the knuckle. "How about if I collect the leaves while you weave them together to start?"

"Sounds like a deal."

Teuila demonstrated one more time how to properly twist and join the shoots, then I sat down on a broken tree stump while she began to tear and separate the leaves. After a half hour or so, I'd assembled a decent pile of arms-length twine, and I shook my wrists trying to relieve the muscle cramps in my hands.

"That's a pretty impressive length of cordage," she said. "I think we're about halfway there. Would you like to switch positions for a while to rest your aching fingers?"

"If you think you're up for it," I nodded. "I'm not used to doing this amount of physical labor with my hands. I better pause for a while before I get repetitive stress syndrome."

"Repetitive *what*—?" Te' asked with a puzzled expression.

"It's another frailty of our Western culture. A lot of people sit around hammering away at computers all day long and develop sore wrists and hands. Something tells me this is not an affliction known to native Anutians."

"I've never seen anything like that," Te' said, shaking her head. "We tend to do most things around here in measured doses. There's plenty enough work to keep everybody busy doing different things at any one time. Between fishing, planting, cooking, swimming, and dancing, we keep our bodies fairly limber."

"I noticed," I said, watching Te's lean legs flexing as she stooped down to cut another bunch of leaves from the base of the plant. "I wouldn't mind switching positions for a while if you're up for it. I'd like to learn how to do everything your culture does. You never know when I might be stranded on another deserted island."

13

Te' and I worked for another hour or so splitting and weaving the leaves until we had an impressive pile of shiny green twine.

"That's a lot of rope," I said, wiping my brow with my forearm. "What do we do now?"

"Now for the *fun* part," she smiled. "We begin building our house in the clouds. Grab a pile of rope and let's see if we can find a suitable location."

As we began walking deeper into the forest, Teuila swiveled her head from side to side, scanning the thicket of trees.

"What are we looking for exactly?" I asked.

"Ideally, a tree that's not too far from the lagoon, but still out of sight from the beach. One with high, sturdy branches and a thick canopy to provide cover from the elements and any search parties. We can build the rest."

While we continued foraging through the forest, my mind wandered to the story of The Swiss Family Robinson, who built such a beautiful and intricate treehouse on their deserted island. But something Teuila mentioned bothered me.

"If we're going to be out of sight from the beach, how will my charter boat crew know where to look for me when they return?"

"I have an idea about that," Te' said. "The trick will be to build a marker that they can find, but my father won't so easily see. We'll focus on that tomorrow. Our priority today is to build a safe hiding place."

I glanced around the forest and noticed a tall mushroom-shaped tree standing in a clearing a few hundred feet away. It had a thick golden trunk and long stringy vines hanging down from its domed canopy. Broad horizontal branches radiated out in every direction about fifteen feet off the ground.

"How about that tree?" I said, pointing to the unusual specimen. "It looks pretty sturdy and well camouflaged."

Teuila turned in the direction of the tree and nodded when she caught sight of it.

"That's a banyan tree," she said. "It's perfect. It's even got a built-in elevator."

"If you're referring to those vines hanging down from the branches, that's not exactly what I'd call an *elevator*."

"Yes, but they're a lot less obvious than a ladder. If my father comes around, nothing will look out of place. He won't have any reason to believe we're hiding in the trees."

Te' walked up to the tree and grabbed one of the hanging vines, pulling herself up hand over hand until she reached the bottom of a branch. Then she grabbed the limb and flung her body upward in one quick motion, placing her feet on the branch and standing up.

"*Damn*, girl," I said, shaking my head at how nimble she was. "You make that look like Tarzan. You really do know your way around this jungle, don't you?"

"It's easy, once you get the hang of it," she said. "Now you try it."

I grabbed the vine with two hands, then wrapped my legs tightly around the cord and pushed up. It took me a minute to shimmy to the top, and when I reached the branch, I couldn't pull my body over it like Teuila had, so I flung one of my legs over the bough and awkwardly rolled myself on top.

"Not quite as elegant as your technique," I said, standing precariously on the limb, holding an adjacent vine for support.

"You'll get the hang of it soon enough," she said, brushing some loose debris off my bare breasts. "You just need to learn how to climb the vine with less rubbing. Otherwise, it won't just be the bottom of your *feet* that get scraped up."

I glanced above me and noticed some teardrop-shaped fruit dangling from the branches.

"Are those *figs*?" I said, widening my eyes in excitement.

"Yes," Te' nodded. "And they look nicely ripe. Have you ever tried one fresh off the tree?"

"If they're half as good as your fresh pineapple and mango, I can't wait."

Tequila picked one of the purple pods off a nearby branch then pinched the skin with her fingernails and separated it in half, placing it under my nose. The pulpy seeds glistened in the crimson-colored syrup of the berry.

"It smells heavenly," I said, closing my eyes as I savored the floral aroma. I cradled the dewy husk in my hands and bit into it softly.

"Mmm," I hummed. "This is almost as good as sex. Sweet, juicy, and succulent. Just like you."

Te' plucked another fig off the branch and bit it in half, squeezing the moist nectar over her hand.

"I see what you mean," she smiled. "This is definitely getting me in the mood. Let's hurry up and finish building our nest so we can have some more fun."

As I finished eating my fig, I looked up at the web of golden branches above us, marveling at how far the crown extended out in all directions.

"At least we've got pretty good protection from above. Will those leaves keep us dry when it rains?"

"Only during light showers. We'll have to build a thatch over our heads to channel heavier rainfalls away."

"What about *beneath* us?" I said, wobbling on the thin limb. "What will keep us from falling between the branches?"

"We'll have to put some additional support beams in place. We'll use the twine to hold them together. Come on, it's time to go gather some more supplies."

Teuila led me back into the brush and we hacked down a handful of ten-foot-long poles about three inches in diameter. We carried the poles back to the banyan tree where she tied three crossbeams between two overhanging branches about fifteen feet off the ground. Then she placed the longer poles over the crossbeams, creating a webbed floor in the shape of a fan spanning between the radiating branches. After she taught me how to wrap and tie the twine so that each connection was tight and secure, it only took us a little over an hour to secure the floor. When we were done, she stood on top of the latticework and held out her hand.

"What do you think?" she said, inviting me to join her on our newly installed deck. "Does this look more comfortable than lying in a pit for the evening?"

I stepped gingerly onto the web of poles and flexed my knees to see if it would support my weight. The poles bent slightly, like a firm mattress.

Te' sat down on the web and smiled.

"Lie down beside me and see how comfortable it is."

I lowered my body onto the lattice, then lay on my back. The hard poles pressed into my flesh, especially where we'd lashed the ties around the connections.

"Not quite as comfortable as my mattress back home, but at least it's less lumpy than lying on the ground."

"We're not finished yet," Te' said. "We still haven't laid the carpet for our new home."

"*Carpet?*" I said, pinching my eyebrows imagining how the rough surface of our jerry-rigged deck could be converted into something as smooth and comfortable as the broadloomed floor of my house back home.

Teuila took my hand and we shimmied down a nearby vine, then she led me a little deeper into the forest where she hacked off some wide strips of bark from a mulberry tree. Then she climbed a coconut tree and passed down a handful of long palm fronds. When we returned to the banyan tree, we cut and lay the thick pieces of bark horizontally across the webbed floor until all the gaps between the poles were covered, then we sat down again.

"Better?" Te' asked.

"Definitely," I said, surprised at how similar her construction technique was to the conventional wood-frame houses I'd seen built in the Midwest. "It's still a bit hard though. Will we sleep on it like this?"

"There's one last step," she said, handing me one of the palm fronds. "Now we're going to make the carpet."

She began tearing the leaves into one-inch-wide strips, laying the strips on the floor in neat parallel lines. Then she placed another strip perpendicular across the leaves and deftly wove it over and under each of the underlying strands. With each successive strand, the leaves began to form a beautiful two-foot-square mat of interlaced leaves that looked as pretty as any placemat I'd find at Crate & Barrel or Target. When she finished, Te' lay the mat over the bark and asked me to sit on it. The soft leaves absorbed my weight and felt as soft as carpet.

"This feels almost as comfortable as my broadloom back home," I said, running my hands over the cushiony mat. "But it's much *prettier*. The two of us might be able to find a whole new vocation when we return to the United States. People would pay big bucks for this kind of natural fabric. What *else* can you use this stuff for?"

"We use the same weaving technique to make baskets, handbags, fishnets, all kinds of useful objects," Te' said.

I shook my head at the myriad uses of the island's natural resources.

"You guys really are self-sufficient on this little island, aren't you?"

Te' smiled at me as she thinned her eyes.

"Are you sure you want to go back to America?"

"Ask me in another week or two. I'm growing more fond of this lifestyle with each passing day."

"Help me weave some more mats then," Te' said, happy to see me beginning to enjoy the crafts of her tribe. "We need to cover the whole floor and add a few more layers for extra cushioning."

"Our very own wall-to-wall carpet," I nodded.

As the two of us continued weaving our natural-fiber mats, I looked up at Te' and smiled with a silly grin.

"What are you thinking?" she asked. "You look like a child who's just discovered her first pearl shell."

"I'm just so happy to be with you," I said. "All this nesting makes me realize there's nowhere else I'd rather be in the entire world."

14

———————

After we finished building our carpet of plant leaves, Te' and I made love until we fell asleep exhausted under the warm canopy of our new home. The last thing I remembered before my lids fell heavily over my eyes was the sight of the luminescent figs gleaming like Christmas tree ornaments in the fading light of the setting sun. In the morning, we picked some more fruit from the branches above us and playfully rubbed the sticky pulp all over our naked bodies before going for a cleansing dip in the lagoon.

As I emerged from the surf gazing at Te's sexy tanned body, I could hardly believe my luck. Fate, or happenstance, had landed me in a tropical paradise with the woman of my dreams. We spent the next half hour spearing fish for breakfast, then she placed the catch in a small holding pen we'd built out of large rocks near the shore.

"No fresh sushi for us this morning?" I asked, wondering why she wasn't filleting the fish right away as she had yesterday.

"I thought this might be a good time to teach you the next essential step in your survival skills. I need to teach you how to build a fire. You never know when you might need one. Besides, fresh fish tastes even better when it's grilled over an open flame."

"I was wondering when we were going to get around to that. But are you sure it's safe? I thought you wanted to keep a low profile in case your father came snooping around."

"There's an art to building a fire with a low smoke signature," Te' said. "Just as there is to building one with a *strong* smoke signal, which might come in handy later. Let me show you how to gather the necessary ingredients."

By now, the soles of my feet had fully healed and all the rubbing on the sandy beach and jungle floor had begun to form a thick, leathery second skin. I was surprised how comfortable it was to scamper across just about any surface without any external protection. More importantly, Teuila's cut had finally closed and she was able to remove her bandage and use her hand freely. Now the only items of clothing either one of us wore was my fading cargo shorts and her tapa-cloth dress, re-fashioned as a wrap-around loincloth. It felt exhilarating to traipse about our corner of the forest completely topless, unconcerned about the judging eyes of our neighbors.

Te' led me back into the forest where we began collecting dead twigs of varying thickness. When we had a handful, we returned to the edge of the beach where she dumped the pile in our old sleeping pit.

"There are three things to keep in mind when building a fire you don't want anybody to see," she instructed. "The first is the *smell* of burning material. We have an onshore breeze today, so at least we're protected from people approaching from the sea. The second is the appearance of the *flame*, which is why we're building this fire in a pit protected from surrounding lines of sight.

"But the biggest danger is from the *smoke*, which can be detected from further distances. The trick is to use the driest and smallest materials, so the fire burns more efficiently and doesn't smother. But first, we have to get it started, and for that we need some special materials."

Teuila grasped the shank of her adze and began scraping the blade along the edge of one of the longer branches, producing thin curly strands of dried pulp. Then she picked up the pile of filaments and rubbed them between her hands, breaking them into finer, shorter pieces.

"They look a bit like the strands we used yesterday to make cords," I said.

"You could use this to make rope also," she nodded. "But since this material is drier and more combustible, we're going to use it as a fire starter. But now that you mention it, we're going to need another three-foot long length of string. Do you think you could do that while I prepare the other elements? This time we'll need the rope to be a little thinner, so use about half the amount of strands for each side as before."

"No problem," I smiled. "After all the rope we created yesterday, that technique is indelibly imprinted on my brain."

While I lifted one of the fronds lying in the pit and began separating it into thin strands, Teuila chopped the long branch she'd shaved earlier into a two-foot length then chopped a small indent into the side of the branch on each end. Then she picked up a shorter dead branch about one inch in diameter and sharpened one end to a sharp point while rubbing the other end against a nearby rock to create a rounded stub.

"That doesn't look like a very efficient spear," I said, twisting the doubled ends of my palm strands into a thin rope.

"We're not going to use this as a spear," she said. "We're going to use it as a *drill*."

"A drill?" I said, raising my eyebrows. "But it doesn't have any thread."

My mind suddenly flooded with images of Tom Hanks' character in the movie Cast Away blistering his palms while he rolled a dry stick in his hands trying to build a fire.

"And what are you going to use to *turn* it? I'd hate for you to damage those pretty hands again."

"Don't worry," Te' said, smiling at me. "My hands aren't even going to touch it. We're going to build a *bow* to create the necessary friction."

While I looked at her with a puzzled expression, she picked up two pieces of flat driftwood and carved a small notch in the center of each board. When I finished splicing the strands of the palm leaf into a three-inch length of braided string, she took the cord and tied each end around the notches in the stick, bending it to create a tight bow.

"This is going to help us build a fire?" I said, shaking my head wondering how she could use the bow to generate any kind of friction.

"Oh ye of little faith," Te' smiled. "Watch and learn, my apprentice."

She took the short beveled stick and placed it against the inside edge of the string then twisted it a hundred and eighty degrees, creating a tight loop around the shaft. Then she positioned the rounded end of the stick into the notch of the larger piece of driftwood and placed the smaller piece of driftwood over the pointed end. Then she angled the bow parallel to the ground and began swiping it forward and back. As if by magic, the beveled stick began rotating rapidly in the shallow hole in the driftwood.

"Holy cats—you weren't kidding!" I said, amazed at the ingenuity of the device. "That way is so much more efficient than the way Tom Hanks did it!"

"Tom who—"

"It's just another one of our crazy Western stories that I'm sure you'd find amusing." I noticed Te' was pressing firmly on the top piece of driftwood as she sawed the bow. "Is there anything I can do to help?"

"When you begin to see smoke, place the shavings around the twisting piece of wood. We'll need to act fast to ensure the heat ignites."

I watched with fascination as Te' jerked the bow forward and back until the lower end of the stick started turning black and small wafts of smoke began rising from the fulcrum.

"Now, Jade!" she panted. "It needs fuel!"

I bunched the dry shavings around the edge of the stick, watching the smoke grow thicker and denser. When tiny orange embers appeared under the shavings, Te' bent down and cupped her hands around the pile, blowing gently into the nest. Within seconds, it erupted into flames as she began piling small twigs onto the pile. Eager to not have all her hard work go to waste in the fledgling fire, I began to throw a bunch of larger twigs and leaves onto the pile, throwing up a large plume of gray smoke.

"Be careful," she said, pulling the material off the flame. "We don't want to smother it. A fire needs plenty of oxygen to burn efficiently. If it has more fuel than it can burn at any one time, it just creates more smoke. The key is to feed it only as much as it needs to keep burning at the desired intensity."

Within seconds, the smoke began to dissipate as the fire steadily grew while she fed it increasingly large twigs and logs. When the flames reached a height of six inches or so, Te' looked up at me and nodded.

"We're almost ready to begin cooking our fish. Can you gather ten or fifteen small rocks so we can build a cradle for the grill?"

"Absolutely," I said, my mouth already watering at the idea of our eating warm food for the first time in three days.

When I returned to the pit with a handful of rocks, Te' placed them in a two-foot-wide circle around the fire then held some long branches above the top of the flame, charring them a dark brown color.

"I think we've got everything we need now," she nodded. "If you bring me two of the larger fish from the pen, I can cut them up and begin grilling them."

I went to the holding pen and snared two fish with a spear and carried them back to Teuila. She placed each one on the large piece of driftwood, cutting off its head and slicing it under its belly, removing the entrails and pulling the flesh away from the spiny skeleton. Then she spaced the charred poles about two inches apart over the top of our fire pit and placed the fillets on top of the makeshift grill. As the flesh began to sizzle, she fed the fire with medium-sized twigs, keeping the top of the flame a few inches below the slats.

"You're a master at this outdoorsy stuff, aren't you?" I said, shaking my head at how seamlessly she'd learned to live off the land.

"You get pretty handy at doing these things when you've been doing it your whole life," she said, turning the fillets over with her bare fingers. "Tonight, it'll be your turn. But for now, let's enjoy our new catch."

As we ate the perfectly charred fillets with our bare hands, I oohed and ahhed at how delicious the fish tasted.

"Ok," I said. "Scrap that basket-weaving idea I suggested earlier. I think your real calling is in the *kitchen*. I think we should open your own authentic Polynesian restaurant when we get back to the States."

15

———————

After we finished eating, Te' and I strolled hand-in-hand along the shore of the lagoon while I stopped periodically to pick up pretty shells strewn along the beach. I marveled at the magnitude and diversity of the beautiful specimens, sprinkled like gleaming jewels across the pink-colored sand. Displaying in all kinds of shapes and colors, I felt like a kid in a candy store as I picked up the fascinating objects and turned them over in my hands.

"I've been to a lot of beaches in my life," I remarked. "But nothing like this. I've never seen such a huge variety and quantity of seashells ever. This is truly a magical island."

"Maybe it's because there's no other islands for hundreds of miles around," Te' nodded. "Or maybe it's just because there's fewer tourists picking them up."

"Is *that* what I seem like to you?" I said, pinching my eyebrows in disappointment.

"Well," she said, squeezing my hand playfully, "I suppose you're still technically a tourist since you aren't officially *living* here. But if you keep learning all of my native island secrets, we'll have to make you an honorary citizen soon enough."

As I continued picking up and examining one beautiful shell after another, Teuila suddenly became silent as she gazed out to sea.

"What's it like on the other side of the ocean, Jade?" she asked. "Will I be like a fish out of water in America?"

I stopped and placed my hands over Te's shoulders as I gazed into her eyes.

"Not as long as you're with me. You speak near-perfect English, and you have an amazing array of practical skills. I can teach you everything else you need to thrive in my country, just like you're showing me here."

"Does that mean you want to stay with me?" she asked with a pained face. "I don't know what I'd do if I lost you again."

I pulled her close to me, feeling her heart beating against my chest. For the first time since my first college affair, I felt that she was the only one for me.

"I will never leave you, Teuila," I said, squeezing her arms. "I've never felt such strong feelings for anybody my whole life. You're the only one I want to be with—forever and ever."

As we held each other close, I peered down at the warm water washing over our feet. Bobbing on top of the surf I saw a skinny threaded shell, shaped like the head of a spear.

"Look at that," I said, pulling away for a moment. "This one almost looks like a unicorn horn."

"A *what*?" Te' said, furrowing her brow.

"It's another one of our silly Western fairy tales. But it also reminds me a bit of your ingenious little fire drill. I think I'd like to keep this one as a memento of my trip to your island."

Te' rolled it around in her palm and nodded as she peered up at me.

"Would you like me to attach it to a wrist bracelet made out of palm twine? That way you won't lose it."

"I'd like that very much," I said, kissing Te' gently. "My very own Anutian charm bracelet."

Suddenly, a larger swell washed over our feet and I peered down seeing a shiny green stone. It was about an inch and a half in diameter and shaped like a heart, glistening in the morning sun. I picked it up and examined it carefully, shaking my head in amazement. Under its emerald-green coating, I could see tiny specks of black embedded in the rock.

"I can't believe," I said, shaking my head. "I think this is a natural Jade stone. What are the odds we'd find it on a remote beach like this?"

Teuila picked up the stone and turned it around in her hand, rubbing it gently with her fingers.

"It's smooth and soft, just like you. What a perfect name for such a pretty stone. Do you mind if I keep this one to remind me of you?"

"Of course not, baby," I said, my eyes tearing up in a swell of emotions. "Do you know what this unusual shape means?"

"Is it from another one of your American fairy tales?"

"In a roundabout way," I chuckled. "It's a powerful symbol of love where I come from, symbolizing the shape of our hearts that beat strongly when we feel especially close to someone. And I can't think of a more perfect memento for you to take away from your native island, because that's exactly how I feel about you."

I paused, as I gazed gently into her eyes.

"I love you, Teuila."

"If that's what all this pounding in my chest is that I'm feeling right now, then I guess I'm in love with you too, Jade. I think the Gods are trying to tell us something."

As I looked at Te' with tears of joy streaming down my face, I noticed some movement at the edge of the cape a few hundred feet offshore. I narrowed my eyes trying to focus on the object, then my eyes flung wide open when I realized it was the bow of a canoe slicing through the water. I grabbed Te's hand and pulled her behind one of the dunes.

"What is it?" she said, recognizing the fear in my eyes.

"It's a canoe," I said, pointing in the direction of the craft. "I think your father is getting closer than we hoped."

Te' poked her head carefully above the dune and peered in the direction I'd pointed, then ducked her head back down, her chest puffing up and down in frantic bursts.

"Is it from your tribe?" I asked.

"It looks like it," she said. "If we stay hidden, hopefully they won't come ashore. We haven't left any visible signs of habitation nearby. They're probably just searching the boundary of the island to see if they can find any sign of us."

As we lay flat against the side of the dune, I heard the sound of rhythmic singing emanating from the lagoon, growing progressively louder, then it began to diminish. After another minute or so, Teuila lifted her head again.

"What are you doing?!" I said, grabbing her hand. "They might see you!"

"It sounds like they're almost past the lagoon," she said. "I just want to see who they sent out to look for me."

Te' peered over the top of the sand for a long moment as her eyes grew wider and wider, then she ducked down again into the pit.

"What is it?" I said. "You look like you've seen a ghost."

"It might as well have been," she said. "Those men weren't from my tribe. They must be from the tribe on the other side of the island. And they weren't singing. Those were *war chants*. I think they have something far more sinister on their mind."

16

—————

"There's another tribe on this island?" I asked. "Why didn't you mention this before?"

"I didn't think it was important," Te' said. "It's a big island and they usually stick to themselves, so I didn't think we'd cross them. But they're venturing further afield than usual and coming from the direction of my village, which worries me."

"Have the two tribes never had contact before?"

"Many years ago, we all lived together in peaceful harmony. But when a power struggle erupted between the chief and my grandfather, my *tama matua* was killed in battle and the chief banished the other faction to the other side of the island. My father became the chief of our clan and built fortifications to keep the other tribe away. Since then, everybody's been content to mind their own business. At least until now."

"What makes you think they mean to threaten your village?"

"It's unusual for them to venture so far from their side of the island. Their normal fishing grounds are to the north, not the west. And they were wearing war paint. But it was what they were *chanting* that worries me the most."

"What were they saying?"

"Something about taking back their land and reunifying their clan. I think they intend to recapture the women and children and kill off all the men. This was probably an advance reconnaissance mission to scope out our village's defenses before sending in their full war party."

"Oh my God!" I said, widening my eyes in horror. "What do you intend to do?"

Teuila paused for a moment as her gaze darted from side to side in thought. Then she looked up at me and frowned.

"I don't think I have any other choice. I've got to warn my father of their intentions before my tribe gets slaughtered. I'd never forgive myself if I didn't do everything in my power to save them."

I peered into Te's brown eyes, considering the implications of her plan.

"But aren't you risking your *own* freedom if you go back? After you've already disobeyed his wishes, he'll never let you out of his sight a second time."

"I can sneak in under cover of darkness and warn my nona. We can trust her to protect our safety. She'll tell my father, then we can retreat back to our hiding place."

"While you worry about the safety of your family? Do you really think you'll be able to stay here while there's a battle raging on the other side of the island?"

Te' looked at me with a pained expression. I could tell she was torn between the loyalty to her family and her love for me. My stomach sank, realizing I was putting her in an impossible situation.

She paused for a long moment as she considered her predicament.

"There might be another way," she finally said. "If I sneak into the other tribe's camp, maybe I can gather information about their plan. If there's still enough time, my father might be able to set up a meeting to defuse the tension. If the other tribe realizes that we know about their plan, hopefully they'll be less likely to attack."

"That sounds almost as dangerous as your *first* idea," I said, shaking my head in dismay. "What can I do to help?"

"I don't think you should go anywhere near either village. Your blonde hair and white skin will stick out like a sore thumb and be that much easier to detect. The best thing you can do is hide out here and wait for me to return. Now that you've learned the essential survival skills, you should be fine on your own for a couple of days."

"Screw that!" I said, fearing for Te's safety. "I'm not letting you go there alone. What if you get caught? At the very least, I can be a lookout and send for help if you get captured. You mean far too much to me. I'm not taking any chances that we'll get separated again."

Te' peered into my eyes and sighed in resignation.

"Okay. You can come with me—but only if you promise to stay further back while I scope out the situation. There's no point in both of us getting captured.

"Besides," she said, scanning my bare breasts, "there's no telling what they'd want to do with you if they got their hands on you."

"It's a deal."

"Come on then," she said, grabbing my hand. "There's no time to lose. We need to be there when the scouting team returns to their village so I can hear their plans."

Teuila picked up her adze and led me through the jungle, staying a few hundred yards away from shore to keep out of sight from the canoe team. Every now and then, a thin break in the brush revealed the wide expanse of blue surrounding the island, and she stopped to earmark the position of the passing boat.

"Do you know your way to their village?" I asked after she paused for another moment.

"Not as easily from this side of the island," she said. "But I've spied on them before on some of my longer hikes from my village. As long as we keep following the canoe, they should lead us directly there."

"Assuming they're heading to *their* village and not yours," I said, wondering if the angry tribesmen were already planning to attack.

"It's not a large enough team to overtake our village, even with the element of surprise. I'm ninety-nine percent sure this was just a scouting mission in preparation for the main invasion."

"It's that other one percent I'm worried about," I said, peering at

Te's primitive hatchet. "If it came to an armed conflict, how would you defend yourself? Shouldn't we have brought the fire bow with us just in case?"

"That wouldn't do much good against an army of hundreds. It's too small to function as a weapon. Besides," she smiled, "that's one skill I still haven't taught you."

I shook my head at how quickly everything had begun spiraling out of control

"And here I thought the people of Anuta were such a peace-loving tribe."

"We normally are," Teuila said. "But some men's egos are easily offended. It appears that this next generation of chiefs still have a bone to pick."

"I just hope it won't be *our* bones they're picking over in the end," I said, re-imagining scenes of cannibalism among the warring tribes.

17

D usk was beginning to set in as we approached a flickering light near the edge of the forest. Teuila held up her hand and crouched low as she peered through the trees. The team of canoeists were pulling their vessel up onto a sandy beach framed by thatch-roofed huts similar to those in her own village. A gray-haired man wearing a grass skirt approached the boatmen, flanked by a group of other young tribesmen. They paused to confer briefly on the beach, then they walked up the path and sat around a large fire burning in the center of their square.

Te' turned around and handed me her stone adze and small filleting knife.

"You stay here," she said. "I'm going to try getting closer to see if I can make out what they're saying."

I looked at the basic implements, batting my eyes wondering how they could possibly serve me better than her.

"What do you expect me to do with these?"

"Nothing, hopefully," she smiled. "They'll just slow me down. But you might need them if I get caught."

"What? To tomahawk the bad guys and cut you free?"

"Don't even think about trying that," she said. "If I don't return within the next hour, can you find your way back to my village to warn my father?"

I paused, looking up at the darkening sky.

"Not at dark, that's for sure."

"It will be easier if you double back to our lagoon, then try to pick up the trail from there. Worst-case scenario, just stay close to the beach and follow the island around until you get to our village. It might take a little longer, but at least that way you won't get lost."

"You're making this sound increasingly ominous," I said, wrinkling my brow. "Please be careful, Te'. Don't go any closer than you have to."

"Don't worry, my love," she smiled. "I've done this many times before. I should be back before the sun disappears over the horizon."

Teuila kissed me gently, then crept into the woods in the direction of the village. As I watched her tip-toeing through the trees, I marveled at how quietly she was able to pass through the dense brush hardly making a sound.

That's my girl, I nodded, peering up at the whispering canopy. *Don't even let the snakes know you're there.*

After a few minutes, she passed out of sight, and I squinted through the thicket, focusing on the circle of tribesmen seated around the fire.

It's true, I thought, remembering what she'd said to me earlier. *Why is it always the men who need to mix things up and create conflict?* I closed my eyes and imagined Teuila and me back in our little tree-house, living a peaceful life in our isolated stretch of paradise. I was in no hurry returning to all the stress and noise of Western civilization.

I picked up her adze and ran my finger gently over the edge of its blade. It was heavier than I imagined, and surprisingly sharp. I studied the head and shape of the handle, admiring how her people had fashioned such an effective tool out of basic materials. The stone head had been filed down to a sharp edge, with the butt of the blade supported by the extended arm of the ninety-degree handle. Tight cords of woven bark wrapped around the shank, securing it tightly to the frame. As I held it up wondering if it could be wielded as a weapon if the need arose, a deep masculine chant suddenly arose from the direction of the fire.

I peered through the copse of trees and saw that the men had raised to a standing position as they danced in a circle around the fire, flexing their spears and chanting loudly, just as I'd seen Manaia and the other young warriors from Teuila's tribe demonstrate a few nights earlier.

Maybe they'll kill each other off and let the two of us live peacefully on our own, I thought, shaking my head at their belligerent behavior.

I squinted my eyes, glancing from side to side to see any sign of Teuila. For the first time in days, I wished I'd had my phone or watch to keep track of time. It seemed like an eternity since she'd snuck off in the direction of the camp.

Where are you? I cursed under my breath, fearing she'd been discovered.

Seconds later, I heard some branches rustling behind me and I ducked defensively behind a bush.

"Jade!" Teuila whispered as I poked my head up.

"Thank heavens you're okay," I said, pulling her tightly against me. Her bare breasts were warmer than usual, toasted from the heat of the enormous fire in the village.

"I said I'd never leave you again," she said, kissing me sweetly on the lips.

I held her closely, feeling her heart beating against mine, then I pulled away and looked into her eyes.

"Did you hear anything?" Do you have any clearer sense about their plans for attacking your village?"

"Yes," she said, tightening her face in concern. "And it's even worse than I thought. They intend to attack two nights from now, during the next full moon. We haven't any time to lose. I have to get back to my village immediately to warn my father."

Teuila picked up the blades from the ground beside me and pulled me back through the forest in the opposite direction of the camp. As we scurried through the brush, I shook my head in dismay. I wasn't sure which posed the greater threat—her father, or this new tribe.

18

———

By the time we wound our way through the dark tangle of jungle to the other side of the island, the first glimmer of morning light had begun to appear over her village lagoon. Teuila paused at the edge of the forest overlooking the main square and peered in the direction of her hut. Everything appeared to be quiet and still, save the occasional squeal of a seabird returning from the surf with its morning catch of fish.

I glanced at Te', shaking more out of fear than from the cool onshore breeze.

"So what's your plan?" I said. "Everyone still appears to be sleeping."

"I'm going to sneak up behind my hut and try to get the attention of my nona. I want you to stay here and keep a lookout. If you see any unusual activity, whistle softly twice in succession."

"Won't that attract the suspicion of the tribespeople?"

"Not if they're still asleep. Just try to sound like one of those seabirds."

"Fat chance of that," I said, realizing I still had much to learn about her island. "What should I do if you get caught?"

"Same thing we talked about earlier. It'll be safer for you to return to our lagoon until things quiet down. I'll steal away when I can and find you."

I shook my head and furrowed my brow at the fragility of her plan.

"You might not have enough time. The other tribe is going to attack in two days."

"Once my father finds out about their plans, I'll be the least of his concerns. He won't be able to spare any extra tribesmen to watch over me. It shouldn't be too hard to break away during all the distraction."

I placed my hands around Te's arms and stared into her eyes.

"Just tell me no matter what happens that you won't stay and fight. I don't know what I'd do if I lost you."

Teuila smiled at me as she cupped my face and kissed me gently. Then she pulled the heart-shaped stone we'd found on the beach out of a pouch in her loincloth and patted her chest with the palm of her hand to symbolize the beating of her heart.

"You'll always be with me, Jade. *Forever and ever.*"

I pulled her close to me and squeezed her tightly against my chest.

"Please be careful."

Te' nodded, then crept quietly around the perimeter of the camp toward the chief's hut. As she disappeared behind the cabins, I glanced toward the beach and noticed Manaia stowing something in one of the village's outrigger canoes. It seemed odd that he'd be up alone at this early hour and I peered back toward Teuila, unsure if she'd seen him. For a moment, I pursed my lips preparing to send a warning signal. But he seemed unaware of her presence and I decided it was best not to risk any further distraction.

When I looked back in Manaia's direction, I noticed a flickering light emanating from inside the hull, as smoke began to rise above the gunwales.

He's setting fire to their outrigger canoe! I realized, pinching my eyebrows in confusion. *Why would he be doing that?*

Teuila had told me how important the village's few outrigger canoes were to their tribe and how long it took them to hollow them out from the thick trunks of the island's breadfruit trees. If they needed them as their sole method of navigation around the island and for deep sea fishing, what purpose would he have in destroying them?

Then it suddenly dawned on me. The timing of his act of sabotage was too coincidental. He must be a *spy* for the other tribe! By virtue of his status as Teuila's chosen mate, he'd have unique access to her father and his plans for protecting the village. He must have been offered some kind of preferential treatment by the other tribe for him to take such drastic action.

I turned back in Teuila's direction just as she slipped behind the rear of her family's hut. If I gave the warning signal now, she mightn't hear me and just attract the attention of Manaia. As I swiveled my head frantically back and forth between the two scenes at opposite ends of the village square, I heard some rustling coming from the chief's cabin. A few moments later, Te's grandmother appeared at the front entrance. She slowly swiped the door covering aside and tiptoed down the front steps toward the back of the cabin.

Te' pressed her finger to her lips when she saw her nona, and two women retreated further up the path away from their hut. I could see the two of them talking quietly at the edge of the forest, then her grandmother began gesticulating wildly with her hands, obviously upset about what Teuila had told her. When I turned back in the direction of the beach, I noticed two more canoes had been set aflame and there was no sign of Manaia.

I wasn't sure if he had escaped into the bush to rejoin his comrades, or if he'd retreated to his cabin to maintain the guise that the other tribe had sabotaged their canoes. Either way, Teuila needed to be warned so she could notify her grandmother of the betrayal within their ranks. I pursed my lips and strained to whistle as loudly as I dared.

It took longer than I hoped to attract Teuila's attention, and by the time she finally looked in my direction, the flap of her hut's front door swung open as her father stood in the entrance, peering from side to side. From her position many yards away from her family's hut, she was unaware that her father had been roused. I wanted to scream out loud to her and tell her to run, but by now many of the villagers had begun to stream out of their huts, attracted by the unusual smell of burning wood.

When the chief caught sight of the burning canoes, he hollered something in his native tongue and a swarm of tribesmen converged on the beach trying to put out the flames with baskets of seawater. But it was too little, too late. By the time they were finally extinguished and the gray smoke stopped pouring out of the hulls, all three of the village's outrigger canoes had been cut in half by the charred ruins of the fire.

When I looked back toward Teuila's hut, I was horrified to see that Manaia had found her and was holding her arms tightly behind her back as her father stormed back up the path in their direction. When he confronted his daughter, they hollered at each other for a few moments as Te' struggled helplessly against Manaia's hold. Her younger sisters and brothers began streaming out of the hut, and the chief muttered something to Manaia, motioning for him to take Teuila inside.

When they disappeared behind the door curtain, the chief castigated nona for helping his daughter then yelled to the tribesmen returning from the beach, pointing into the woods in my direction.

"*Saili latou!*" he shouted, as the angry warriors spread out into the jungle.

19

———

As the tribesmen darted toward me, my mind raced trying to devise an escape plan. All I could think about was Teuila's dream where her father tied me to a stake and burned me alive after he found us. It seemed like an extreme punishment for two lovers following their hearts, but from the crazed look in his eyes, I couldn't rule anything out right now. And with her jealous boyfriend demonstrating increasingly suspicious behavior, I'd have one more enemy wanting me out of the picture.

With the warriors fanning out in every direction, I knew running wasn't an option. I'd quickly be overtaken by their superior speed and familiarity with the terrain. And climbing another tree was out of the question. With so many eyes probing for the white girl, I'd stick out like a polar bear in the dark jungle. My biggest liability was my light skin and hair color. I needed to find a way to blend into the landscape —fast.

Picking up the stone adze Teuila had left behind, I hacked away at the ground, exposing the dark volcanic topsoil. I clawed at it with my fingertips and rubbed it all over my blonde hair and upper body, then shrunk behind a leafy bush as low to the ground as possible. Within seconds, I heard footsteps approaching my position with the sound of sticks beating the bushes.

Lying as still as possible not even daring to breathe, I closed my eyes praying that my clumsy camouflage job would keep me hidden for a few moments longer. The slapping sounds grew louder and louder until it seemed as if one of the searchers was standing right over top of me. Suddenly, something struck the ground next to me and I opened my eyes to see the sharp point of a stone-tipped spear plunging into the bush.

Jesus! I thought, realizing how serious these tribesmen were in apprehending their prey. My mind began to spin with all the possibilities. *Was it really me they were after? Had Teuila's father asked for me to be returned dead or alive? Maybe they thought I was the one who'd set fire to the canoes? Or were they looking for the saboteurs from the other tribe? Had Teuila even had a chance to tell her father about their plans to attack the village?*

While the tribesman continued jabbing his spear into the bush, I watched his dusty feet dancing over the ground not far from the gash I'd made with the adze. From my perspective inches away, it looked like an obvious mark inflicted by a recent intruder. As I lay on the ground with the sharp tool digging into my stomach, I wished I'd had the presence of mind to cover the fresh soil with some leaves.

But just as the tribesman stopped spearing the bush and I thought I was in the clear, I noticed some unusual movement sliding along the ground out of the corner of my eye. It was another three-foot-long snake winding through the brush! All the beating of the bushes in the surrounding area had scared it from its roost, and it was moving directly toward me. And this time, I knew that if it bit me, I couldn't count on Teuila and Nona to nurse me back to health.

As it slithered up over my arm toward my shoulder, I lay deathly still, holding my breath. At least I was aware of its presence this time. If I could just keep from flinching, maybe it would think I was another dead branch on the ground and leave me alone. I watched its forked tongue flickering in and out of its mouth like a divining rod.

When it got to within inches of my face, I closed my eyes and prayed it didn't view me as a threat.

Why would it want to bite me? I thought. *I'm too big for it to eat, and I'm not threatening it in any way.* I remembered my father telling me on family excursions into the cottage country of northern Wisconsin that rattlesnakes were threatened by the vibrations of the earth in their vicinity. *As long as I remain still, it should leave me alone.*

As the snake paused next to my ear, I clenched my neck muscles unconsciously, expecting it to strike. But after a few seconds that felt like an eternity, it continued winding its body over my back and down the side of my torso, until it slithered off into the brush. The moment it left contact with my body, I gasped in a breath of fresh air as slowly as possible, trying not to make any sounds that might alert the nearby posse. I'd been so focused on the serpentine intruder, that I hadn't even realized the tribesman who'd been searching in my area had moved on. As I strained to listen for any nearby activity, I heard the sound of shouting receding into the distance, and I finally began to relax my muscles, pulling the sharp axe from underneath my body.

Now what? I thought, realizing I was still in a dangerous position, surrounded by a small army of warriors on the lookout for any suspicious movement. *How long should I stay concealed in my precarious hiding place? Should I wait a little longer to see what the chief intends to do with Teuila? Will he stop looking for me when he realizes he needs to start preparing for the impending attack?*

I had no way of knowing what kind of arrangements Te's father had made to prevent her escape. She'd told me to return to our lagoon and wait for her to come back, but what if she was tied up or had a twenty-four-hour guard? Maybe I could create some kind of distraction and cut her free.

I looked at my small stone adze and shook my head. With my luck, I'll get myself caught too and be no good for either one of us. I'll just have to spend the night here and see if I could find an opening at first light. I peered up at the bright moon, noticing that it was almost perfectly round.

Either way, we've got less than forty-eight hours before the crap hits the fan and someone's going to get hurt.

20

———

Teuila sat against the knobby walls of her hut with her hands tied behind her back, staring angrily into Manaia's eyes. He returned her gaze with equal intensity, as his lips curled into a menacing sneer. His eyes darted over her exposed body, taking particular interest in her loincloth wrapped tightly around her hips and waist.

She lifted her knees and pressed them against her chest, folding her arms around her legs. The idea of Manaia violating her made her sick to her stomach. Beyond the fact that she was madly in love with Jade, there'd always been something sinister about him that gave her the creeps.

"What do you *want* with me?" she asked in her native Samoan tongue.

"What makes you think I need anything from you right now?" he said.

"The way you're looking at me, for one thing. I've seen that look on men's faces before. I'm never going to let you touch me like that."

"We'll see about that," Manaia snickered, glancing back down in the direction of her crotch. "We'll soon be married and you'll have no other choice. And this time you won't be able to run off with your girlfriend. We'll either find her soon or she'll perish in the jungle. Without you looking after her, she'll die of starvation or get bitten by another snake. Either way, there's no way you're going to escape this time."

Teuila huffed at Manaia, realizing he had no idea just how well equipped Jade was to survive in the jungle with her newfound skills. As long as she could evade the search dragnet currently underway, she should have no difficulty looking after herself until Te' could make her way back to their lagoon.

"You could *never* satisfy me like she does," Teuila taunted. "You men are only good for two things. Making war and making babies. And I have no interest in either of your plans. Her friends will soon come back for her and when they do, you'll never see me again."

"I wouldn't be so sure about that," Manaia said. "Her tiny crew will no match for our tribe of warriors. We'll be ready for them if they return, then remove any sign they'd ever been here."

Teuila thinned her eyes as she studied Manaia's face. Although her father was no fan of Western interlopers, she knew it wasn't his style to kill outside visitors. As chief of the village, Manaia and the others were still bound to follow his commands.

"My father would never do that," she said. "You know as well as he, that that would just invite more external aggression."

"Only if the outsiders have reason to suspect foul play. We have plenty of ways to conceal any evidence of visitation to our island. And besides, your father won't be chief for much longer. Soon, *I'll* be the one calling the shots."

Teuila squeezed her eyes together, unsure what he was alluding to. But right now, she had bigger concerns. She needed to warn her father of the impending attack and make sure Jade got to safety. She'd worry about Manaia later. The smirk on his face soon disappeared when the flap covering her hut's front door swung open and her father stormed into the hut.

"Where is she?!" he shouted angrily, standing over his daughter.

"Who?" Teuila said coyly.

"The Western woman! She can't have gotten far and you must know her hiding places. Tell me now!"

"I honestly don't know," Teuila said. "But you have more important matters to be concerned with right now. The *Tuange* tribe is planning to attack our village tomorrow night. You need to prepare our defenses or take preemptive action."

The chief stepped back, placing his fists on his hips.

"How do you know this?" he asked.

"I overheard their warriors discussing their plans when I followed one of their scouting missions back to their camp. They intend to steal the women and children and kill all of our men. You have to act quickly."

Manaia suddenly stood up and stepped toward me with an angry expression on his face.

"She's lying!" he said. "She's just making up this crazy story to distract our attention while she tries to escape again. We need to focus our manpower on making sure she doesn't get away. What she's been doing with that fair-skinned woman is an abomination."

"Shut up!" the chief said, turning toward Manaia, thrusting his hand against his chest. "*I* make the decisions around here, and we need to listen to Teuila's warning. I know what the *Tuange* is capable of, and we cannot take any chances at being ill-prepared."

Teuila's father swung back around and looked sternly into his daughter's eyes.

"Did they say if they planned to attack by land or sea? Were they the ones who burned our canoes?"

Teuila looked at her father with a confused expression and shook her head.

"They didn't mention anything about destroying our canoes. I got the impression they were going to wait for the full moon before they struck out for our camp. What do you intend to do, father?"

The chief stood for a long moment pondering his options, then motioned to Manaia.

"Gather the other tribesmen in the village square. We will need to organize our battle plans quickly. I will make sure my daughter doesn't escape again."

When Manaia rushed out of the hut, Te' struggled to stand. Her father placed his hand gently on her head and motioned for her to stay seated.

"I'm sorry to have to do this Teuila, but I can't afford to lose you again." He kneeled down and wrapped some thick strands of hibiscus twine around her binds then tied the new rope around a sturdy branch in the side wall. "You'll have to stay here until we sort this other matter out. And this time Nona won't be here to help you."

As her father stormed out of the hut and Te' struggled against the sharp twine digging into her wrists, a lone tear dribbled down the front of her cheek. It looked like regardless of the outcome of the looming war between the tribes, she'd soon be bound into the arms of one power-hungry man or another. She wiggled her leg and felt Jade's stone rubbing against her thigh.

Stay safe, my love, she thought. *Hopefully at least one of us can escape this madness.*

21

———

I woke up at first light the following morning with a growl in my stomach. It had been twenty-four hours since I'd eaten anything, and I swallowed hard realizing I was left to my own devices to feed myself. But I had more pressing immediate matters to attend to. I needed to see what had become of Teuila and find a way to extract the two of us safely from the village. We only had a little over thirty-six hours before all hell would break loose in the camp. The safest place for both of us would be as far away on the other side of the island as possible.

I slowly lifted myself up and parted the leaves of my bush, peering in the direction of the village. The square was busier than usual for this time of the morning, with sentries posted at opposite ends of the esplanade. A large group of tribesmen sat in the middle of the square sharpening stones, tying them carefully to the ends of long spears and arrows. Manaia paced around the circle, gesturing and barking orders like he was in command.

I glanced in the direction of Te's hut and saw that a guard was standing on all four sides of the structure. There was no sign of Nona or the chief, and from the stillness of the cabin, I assumed that Teuila and her family were still sleeping. After another twenty minutes or so, her father stepped through the front door and called to one of the tribesmen in the working group. He walked to the bottom of the steps, and as Nona and Teuila's siblings streamed out the front entrance, the chief motioned for them to follow the tribesman toward the lagoon. I took this to mean that Teuila had notified him of the other tribe's invasion plans and that he was taking no chances leaving the women or children unattended.

At least he's aware of the danger now and is taking necessary precautions, I nodded.

But where was Teuila? Why hadn't he sent her down to the lagoon with the rest of her family to attend to her morning ablutions? Was he going to leave her under armed guard in the hut all day, where she'd have to take care of her private affairs in a bowl?

I shook my head at the barbarity of his decision.

He's not taking any chances with her, I thought. *It's going to be next to impossible for her to escape with an armed guard surrounding her cabin and with her grandmother not allowed to go anywhere without an escort.*

I glanced toward Manaia again, wondering what he was up to. After destroying the village's only means of marine navigation, instead of slipping into the forest to join his comrades from the other clan, for some reason he'd chosen to stay behind and help his tribe prepare for the attack.

Was he going to join his tribe in battle, then turn on them at the last second? Or was he waiting for the right time to slip away and alert the other tribe that his village had been forewarned of their intentions?

I still wasn't sure if the chief intended to defend his village against the attack or if he planned to take preemptive action. Either way, Manaia couldn't be trusted. I needed to find a way to warn Teuila and her father before it was too late. The other tribe looked to be at least twice as large as Teuila's. The only chance her group would have to prevail in the looming battle was to maintain the element of surprise. Manaia surely would have already informed the other side of her village's defenses and battle readiness. If he were to switch sides in the heat of the fight, that could easily turn the tide in favor of the other clan.

But how could I get close enough to her hut to send her a signal? Trying to whistle again was out of the question. After my last pitiful attempt to mimic the local wildlife drew her father's attention, I couldn't risk betraying my position again. My only chance was to leave some kind of message with her grandmother. But how could I draw her attention when she was being watched so closely?

I paused to rack my brain with every possibility. Then it suddenly dawned on me. Teuila had told me she'd studied many of the same subjects as me during the time missionaries visited the island. What if she could *read* English as well as she spoke it? If I could get her grandmother to pass her a note, I could warn her about Manaia's intentions and see if her father might relax his restrictions.

But how could I write her a message? I didn't have any writing material, and I'd left my phone in my bag in her hut when we escaped three days ago. I looked around for any object that might serve as a writing tablet, then I noticed a mulberry tree like the ones Te' said her tribe used to make their skirts and dresses. I knew that the inner layer of its bark was thin and pale. If I could strip a piece off, maybe I could carve a message into its pulp-like skin.

I got up on all fours and crawled toward the tree, keeping a close eye on the village square to make sure nobody saw me. When I reached the tree, I used my small paring knife to cut a four-by-six-inch piece of bark off the trunk, then I lay it flat on the ground and found a small sharp stone nearby. Realizing I wouldn't have long before Nona and the rest of Te's family returned from the lagoon, I scrawled a rough message into the backside of the strip.

Watching close by. Manaia burned the canoes. Warn chief. Will wait for you at our lagoon.

I hid my adze and knife under the bush then stuffed the piece of bark in the back of my shorts and carefully circled around toward the lagoon. By now, I had a decent understanding of the layout of the village, and it didn't take long to wend my way through the woods near the trailhead to the bathing lagoon. When I got there, I saw

Nona and the children walking single-file up the path with the tribesman urging them on from the rear.

I waited until she was close to my position, then I shook the branch of a low-lying tree to get her attention. She glanced in my direction and when she saw me hiding in the brush, she paused as I tossed the piece of bark toward her. The guard yelled something to her, then she kneeled on the ground and leaned over, pretending to be sick. The tribesman hurried past her with the rest of the children as he grimaced in her direction. Nona picked up the piece of bark and noticing the strange writing symbols on it, tucking it under her tapa dress. Then she nodded toward me and joined the rest of the group while the guard waited impatiently.

As the group continued marching up the path toward Teuila's hut, I doubled back to my previous hiding place and waited for her grandmother to deliver the news. When they returned to the hut, the chief stood on the front porch with his arms crossed and ordered them all back inside. A few minutes later, Nona stepped through the front door carrying a large wooden bowl and the chief jerked his head in the direction of the jungle. She tiptoed down the steps cradling the bowl carefully, then disappeared behind the hut and returned a few minutes later, sprinkling some loose sand inside the container.

So it's true, I grimaced in disgust. *The chief is making her do her business in a pail. At least it's affording her a little privacy to receive my message.*

Nona disappeared back inside the hut for a few minutes, then she stepped out and spoke quietly with the chief as she glanced nervously in Manaia's direction. The chief shook his head angrily, then he flipped open the door flap and stormed back into the cabin. I could hear he and Teuila talking in strained voices, then her father stepped out onto the porch and motioned for Manaia to join them in the hut. For the next minute or two, the sound of angry voices emanated from the building as the rest of the tribesmen turned and looked at one another in confusion.

Finally, the two men stepped out of the cabin and the chief said something to Manaia as he pointed toward the men working in the square. Manaia scurried to join them, but this time he sat quietly among them, joining them in their labor. Then the chief sat on his chair on the porch, motioning for the four guardsmen guarding his hut to maintain their positions.

That's it? I thought. *He's letting Manaia off scot-free? What about Teuila? Is he just going to leave her in there? Didn't she tell him about Manaia's treacherous behavior?* He must have convinced the chief that she was making it all up to drive a wedge between them in the hope of rejoining her white girlfriend.

It looks like we're on our own again babe, I sighed.

At least it looked like her father had temporarily demoted Manaia and was going to keep him in his sights for the time being. However he chose to address the coming assault, I couldn't help much sitting here in the crossfire between the two tribes. Besides, my stomach was getting increasingly noisy, telling me I had to get something to eat soon. I decided to head back to our private lagoon and try to catch some fish while I planned my next steps.

22

It took me longer than expected to find my way back to our lagoon on the other side of the island. After getting lost a number of times, I had to retrace my steps more than once to get back on the trails that Te' had marked. By the time I saw the familiar shape of our crescent-shaped beach, the sun was almost setting over the horizon. I knew I wouldn't have long to catch some fish in the fading light, so I grabbed a spear from the treehouse and waded into the shallow waters of the lagoon.

Without Te' herding the fish toward me with the big rake, it was hit and miss trying to spear one, but I got lucky when a big grouper ambled nearby and I snared it on my second attempt. By this time, I was so hungry that I didn't bother trying to build a fire and instead tore open the flesh with my paring knife and dug into it like a grizzly bear eating fresh salmon.

When my stomach finally began to quiet down, I paused to consider my options. I knew that I could spend the night holed up in our treehouse in the hope that Teuila would find a way to steal away from her camp under the cover of darkness. But what if she couldn't escape? And what if her tribe lost the battle? What would the other tribe do to her? Even if her clan won, her father wouldn't be likely to let his guard down as long as I was on the lam.

I had to do something. I couldn't just wait here and pray that the odds rolled in our favor. There were far too many variables that could swing this in the wrong direction. With Manaia working to undermine his own tribe, there was no telling which way the battle could go. At the very least, I could keep an eye on the other tribe and send a warning to Nona and Teuila if I recognized any change in their plans.

I grabbed a few figs from our banyan tree to wash down the sushi, then I went for a quick swim in the lagoon to wash all the filth from my body. It felt refreshing to be clean again, and for a moment I thrust my hand down the front of my cargo shorts remembering the image of Teuila's naked body walking toward me in the lagoon. Then I quickly buried my leftovers and picked up my adze and pocket knife, following the trail toward the other tribe's camp.

With the light beginning to fade over the horizon, I struggled to remember the path Teuila had taken to make her way to the other village. After an hour or so, I became lost again and headed toward the shore to follow my way around the edge of the island. I knew the other tribe's camp was in a clockwise direction from our lagoon. If I just followed the shore, sooner or later it would lead me to their camp.

As I stumbled along the rocky shoreline, trying not to step on any sharp shells or sea urchins, I glanced up toward the sky. The moon was almost full, casting a bright glow over this side of the island. At least I could see what I was stepping on for the most part. The last thing I needed right now was to crack open the soles of my feet again. Whatever was going to go down over the next twenty-four hours, I knew I needed to remain fleet of foot and nimble.

As the moon continued rising over the shimmering sea, I began to hear the sound of men chanting in the distance. I peered to my right and saw the flicker of a fire burning in the distance. Recognizing I was getting close to the other tribe's camp, I stepped off the rocky shore and began to wind my way through the thick woods in the direction of the light. When I got to within a few hundred yards of the camp, I paused near a tree and crouched down low to get a closer look at the tribesmen assembled around the fire.

A large twig suddenly snapped underneath me, and I cursed under my breath for not being more careful where I stepped. Teuila had made it look so easy passing through the thick brush like a jungle cat, barely making a sound. Apparently, I still had a lot to learn about how to behave like a true Anutian.

When I looked back in the direction of the campfire, the number of tribesmen appeared to have thinned somewhat, and I wondered if they were sending out another reconnaissance mission to Teuila's side of the island. At least Manaia was nowhere to be seen, I thought. He's probably too afraid to try slipping away now that Teuila's father suspects him of foul play. He's undoubtedly waiting until the last moment to see which way the battle is going before he chooses which side to fight on. My lips curled into a sickening scowl imagining Te' wedded to that coward.

Suddenly, I heard some bushes rustling behind me and I twisted around to see what it was. Peering up in horror, I saw a band of painted warriors surrounding me with their spears raised over my head.

Damn, I thought, immediately recognizing I shouldn't have been so eager to bathe in the lagoon. My white skin and yellow hair were shining in the moonlight like a beacon atop a lighthouse.

23

As the tribesmen shouted at me, angrily stabbing their spears in my direction, I shrunk back against the tree, fearing for my life. I had no idea what they would make of a half-naked white woman spying on their camp. From Teuila's description of the rift between the clans, I wasn't even sure they'd seen a Westerner before. One thing was for certain—they were in no mood for a peaceful welcoming committee.

One of the warriors noticed my adze lying on the ground and he picked it up, shouting something at me. I shook my head indicating I didn't understand what he was saying. He motioned to two of the other tribesmen and they lifted me up, finding my steel paring knife tucked under the waistband of my cargo shorts. He ran his fingers over the sharp blade and flinched when it drew blood.

Great, I thought. *Their first exposure to a white person, and the first thing they find are two weapons of mass destruction.*

The lead warrior said something to the other tribesmen, and they grabbed my arms, dragging me in the direction of the village. As I stumbled to catch my footing, I peered toward the large bonfire burning in the center of their camp. All my fears of being burned alive and eaten by cannibals were suddenly rekindled. I twisted and screamed for them to let me go, but the two men just tightened their grip on my arms until they were throbbing in pain.

As we approached the main camp, the tribesmen sitting around the fire turned toward me with puzzled expressions on their faces. Everyone was wearing grass skirts with war paint streaked across their naked upper bodies and faces. An older man with a beaded vest and elaborate headdress stood to greet the search party. The two tribesmen holding me marched me within three feet of the old man, then they forced me to kneel on the ground in front of him. I peered up at him and they shouted at me, pushing my head back down. I shook my head, unsure what they wanted me to do and the guards puckered their lips, tilting their heads in the direction of the man's feet.

This must have been some strange island ritual that I'd been spared at the other camp because of my infirm condition. I knew based on the superior elevation of Teuila's father's hut that the Anutians placed a high value on the height difference between individuals as a reflection of their relative power standing. It was obvious that this was the other tribe's chief and that as an unwelcome outsider I'd have to pay homage by submitting myself to his lowest level.

I looked at his dusty feet and leaned forward slightly as the two warriors nodded. Pinching my lips tightly together, I bent down and touched my mouth to the top of each of the chief's feet. He then motioned to the two tribesmen to lift me up, but when he saw that I stood three inches taller than him, he instructed them to push me back down onto my knees.

"*O ai oe?*" he said, grabbing my jaw and thrusting my face up to look at him.

"I'm sorry," I said feebly, "I don't speak your language. I'm from America."

"Amerika?" he asked, with a puzzled expression, peering at my faded cotton shorts and bare chest. "*Uana oe lava?*"

He seemed confused by my unusual appearance. I was pretty sure that if he'd ever seen a Western woman before, she would have been fully clothed.

The lead warrior stepped forward and presented my knife and adze to the chief, mentioning something as he motioned to me. The chief pinched his thumb gently over the end of the knife then turned the adze slowly around in his hands, noticing that it was well worn.

"*O fea na mua?*" he said, jutting it toward me with a furrowed brow.

He must have wondered what a naked Western woman was doing so close to his camp carrying one of their local tools. I wanted to tell him that I meant no harm and that Te' and I had noticed his tribesmen while bathing in our lagoon, but it was obvious that no one among the group spoke English.

"English?" I said, swinging my fingers from my lips, feigning a speaking motion. "Does anyone here speak *English*?"

The chief paused for a moment, then motioned to one of the tribesmen to fetch someone from one of the huts overlooking the square. A few minutes later, he returned with a native woman walking a few paces behind.

The chief mentioned something about *iglisi* to the woman, then he jerked his head in my direction.

"Do you speak English?" she said, looking at me.

"Yes, thank God," I sighed. "I mean you no harm. I'm here alone—"

The chief yelled something at the woman and she turned back to face me.

"What are you doing here?" the woman asked. "How did you get on this island?"

"I came on a chartered cruise from New Zealand. When our crew stopped to visit your island, I got lost and they left without me. I've been here alone for the last week or so."

The chief shook the adze angrily as he shouted at the woman.

"*O fea na mua!*" he repeated.

"Where did you get this axe?" the woman said. "It looks like one of ours."

I paused as I peered at the chief unsteadily. I wasn't sure how much I should disclose about my knowledge of the other tribe with so much tension brewing between the two clans.

"I met a native girl from the other side of the island," I said. "She taught me how to use it."

The woman said something to the chief, then he looked at me suspiciously, trying to discern my intentions.

"*Oe sakina mo latou?*" he said.

"Were you spying for them just now?" the woman translated.

"No," I lied. "I was returning from my camp when I got lost. I meant you no harm—"

The woman repeated what I said to the chief and he paused for a long moment, studying my face. I knew my story sounded improbable, but I hoped that he would find a naked Western woman carrying a stone axe as no threat.

He reached down and ran his hands over my head, rubbing his fingers through my hair. Then he leaned over and caressed my face, running his hands over my shoulders onto the front of my chest. Suddenly I felt less afraid and more embarrassed with so many male eyes ogling my naked figure. The chief cupped my breasts and squeezed them with his hands.

"*Fata masali!*" he shouted, peering around the campfire at his fellow tribesmen. They all laughed as he continued running his hands down my body. When he reached my shorts, he paused, feeling an unusual object under the cloth. He reached into my right pocket and pulled out the spiral unicorn shell that I'd found on the beach with Teuila.

"That's mine!", I shouted, reaching out to take it back.

The chief peered up at the translator, and when she told him what I'd said, he scoffed and threw the shell far to the other side of the sandy courtyard. Then he motioned for the two guards who'd carried me down the hill to tie me to a large pole standing in the middle of the square. As they lashed my hands tightly behind my back around the pole, I squirmed, screaming at the top of my lungs.

"What are you doing with me?" I cried. "I'm innocent! I don't have anything to do with the other tribe. Let me go!"

As the tribesmen reassembled around the fire laughing amongst themselves, the native woman paused, looking at me.

"Why are you doing this?" I said to the woman. "Can't you see I mean you no harm?"

"You're aligned with the other tribe. Our chief will keep you here until our grievance with them is settled. It's best that you don't resist. It will just make things more difficult for you."

As she walked back to her hut, I glanced at the group of tribesmen leering at my bare breasts. I had no idea what they intended to do with me, but the look on their faces gave me a sickening feeling in the pit of my stomach. I wasn't sure which would be a worse—being burned at the stake or getting raped by these savages.

As I dropped my head to my chest in resignation, I caught a glimmer of light reflecting off the sand near the edge of the fire pit. It was my unicorn shell.

"I'm sorry Te'," I said, realizing she'd have no way of finding me if she managed to get herself free. "I wanted to be with you. Hold close my love if I never see you again."

24

———

Teuila shifted her weight uncomfortably on the woven mat covering the floor of her hut. It had been twenty-four hours since she'd last seen Jade, and the crunchy sound of the leafy fibers reminded her of the first time they made love after building their treehouse. But the tight twine digging into her wrists quickly dispelled the pleasant memory as she began to focus on their current predicament.

She was pleased that Jade had evaded her father's dragnet and managed to pass word that she was returning to their lagoon, but there were still too many immediate threats that placed them both in danger. Compounding her anxiety, she didn't have any idea what her father's plans were for defending the village. If he decided to dig in and try to hold off the other tribe's attack, there was no way of knowing which way the battle would go. And if he chose to make a preemptive attack against their village, she'd be left here alone awaiting the outcome.

And with her father not believing Jade's story about Manaia's suspicious behavior, it was looking increasingly likely that either way, she'd be tied to him as long as she remained on the island. Even worse, Jade would be left to her own devices, with no way of protecting herself if Manaia mounted another concentrated search. Although she was capable of feeding herself and knew how to build a fire to stay warm, Jade didn't have Teuila's knowledge of the island or her ability to blend into the terrain. It was only a matter of time before either her father or Manaia would find her.

Jade's only chance now was for her sailing crew to return to the island and find her before the others did. But how would they even know she was still alive or where to search for her? Teuila wished she'd taken the time to help Jade build a marker atop a nearby hill to draw the attention of passing vessels. And what if she was bitten by another snake or stepped on a sea urchin? she thought. Jade didn't have Te's knowledge of the local plants to heal herself back to health.

Things were looking increasingly bleak for a happy reunion. Either Jade would be rescued by her Western friends or she'd be recaptured and sent home on the next cargo ship. Or worse, if she was found by Manaia. There was no telling what he might do to dispose of her in a more expedient manner. As Teuila's face contorted into an anguished grimace, the flap covering the hut's entrance swung open and the chief stepped into the hut.

Thank God! Te' sighed, thankful to finally have another chance to talk to her father.

"Father," she pleaded, twisting against the ropes tied behind her back. "Why are you treating me like this?"

"I'm sorry, Teuila," he said, squatting down into a cross-legged seating position in front of her. "But I can't trust you to not try running away again."

"So what if I did?" Teuila said. "What's so wrong about wanting to be with the person you love?"

Her father sighed as he shook his head dismissively.

"It isn't right for a woman to be with another woman that way. It's your duty to marry a man when you become of age and produce children to keep our community alive. Besides, running off alone breaks with our longstanding custom of aropa, where we've always shared everything communally."

"But I *love* her, father! I don't want to be with anyone else. If you loved me, you should want me to be happy."

The chief paused for a long moment as his face tightened with anguish.

"What makes you think this Western woman would be happy staying on this island with you anyway? She's ignorant of our customs and would soon begin longing for her material things. Eventually, she would just pollute our culture like the missionaries before her."

Teuila sighed, hesitant to tell her father of Jade and her plans to leave the island when her friends returned. She knew he'd never permit her to leave her family and the island. Beyond the insult to his personal authority, it would set a dangerous precedent for other members of the tribe. If she was allowed to go west, what would stop others from wanting to experience the temptations and luxuries of more developed societies? But she knew her father was right that Jade would likely soon miss her life on the other side of the ocean if they tried to stay.

"We've had a very happy couple of days living on our own on the other side of the island. Jade is beginning to appreciate the quiet comforts of our life on Anuta. But even if we did decide to leave, our community is strong enough to survive without me. Aren't you interested to know what life might be like outside our sheltered little island?"

The chief slammed his fists angrily on the floor of the hut, shaking the entire structure.

"You're already betrothed to Manaia!" he said. "No one is leaving this island. Our tribe has lived here in peace and harmony for hundreds of years. You are my daughter. I simply won't allow it."

Teuila gritted her teeth as she peered at her father impassively. She suspected his decision was based far more on his desire to protect his authority over his clan than a desire to maintain internal peace and harmony.

"What about this new aggression by the other clan? The peace is soon to be violently disrupted. How can you continue to protect us without outside help?"

"I have a plan for dealing with these renegades. We will attack them when they least expect it. I'm preparing a team to advance on their camp this evening. They will be too busy making their own battle preparations to anticipate our preemptive strike."

Teuila squinted at her father with a worried expression.

"Will Manaia be going with you?"

"Of course. He's one of our most powerful warriors."

"Do you really think you can trust him based on what Jade saw him doing earlier this morning?"

"That's just lies!" the chief said, flaring his nostrils. "She's making this up to drive a wedge between the two of you. Why would he do this?"

"Maybe he's been talking to the other tribe. If he knew of their invasion plans, this act of espionage would help protect him if they win. How can you be so sure he's not working for the other side?"

"I'm not completely sure he isn't," her father said. "Which is why I'm keeping a close eye on him until we leave. We'll know soon enough if he's a traitor. In the heat of the battle, he'll have to choose sides. Either way, he won't have a chance to inform them that we're coming. We still have the advantage of surprise."

Teuila thought for a moment about her father's plan. There was something about the idea of including Manaia in the campaign that gave her pause.

"Let me come with you, father. I know the configuration of their camp and I'm skilled using a spear and arrow. You're going to need all the help you can muster against their superior numbers."

"This is a job for *tangata*," the chief said. "We can't afford to lose any more women from our tribe. Besides, I can't trust you to use this as another excuse to slip away."

Te' looked at her father with a painful expression.

"Father, you know I'd never abandon my tribe in a time of need such as this. Do you really think so little of me to believe that I would shrink from my duty to protect my village?"

The chief reached out his hands and cupped Teuila's face gently.

"I know you want to do what's best for your community. But leave this to us. I promise we will come back for you soon. I'm going to leave a small contingent behind to protect the village from any interlopers. When I return, we'll talk further about your plans. This will all be settled soon enough."

Te' twisted against the tight cords binding her hands.

"Can't you at least untie me while I'm under guard?"

"I'm sorry, Teuila. This is for your own safety. You're far too crafty. It's safer for you to remain in the village than be roaming over the island with so many dangerous elements on the prowl. We will celebrate our victory when we return with a wedding ceremony to join you and Manaia in marriage."

The chief kissed Teuila on her forehead then stood and exited the hut brusquely. Not long after, she heard the sound of warriors chanting war songs in the village courtyard. She peered through a gap in the wall of her cabin and noticed Manaia waving his spear menacingly as he glanced in her direction.

You might possess me soon, she thought, noticing the heart shape of Jade's stone pressing against her loincloth. *But you'll never own me.*

25

———————

Teuila squinted through the narrow gap in the wall, watching the band of warriors dancing around the bonfire in the middle of the square. As their chanting progressively escalated in volume, her father exhorted them to be strong and brave. Whenever Manaia circled around and gazed in her direction, he seemed to have a crazed look in his eyes. Even though she knew he probably couldn't see her through the thin breaks in the wall, it seemed as though he was staring right at her. Then with a final flourish, the chief waved them forward, and they charged into the jungle.

Te' paused for a few moments, listening to the sound of silence, save the cackling of the fire outside her door. She couldn't see any further sign of movement through the slits in her cabin, and she wondered where the rest of the villagers were. She remembered that her father had said he would leave a few tribesmen behind to guard the village, but where was her nona and the rest of her family? Had they been sequestered to another hut to prevent her aiding Teuila's escape again? It was strange to see her village so eerily silent at this early hour.

"Hello?" she called out, checking to see if anyone was guarding her hut. "Is anyone there? Who's protecting our village?"

"Be quiet, Teuila!" a young tribesman replied from outside the front entrance to her hut. "We don't know if there are spies watching us. We don't want to betray the location of the remaining villagers."

Okay, Te' nodded. *So I know I have at least one guard. It was clever of father to concentrate the women and children in a few huts. That way if the other tribe attacks, the remaining defenses can be concentrated on protecting a smaller perimeter. I guess I'm on my own until the war party returns.*

"Is there anyone else with you?" Teuila whispered to the guard outside her gate, fishing for more information. "How many warriors are left to protect our village?"

"There are five of us," the tribesman replied. "But don't get any ideas about trying to escape again. We have every side of your cabin under surveillance, so even if you were able to untie your binds, you'll be unable to leave the hut. Now shut up and let us focus on keeping an eye out for other threats."

Teuila paused to consider her options. She could stay holed up here and wait until the battle was decided before she made her next move. There'd be plenty of other opportunities to steal away into the jungle after things quieted down. Her father couldn't keep her tied up forever. She could try to escape and rejoin Jade in their private lagoon and fortify their defenses to avoid detection from any further searches. Or she could unite with her father in the attack on the other village and keep an eye on Manaia to make sure he didn't stab the chief in the back.

The more she thought about it, the less appetizing the idea of waiting it out seemed to be. There were far too many variables at play for her to risk the lives of her loved ones. Besides the threat to her father and the rest of his war party, there was her family and the rest of the villagers to think about. If her father lost the battle, there was no way of knowing how the victors would treat the remaining women and children. She knew they intended to kill all the men, but did that mean the young *boys* as well? And would the remaining women be simply absorbed into the new tribe, or would they be treated as sex slaves for the enjoyment of the conquering heroes?

And what of Jade? Even if she was able to find her way back to their lagoon and remain hidden, how could Teuila be sure she hadn't left a trail back to their hiding place? Te' knew how to use the riverbeds to hide her footprints, but Manaia and the other tribesmen were excellent trackers and would sooner or later pick up Jade's trail. Whether it was her tribe or the other clan that eventually found her, neither could be trusted to keep her safe and protected.

She knew that one way or the other, she'd have to find a way to escape to make sure that Jade was safe, then join her father and do whatever she could to ensure the success of their mission. But how could she escape from her hut if it was being monitored on all sides? It wouldn't be as simple as slipping out the back with the help of her nona. The first order of business was finding a way to break her bonds. She wouldn't be much use to anybody if she couldn't free her hands.

Te' wiggled her body along the floor until she found a sharp spur on one of the posts supporting the wall. Then she began rubbing the cords binding her hands as quietly as possible against the knob, trying to splinter the twine. She could hear the fiber pulling and tearing, but it took fifteen minutes before they finally snapped and freed her hands.

Now what? she thought, rubbing her aching wrists. *How am I going to get out of here with five people watching me?*

She peered through a gap in the far wall of her hut and noticed the diminishing reflection of the moon on the water, indicating it was moving higher in the night sky. Time was running out if she was going to have any chance to help her father. She already knew where the weak spots were in her hut, and for a brief moment she considered wedging out the back and making a dash into the woods. But if she got the timing wrong and was caught, she wouldn't have a second chance at her escape.

As she peered down at the leafy mats covering her floor, she reflected back to when she and Jade had built their own improvised house in the trees. She knew the floor of her hut was built the same way, with lashed poles supporting the foundation. If she could get underneath the webbed floor, the guards might not be able to see her while she planned her escape route. Teuila peered in the direction of the front door, watching the guard swiveling his head from side to side as he looked up and down the courtyard for any sign of suspicious movement. Then she pulled back a few of the leafy mats to inspect the floor more closely.

Each of the poles was spaced about an inch apart with tight binding connecting them every foot in length to keep them from separating. She would have to remove the ties from at least a dozen joists for a distance of three or four feet to have any chance at bending them enough to give her space to wiggle through. At least the ties were made from flat strips of inner bark instead of braided leaf strands, which would make it easier for her to dig her nails into the fiber to loosen the knots. But each of the ties were made in the form of a double constrictor knot, which made them all the more difficult to untie.

Te' cursed, realizing it was going to take longer than she hoped to disentangle the posts. She chided herself for not keeping the small paring knife for herself, but she realized Jade needed it as much as she did.

I guess we'll just have to do this the natural way, she thought.

For the next half hour, she painstakingly pinched and pulled each of the ties until they fell away to the floor of the pit six feet below the raised platform. Then she pulled two of the poles in opposite directions until the posts bunched together, leaving a narrow hole to squeeze through. Taking one last glance in the direction of the front door to make sure she wasn't being watched, she squeezed her legs and upper body through the hole, then dropped silently to the ground below, flexing her knees to absorb the impact.

Fortunately, the foundation of her hut was surrounded in leafy thatch similar to the kind coating the walls, so she had a modicum of cover concealing her from prying eyes. She crept to the back corner of her hut and parted the leaves carefully, peering out the crack. There were two guards standing at opposite sides of the hut keeping a close watch on the edge of the jungle for any suspicious movement.

With a good twenty feet from the edge of her hut to the forest, there was a good chance she'd get tackled before she was able to reach the brush.

She'd have to create some kind of diversion to distract the guards, then slip over to the adjoining cabin from which she'd have a better chance to steal into the jungle. She looked around the base of her hut and found a large rock then picked it up and parted the curtain. She waited until both of the guards were looking in the opposite direction, then she threw the rock as far as she could straight into the opposite brush. The guards looked at one another, then one of them motioned for the other to check it out.

As the first guard stepped into the bush to investigate the disturbance, Te' pulled the leaves covering the side of her hut aside and sprinted across the lane, diving underneath the adjacent cabin. She waited a moment to catch her breath, then she parted the covering at the back of the new hut to see if the coast was clear. By this time, the other guard had returned to his position, shaking his head to indicate that it was likely just a bird rustling the leaves. From her new position, Te' could see that she was still too close to the guards to attempt a dash into the woods, so she crawled across the laneway separating the next two huts and took shelter one cabin further away.

But with each cabin further from the chief's signifying a lower status in the tribe, the floor of the third cabin was only a couple of feet off the ground, and she had to crawl on her elbows and knees to reach the furthest side away from the guards. As she rustled through the leaves, she could hear children's voices above her, so she knew this was one of the cabins that was being used to hide the remaining villagers.

But she didn't have any time to check on their wellbeing. She lifted the grass skirt at the far end of the cabin, then crawled out into the laneway, crouching low as she peered in the direction of the guards. She waited once again until they were looking in the opposite direction, then she prepared to sprint to the cover of the woods. Just as she was about to leap forward, she felt a hand touch her on the shoulder. Turning around fearing she'd been discovered by one of the guards, she was surprised to see the face of her grandmother peering through the slats in the wall, reaching out her arm toward Teuila.

Teuila squeezed her hand and Nona nodded silently toward her, blowing her a kiss with her other hand. No words needed to be spoken between the two women. They both knew where Teuila was going, and her grandmother simply wanted to wish her well. Te' looked up at Nona and lifted her finger to her lips, instructing her to keep the children quiet. Then she glanced in the direction of the tribesmen guarding her hut and leaped to the edge of the forest, disappearing quietly into the jungle.

26

———————

Teuila knew she'd lost precious time fashioning her escape and that she'd be hard-pressed to catch up with her father. There was no time now to check up on Jade to make sure she was safe. She had to assume that she'd found her way back to the lagoon and that she would wait for Te' to return as she'd promised. There'd be plenty of time to attend to Jade later. Right now, her priority was to catch up with the war party and make sure Manaia didn't stab her father in the back.

The good news was that by now she was familiar with her way to the other tribe's camp and was able to cover the distance in half the time. Still, it took her almost three hours to traverse the island, and by the time she neared the other tribe's camp, the moon had risen almost directly overhead. As she neared their village, she heard the sound of tribesmen singing and chanting around a flickering light in the distance. Not wanting to set off any warnings in case her father was still preparing to attack, she found a point on top of a hill over-looking the village and peered around the woods trying to locate the position of the war party.

She couldn't see them on any of the high ground, but as she glanced down the slope, she saw the backs of warriors creeping through the jungle in a semi-circular formation, closing in on the tribesmen prancing around the fire. When she turned her head to make sure the other tribe was unaware of the encroaching invasion, her eyes suddenly flung open when she caught sight of a familiar blonde figure tied to a stake in the middle of the square.

It was Jade! How had she managed to get captured by the other tribe? And what were they planning to do with her?

Teuila could see logs and kindling spread around the base of the post she was tied to in the familiar shape of a fire starter.

Oh my God! Te' thought. *They're planning to burn her alive! Just as she'd feared in her wildest dreams!*

But as she watched her father's war party creep closer to the fire pit, she realized Jade was in grave danger of *another* threat, just as severe. Her position next to the band of targeted warriors placed her in the middle of the coming crossfire. Teuila had to get her out of there as quickly as possible. As she began sprinting down the hill in the direction of the camp, she heard the war party scream as they surged out of the woods, flinging arrows and spears in the direction of the tribesmen.

Hold on, my love, Te' thought as she crashed through the underbrush. *I'm coming for you!*

27

—————

My legs trembled in fear as I watched the chanting tribesmen circling around the fire. I had no idea what they were saying, but judging from the brightly colored war paint adorning their faces and the intensity of their intonations, they must have been preparing for something big. But I knew their attack on Te's village wasn't due for another twenty-four hours. Was all this in preparation for the planned invasion, or were they getting worked up for something else?

I peered down toward my feet and got a sick feeling in my stomach. The twigs and logs assembled around the base of my stake looked threateningly similar to the type Teuila had used to start the fire in our lagoon.

Were they really going to burn me alive? Simply for stumbling onto their camp carrying a few small tools?

I'd always been reluctant to travel to third-world countries because I wanted to have the rule of law to protect me in case anything went wrong. But this was taking the abuse of human rights to an entirely new level. *What kind of barbarians would treat another human being in this way?*

At least they haven't raped me, I thought. *Yet.* Then I shuddered at another possibility. *Maybe they're planning to cook me in preparation for a special feast.* My charter captain had dismissed the notion of cannibalism being practiced in this region of the world, but Teuila hadn't explicitly denied it. Maybe these villagers looked at the odd stray Westerner who washed across their shores as a rare delicacy to be enjoyed in the same way we looked forward to the occasional roast turkey or rack of lamb.

I cursed at my stupidity for ever having strayed from the group hiking inland after we'd set ashore. But then I'd never have met Teuila, who was the most special person I'd ever known. I'd never have known a love as strong and pure as the kind I'd experienced in the short time we'd been together. There was something sweet and innocent about her, unvarnished and uncorrupted by Western civilization. The ironic thing was that we'd *both* stretched the boundaries of what we'd previously imagined possible by being thrown together in this unlikely place.

It was this clash of cultures that had brought me both the greatest joy in my life and the greatest despair. And now it was all about to end in the most horrifying way imaginable. Even worse, there'd be no way for Teuila to know what had become of me. She'd have to live the rest of her life thinking her lover had abandoned her without even saying goodbye after her friends returned to pick her up. There would literally not be a single human remain left of me for her to put the clues together. I closed my eyes and said a prayer, asking God to make the ending quick and to look after Teuila.

But just as I began my supplication, I heard the loud shouts of tribesmen approaching from the woods. I opened my eyes to see scores of painted warriors closing in on the men around the fire as they flung arrows and spears in their direction. The local group turned to face the attacking horde, hurling their own spears in self-defense. Within seconds, the attacking group had closed in on the surprised tribesmen, engaging in hand-to-hand combat with their makeshift axes and knives.

My eyes suddenly flung open when I recognized Teuila's father grappling with one of the tribesmen on the dusty ground. They rolled side-over-side a few times in the sand until Te's father gained the superior position. Then he raised his adze over his head and slammed it down, splitting the other man's skull in half.

Suddenly I heard the sound of another warrior's scream, and I looked up to see the crazed face of Manaia running toward me holding a flaming spear. Just as he reared back to fling the spike toward my helpless body, his face contorted in agony and he flopped to the ground with a large arrow sticking into his back. Standing a few feet behind him, Teuila stood wearing a lopsided grin. She nodded toward me, then she reached behind her back and grabbed a series of arrows from her quiver, felling the few remaining warriors still standing from the other tribe.

Within minutes, the battle was over as the warriors from the other clan lay sprawled on the ground around the fire with one or more stone objects embedded in their lifeless bodies. Te's father lifted himself off another dead tribesman, and after satisfying himself that the threat from the other side had been neutralized, he noticed Te' and approached her with an angry expression.

"*O lau o fae inerti?*" he shouted, acting surprised to see her.

"*Mea tau!*" she replied, holding her bow up and pointing toward the tribesmen she'd killed with her arrows.

The chief nodded in appreciation, then he recognized Manaia's figure lying on the ground and turned him over. Manaia groaned as he reached around toward the arrow still embedded in his back. Teuila's father said something to him, then turned him over on his stomach to inspect the wound. Then he grasped the shaft of the arrow and pulled it out of Manaia's shoulder and flung it onto the ground. He motioned to one of his men to bring him a tapa-cloth sling and Manaia sat up gingerly, placing his injured arm in the pouch. He glanced up at Teuila, pinching his eyebrows suspiciously, and she looked away from him disdainfully.

Te' strode up to my stake and began loosening the binds holding my hands behind the pole, but she paused when her father barked a command to her. She protested whatever he was saying, then he stormed toward me and pulled her hands away from the pole.

"What's going on?" I said, peering into Te's eyes. "What is he saying?"

"He wants to leave you tied up until he figures out what to do with you. He doesn't want to take any more chances that either one of us will run away."

"Oh Te'," I suddenly cried, overwhelmed to see her again. "I thought I'd lost you forever."

"Not as long as I live and breathe," Te' said, clasping the side of my face with her hands and kissing me firmly on my lips.

For now, at least, we were together again. But from the angry look on her father's face, I had no idea for how much longer it would last.

28

For the next fifteen minutes, the chief huddled with Teuila and Manaia as they gestured toward me in a heated discussion. Manaia seemed particularly agitated, pointing back and forth between me and Teuila like he was blaming us for the interclan rivalry. He walked over to where her father had discarded the arrow fired into his back and inspected it carefully, then he carried it back to the chief, shaking it angrily in Te's face. The chief muttered something to Teuila and she dropped to her knees in front of him, begging him to accept her version of the story.

Finally, he swept his hands in a dismissive motion and gestured to one of his guards to attend to me. The guard pulled a sharp adze from the side of his skirt and began walking toward me in a threatening manner. I could only assume from Te's anguished expression that her father had instructed him to kill me, and I closed my eyes, steeling myself for the worst.

At least it will be quick this time, I thought, tensing my body in anticipation of the final blow.

But instead, the guard circled around behind me and began sawing at my ties until my hands were free. I looked up at Teuila, breathing a sigh of relief, but she just peered back at me sadly, shaking her head. The chief said something to the guard and he pulled my hands behind my back and retied them, then he connected a longer cord, which he wrapped around his hand. Te's father pointed to three more guards and motioned toward the remaining villagers cowering in their huts, then he lifted his hand and waved it in a circle, indicating that it was time for the rest of us to return to the village.

The tribesmen got in formation behind the chief and the guard who was bound to me pushed me in the back with the butt of his adze, instructing me to join the line. Te's father said something to Teuila, then she led the way back into the jungle with the rest of the troop following dutifully behind. As Manaia took up the rear position, I looked back at the sad faces of the women and children peering on from the entrance of their huts and wondered what would become of them. The whole scene reminded me of something out of a Vietnam War movie, with me taking the place of the captured soldier having to do a forced march back to the prison camp.

―――――

By the time our band returned to Te's village, the morning light was beginning to stream over the lagoon and the women and children raced out of their cabins, overjoyed to see that their side had won the battle. The men were exhausted from the night-long march, but Te's father pointed to the middle of the square, motioning for them to begin work on something. The guard who was tied to me escorted me to the location where the chief had pointed and forced me to sit down in the sand. Then the rest of the group disappeared into the woods as they began hacking down trees and branches of different sizes.

When they returned, they dug four deep holes in the sand on either side of me, then they placed a long stake in each pit, being careful to shore each one up so that it stood firm and steady. I watched dumbfounded as they began erecting a webbed scaffold all around me from the smaller branches, tying the posts tightly together with cross-ties of threaded bark. As they scurried up and over the structure like spiders, Te' reached out her arm and held my hand while the wall slowly rose between us.

"What's happening, Te?" I said, horrified they was caging me up like an animal.

"My father doesn't trust us to be together," she said. "He plans to keep you in this enclosure under close guard until either your friends return or the next cargo ship passes by our island. He doesn't want to take any more chances that either one of us will escape before then."

I glanced up at the lattice of poles rising above me and noticed they weren't building any kind of door into the structure.

"Don't you think this is a bit extreme?" I said. "How am I supposed to go to the washroom?"

Te' frowned sheepishly as she pointed toward the back corner of my cage.

"There's a small opening at the base of your enclosure through which we can pass a bucket and plates of food. I'll make sure you're kept as clean and well fed as possible until the ship arrives."

I reflected back on the image of Nona carrying a bowl in and out of her hut while Te' was being held in detention. At least there she had the advantage of covered walls to protect her modesty.

"They want me to do my business in plain sight of all the other villagers?" I said, hardly believing my ears. "Jesus, Te'—this is worse than a Turkish prison. At least there, you have a modicum of privacy."

Teuila squeezed my hand as she looked at me painfully.

"I'll talk to my father about placing a drape over your enclosure. I know it seems harsh, but he could have decided on a far worse course of action. As long as you're still alive, there's a chance we can find a way to be together."

I glanced behind Teuila and noticed Manaia conferring quietly with the chief as they watched us suspiciously.

"What about Manaia? Doesn't your father believe our story about him being a traitor?"

"Unfortunately not. He thinks Manaia comported himself bravely in battle and that his injury was further evidence he was fighting for our side."

I allowed a slight curl to form in the side of my mouth.

"So he doesn't know that you shot the arrow that injured him?"

"He has his suspicions, but there were a lot of arrows flying in every direction during the battle. My father is convinced that it came from one of the other tribesmen."

"And I suppose he also doesn't believe that Manaia was trying to kill me just before he was injured?"

"There were too many people running around, and he was busy fending off his own attackers. It's my word against his."

"And he believes *Manaia* over his own daughter?!"

"Unfortunately, he's already seen where my allegiance lies, which is with you. He has no reason to believe Manaia had any motive to betray his own tribe."

"So what happens now? What will become of you once your father gets rid of me?"

Teuila glanced down toward my feet as a tear dripped down her face onto the sand.

"He intends to marry me to Manaia tonight after everyone is rested, in celebration of our victory over the other tribe."

"Even though you've made it clear that you want nothing to do with him?" I said, shaking my head in dismay.

"It's no use. My father doesn't understand how two women can be in love the way we are. He insists on following the custom our tribe has practiced for hundreds of years. He expects Manaia and me to produce lots of babies and live happily ever after. He's convinced that once you're out of the picture, I'll regain my senses and settle in to a normal family life here in Anuta."

My face tightened into a painful expression as I peered into Te's eyes, realizing how hopeless our situation had suddenly become.

"Maybe he's right," I sighed. "Maybe I'm just pulling you away from what is natural and right. Maybe I'm just another Western intruder chipping away at your culture, leading you down a path of destruction and heartache, like the explorers did with the people of Easter Island."

"No Jade," Te' said, clasping my arms with both hands. "It's just the opposite. You've opened my eyes to the joy of true freedom and helped me recognize the opportunities outside my tiny sheltered island. It's my *father* who's been oppressing me and my people. I'm just expressing my free will and following my heart to be with the person I love."

"Oh Te'," I said, reaching between the poles and pulling her close to me as the last of the tribesmen stepped away from my completed cage. "I love you more than you'll ever know. I just don't see how—"

Seeing that my enclosure was now fully secured, Te's father stormed up the path and grabbed her arm, pulling her away from me.

"*Alu mai te ai!*" he shouted, glaring angrily at me.

As he dragged Teuila kicking and screaming back to their hut, Manaia locked eyes with me and sniggered a lopsided grin. I collapsed my body against the webbing of my enclosure and began sobbing, knowing I'd never have another chance to run away with my island girl.

29

After Teuila left, one of the tribesmen planted himself in front of my cage and stared at me impassively, while the rest of the village resumed their usual activities. Every now and then, some small children ran past my enclosure, pointing at me and giggling. Most of the men had retired to their huts to get some rest, but the women were busy moving about the courtyard with handfuls of provisions, preparing for the big celebration later this evening. I glanced in the direction of Te's hut and noticed her grandmother shaving some taro root on the porch, trying not to look at me. Her hut was surrounded on each side by a guardsman holding a spear. Inside, the dwelling was quiet and still, and I wondered if Teuila had been tied up again to prevent her escape.

So that's how it's going to be, I thought. *The chief is going out of his way to keep the two of us separated and confined.*

I looked at my guard and shook my head. I felt more exposed than ever with my bare breasts on display for everyone to see, like some kind of hooker standing behind the glass in Amsterdam's Red-Light District. I crossed my arms over my chest and sat down in the sand, and before long fell asleep from sheer exhaustion.

A few hours later I woke to the sound of chatter and noticed some tribesmen erecting a long trellis-shaped structure in the middle of the square. A band of women followed closely behind, decorating the lattice with garlands of flowers. My skin felt hot from the overhead sun beating down through the open bars of my cage, and I pressed my fingers against my flesh realizing I was beginning to burn. I picked up some sand from the base of my pit and tried to coat my body with it, but it just fell off my skin like dry confetti. Peering up at the sun, I estimated it was around noon, and I wondered how these people expected a pale white woman to survive all day long, exposed in the tropical sun. It had also been almost thirty-six hours since I'd had anything to eat, and I clutched my stomach from the gnawing feeling in my gut.

Te's father disappeared into their hut, then a few minutes later he came out carrying a few bowls and some folded objects. He spoke with Nona and pointed in my direction. Nona placed some items in one of the bowls, then she took the materials from his hand and began walking toward me. Upon reaching my cage, she bent down and slid one of the bowls through the narrow hole at the bottom of the enclosure.

When I saw that it was filled with fresh fruit and vegetables, I picked it up and gobbled it down like I'd never seen food before. Nona nodded toward me and passed a hollowed-out coconut shell filled with water through the bars and I emptied it in three gulps. As my stomach began to settle, I looked at her and smiled, placing my palms together and bowing to thank her for her act of kindness. Even though I knew she couldn't speak English, I hoped she'd be able to share some news about Te'.

"How is Teuila?" I said, pointing toward her shack. I swiveled my wrists together in a shackled motion. "Is she tied up?"

"*Eh le lelei,*" she nodded, recognizing her granddaughter's name. Then she placed her hands over her heart and spread her palms in my direction. "*Na te misia oe.*"

I choked up understanding her meaning and swallowed hard, knowing that Te' was thinking of me. I looked at the other materials she'd placed on the ground outside my cage and recognized some woven mats similar to the ones Te' and I had made to line the floor of our treehouse.

"Are those for me?" I asked, motioning to the mats.

She nodded then said something to my guard, and he unfurled the mats and threw them over the top of my cage like two long table runners, one on each side. Nona straightened the leafy curtains until they extended all the way down to the base of my enclosure, then she slid one of the drapes aside so we could see each other.

"*Mai le Teuila,*" she said, pointing to my newly created canopy.

I returned Nona's gesture, placing my hands over my chest and extending them toward her in gratitude.

"Thank you."

Then she picked up the last object on the ground, which looked like a small hollowed out stump. She placed it between her feet and half-squatted over it, nodding and pointing to me. I nodded back, understanding her meaning, then she pushed it through the little hole at the bottom of my cage and rearranged my curtains so that I was almost completely covered.

I placed my hand over my heart again and blew her a kiss, then she walked slowly back in the direction of Te's hut. As I watched her walk away, I reached out and rubbed a piece of the leafy matting between my fingers. The strands were still bright green and pliant, like they'd been recently harvested, and the weaving pattern was exactly the same as the one Teuila had shown me days earlier. I leaned my body forward and closed my eyes, breathing in the fresh scent of the pandanus leaves. For a moment, I imagined I could smell Te's scent on them too, and I wondered if she'd had a hand in making them. Either way, I was grateful she'd sent them to me as I sat down in the dark shade of my little hut and finished off the rest of the food Nona had brought me.

At least they're not going to let me starve out here, I thought, grimacing at the makeshift toilet bowl. *Looking after my other personal needs is going to be a whole other nightmare.* But the shade from my leafy umbrella was already starting to cool the inside of my cage, and

I soon fell asleep dreaming of making love to Teuila on the floor of our treehouse.

I awoke many hours later to the sound of singing and chanting coming from the courtyard. I pulled my curtain aside and saw the villagers seated in long rows on opposite sides of the floral-decorated trellis leading toward a giant bonfire burning in the middle of the square. The flames reflected off the face of Te's father sitting atop his chieftain's chair, flanked by his children sitting squat-legged on the ground beside him. As the tribesmen hopped and skipped around the fire, the women and children sang gleefully at the top of their lungs.

Standing stoically in front of the chief with his arms folded over his chest, Manaia peered expectantly down the path in the direction of the trellis. He wore a long grass skirt like the other tribesmen, but unlike the rest of the bare-breasted warriors, he wore a beaded vest festooned with brightly colored sea shells and an elaborate feathered headdress. Posing like a flamboyant peacock, he looked ridiculously overdressed for the occasion. But with his exaggerated sense of self-importance, it seemed to fit his personality perfectly. I fingered the unicorn-shaped shell that Teuila had reclaimed from the sand of the other village, wishing it were a dagger I could throw at him instead.

But Teuila and her grandmother were still nowhere to be seen. As the singing and dancing slowly increased in pitch and volume, I recognized some movement on the front porch of their cabin. Nona swept the front door mat aside, then Te' stepped out onto the portico looking like an angel from heaven. Wearing a white tapa dress dyed in a pretty floral motif, she wore a long wreath made of frangipani and jasmine around her neck and a crown of orchids atop her head. Her face shimmered in the moonlight, with a greenish-yellow dusting of turmeric powder and flower pollen coating her upper eyelids. I gasped at her beauty as her grandmother took her arm and escorted her down the front steps of their cabin.

As they strode toward the trellis marking the entrance to the reception, Te' glanced in my direction and I slunk back toward the rear of my cage. For some reason, I didn't want her to see me watching her as she prepared to get married. Whether it was from my own sense of dread at losing her once and for all or from some misguided feeling of not wanting to ruin her big day, I lurked in the shadows, closing my eyes listening to the chanting of the wedding participants. But after another minute or so, I couldn't resist the urge to see her one last time, and I pushed my screen aside to see the two of them walking under the trellis toward the fire in the direction of Manaia, who was grinning in front of her father like a Cheshire Cat.

So this is the way they do it here in Anuta, I thought, nodding at the similarities between the Polynesian wedding and those in the West. *The groom waits patiently by the altar, while his bride-to-be tantalizes him by slowly walking up the aisle as their loved ones eagerly look on. The only difference was that the mother of the bride, or in this case her grandmother, gives the girl away. Typical male-dominated culture, where the patriarch sits on his high horse as he watches his daughter given away.*

The two women walked together through the floral-covered trellis, then Nona disengaged and joined the rest of her family as Teuila approached the raging fire.

How appropriate, I thought, watching the shadows flickering over Manaia's smug face. *From the mother's arms into the fire.*

I half-expected Teuila to leap into the flames and self-immolate to escape the clutches of her treacherous groom. But then I realized that her father still had me to use as leverage to force her to go through with the ceremony. It was probably no accident that he'd placed me in the middle of the courtyard for everyone to see as a reminder of his absolute power over the rest of the village. He'd probably threatened to kill or torture me if Teuila didn't abide by his wishes and marry Manaia.

When Teuila got to within arm's reach of Manaia, he reached out and took her hand then they both turned around to face the chief as a hush fell over the crowd. Her father muttered a few words to them both, then he threw up his hands in exaltation, shouting to the rest of the crowd. Suddenly, the women and children poured off their benches, as they joined the tribesmen in excited dancing around the fire. At first, Te' seemed reluctant to join the festivities, but Manaia grabbed her hand and swung her boisterously around the fire with all the other celebrants. Whenever she came back around facing in my direction, I could see her glancing at my enclosure, but I squinted through the narrow breaks in the leaves, remaining hidden. I was too ashamed for her to see me trapped like a rat in my dark and dirty cage.

For the next two hours, the entire village sang and danced and feasted in celebration of Teuila and Manaia's union. After a while, I could no longer bear witness to the tragedy of the spectacle, and I curled up on the sandy floor of my cage, holding my hands over my ears trying to block out the sound of all the merrymaking. Eventually, the cacophony began to subside and I pulled my curtain aside, noticing the villagers slowly returning to their huts. Manaia and Teuila sat with her siblings finishing the plate of food laid out on the buffet, then her father said something to them, nodding toward one of the huts next to his own.

As the bride and groom stood up and began walking hand-in-hand across the sandy courtyard, I couldn't help noticing the bounce in Manaia's step as Te' dragged her feet through the sand. He seemed determined to consummate their marriage as quickly as possible, pulling her by the arm as she lagged two feet behind. They stopped at the base of the steps leading up to the cabin next to her own. Like the chief's, it was elevated much higher above the ground, signifying their newly elevated status.

Unbelievable, I thought, shaking my head in disgust. *All he has to do is marry the chief's daughter to elevate his status to second-in-command within the tribe. It's only a matter of time before he finds a way to take over command of the entire island.*

Manaia pulled Teuila reluctantly up the steps of their cabin, and just before they disappeared inside, she turned and glanced in my direction. My heart leaped out of my chest, and for a moment I considered flinging my drape aside and crying out to her to tell her how much I loved her. But Manaia yanked her inside and within minutes I heard the sound of pounding floorboards as he had his way with his new bride.

I closed my eyes and prayed forgiveness for ever having planted the seed of doubt in Te's mind. If it hadn't been for me, she'd never have known any other way than that of a man. I'd ruined it for her for the rest of her life. Teuila would forever pine for my tender touch as long as she remained on this far-flung island. I collapsed to the ground and sobbed, watching the tiny rivulets of tears roll away over the sand.

30

The next morning, I woke early with a sick feeling in my stomach. I'd dreamt Te' and I were swimming in our lagoon when a sea monster breached the surface and pulled her underwater. I reached out trying to grab her arm, but all I could do was watch the sad look on her face as she faded away into the depths. Realizing how accurately my dream mirrored the reality of our situation, I leaned over and retched into my wooden toilet basin.

Looking for a bit of light to pull me out of my depression, I pulled the blind across on the south side of my crate and noticed another guard sleeping in the sand a few feet away. I checked the other side and saw that my original guard was lying still on the sand with his eyes closed. The sun was starting to peer over the horizon at the far end of the lagoon, and with the village still quiet, I began to think about an escape plan. If I could just find a way to break out of my pen and sneak past the guards, I could return to our hiding spot and wait for Teuila to rejoin me. Once she knew I was free and safe, there would be nothing holding her back from escaping on her own.

I surveyed the construction of my cage and pushed it firmly on the side to see if it would give. But the heavy posts embedded deep in the sand at the four corners meant it wouldn't be as simple as toppling the tightly strung structure onto its side. I kneeled down and burrowed under the base of the enclosure with my hands, but the soft sand quickly backfilled into the hole. The guards were beginning to get restless, and I didn't want to take any chance at the digging sound pulling them out of their slumber. My only chance would be trying to untie the straps holding the poles together and slip out before they woke.

As I dug my nails into the cords and began loosening the ties, I kept a close eye on the guard on the south side of my crate. There were fewer huts between me and the forest on this side, plus I could use the shelter of the lagoon if necessary to hide underwater as Teuila and I had done at the swimming hole. But my finger slipped while untying one of the knots, and I squeaked in pain as it twisted against the wooden pole. The guard suddenly stirred and when he saw what I was trying to do, he leaped up and yelled at me, flinging a handful of sand in my direction. Some of the grains landed in my eyes, and I staggered back against the other side of my cage as they welled up in pain.

I batted my eyelids as tears streaming down my face, and within a minute or so I was able to recover my sight. The drapes had been pulled to the side of my enclosure, and the two guards barked at me as they thrust their spears in my direction. I slunk back onto the sand at the base of my pit while the guard on the lagoon side refastened the loosened ties, pulling them extra tight with double knots.

A few minutes later, Teuila emerged from the front of her hut and she began walking toward me carrying a few items. I smiled at her as I wiped the tears from my face, throwing a handful of sand into my bucket to cover up the smell of my vomit. As she approached my enclosure, she noticed the redness in my eyes and furrowed her brow with a worried expression.

"Good morning, Jade," she said, trying to cheer me up. "I brought you some fresh food and other provisions. How have you been holding up?"

"As well as can be expected under the circumstances," I smiled weakly.

Te' pulled the shades back across my enclosure, glaring at the guards for not giving me enough privacy. For a moment, I considered telling her about my failed escape attempt, but I figured it would just inflame their already raw emotions even further.

"Are you finding the drapes I made for you are keeping things a bit cooler in here?"

"Yes, thank you," I said, happy to hear that at least she wasn't being tied up in her hut.

"I thought you might like a bit more protection against the sun and the prying eyes of the villagers," she said, handing me a folded white cloth through the bars.

I unfolded the garment and smiled, seeing that it was a dress similar to the one she'd replaced from the previous night's wedding ceremony. I pulled it over my head then pressed against the bars, desperate to feel her touch. She reached out and squeezed my hands as we pressed our foreheads together.

"Te'," I moaned. "I've been thinking of you so much. I watched the ceremony last night, then I heard you with Manaia in the hut—"

"Don't pay any mind to that," she said, pulling back to peer into my eyes. "He may possess my body, but my heart will always belong to you. We just have to wait a few more days until things quiet down, then we can find a way to escape this god-forsaken place."

"What about the two guards?" I said, noticing the tribesmen still scowling at me. "How can we hope to escape with them watching me twenty-four hours a day?"

I glanced in the direction of her hut, fearful that Manaia or her father would see her with me.

"And what about Manaia? What if he finds us? I have a feeling that he and your father won't be as lenient if they were to catch us again."

"Let *me* worry about them," Te' said. "I know how to keep Manaia distracted. He's sleeping right now. We'll have plenty of opportunities soon enough. They'll never find us on the other side of the island."

I shook my head, remembering how easy it had been for the other tribesmen to catch me.

"Have you seen any sign of my sailing crew? The sooner we get off this island, the better. I think I've had quite enough of the tropics for a little while."

"There's been no sign of them. But my father says a cargo ship is due to pass by any day now. We won't have long before you're sent away."

She lifted a bowl full of figs and sliced pineapple, and I closed my eyes, breathing in the heavenly aroma.

"Are you hungry?"

I nodded, and she pushed the bowl through the hole in the bottom of my crate.

"This reminds me of our first day in the lagoon," I said, lifting the sweet fruit to my parched lips. "I remember waking up to the fresh scent of these hanging above our treehouse after we made love that night."

"It's all I can think about too," Te' said, squeezing my hands so tightly they began to turn red. "It's the only thing that keeps me going."

I looked at Teuila with sad eyes and frowned.

"I'm sorry, Te'. I should never have come to this island. If you had never met me, you'd never have known anything different—"

"I'd still know what it feels like to be abused by a man," she said. "If it weren't for you, I'd have never known what it feels like to be truly loved by someone."

"Oh Te'," I cried, thrusting my body against the front of my crate and throwing my arms around her. "I don't want to lose you. I can't imagine my life without—"

Suddenly, the flap covering Teuila's hut swung open and Manaia turned to face us, glaring angrily in our direction. He quickly descended the steps and began running in our direction, and Teuila turned around and began running toward the woods. But he already had a healthy head start, and he quickly closed the distance, tackling her in the sand. Then he picked her up and threw her kicking and screaming over his shoulder, snickering at me as he strutted back up the steps of his hut. Soon after, Te's father emerged from his cabin and nonchalantly sat down on his rocking chair.

Teuila wasn't kidding about the men on this island, I thought.

As the thumping sound resumed in Te's hut, the chief leaned back in his chair and began to rock it slowly, nodding to my guards to keep a close watch over me.

31

———

For the rest of the day, I didn't hear from Teuila and wondered if Manaia had tied her up in their cabin to prevent her from communicating with me. Fortunately, Nona kept me well fed and hydrated, emptying my toilet bowl every few hours to keep my enclosure tolerable. I had plenty of time to ponder my situation, and the more I thought about it, the more hopeless I realized our predicament had become.

It would be nearly impossible to escape from my cage under twenty-four-hour guard. And with Manaia keeping a short leash on Teuila, she'd be hard-pressed to find a way to slip away before the cargo ship arrived. Almost as worrisome, I wondered why my sailing crew hadn't yet returned for me. It had been almost two weeks since they'd abandoned the island, and I couldn't understand why they'd left in such a hurry.

Had they run into members of the other tribe who threatened to harm them if they didn't leave immediately? Had they aborted the search once they realized how large the island was and how much ground they'd have to cover to search all of it? Had Teuila's father convinced them that I was likely dead after they'd stopped by the village? Or were they going to get reinforcements to search for me more thoroughly?

Either way, I didn't have much time before this was going to be out of my hands. There'd be very little I could do to salvage my relationship with Teuila once I left the island. It wasn't like I could come back with a team of mercenaries and forcibly abduct her. For all intents and purposes, Anuta was a sovereign nation and I'd be flaunting the rules of maritime law by interfering with their right to privacy.

And once I left, what chance would Teuila have escaping the island on her own? Even if she managed to evade Manaia's clutches, he and the rest of the tribe would hunt her down until they found her. With hundreds of miles of open ocean surrounding Anuta, there'd be no way for her to navigate to friendlier waters using one of the few remaining outrigger canoes.

The isolated beauty of the island was both a blessing and a curse. It was the tropical paradise where I'd found the love of my life, but it was also a refuge from which few could ever hope to escape. What right did I have invading their personal space, thinking I could steal away their most important daughter? Anutians had lived for centuries in peace and tranquility until I arrived. Teuila wouldn't even have known what it felt like to experience lesbian love if I hadn't contaminated their culture with my promiscuous Western values. I was acting like the typical arrogant American, thinking I could impose my superior Western mores on their backcountry civilization.

I slept fitfully that night, tossing and turning while trying to reconcile my selfish desire to hold on to Teuila with my knowledge that I had no right to intervene in the tribe's personal affairs. I awoke the next morning to the smell of fresh sea breeze wafting under the curtains of my hut. I pulled the blinds aside and watched the sun gleaming off the pristine waters of the lagoon as children ran playfully across the sand. Their mothers and grandmothers looked on from the porches of their huts as they prepared another healthy breakfast of fresh fish and locally harvested vegetables. On the beach, a team of young tribesman were busy chipping away at the trunk of a felled breadfruit tree, hollowing out a new canoe.

I smiled at the bucolic scene, realizing I had no right trying to interfere in their tranquil life. Suddenly, I noticed movement in the direction of Te's hut and I saw her grandmother walking toward me with a heightened sense of urgency. She had a strange look on her face, like she knew something foreboding was coming. When she approached my cage, she glanced at the guards nervously as she passed me a handful of fruit. A curl of bark fell to the sand and she gestured for me to pick it up. I leaned down and unfolded the husk, noticing some writing had been etched onto the inner skin.

"*Mai Teuila,*" she said, placing her hands over mine. Then she turned around and hurried back to her hut past the imposing figure of Manaia, standing on his veranda with his arms crossed.

I unfurled the parchment and read the message scrawled into the pulp.

Cargo ship on the horizon. Will be here within two hours. Manaia is not letting me leave the hut. If I don't see you before you leave, find your way back to our treehouse. I'll meet you there as soon as I can. Thinking of you always, love Teuila.

As I stood reading the message, my heart beat a hundred miles an hour. I wanted to scream out across the courtyard to tell Te' I loved her and would never forget what we'd shared. But that would betray the vow that I'd made not to meddle any further in their affairs. But I couldn't just leave without saying goodbye. I had to let her know what she meant to me. I ran my fingers through the sand at the base of my enclosure and found a small stone. Then I peeled off the top layer of the bark and placed Te's message in my pocket. I sat down in the sand and began to scratch a new message on the parchment.

Dearest Teuila,

I'll never forget the delicate love and tenderness we shared during my short stay on your island. I'll carry the precious memories with me as long as I live. But I don't want you to pine for me after I leave. Your people share this wonderful culture of aropa, and in time I believe you will grow to appreciate the peaceful comforts of your community. I'll always be with you in mind and spirit.

I signed the note with a heart symbol and the letter J scrawled inside. Then I pulled the curtain aside on the side facing the chief's cabin, noticing Nona weaving quietly on the front porch. I feigned a cough and she looked up in my direction. I looked around to make sure I wasn't being watched, then I motioned with my hands for her to come back toward me. I knew this would be my last chance to leave a message with Teuila before the ship arrived.

She placed some fruit in a bowl and carried it back to me, and when she slid it through the slot in my cage, I dropped the husk in the pot and looked up at her. She paused for a moment, and I nodded as she slid the scroll under her dress.

"For Teuila," I said, pointing to her hut. "Thank you for all your kindness."

I steepled my palms in front of my chest and smiled, bowing in gratitude.

At least Teuila won't be entirely on her own once I leave, I thought. *She'll still have the love of her siblings and grandmother to keep her spirits buoyed.*

As Nona walked back toward her hut, I closed my blinds and sat down on the sand of my crate and began to sob uncontrollably.

32

For the next couple of hours, the village square was a bustle of activity as the children pointed excitedly toward the horizon and the men began bundling up piles of shark fins they'd caught on their recent fishing expeditions. A foghorn sounded from the direction of the lagoon, and my guards began dismantling my crate. Soon after, the bow of a large cargo ship glided into view beyond the cape. As a small skiff jetted toward the beach, Te's father and grandmother emerged from their cabin. Nona was carrying my handbag, and as they began walking toward me, I realized this was to be my final sendoff from the island.

I glanced in the direction of Te's hut and noticed that it was eerily still. It was obvious that Manaia was keeping her from me, and I suddenly began hyperventilating at the thought of not seeing her again. It seemed unimaginably cruel of him and Teuila's father to deny us the opportunity to say one last goodbye.

When the guards pulled the last of the ties away from my crate, they each grabbed one of my arms as Nona handed me my handbag. It was obvious that Te's father wasn't going to take any chances that I wouldn't be getting on the boat. I looked inside my handbag and noticed that everything was just as I had left it. It felt strange and surreal to see all the usual trappings of my old life lying in the bottom of the bag. There was my bikini, a bottle of sunscreen, my smartphone, and of all things—a business card, which must have fallen out of one of my travel guides as a bookmark. It was hard to imagine returning so abruptly to my privileged life on the mainland.

The guards escorted me down the courtyard toward the beach, and as I began stepping into the boat, I turned around one last time, hoping to catch sight of Teuila. Suddenly, she leaped out the front door of her hut with Manaia in hot pursuit and began running down the path toward me. This time she was the one with a head start, and it only took a few seconds before she traversed the full length of the courtyard and flung her arms around me. As Manaia pulled up behind her breathing heavily, the chief held up his hand and nodded, indicating he was going to permit us a few moments to say our goodbyes.

"Jade," Teuila cried with tears streaming down her face. "I got your message, but I don't understand. Don't you love me anymore?"

I pulled away and cupped Te's face gently in my hands.

"Of course I do, baby. I'll never stop loving you. I just wanted you to see the inevitability of our situation. You belong here on Anuta." I glanced at her grandmother and her siblings looking on from the porch of their hut. "You're surrounded by people that love you."

"But what about *you*?!" she said. "I thought you said you were starting to like it here? We could hide away on the other side of the island."

"If we stayed here, we'd eventually be hunted down. And your father will never let you leave this island."

I choked up, fighting to say the words.

"It's time to move on. I'm sure that once I'm gone, everything will quiet down and return to normal. You can still live a good life in this beautiful place."

"But I don't *want* to stay!" Te' cried. She turned to face Manaia and scowled. "I will *never* love that man. You're the only one that I want."

"Oh Te'—" I said, trying to hold back my tears.

Te's father suddenly motioned to the guards, and they grabbed her arms, pulling her away from me. I despaired at the thought of never speaking with her again and reached into my handbag, passing her my card.

"I don't know if you can send mail via the cargo ship, but this has my address if you want to keep in touch."

The boatmen started up the engine and pushed the skiff off the beach, and my face tightened in anguish as Teuila screamed and flailed, trying to escape the guards' grasp. I blew her a kiss and mouthed the words I love you, then the boat turned around and headed toward the cargo ship over the bumpy surf. When we reached the big ship, they threw a rope ladder over the side and I leaned over the gunwales, retching into the sea. I couldn't bear the thought of never seeing my island girl again.

After I got on deck, I peered over the railing toward the village lagoon, but Teuila was nowhere to be seen. For a brief moment, I considered asking the crew to drop me off on the other side of the island, then I realized I'd just be prolonging her agony. I asked the porter to escort me to my stateroom, where I cried myself to sleep.

33

It took me four full days to return home to Chicago. I had to have new credit cards delivered to a branch of my bank in Honiara, then take three flights to transport me from the Solomon Islands back to the continental USA via Sydney and Hawaii. But I was in no hurry to return to the comforts of my previous life. I didn't even buy new clothes en route to the States, happy to wear my tapa dress for a few more days as my fellow fliers looked on curiously.

It wasn't until I'd been home for a few weeks that I began to settle in to my normal routine. But I never stopped thinking of Teuila. Whenever I passed the pineapple stand in my local grocery store, I smiled recalling how she'd scaled the prickly tree to harvest some fruit for us to eat near our favorite waterhole. I cooked seafood on my barbeque and marinated it in lime juice, trying to remember how good the fresh-caught grouper tasted after we'd trapped it in the lagoon. But the only tangible memento I had of her was my little unicorn shell, which I placed on my office desk and gently caressed whenever I needed to let my mind wander back to the pristine waters of our private paradise.

One particularly lonely day, I opened the photo app on my iPhone, intending to browse through the few pictures I'd taken of

Anuta before getting lost in the jungle. I knew that I didn't have any photos of Teuila, but I wanted to see the pink sand and big leafy trees of the island again to remind me of the few blissful days we'd shared in our lagoon. I smiled at the pictures of Captain Ben and the rest of the crew of our sailing vessel, and my heart skipped a beat looking at the images of my fellow passengers enjoying our first catch in the lagoon.

But as I flipped through the pictures, my eyes suddenly widened when I came upon some photos of Manaia hunched over one of the village's dugout canoes as smoke poured from the inner hull. I paused for a moment, dumbfounded at how the villagers had figured out how to use the sophisticated electronic device. I knew that young children could quickly decipher the graphical user interface, and I assumed that one of Te's siblings had picked up my unlocked phone and begun playing with it before it ran out of battery power. The camera app was at the top of the screen, and they must have accidentally tapped the capture button while running around the courtyard.

I studied the photos for a moment and spread my fingers to zoom in on the images. The pictures provided unmistakable proof that Manaia had sabotaged the canoes shortly before the battle with the other tribe. But what could I do with them? I could try printing the images and sending them back to Teuila and her father. But how would that change anything? He'd just think it was another trick by the jealous American, who was manipulating her Western technology to accuse a rival of violating their custom of Aropa.

But I couldn't just stand by and do nothing. If there was the slightest chance to use the pictures to convict Manaia of his crimes, maybe the chief would excommunicate him from the tribe, or at least annul his marriage to his daughter. And if the wedding was overturned, this could open a window for me to return to the island and reclaim my girl. I rushed to the nearest photo shop and asked to have the pictures developed immediately then called the shipping company that had picked me up from Anuta to see when the next ship would be passing by the island. They said another ship was scheduled to return the following month and that they could deliver a package to the island for a fee.

I mailed them the photos together with a bank draft for two hundred dollars, with explicit instructions to deliver the package to the chief's daughter only. Concerned they might just take my money and run, I told them if they could return a note from Teuila, I'd send them another two hundred dollars as proof of delivery. Four hundred bucks was a pretty steep price to send a package overseas, but it would be worth it for my peace of mind knowing that her father at least had tangible proof of Manaia's treachery.

I waited over a month for some kind of word back from Teuila. Then another month passed. And another. Eventually, I resigned myself to the fact that there was nothing further I could do to convince the chief of Manaia's lack of fitness for his daughter. For weeks, I cried myself to sleep every night pining for my lost love, realizing that I'd never see her again. It seemed ironic that *I* was the one having difficulty letting go, not her.

Then one day, returning from running some errands, I noticed a shiny stone lying atop the welcome mat in front of my front door. I squinted at the object, then widened my eyes, recognizing the familiar shape. I picked up the gem and ran my fingers around the edges as my heart began to thump in my chest. It looked just like the stone Te' had picked up off the beach of our lagoon and said she'd keep it as a memento of our love.

I suddenly gasped and swung around to see Teuila's pretty face smiling at me.

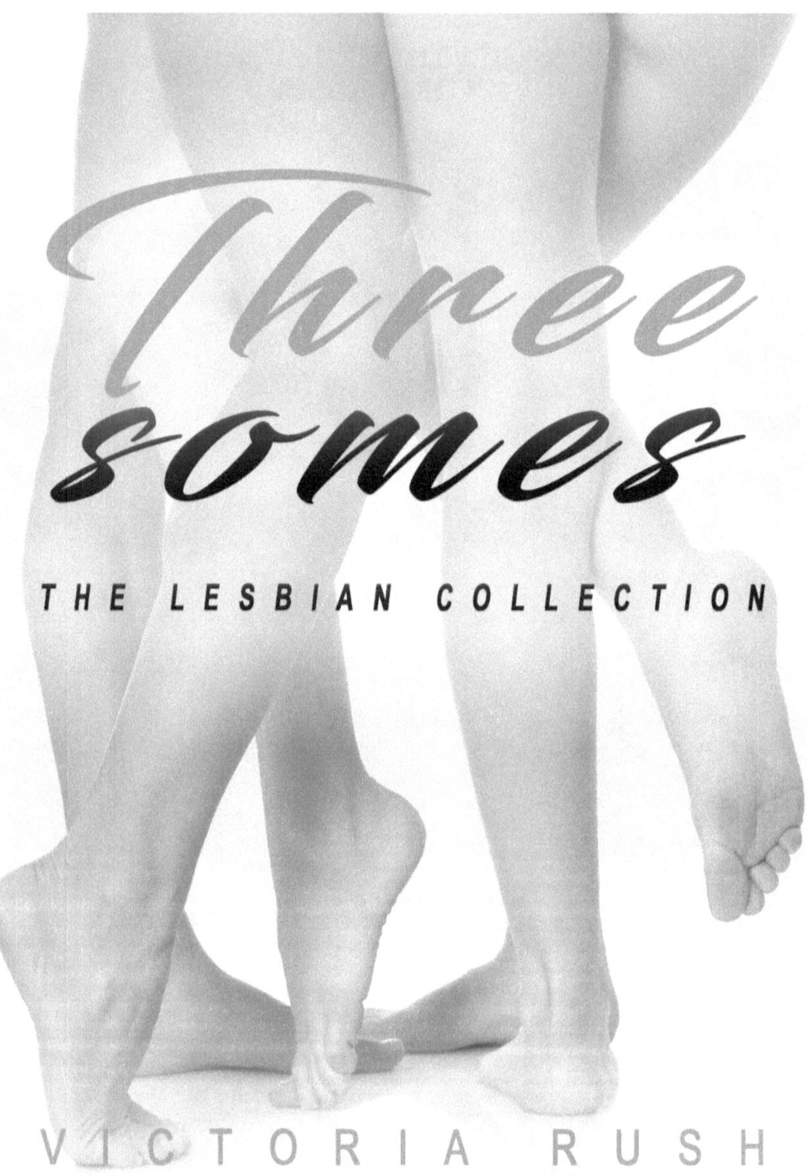

Threesomes

THE LESBIAN COLLECTION

VICTORIA RUSH

2 + 1 = a hundred ways to have fun...

Sometimes the biggest turn-on is knowing you might get caught...

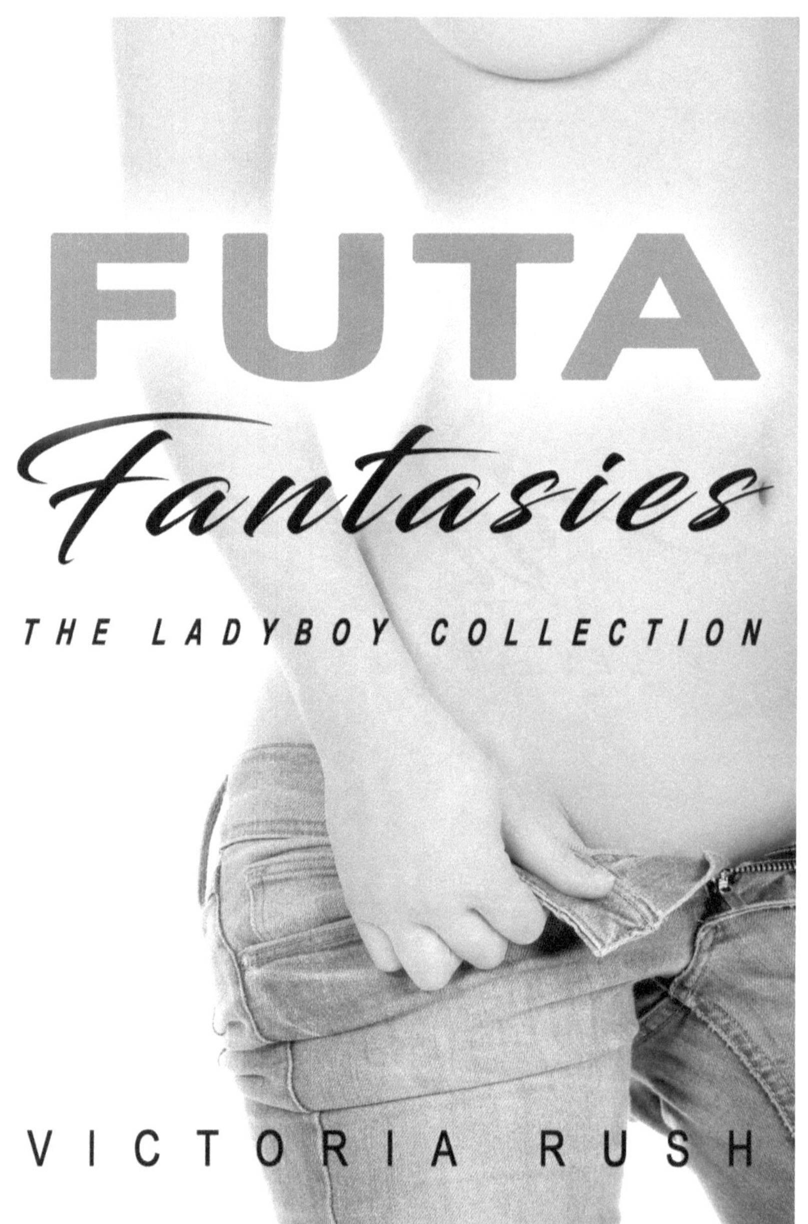

FUTA

Fantasies

THE LADYBOY COLLECTION

VICTORIA RUSH

Some girls have got a little more to work with than others...

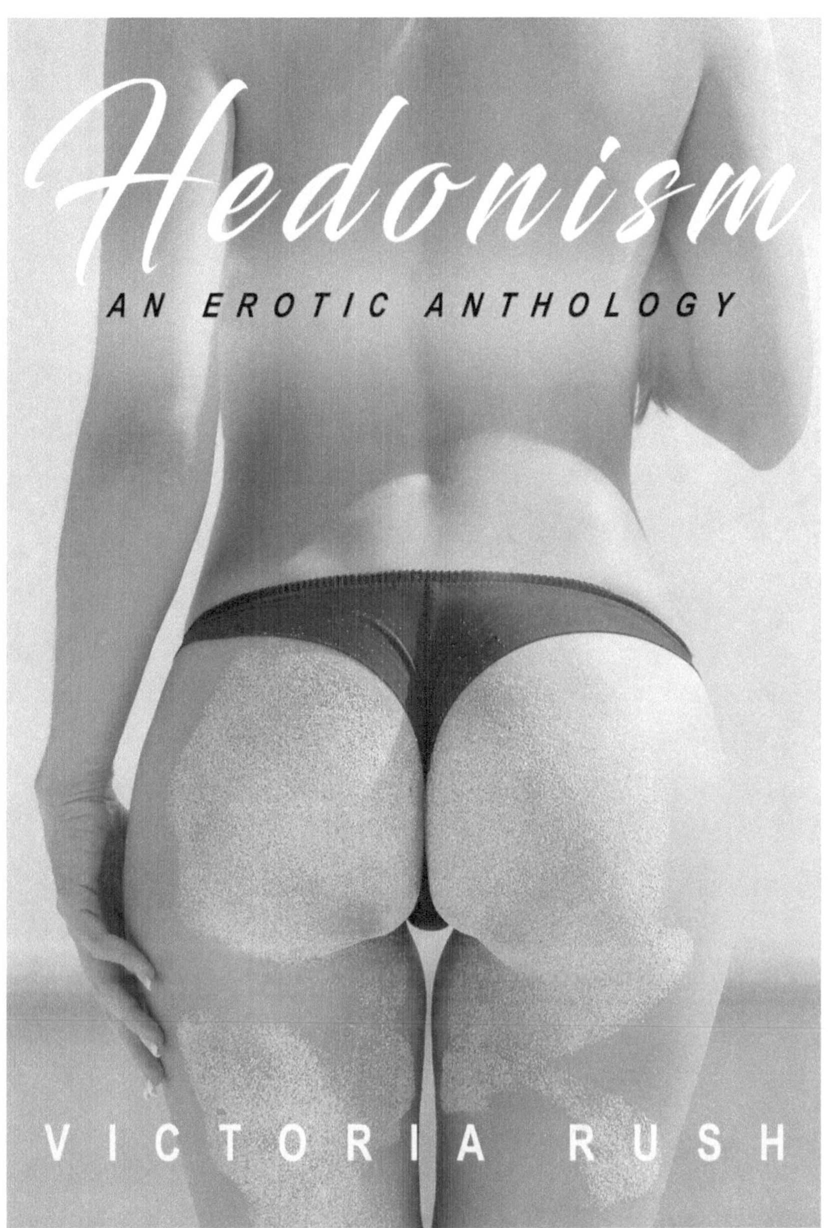

Hedonism
AN EROTIC ANTHOLOGY
VICTORIA RUSH
Sometimes all you need to spark up your love life is a little change of scenery...

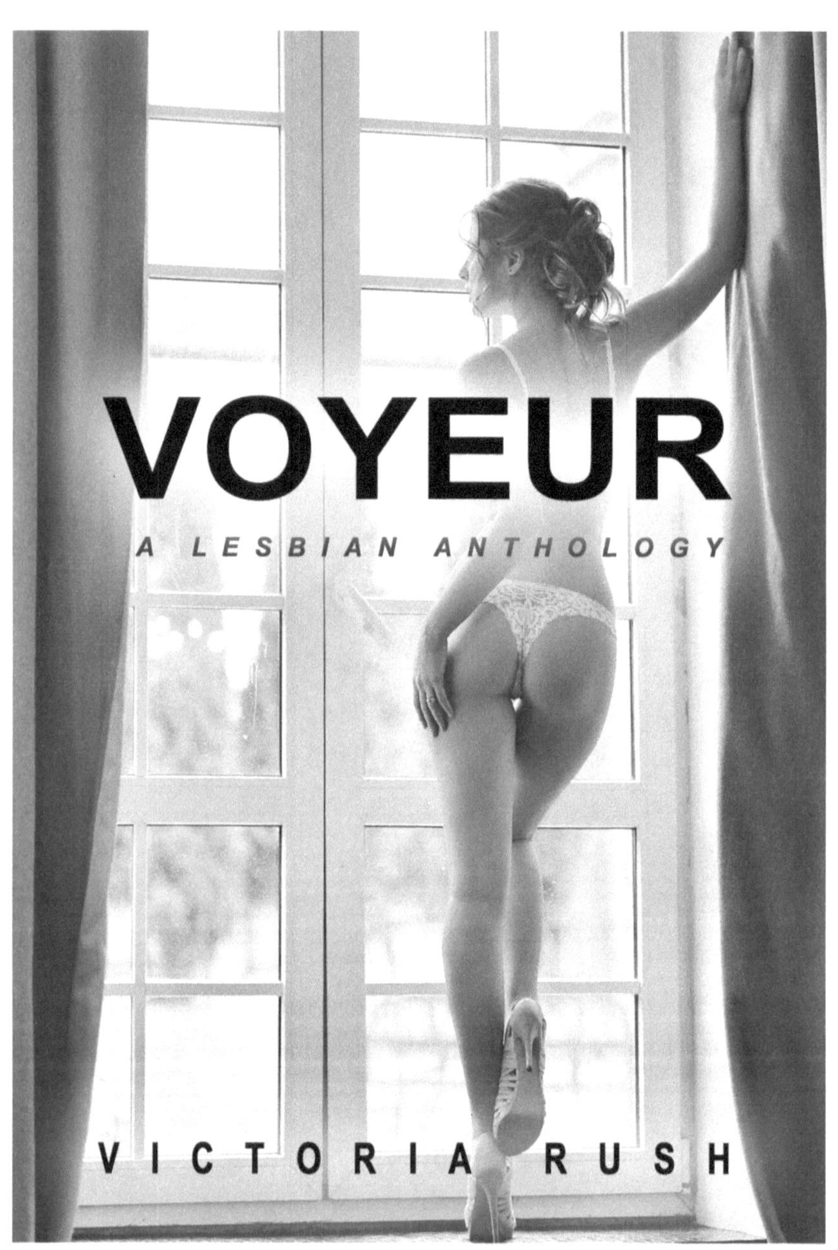

VOYEUR

A LESBIAN ANTHOLOGY

VICTORIA RUSH

Sometimes it's more fun to watch...